Jocasta and the Cruelty of Kindness

SISTERS OF CASTLE FORTUNE 2

ALICIA CAMERON

To Matthew's Mum from Holly's Mum

Contents

1. The Problem of Jocasta   1

2. The Demon's Second Move   11

3. Another Drive   20

4. The Baron's Intentions   37

5. A Polite Rescue   41

6. Family Friend   48

7. TutelageBegins   60

8. NewArrivals   70

9. QuarrellingCouples   86

10. Parental Interference   96

11. The Beginning of Partiality   108

12. The Practice of Obfuscation   128

13. A Spirit of Independence   138

14. The Beau Monde Wonders ... 148

15. Friendshipand its Foibles ... 162

16. The Triangular Conundrum ... 172

17. Miss Montgomery's Idol ... 183

18. Another Fortune Sister ... 207

19. A Distressing Breach of Etiquette ... 222

20. Jocasta vs the Spanish Beauty ... 235

21. Visiting the Invalid ... 248

22. Confusion and Rage ... 259

23. Cat Among the Pigeons ... 273

24. Love in Unexpected Places ... 286

25. Resolutions ... 301

26. Regis and the Demonic Plan ... 310

27. Epilogue ... 324

Also By Alicia Cameron ... 331

About Author ... 337

The first chapter of the Fentons series to tempt you... ... 338

CHAPTER 1

The Problem of Jocasta

The figure that lolled against the pillar in the ballroom earlier that evening had been most remarked. His hair was longer than fashion decreed, his evening coat cut for ease not style, his cravat knotted too carelessly for dress attire. Nevertheless, it was hard to disguise the powerful shoulders, slender waist and long legs of an athlete. The long hair was dark, but his brows were even darker, and their remarkable dexterity of movement added a fascination to a face of chiselled lines. Now, they expressed his quizzical look — which caused the centre points almost to meet high on his forehead and make a wavy scroll downward. High cheekbones, a strong jaw, and deep-set eyes, a riveting colour between green and gold. He had been missing from town during the Season this last year, but most gentlemen in the room still remembered that it was no use competing in any sport against Sir Damon Regis, for you would lose. Thankfully for Regis' pockets, some still took up the challenge — and duly lost their bets. He had not had to buy a carriage horse for years; his stable was full of horses bet by once-confident owners.

'Oh, Mama — whoever is that gentleman?' said the plump Miss Amethyst Bailey, arrested in mid-chatter, to her parent.

Lady Bailey looked and said, in her firmest tone, 'No one who need concern you, my dear. Do not, I beg you, catch his eye.'

Amethyst shivered. 'I should be too afraid to. He looks so fierce...'

'And yet you stare,' her brother James scoffed. He leaned towards her ear. 'Get too close to that gentleman, and you get burned.' Amethyst turned her back quickly, too shaken to start up her inane chattering again.

'The Demon King is back, I see,' remarked one gentleman to another at the other side of the room.

'Can't have been for long. No tales of fire and brimstone have reached me as yet,' said his tall, elegant companion.

'Watch his eyes. He's looking for something.'

'One can only be afraid for whoever that may be.'

The gentlemen were distracted by other business, and therefore did not see those fascinating eyes suddenly arrest on an object. It was a figure of a lady, somewhat surrounded by young bucks in the hopes of conversation and a dance. She was a little sprite, with dark blonde ringlets atop her head, huge eyes in a pointed little face, wearing a deceptively simple white gown which was made up of only three sheer layers of muslin, adding to her ethereal grace.

'Who takes your attention, King?' said a voice beside him.

Without moving his eyes, Damon asked, 'Who is *that*, Hugo?'

'Ah, that is Miss Jocasta Fortune. At the moment she is unquestionably the ballroom favourite — for Miss Julia White is absent from town and her fickle court have found a new queen. I am interested to see what transpires when Miss White returns, though I shall be back to the regiment before then.'

'After events at Fontainebleau, is that still necessary?'

'There are some loose ends to be handled, though the pest of Europe be exiled.'

'I cannot recognise a fortune hunter among the little one's court,' Regis remarked, returning the conversation to his object, whom he had never ceased to view.

'No. She is one of Baron Fortune's interminable daughters. Only a respectable portion, I hear.'

'Unfortunate, but that may prove advantageous to me, if handled correctly,' said Damon, his eye still on the doings of Miss Fortune. 'There is an interesting look in her eye.'

'You can see her expression from here?'

'Oh yes. She is playing with her suitors, and she has some skill, but is a little obvious. If she be intelligent, she'll respond to training.'

His companion shrugged his shoulders. 'Training...' he drawled. 'I do not know what devilry you have afoot, King, but it is just a child.'

'Oh, but it will be to her advantage, I assure you. I mean her no harm.'

His companion, the tall, magnificent figure of the Earl of Grandiston, moved off, saying mildly, 'I should not converse with you, Demon, if I believed you would *mean* harm. Your impulses however...! Try not to set too many fires this visit, King. I like having you around.'

3

For the next half an hour, the lounging baronet never took his eyes from the tiny expressive figure of Jocasta Fortune. 'She'll do,' he said to himself, and with some energy moved towards her.

He saw, on the outskirts of her group, a friend. 'Justin, introduce me to Miss Fortune.'

A look of fright came on the handsome face of Sir Justin Faulkes, and he gazed in horror at Regis. 'Why?'

'Why ever not?' asked one flying eyebrow.

'I can't think of a reason, but there is one,' hissed Faulkes.

The lowered conversation had reached the centre of the coterie, and Miss Fortune's large blue eyes moved to the newcomer with a slight jolt (for his eyebrows had drawn down in a threatening 'V' shape) then a mild look of enquiry. Sir Justin felt impelled to say, 'Miss Fortune, might I introduce you to Sir Damon Regis, newly returned to town.'

Jocasta Fortune smiled slightly as Regis said, 'Miss Fortune. I shall call on you tomorrow if I may.' There seemed to be a decision rather than a request in this, and it was evident that the young girl did not quite know how to proceed, but merely nodded. To everyone's surprise, Sir Damon Regis then turned and moved with a peculiar energy towards the great doors that led out of the ballroom.

Sir Justin watched as Jocasta's wondering eyes followed his figure and said to himself, 'Oh Lord. What is he about?'

No one thought of Jocasta Fortune, including herself, as a female of depth or complexity. Admired for her looks and vivacity, here was many a gentleman's ideal. Nothing very much to tax the brain, but a great deal to tempt the senses. Disappointing fortune, perhaps, but of excellent descent. She would make some lucky man a decorative and easy spouse, supposing his estate was as far away from his father-in-law as possible.

She had been in town again for four weeks. She remembered her excitement and pride last season — escaping Castle Fortune and attending so many social events was a great adventure, and she had been courted by many gentlemen in a very flattering way. She had come to think of it as a great game, and as her due. But the spirit in which she played the game this season was vastly different, for at a house party at her castle home, she had finally lost.

She thought idly of those suitors, especially Lord Bryant, a very young man who had been devotedly at her feet until Lord Paxton had begun to seek her out at the end of last season. She had played one off against the other, in a teasing manner, and it had increased Paxton's interest. But this season Bryant affected not to notice her. She had once looked at his face and saw pain there, and was deeply sorry. For now, she had felt the pain of not being preferred herself — Paxton having visited the castle to pay court to her, and instead falling for her sister Portia.

Jocasta now observed herself in the mirror. There was not much difference in her appearance, but she knew how different she was in herself. She adjusted her dress as she always had, choosing hair ornaments or ribbons with care, but it was as though she added some detail to a drawing to enhance it — she regarded herself distantly.

She played the ballroom game as she had before, but was cautious indeed of what she said, so as to hurt no one. She was careful of hearts other than her own, and this was new to her. Castle Fortune had never been swimming in affection, and she had not sought it. So, she had never given it.

Now, residing in the same London house as Portia, she saw her passionate sister give and receive real affection, and Jocasta was jealous. It tore at her, but she kept her face bland throughout. She would never let them see how they had hurt her. She had not really wanted Paxton, she supposed, but the idea that she was not enough for a man, that they might want something more, had crushed her spirits and rent her confidence. And with Paxton constantly near — when he smiled at Portia as he had once done to her — she suddenly craved that smile, even though she had been only mildly flattered before. In fact, his passionate nature had frightened her a little, and his expressed idea of her character had been so far from her own self that she had been slightly repulsed. But now, every touch or word he gave to Portia jabbed at her.

Her feelings for Portia remained the same. She was of little interest. They were sisters, and not friends, like all the ten Fortune sisters, she believed. As such, Jocasta had once fallen from a horse in an effort to stop Portia's mount running off with her (for Portia had stolen a ride on brother George's stallion Falcon, before she was ready for it) and she would do so again, she supposed. She felt no extra animosity to her sister. Portia had not sought to steal his lordship; she was just more suited to him. This, the practical Jocasta understood. However, it did not stop the pain.

Another thing that hurt her was not, as any auditor might suppose, her father or her brother George's thoughtless (or sometimes spiteful) remarks about the situation. That hardly stung at all, since it was to be expected. No, it was encountering *kindness* that killed her.

Everyone who had been at Castle Fortune's house party knew of the situation — at least those who had their wits about them. Also, Jocasta suspected that many people in town may have already known of the purpose of the party — to throw Paxton and Jocasta together. She could detect, in the more compassionate people, a look not just of sympathy, but of pity. At every ball now, she had to suffer the compassion of Frederick and James Bailey, her old neighbours, Colonel Bellamy, one of the Castle Fortune house party guests, and Sir Justin Faulkes — friend of The Marquis of Onslow, her sister's husband — all of whom danced with her at least once at any new assembly. To buoy her spirits, she supposed. Actually it depressed them, and the energy it took to pretend to be happy and relaxed before those who knew of her humiliation almost exhausted her sometimes. She wished they would stop.

She could do this, she could keep her face, if only they would not be kind.

Baron Fortune, her papa, was still not disposed to spend a great deal on his daughters, even though Portia Fortune, newly turned sixteen, and enjoying her first visit to town, knew he had funds. This was not simply from the estate of Castle Fortune — that hardly kept he and his heir in gambling debts — but from the advantageous settlements he had only some months ago achieved, in having another two of his daughters affianced to the wealthier aristocracy. Indeed, to her papa's amazement, Georgette Fortune was now the Marchioness of Onslow, her husband the marquis having seen no need to delay his wedding in the slightest. Portia, too, was engaged to Lord Robert Paxton, a peer of the realm who was the heir to an earldom. Portia could not care a fig for that, but was much more interested in his beautiful face, melodic voice and poetic soul. Her Robbie was perfect, it was true, and she was really, really, happy ... most days.

However, the house that the family was renting for the season had heavy old furniture and smelt of must — all it lacked to be her country home were ramparts, turrets, and mice. It was a respectable address to house the baron's two daughters and himself for the Season, and there had been an addition made of an old aunt as chaperone, but Aunt Hortense mostly slept in a seat by the fire, pretending to set stitches. She was a poor relation from Papa's side of the family, but while Portia had heard that poor relations were often put upon and treated as underlings, Aunt Hortense had both girls and all the servants running after her. "*Portia, my dear, pray send for more water, for the tea is sadly cold. And some cake — and Jocasta, could you pass me my work? My rheumatism is oppressive today. I am a martyr to the pain, I assure you, girls.*" All of this was said in a soft tone and was accompanied by a trace of a smile, in which, Portia thought, no affection was discernible. This did not much daunt her, the Fortune girls had little affection in their lives since the death of their mother nearly six years since. What daunted her most was that her brother George was letting his rooms in London go (in an effort at economy, her father said) and moving into the hired house for the season. As the house was small (only six bedrooms over three storeys, and several public rooms on the ground floor) it would be completely oppressive to have to deal with the presence of George. One Fortune male, Papa, was surely enough.

Portia was naturally enjoying being in town, and all the accoutrements for her come out, with morning dresses, carriage dresses and ball gowns, and all things related, being part of the excitement. She suspected that all but the first of the bills for her new wardrobe had been sent to Paxton, and was a little ashamed, but also a little proud.

Being allowed more time with Paxton was also exciting, but as he insisted on Aunt Hortense, or a maid, or his sister, the elegant Lady Sarah Alderly, accompanying them at all times for respectability's sake, soft words between them were strictly limited. And there was, of course, another fly in the ointment. Jocasta.

The quick tale was simply this: Jocasta had met Lord Paxton at the end of the last season, while Portia was still practising piano in the blustery Castle Fortune and not in town at all. Paxton was disposed to admire the fairy princess Jocasta and her father conceived of the house party at the castle, and it was there that Portia and Paxton met and fell in love.

Even if no words of love had been exchanged, or promises made, between the original pair — still, the purpose of the party was widely known. Jocasta had been, if not shamed, then embarrassed, by Paxton's change of heart. Jocasta had rejected him before he could explain himself, and he had then (immediately) offered for Portia. But Portia was happy and thankful — but guilty too. Jocasta had never been her best friend, but she *was* her sister. After the first giddiness, Portia had not found a way to be easy in the situation.

Paxton was a frequent visitor to the house, and Portia saw how his delicacy of feeling was affected, too, and how he looked at Jocasta with fright, pity and guilt in equal measure. The fright was owing to Jocasta's demeanour with him, which changed each time she met him, as though she was trying out various expressions. One was icily polite, one was overly friendly, one was disdainful, another detached and distant — as though hardly aware of his existence. The waters of Jocasta's temperament chopped about enough to make one seasick. If Paxton looked guilty or concerned, Portia was secretly cross, for his attention to another woman's feelings was not what one expected from a first love. That this was her punishment for stealing her sister's suitor, however unplanned it had been, Portia had no doubt.

Even if Jocasta had not loved, and Portia was almost sure she had not, it was still a difficult situation. At home in Castle Fortune, they had largely spent their time separately after the house party had broken up, but here in London they were rather on top of one another, with few hiding places. And of course, the girls went to the same social occasions and were thus thrust together at a family party.

And now their brother George was coming too. Portia hoped that she could bear it.

CHAPTER 2

The Demon's Second Move

The Marquis and Marchioness of Onslow were seated on an elegant sofa in an attitude of either relaxation or exhaustion. The butler who had just placed brandy on a side table beside the marquis, and some hot wine on another table beside the marchioness, looked back before he closed the door and saw them in the pose of a perfect triangle. Their shoulders touched, and the marchioness' pretty head rested on her husband's. But both sets of legs went in the opposite directions at either end of the sofa, propped up on silken footstools, that they had not bothered to have moved. The butler smiled to himself and closed the door silently.

The marchioness wriggled her toes, finely covered by silk stockings. 'Oh, that's better, my shoes pinched,' she said idly. The pair were richly dressed in evening wear, the marchioness' green silken dress swept the floor, the gems at her wrists and neck sparkled in the light from the candelabra, the marquis' knee breeches fit his athletic form perfectly, but he had dispensed with his coat and sported only a white silk waistcoat with a high collar over the ample folds of his fine linen shirt. The only sign of the exertions of the ball were that his blond curls had fought against the pomade that had restrained them at the beginning of the evening, and now fell over one eye.

'Who dares make shoes that pinch my wife's toes? That shoemaker shall be summoned and beheaded.'

As this was said in the same exhausted tone as her own, the marchioness only grinned. 'Oh, they are not my shoes. I swapped with Jocasta.'

'Swapped is a very vulgar word, my dear. Are you a merchant?'

'Exchanged then. She liked mine so much because of the paste gems on the top, and we put some cotton in the toes so they would fit better.'

'The gems are not paste.'

'Diamonds?' gasped his wife. Her body gave a twitch as though she would rise at this, but the marquis' blond head fell onto her brunette top knot and she relaxed. 'Why on earth must you continue to deck me out in such stuff?'

'*Rings on her fingers and bells on her toes* ... only the best for my marchioness. Assume your position, my lady!' He lapsed into a sigh. 'Will Jocasta return the shoes?'

'Oh yes, for she told me the cotton bunched up and became uncomfortable when she danced.' Her tone dropped, 'But we probably should not tell her the paste gems are real.' A smile, addressed to the wall in front of them, crossed both their faces.

12

'Your family!' remarked the marquis. A muscle pulsed, as though to move. 'Shall we retire now?'

'Stay a bit longer, Lucian. For my toes to recover. It was a prodigiously good ball, but I really didn't like what I saw there.'

'Jocasta and her court, I presume?' remarked her husband cautiously.

'You saw it too! Was her behaviour to her suitors just vivacious, or too flirtatious? It reminded me of—' the marchioness stopped.

'Miss White. Yes, though Julia is a little more skilful than Jocasta.' He added in a vague voice, 'I didn't see Julia White around the ballroom this evening.'

As the marquis could once have been relied upon to be aware of Miss White's every move, it was comforting for a wife to know that he had not remarked Miss White's absence from the town for a whole three weeks.

'She is in the country and expected to return soon. The death of an uncle, I think.' The marquis made a sound. 'But I'm afraid Jocasta will get herself in trouble, and there is no use applying to Papa. He brings along whatever lady he may to chaperone. One night it is the antediluvian strictness of Viscountess Swanson, and another it is the utter laxity of Mrs Shipman, who had no idea whereabouts in the ballroom Jocasta was all evening.' There was a pause of a very long ten seconds. '*Lucian...*'

'*No*, Georgette!'

His wife seemed to shrink, but the marquis was not fooled.

In an exceedingly small voice, she remarked to the wall, 'You said you were going to enjoy my family—'

'Yes,' he said colourlessly. 'Occasionally. And from a distance.'

His wife grinned in appreciation. 'But Jocasta is so hurt...'

'If I thought that your sister staying here would add to your comfort, Georgette, it would be one thing. But you are hardly confidantes.'

'No, the Fortune sisters are a strange pack. We are somewhat savage, you know.' She said this last with some pride, and the marquis sighed.

'Are they both to come, then?' said the marquis in a resigned voice. 'Portia too?'

'No. Just Jocasta. The point is to separate her from Portia and Paxton.' Georgette turned her head to look at the chiselled profile she knew so well. 'I'll tell Papa that I feel she needs a dedicated chaperone.'

'If you say that, I have a happy life to look forward to. Next is the come out of Katerina, then Leonora and Marguerite. Your papa will assume that we will continue to house the whole pack for years to come...'

'I'll make sure not to suggest it, I promise!' Georgette said, with a clutch on her husband's waistcoat.

'No suggestion will be required. Your papa is given an inch and takes ...!' he halted himself. 'We barely escaped having the baron and the girls stay here for the Season as it is.'

'I know. His hopes of avoiding renting rooms! And we might have had George, too, I believe *he* has given up his rooms as an exercise in economy,' she said, speaking of her brother. 'It doesn't bear thinking of.' She turned her head to look at the marquis. 'But I am not *at all* going to insist on the others. They are Papa's affair.' The little voice that preceded his downfall returned. Georgette said, 'I did forget to mention that my sister Cassie might visit in a few weeks' time...'

Her voice trailed away, and her husband rose swiftly. 'And the baron's rooms cannot accommodate her?' He frowned down at her, and his wife looked up at him with soulful eyes, her mouth making a little moue. 'Let us discuss this upstairs,' he said, standing up and pulling at her roughly. The marchioness giggled and followed as he yanked her hand, skipping in her stockinged feet.

The figure that was led into the presence of Jocasta and Portia Fortune in the hour after breakfast on the following day had removed neither his coat nor gloves, the only concession to manners being that his curly brimmed beaver was in his gloved hands. He seemed in a hurry.

'Sir Damon, is it not...?' began Jocasta Fortune. 'You are an early caller.'

He bowed swiftly to her, and adjusting his position, to Portia, who had laid aside her work and looked up at him.

'This is my sister, Miss Portia—' offered Jocasta.

'Yes,' interrupted the strangely powerful baronet, disinterestedly. He had turned his attention back to Jocasta. 'Shall we drive, Miss Fortune?' Jocasta realised with a jolt that *she* was Miss Fortune now, the eldest unmarried Fortune sister. For a girl who had six sisters above her in age, it was strange.

'I had not thought...' said Jocasta, flustered. 'I am not dressed...' Her muslin gown of jonquil stripes was lovely, but light.

The baronet looked at it without interest, saying, 'The day is fine. A warm pelisse over it will suffice, I believe. If you have no other objection, I shall await you in the phaeton. The horses will be restive.' With this, he turned on his heels and was gone with that same sense of purpose she had observed in the ballroom.

15

'Well!' exclaimed Portia. 'Whoever is *he*?'

'Sir Damon Regis,' Jocasta answered, still a little shocked. 'Sir Justin introduced him to me last night.'

'Oh well if Sir Justin ... But his manner is so peculiar. Did you expect him?'

'No. Yes. He said he would come. I did not expect to drive, however.'

Lord Paxton entered, followed by an out-of-breath little maid. 'The gentleman said to bring you this, miss.' She handed Jocasta a wool pelisse and her bonnet, which Jocasta began to put on, rather as an automaton.

'Was that Regis I saw outside?' asked Lord Paxton.

'Yes, my lord. Excuse me, I must go.' She gave the smallest of curtsies and then ran from the room.

She heard Paxton say, as she put on her bonnet in the hall, 'Send a maid in, will you?' Always a thought for Portia's reputation, though he had frequently sought to be alone with Jocasta at the castle, meeting her in the summerhouse. Jocasta was glad, glad to be out of this house.

Before the maid arrived, and even although the door remained ajar, Portia had run to him and grasped his hands, 'Good morning, my love.'

He held her off reluctantly. 'Do not, my sweet! You know I cannot bear it...'

'*When* will you let us marry?'

This was a daily question, and Paxton had formulated his answer and replied, looking at her strictly, 'When you have had your Season, when you have had a chance to dance with others, when I am sure I do not take advantage of you.'

'This is all nonsense,' said Portia, pulling her hands from his restraint and throwing herself at his chest, 'this is for other loves than ours.'

He could not help but take her in his arms then. 'I know, I know. You are so much older than me and wiser in many ways, my darling, but in the eyes of the world you are still a child.'

'I am sixteen now. A fine age to be married.'

'But...'

'Only think of it, Robbie,' Portia said, looking up at him with the passionate eyes that could be his undoing. 'We might honeymoon this summer in Florence, now that the monster of Europe is gone! Together for three months under the sun, my darling, to paint and draw and write and visit galleries. To lie under the lemon trees that you told me of, just us, united in body and soul.'

Lord Paxton, almost sucked into her gaze, did an unexpected thing. He nipped her arm. She pulled away, shocked. 'Robert!'

'Do not tempt me so, Portia. Behave yourself! Or I shall not marry you.'

'Robbie, never say those words to me...' said Portia, her eyes filling.

'Oh, *darling*...!' He took a step towards her again, full of repentance.

There was a cough outside the door as a precursor to the entrance of the little maid, bearing a needle and some linen. She found her mistress seated, and Lord Paxton leaning one hand on the mantelpiece, staring at the coals in an aspect of reverie. The maid slid into a seat in the corner and began to sew. Her dropped head hid her smile, and she bit her lip to stop it.

There was something restful about the drive with Sir Damon Regis, Jocasta considered. Not pleasant, just restful.

She was a little afraid of him, at first. He was so peculiarly energetic, even when he was relatively still, and she had wondered if, like other gentlemen, he had brought her out to flirt with her. His presence was so powerful that she doubted her ability to joust with him as she did with others — turning off their compliments lightly — she feared he would not be so easily turned off from any purpose he set himself to.

They were silent until they achieved the park, Regis hardly minding her, it seemed. When the quiet began to seem impolite, Jocasta made a light enquiry. 'How long have you known Sir Justin, sir?'

'School,' he replied.

'Oh, then you must also know my brother-in-law, Onslow, well.'

'Yes,' he replied, bored.

Feeling that she had done her duty, and that no more was required of her, Jocasta began to relax. He hardly glanced at her for the next hour, and when he did, he had no gleam of admiration in his eye. Jocasta looked at the park view: the trees and flowers in pleasing order, the carriages, the qualities of the horses, the pedestrians and their exchange of greetings — and the time passed easily. From time to time, he addressed her: to point out a beautifully matched pair, or to ask whether she would be at Mrs Sloane's ball on Thursday. If it were any other gentleman, she might have considered this last question a pursuit, but Regis did not appear particularly interested in her answer. Or in anything else about her at all.

She was not his type, she was sure. Therefore, she did not really know why she was in his carriage, but it did not seem to matter.

Jocasta regarded his profile with a detached interest. He was handsome, very. He was masculine, very. This did not cause her to feel a pull towards him. It was his disinterest that did, the way his eyes glanced over her without sticking, the lack of compliments, the coolness of his conversation. She, in turn, had no need to respond with more interest than she felt. Nothing was expected of her here.

It felt — safe.

CHAPTER 3

Another Drive

O n the following morning, after a pleasant ride with the Onslows, Jocasta had to bear a breakfast with Papa, Portia, Paxton and her brother George. It tired her out before nine of the clock.

During the usual interrogation about her suitors, a subject that Jocasta was determined to be non-committal about, Portia had looked her sisterly regret, and Paxton had resorted to becoming a stiffened board. It was impossible to beat Papa. One could only suffer his remarks.

'Has Lord Bryant paid a morning call yet? He looked like a promising runner last Season,' said George, adding to her misery.

'Lord Bryant has not even danced with me this Season, so it is safe to say that he has no interest in me,' Jocasta allowed herself.

'He may well have been hurt at your preference for Paxton,' said George, effectively humiliating everyone at the table, excepting his father. 'Give him a smile to coax him back to the fold.'

'Yes, Jocasta!' added her papa. 'Encouragement, that's what we want. I daresay his father is the richest man in Suffolk.'

'Yes, father,' said George, 'but Jocasta has already shown herself a flirt, and he may very well feel disgust. It cannot be helped.'

Jocasta grasped her cutlery for support. Fortunately for George, it was just a butter knife.

Paxton looked like he might wish to say something, and Portia grasped his hand to stop him, looking at Jocasta with genuine sympathy.

Last year, Jocasta was sure, Papa's strictures and George's remarks had only been merely embarrassing and absurd. This year they cut to the quick.

'I'll leave the table, Papa,' she said briskly, 'I still have some things to attend to in my packing.'

'Yes, go to your sister's! It saves me the trouble of finding a chaperone for every occasion. But do not think I will not have my eye on you, my girl. No other daughter of mine shall run off with a pauper to Bath — mark my words.'

'Yes, Papa.'

'Well, you're a sensible one.'

It was the most affectionate thing Jocasta had heard from her father all Season.

At Onslow House, breakfast had not yet begun.

'What are you doing here again?' asked the Marquis of Onslow, seeing Sir Justin Faulkes seated in his drawing room.

'Flirting with your wife,' Faulkes replied brightly.

'Thank you, Justin,' smiled Georgette, 'it takes me back to my life as an unmarried woman.'

'All of five months ago,' reminded her husband.

'The shackles of marriage have *surely* been chafing me for longer than that?'

'The joke has ended. I'm now wounded,' said the marquis blandly. 'What have you two been up to at any rate?'

'Since you had to see your man of business,' answered the marchioness, 'I rode with Justin.'

'Made yourself the talk of the town, I suppose.'

'No, for Jocasta and Portia rode too. It was a treat for us all to be able to ride together. We never could at home.' She saw her husband was looking mollified and added naughtily, 'But of course, I spent the *majority* of the ride with Justin, whose Solomon could keep up with my Spirit.' The marquis met his wife's pert look with an awful frown, and she laughed.

'Are you going to the Four Horse Club meeting today, Lucian?' enquired Faulkes.

'Yes, are not you?'

'If you are, I'll take Georgette out and let her take the reins on my bays this afternoon.'

'What—?' started the marquis, in more genuine irritation.

'Really?' said Georgette, delighted. 'Do you think I could, Justin? Onslow says I'm not ready for his greys.'

'Nonsense.' The baronet smiled at her delight. 'You'll do well.'

'Now look here—' Onslow threw a look of dislike at his friend, and Faulkes picked up a sporting journal and read it, crossing his legs at ease. The marquis changed tack, 'Since that arrangement is for the afternoon, why are you still here?

'Breakfast,' said Faulkes, not looking up from his paper.

'Yes, let us go in,' said Georgette happily.

As they wandered into the dining room, Justin said to his friend. 'I, too, am wounded, Lucian. You used to seek me out, and now you are different.'

'Stop flirting with my wife then.'

'Ah, but the prettiest marchioness in London must have a court, you know. It is all the rage. And I am not alone in my devotion.'

'But the others are not admitted to my house. You abuse your rights as a friend shamefully to spend part of every day with my wife. Find your own wife.'

'Ah, that is just what we are going to do, you know,' said Georgette. 'I am determined to find Justin a wife this Season. I am making plans.'

'Yes, and she and I will have to meet together *often* to discuss them,' said Faulkes, showing Onslow his most innocent face.

'You are both shameless.'

'Onslow,' said Georgette brightly, changing the subject, 'am I really the lady of this house?'

'Of course, you are, Marchioness.'

'Then should you object if I turned the smallest sitting room into a breakfast room? I feel that for just the three of us this room echoes so, and the table is much too long, even after they removed the leaves.'

'Three of us? Justin does not *live* here. Though he might as well do so.'

'Well, but Jocasta will be here soon. I spoke to Papa. She agrees, and will arrive today. I could see she was relieved.'

'At least with your sister here,' said her husband resignedly, 'your suitor will not have occasion to talk sweet words with you.'

'You think a man of *my* address would be hampered by that?' said Faulkes with a patronising smile.

'What I've always liked about you, Justin, is that you are a man of the world,' said Georgette approvingly.

'Talking of a bride, why not take Jocasta?' said the marquis affably. 'It would solve all our problems at once.'

'Excuse me my frankness, but to the devil with that idea. A young bride is exactly what I could not handle,' answered Faulkes. He reflected. 'Well ... perhaps, but not Miss Jocasta Fortune. I am not man enough to brave a Fortune sister. You wed the only sensible one among them, Lucian.'

Some days later, Sir Justin Faulkes, having seen Jocasta twice this week in Sir Damon's carriage in Hyde Park, decided to pay him a visit.

'I had the devil's own job to find you,' he remarked as he was led into the rooms by a military looking valet.

The valet looked at his master, and as he received Sir Justin's hat and gloves, ventured to reply to this in his master's stead. 'Regis House is rented out this Season, sir, for we had not planned to attend the Season.'

'My plans changed unexpectedly,' smiled Regis lazily. 'You find me at breakfast, Justin. Do you want some? Mr McKay can easily fetch more.' Justin knew that the designation "Mr" before the name of the servant had been given as a continuing token of respect, since the man had more than once saved Damon's life in battle. His friends adopted the title too, and it made Mr McKay unique among the serving class.

'I have eaten already, thank you, Mr McKay.' The little valet brought a coffee cup to him as he sunk onto the chair opposite.

Regis kept eating as Faulkes eyed him appraisingly. His host finished his plate after some silent minutes and finally put a coffee cup to his mouth and eyed his friend.

'You are not going to make this easy on me, are you?' said Faulkes. Damon sipped from his cup, his eyes yellow and wicked. 'I came here with a purpose. But now that I am here, I do not know how to commence.'

'That is because you are burdened with exquisite manners, my friend.'

That made Faulkes abandon them. 'Dammit, Damon, what are you about?' A look of innocent wonder overtook the dark face of the host, and Justin growled. 'Stop it! Drat it man, *I* introduced you.'

Regis' face took on the air of dawning realisation and his eyebrow scroll rose on his forehead.

'Ah, you are referring to the subject of Miss Jocasta Fortune! Don't worry, she'll come to no harm at my hands.'

'But I do worry. I have no idea why women take to you — but they do. You would think they would know better, or that your ugly face—' here Regis grinned, 'would deter them. She's just eighteen and she hasn't had the best time of late—'

'Jocasta Fortune has no more interest in me than I in her, if it makes you feel any better.'

'Then why take her driving, or stand up with her at Assemblies?'

'That is my business,' said Regis shortly. Faulkes had never known his friend duplicitous, but nevertheless he regarded him now closely, and Regis laughed. 'I should not have to repeat myself, Justin, but she will come to no harm at my hands.'

'But who knows *what* ideas young ladies take into their heads? And since the party at Fortune Castle, Miss Jocasta—'

'Yes,' interrupted Regis, 'what *did* happen at that party? Bellamy said something strange about it too.'

'Are you friends with Colonel Bellamy? I'd as lief Miss Fortune was being driven around by you as he...'

'Bellamy? He's the best of good fellows, I assure you. I met him when I had business in the East Indies. What would make you say other?'

'Nothing. That is, he may have been acting a trifle out of character at Castle Fortune ... Anyway, *he* isn't pursuing Miss Fortune, though he does dance with her. You, on the other hand, are taking her driving in the park. Someone asked me about it at the club.'

'Why would they ask *you*?' said Regis, throwing two long legs over a footstool.

'Because she is staying with the Onslows. The marchioness is her sister.'

'I gathered. Mmm — I suppose the world thinks you up on all the news on Onslow and his family.'

'Whatever the reason, I still have had no real answer from *you*.'

'Miss Fortune has driven with me three times. I believe she has driven with others, too. Possibly more frequently. Are you visiting them all this morning? I must say, you sound as though you have an interest there yourself.' He laughed at Faulkes' annoyance. 'I was teasing. She doesn't seem your sort at all.'

'She isn't. But since the party—'

'What *did* happen at that house party?' Regis' voice was enquiring, but with none of the sardonic affectation he had used earlier.

'A great deal happened,' said Faulkes with a sigh. 'It was, in fact, packed with incident. Three engagements took place, which have resulted in two marriages.'

'But I understood that it was only months ago.' Regis regarded Faulkes' answering nod with some amusement. 'Ah, three *love* matches. Busy indeed.'

'Yes, Onslow and Georgette Fortune, Lord Bucknell — do you know him, King? — met a Miss Maria Bailey, who is now Lady Bucknell—' Faulkes paused, 'and lastly, the engagement of Miss Portia Fortune, Miss Fortune's younger sister, to Lord Paxton — Alderly's heir, you know.'

'I do know him, but I cannot understand why you mentioned this last in the tone of doom. Are they not suited to each other?'

'Extremely suited, I should say. But Baron Fortune's purpose in giving a house party in that wreck of a place was to further the interest Paxton had previously shown for Miss *Jocasta* Fortune.'

'Ah, so that is why her guard is up. I understand now. Was she much hurt?'

'How can I say? I see her more now that she lives at Onslow House, but I was barely acquainted with her before.'

'I see. Thank you, Justin, you have been a great deal of help to me, and now must take your leave, for I have work to do.' Regis' customary energetic movements made Justin jolt upright and the valet took this opportunity to hand him his hat and gloves.

'I did not tell you all this so that I could pave your way to whatever devilment you are planning, you demon,' protested Faulkes, being propelled to the door by a firm hand on his shoulder.

'But you have. Goodbye, Justin.' A devilish grin and one side of inverted "v" of a raised eyebrow, and Regis looked at Faulkes' annoyed face across the threshold.

'If I tell Onslow,' threatened Faulkes, 'he won't like it, you scoundrel.'

Regis, still grinning, shut the door on him.

What Regis had to do, as it turned out, was to meet with Miss Jocasta Fortune for another carriage ride.

'I don't suppose that you will let me drive today either.'

'You are correct.'

'You think, perhaps, that I do not have the skill for it.'

'On the contrary, I have seen you drive Burlington's bays, and I am quite sure you have. It is merely that no one drives my cattle but me.'

'It is a pity.' She looked at him, frankly. 'For me, I mean.'

He regarded the distant expression on her little pointed face and asked suddenly. 'Why do you consent to drive with me, Miss Fortune?'

'Because you ask me, sir,' said Jocasta, matter-of-factly.

Regis was surprised into a short guffaw. 'That is a dangerous basis for a young lady to conduct her affairs.'

The full import of his words was lost on Jocasta, but she continued, truthfully, 'And I find it restful. You neither admire nor pity me. Usually, you do not speak much, and when the weather is so fine it is better to be outside than in, after all.'

Regis laughed again. 'My sentiments exactly.'

'Mmm,' said Jocasta. 'Not that I mind, but now that you have asked me, why do *you* drive with *me*?'

'I have a purpose,' he said amused. Then he added, 'I am glad not to have misled you, but *why* do you say I do not admire you?'

'At first I was nervous that you did,' Jocasta Fortune confided calmly, 'for you are not the sort of man I admire at all.' She looked at him blandly. 'Should I apologise for saying so? Only I find today that we are being frank.' He inclined his head, smiling, and she continued, 'I can see now, though, that you are an intense sort of man. You would want your wife to read books, and be intelligent and witty and sophisticated, I can tell.'

'How can you tell?'

'By the women you spend time with at balls. Mrs Norton, Lady Jersey and the like. All *we* would have in common is horses.'

'Not much to build a relationship on, it is true. I am glad we have had our talk today, it worried me a little that you might—'

'Hold a *tendre* for you?' said Jocasta, but with no real inflection in the dead calm of her voice. She looked him up and down in a speculative way that he found made him slightly uncomfortable. 'No,' she said with finality.

It was the answer Regis wanted, but its very certainty had a slightly depressing effect on his self-esteem. However, he said, equally matter-of-factly, 'Good.' He hesitated. 'Perhaps we have discussed my purpose enough for today.'

'We have not discussed it at all,' said Jocasta, and Regis noted that her voice was once again flat.

'I think, Miss Fortune, that you are not much engaged in the events of this Season.'

'I have *several* appointments every day,' answered Jocasta with a lofty chin.

'I have observed that you are *busy*. But I said, not *engaged*.'

She sat for a moment, as though wondering whether to reply, but finally answered. 'This Season feels quite different than the previous, I confess. But it is my last, so I must do my duty.'

'Your last?'

'There are a great many Fortune girls. We each get two seasons in London, my papa has decided.'

'But you are not in your usual spirits this Season?' Regis said, somewhat gently.

Jocasta glared at him and the plaintive look that his eyebrows gave him when he was concerned, pulling the corners of his eyes down, was like a mask of all the pity that was driving her to lose her reason at this time. 'You *know*!' She closed her eyes briefly as though to contain herself. 'I did not expect Sir Justin to be such a tattle-tale.'

'He was concerned for you ... in case my purpose was to play with you. That is the only reason he mentioned it.'

'I do not wish for his concern or pity. Or yours. These rides with you, because you are so cold, were the one spot of freedom in this dreadful Season. *Now ...!* You may not call on me again, sir.'

Regis was taken aback by her venom. He looked down on her just as the first spots of rain came on, wilting the feather on her handsome bonnet. 'I do not pity you,' but as he looked at the little face, so full of rage and hurt, he thought he might be lying. He leaned nearer, threateningly. 'I want to *use* you.'

Regis' face, thought Jocasta at that moment, looked every inch the Demon King she had heard him called. His yellow eyes held hers, and his eyebrows frowned dramatically downward, so that he seemed dangerous and evil. Somehow, it salved her spirit. Better this than ... 'Why me?' she asked.

'Let us go to the Coffee House nearby and shelter. We are bound to find some lady we know to take refuge with, and stop any chatter.'

Jocasta shrugged, resigned, as they did so. But when Regis placed her hand on his crooked arm, elbowed his way through the sheltering throng of the Coffee House and hit upon a table already occupied by two dames, she threw him a glance of deep dislike.

'Viscountess!' he was saying. 'I was driving Miss Fortune when it came onto rain. I wonder if we might join you.'

Viscountess Swanson, that stickler for propriety, nodded regally. 'Miss Fortune!' she said, bowing her head, infinitesimally, to Jocasta.

Jocasta replied, colourlessly, 'Thank you, my lady.'

'I've just sent for my carriage, Sir Damon. I am able take Miss Fortune to Brinklaw Gardens.'

'I was to take her to Onslow House, where she has moved to stay with the marchioness, my lady.'

He could see the viscountess saving this tidbit for later, for it was not yet generally known. 'It is convenient for me to go there,' said the old lady loftily.

Sir Damon, ignoring with difficulty the pinch that Jocasta was inflicting on his arm to detain him, detached himself, bowed low and was gone.

Georgette was tripping down the stairs when the door opened, and Jocasta entered. The marchioness could see the closed carriage on the street, just before it drove off. 'Was that the Swanson crest?' Jocasta gave her sister a sulky look. 'Then did *Viscountess Swanson* drive you? I thought you were to come here after you drove with one of your friends?'

'I did so ... has the rest of my baggage arrived?' When her sister nodded, Jocasta added, '...but it came on to mizzle and we drove to a coffee house for shelter. He left me with that old witch.'

'Jocasta!' protested Georgette.

Jocasta rolled her eyes. 'You do not know what I have had to endure these past minutes, Georgie. She has disparaged me, my manners, my dubious choice of companion, my family — excepting of course Papa, whom she regards as a saint—' At this last, the marchioness permitted herself a snort. Had it not been Viscountess Swanson who was being talked of, Georgette might have asked her sister about the dubious companion. But as it was, Georgette immediately discounted every insinuation. Seeing her sister seriously discomposed, and now that she was divested of her bonnet and pelisse, Georgette took her by the waist and led her into an elegant salon, 'Come and sit and I shall send for refreshments. It is not like you to let yourself be upset by that — by the viscountess.'

'Stop being either a marchioness or my mama for a moment, Georgie, and just be my sister,' sighed Jocasta. 'The viscountess is the vilest cat imaginable, and you know it.'

'A prying busybody!' agreed Georgette, joining in.

'A pimple, no, a boil, on the face of the earth!' added Jocasta with relish.

'A poisoned toad!' enjoined Georgette.

'A ... sinuous snake!' was all Jocasta could summon.

'*That trunk of humours, that bolting house of beastliness, that swollen parcel of dropsies—*'

'Oh, that *is* good. Where had you that from?' asked Jocasta, diverted.

'It is from Shakespeare, part of a very long insult that I memorised to say to myself silently, if Papa or George were chafing me too much.'

'Georgie!' said Jocasta, shocked. 'I thought you the calm one. I never knew ... How does it continue?'

'*...that huge bombard of sack, that stuffed cloak-bag of guts, that roasted Manningtree ox with pudding in his belly, that reverend vice, that grey iniquity, that father ruffian, that vanity in years!*'

'How splendid!' laughed Jocasta, finally in a better mood. 'I too, shall have to memorise it. Who ever thought that *Shakespeare* could be so useful? It is George to a "t" until the last part.'

Very seriously, Jocasta requested that Georgette wrote the insult down so that she could con it. Georgette did so, laughing, glad about the leavening of her sister's spirits.

'Oh, and you received a missive — from Katerina!' said Georgette, reminded.

'I did?' said Jocasta.

'You did, directed here since I had written her of my plan.' Georgette tilted her chin and gave Jocasta a resentful look. 'I am green with envy. I write to the castle every week, and only the twins reply.'

Jocasta broke the wafer, leaning back and curling her legs beneath her as though she were already at home, Georgette was happy to note.

Dear Jocasta,

If this letter smears your fingers, or stains one of your fine gowns, I cannot help it. While you and Portia kick up your heels, our life is a dust field, with every nook covered with an inch layer. You did not think Castle Fortune could get any more inconvenient, did you? Well, try it when the roof is removed in sections and all our hiding places are covered in dirt and the intrusion of icicles.

Do not fear for us, though. We moved from room to room, and all was misery, so we tried to take refuge at Great Aunt Hester's, but she wanted us out quickly, all because of Leonora interrogating her incessantly about London life. But our Lion's concerns are not dresses, and balls, but the occupations of gentlemen in town. Strange, but you know Leo when she becomes fixed upon something.

If only I can persuade Papa to send the twins next year, I need not go there at all. As the castle freezes us, it seems ludicrous to wish to remain here, but it is so. It is not London I object to, but all the social occasions — I do not think I could bear it. Anyway, we no longer freeze at night because of Georgette's suggestion. The little sitting room that used to be hers (and Mama's of course) has a chimney to the side of the house, not on the roof, and we can light the fire and have brought every comforter we could find to lay out for sleeping. It works well, though Marguerite takes the centre spot and is by far the warmest. I have noticed that her sweetness contains a strong vein of self-preservation, you know. When we seek the kitchens, she steals food with an unladylike stealth, and the servants blame Leonora or me, never the angel Marguerite.

This was all very loquacious for Katerina, the most reserved of all her sisters. But the next line gave Jocasta a hint of why.

Moving away from Papa must be a relief. You have exchanged one sister for another, but that cannot be helped, and I am sure the visitors at Onslow House are less tiresome.

Here was the crux. She referred, of course, to Lord Paxton. Even Katerina felt she needed sympathy. Somehow, from this distance, she forgave her sister, and even found this unusual bit of noticing behaviour comforting. Katerina always seemed to care for nothing or no one, but she casually shared her food, or offered you the warmest blanket, or diverted George's ire away from you, to herself. Her red hair had never denoted any obvious spirit, but Jocasta always thought it suited her. For Katerina was unique amongst all the sisters, straight-faced, flat toned, but unexpectedly understanding.

I hear you have a great many suitors. If you think that a great thing, then I am glad. Choose someone kind if you can, Jocasta, whatever Papa might want.

Send me books on the new sciences, will you? We have nothing here at all.

The twins think of you and Portia much more often than I do, and no doubt they will write to hear of all your balls and parties and dresses. Do not reply to me unless you have visited a museum or something, at least, interesting. I do not wish to know about <u>people</u>.

Your sister,

Katerina.

35

Jocasta found Georgette, and put the letter in her hand asking, 'What are the new sciences?'

Georgette shook her head. 'I am unclear about the old sciences, too! We shall have to ask Onslow.'

'Or Regis!'

'Who?' asked Georgette.

'Never mind,' said Jocasta. 'I probably won't encounter the gentleman again.'

CHAPTER 4

The Baron's Intentions

B esides his own amusements, Baron Fortune, owner of Fortune Castle and father to a brood of ten daughters (five still unwed) and one heir, came to London annually with a purpose. For some years now (since the first of them had reached the age to be wed) it had been important to attend the entire Season. He generally brought two of his girls and tricked them out prettily, in order to get them off his hands at a later date. After the debacle of his fourth daughter, Mary, running off with the music master, he kept a reluctant eye on their swains. A poor marriage meant no settlements. In this regard, it had been a bountiful year. Both Alderly (the earl, and Lord Paxton's papa) and Onslow had been generous. Large sums had been settled upon him and Onslow had included a smaller, but welcome, yearly allowance. However, his man of business had stipulated that his funds, at his rate of expenditure, would not last the year out. There had been debts to pay, of course, which had turned out to be much greater than he thought when one added up every little piece of paper; he had paid off staff whose wages had not been forked over in full for a number of years, and agreed to some essential (a surly man-of-work had informed him) repairs to the roof of Castle Fortune. "Else the whole thing'll crumble in a year or sooner." The baron, with funds on hand, gave in, and his residual daughters Katerina, and the twins Leonora and Marguerite were now living in a cloud of dust and stones as the construction work took place while the rest of the Fortunes were in town. But it was a bit much to have to curtail his own delights. His visits to town were to indulge all the tastes of a gentleman. The baron had a tall, powerful frame which had thickened considerably as he aged, but he still rode his horse King every day, dröve a handsome high-perched phaeton around town, and also stabled his travelling carriage and a curricle. He dressed himself as became his station, he drank with his cronies in gin dens where sportsmen mixed with gentlemen, for the purpose of discussing the odds on upcoming events such as boxing, cockfighting or racing. Town had special spectacles too, such as boxing bouts between female bruisers (clad only in white stockings and short petticoats above the knee) which were to be found in the sleazier parts of the city. He also belonged to many gentleman's clubs, and gambled heavily there. Indeed, it was said of him that he would put a monkey (the cant phrase for five hundred pounds) on a pea counting contest. Drinking, sporting, gaming and visiting discreet houses for a particular type of female companionship, all cost a great deal of money. On top of that, he had had a run of bad luck these days, so his Man of Business' words had struck home.

It was all the fault of George. His son was as tall and broad as he, and much more handsome: with his youthful build and strong jaw he was his father's pride. As to amusements, George followed in the footsteps of his père. Recently however, keeping George's stable, rooms and paying his gaming debts had palled. Once the baron heeded the warning from Mr Tippet, he berated George, had him move from his rooms and sell two of his carriages to save on cost, leaving him only a phaeton of his own, and warned him strongly against his gaming. 'For I will not frank your losses, sir. I shall no longer do so.' In this he was moved by a look of steel he had seen in Onslow's eyes as the settlement papers were signed:

'I hope that I have been more than generous as a response to my receiving into my care your precious daughter, sir,' the marquis had said.

The Baron, nodding his shaggy thatch of hair had replied, 'Yes, yes, my boy. Most generous.'

'Good. And you understand the rules of play sir. Gaming debts are the responsibility of the loser, and I myself never play where I cannot pay.'

It had been a warning, and the baron knew it. This well had run dry. With a lesser man, the baron might have thought this an empty threat, but he was convinced by Onslow's eyes. Usually mild or sometimes cool, that day they had been hard. The Earl of Alderly, too, would brook no further claims. No. It was for Jocasta to enlarge his coffers once more. He was sorry she had left the house, so that he could no longer reiterate this to her on an hourly basis, but he would watch to see what was the richest prize he could capture for her.

Portia, engaged, was nothing to him now. He seldom spoke to her. But Jocasta, now. He must turn up to Almacks a few times to see how she fared.

She was prettier than Georgette after all (Georgette's husband would violently disagree with this assessment) — and Georgette had nabbed a marquis.

CHAPTER 5

A Polite Rescue

'Thank you for the rescue.'

'You are just fortunate that I was driving, rather than riding, today, Miss Fortune. It would have been a great insult indeed to Mr ... what was his name?

'York. Mr York.'

'Why was rescue needed? I do not object, but why—?'

'I find being admired so very tiring these days. I wished to be with someone who does not like me.'

Regis reflected that she wished to be with someone whose opinion matched her own. 'I do not dislike you.'

'Perhaps. I feared a change in you after our last meeting, but seeing you again reassured me. You are quite gloriously indifferent, at least. It makes me content.' Jocasta spoke in a removed tone, but saw the change her words had made in Sir Damon's hard face. It might be

41

concern, but it could be disdain. 'Oh, do not look so! I am aware that there are a great many gentlemen in town who view me with indifference, I do not think so highly of myself as to believe I am universally admired. But *they* do not call upon me, or spend time with me, as you do. Therefore, *you* are my only refuge of indifference.'

'I have never figured as such before.' He regarded her with a sad amusement. She was too young, he considered, to be quite so disillusioned. 'I think it is time to tell you *why* I spend time with you.'

'Is it?' asked Jocasta blandly.

'You do not seem to be interested in the reason.'

'What difference does your reason make to me? *I* have a purpose for *you,* and that suffices.'

'You might also allow me to have a purpose for *you.*' He saw a fearful look cross her face, and added swiftly, 'Not a usual one.'

'What are the usual ones?' Jocasta enquired.

'A prospective suitor. Or, at least, because I find you entertaining and amusing — as an object of dalliance.'

Jocasta shrugged. 'I am not at all amusing. I do not know how to be. I believe Georgette is amusing. I never really needed to *amuse* gentlemen. The gentlemen do all the conversational gambits. They do not seem to require it of me. All I need do is smile at them, or laugh at an amusing remark. At first, at any rate. I believe some find me disappointing as a companion, in the end.'

Damon observed the serious, pointed little face. 'This cannot be. Why, then, do so many men pursue you?'

'I am accounted pretty, I suppose, and the words *"fairy princess"* are said of me. I think that some have a romantic notion of me when, in truth, I am not even a little romantic. They make all the romance up in their heads.'

'Have you no responsibility for all that?'

'Because I smile at them and talk civilly?' said Jocasta, those large serious eyes regarding him in genuine enquiry. 'Should I not?'

He was taken aback by her straightforward enquiry. 'I beg your pardon, Miss Fortune. I should not have said so much. It is not my wish to offer you criticism'.

'I am truly desirous of knowing, sir, I assure you. How *should* I conduct myself? Tell me a better way forward. I find myself at a loss.'

She was not the only one. Regis, too, was at a loss, but his primary instinct was to offer reassurance. 'I have never witnessed you do aught that was either ill-natured or too coming. You comport yourself as a young lady should, I believe.'

'Thank you,' said Jocasta with feeling. 'I was afraid that I did ill without knowing.'

'Do you really have no interest in me or my motives, Miss Fortune?'

'I have very little interest in anyone's motives. My brain is not inquisitive, and I am shockingly selfish.'

He laughed. 'We share the latter trait then.'

They drove on in silence for a minute, while Jocasta put her head to one side in thought. 'Oh, there is *one* thing I'd like to know.'

'*Perhaps* I may answer you,' he said with one of his mobile brows flying into the air, making the scroll shape again.

Jocasta seemed to find this vaguely amusing. 'I have heard you called the Demon King; how did you earn that name?'

'I have done all sorts of devilish deeds!' His answer was flippant and roguish, but it did not seem to interest her, so he added, more prosaically, 'Some wag at school called me that. Demon because of my Christian name and my devilish looks, and King after the meaning of my surname — Regis means King, of course. I tried hard to live up to it in later life.'

'It is a name a schoolboy would love, I suppose. Better than Prissy-Missy, which is what the Fortune girls nicknamed my brother George.'

Regis considered the picture of the tall, handsome George Fortune in his head. 'It does not seem to fit.'

'You only say that because you have never lived with him. He nit-picks all our actions, and none of his own. It may not fit his looks, but Cassie, my sister Cassandra you know, just chose it to annoy him. We rather gave it up when she left home. She was able to shout it from a great distance, so that she could run before he caught her. The rest of us do not have her volume.'

He was amused despite himself. '*That* is all you wish to know? The origin of my nickname?'

'Yes - what else?'

'My reason for our drives and spending time together.'

She looked ahead at some trees, disinterested. 'I have already told you. Since they suit me, I have no need to know why they suit you.'

'It is more than that...' he said speculatively, 'you do not *wish* to know. Why?' She did not answer him. 'You are very strange, Miss Fortune. Have you *none* of the inquisitiveness natural to a female?' Again, she was silent. 'What,' he ruminated audibly, 'have you to lose by knowing my reason?' He jerked her arm with an elbow so that she turned to face him. His eyes commanded her, and she let out a little sigh.

'Your company. If you tell me, perhaps it must all end.' The look that she gave, as she said this to him, was not lover-like or admiring, just raw and open. He began to understand the depth of her wound.

'Nevertheless, I must tell you today.' She looked away again, waiting for the inevitable, it seemed. 'It was not my intention to discuss this with you, but it was an impulse to take you up. The world will tell you that I am famous for my impulses. I wished to make a friend of you, so as to throw you in the way of another friend.'

'If you wished to make a friend of me, you were not very pleasant.'

'I did not wish you to misunderstand me.' His gaze sought hers and he saw her blush a little.

'Well, I have never done so. But you did not succeed in making me a friend.'

'I should have said, I sought your acquaintance merely. Enough of it to introduce you to my friend.' He paused as he saw her think about this. 'You do not know him; he is not yet in town. He was supposed to arrive earlier.'

'Has that lengthened our acquaintance then?' Regis pursed his lips. Jocasta looked away. 'You wished to introduce me to someone? To what purpose?'

'A devilish purpose, as befits my reputation,' Regis said frivolously.

'I see,' Jocasta replied, coolly. 'And how would this help you?'

'I chose you as a young lady who represents his ideal. He admired Miss White's beauty last year, but her sophistication repelled him, I believe, however much she tries to hide it. That makes him nervous. He likes young, innocent beauties. I thought you just his type.'

'It sounds as if you wished to sell me in a Turkish Bazaar, sir.' Her tone was derisive, but he heard some hurt behind it.

'Perhaps. He is betting on another innocent young beauty at present, and I cannot let him win her.' He laughed a harsh laugh, 'and demon that I am, I did not scruple to think to use you as my weapon.'

She looked to the side, with her eyes distant. 'Why is he not good enough for your ... friend?'

'He is young and inconstant, I believe.' Jocasta's eyes became even cooler, looking further from him. '*You* were in no real danger.' He knew that he was offering an apology, an excuse perhaps. This was not usual to him, and he surprised himself at his need to explain. This would all have been so simple if Jocasta Fortune was really the vivacious sprite she portrayed in the ballroom, and if the advent of his target had not been delayed. 'I merely wished to demonstrate to that lady the young man's tendency to flirtation. She has been too much sheltered, and I feared she may trust him too much.' When Jocasta did not reply, he added, 'So many others flirt with you, it would make no difference to *you*, I supposed.' She did not look his way and he waited for her ire. 'You have your family to protect you, after all. The baron, and your brother.'

'Of course,' said Jocasta bleakly, 'The baron, my brother.' She seemed to gather herself, and said in a false, bright tone, 'Is the gentleman eligible?'

'He is a duke.'

'Then my father and brother would offer me no protection,' she said flatly. Damon reeled. But her soft voice continued, in tone she reserved for him today, 'however, if the gentleman is presentable, introduce him, then pursue your love.'

'She is not my love — precisely. More my obligation, as she has no family of her own.'

'Since he is a man of rank and fortune, I may be obliged to you for the introduction, Sir Damon.' She put up her parasol. 'It hardly matters, after all.'

CHAPTER 6

Family Friend

D amon Regis felt like the very demon he was named for. He had striven to make the connection with Miss Fortune so that the introduction of his young friend the Duke of Enderby would be perfectly natural. Before he carried out his devilish deed, he had spent time with her, making sure that he would do as little damage in the commission of his purpose as he could. He had been cold enough to forbid her to mistake his attentions for romance. He had wanted to understand her, to better aid his plan. Now he understood her too well. She was not the frivolous young girl of the ballroom; she was hurt and scared and newly unsure of herself and the attention paid to her by her beaus — only because one romantic idiot had hurt her pride. He had seen Jocasta Fortune talk to Lord Paxton awkwardly at social events, and he did not believe she ached for him. She was a female who kept herself well in check, however — so perhaps he was mistaken. But in regarding Miss Fortune, he had begun to think that he alone could see what was behind each expression in those huge blue eyes. They sparkled in amusement, and smiled at the remarks of gentlemen who came her way, but the look beneath was sometimes wary, sometimes exhausted. He wanted to tell her that it was not *all* false, as she believed. That Sir Eamon Dalton really cared for her, that Mr York actually admired her. But Miss Fortune evidently believed they admired a false vision of her — and she was not all wrong. They saw the light and breezy fairy, and he saw a sad little girl only.

Today, whatever he had told himself about his purpose in telling her the truth, he saw that *he* had wounded her more. If Cecilia Montgomery had not been delayed by a week, he would not now know all he did of Jocasta Fortune, and he could have fulfilled his purpose with little thought or regret. But now he remembered her saying, her face closed to him, *"It hardly matters, after all."* And he knew that she meant that *she* hardly mattered, and he was pierced with remorse. All at once, his plan fell into ashes. He would have to think of another way to show Cecilia the duke's true colours.

Somehow, though, he would have to undo the harm he had already done to Miss Fortune. He could not be the man to add to the early cynicism of such an innocent. She was just lost, that was all. He thought of her bleak little face (that he had been permitted to see only because she dropped the social pretence when with him), her tiny frame, her sadness and fear — and he could hardly bear it. The Marchioness of Onslow seemed like a sensible young woman. Why could *she* not see, not understand?

But of course, the marchioness was one of those from whom it was important that Jocasta Fortune hid her feelings. Expressing some things to him, (who after all did not matter in her life) had been easy.

She had to hide her pain from those who would pity her. But now he, Regis, sincerely pitied her, and her predicament. Some of it was her own pride, of course, and that she was so young she could not think of a way of protecting that pride, and continue to enjoy her young life. But still, he pitied her. He had never liked George Fortune, whom he considered a handsome vaunter of nought, and he was beginning to think that he may have been cut from his father's pattern, which did not auger well for Jocasta Fortune's protectors.

The Marquis of Onslow was certainly a man who could be trusted. But he was newly married, and though he now housed his wife's sister, he may not notice her predicament. How Regis might bring the subject up with Lucian, or even with his ever-present best friend Faulkes, was questionable. It was suspicious, at all events, for him to express such interest, to explain how it was that he was now worried about Onslow's sister-in-law. It might land both himself and Miss Fortune in hot water. And he knew, if he told Justin Faulkes, that it would arouse just such pity as Jocasta Fortune could not bear.

No, if she felt Damon Regis' pity, she would cease to talk with him, and thus he would not be able to help her through this morass. He knew that *all* of this defied convention. His interest in aiding a young lady find her way once more was inexplicable by society's rules. If he was not family, or family friend — if he was not intending her for his bride, then Miss Fortune was very definitely *not* his concern. Damon had never much cared for convention, though, and whatever way he regarded it, just by driving Miss Fortune into herself more deeply, as he had today, he now had a moral duty to help her. She had kept so much hidden — it was difficult to see anyone else who could.

It was the Carmichaels' Rout tonight and she was to attend, she had said, indifferently chatting as they had driven home. Her bright manner had been more frightening than anything that had come before it. He had become to her no more than Mr York. He would not live in that false place, and he would not allow Jocasta Fortune to do so much longer. He did not have an invitation to the rout, but he would hardly be denied admission to such a hodgepodge occasion. He asked for an early dinner, and went upstairs to change.

The Carmichaels welcomed their unexpected guest with warmth. 'Sir Damon!' Lady Carmichael lied smoothly after he had apologised for his arrival, 'I did not know you were in town, or I would surely have sent you a card.'

The ballroom of the house glittered with candelabra, with tables strewn across the floor somewhat informally and Chinese lanterns slung between pillars and trees in the garden beyond the open doors. Sustenance was available on tables here and there, Regis saw, and there may be dancing later, for a few musicians were tuning up on a raised dais. A rout indeed, a casual occasion with entertainment made to look ad hoc, but carefully contrived by the hostess.

'Thank you, my lady, you are too kind,' drawled the baronet.

The buxom Lady Carmichael, a plump dame in her forties, exchanged a knowing glance with him. 'Why are you *really* here, sir? Have you some devilish business with one of my guests?'

'Oh, my reputation!' said Regis, suavely. He leaned down towards her and said confidentially, 'You have found me out. I have a bet with Onslow that must be settled this evening.'

'I knew it!' she cried, clapping her hands in delight. 'I shall not ask for your gentlemen's secrets, but you cannot deceive such an old hand as I.'

Regis bowed. 'You look just the same as when I first saw you. I had a huge *tendre* for you, you know, my lady, when first I came to Town, but alas, you were already married!'

'And ten years your senior! You are a demon indeed sir!' Her eyes admonished him, but she had flushed none the less, and walked off happily, to greet a new guest.

Damon sought the Onslow party and saw them almost at once. He walked to them with purposeful energy, and joined them, greeting Onslow with a warmth that raised the marquis' eyebrow.

'What is amiss with you, Regis?'

'Just *glad* to see an old friend, Lucian,' Damon said, with a warm slap on the marquis' shoulder. Onslow's brow did not go down, and he turned his head to regard Regis' hand. Regis squeezed. 'And your beautiful marchioness, of course.'

Georgette smiled, but Onslow said, 'That does it! What are you up to, King?'

The encroaching hand fell away, and Regis' face became as innocent as he could make it. 'Swearing on the dead body of Pet,' Damon said, referring to a dog that both he and Lucian had played with as children, 'That I am up to nothing.' His mobile brows did a strange quizzical dance as his eyes looked upwards, as though examining his conscience. 'Or at least, nothing that you would dislike.'

'I am not so sure about that.'

Georgette was more direct. 'Does this have anything to do with my sister?'

'Yes,' Regis said directly, meeting her eyes. She held his for a second, and then exchanged glances with her husband. 'But not,' Sir Damon continued, 'anything that you may be imagining.'

Georgette's eyes followed Jocasta, now dancing with Sir Justin in a country dance set. Her sister smiled politely when Sir Justin came forward, but the smile dropped as he turned away. 'You should not pursue her sir, if you mean nothing *that I can imagine* by her.' This was not quite polite, but Damon met her admonishing eye, taking to his friend's wife at once.

'I can see why you would think that,' said Sir Damon, and Georgette considered that he looked at his most wicked. 'That is why,' and here Regis' eyes sought Onslow's, and his voice lowered confidentially as he leaned forward, 'I mean to become a Family Friend.'

'This,' said Onslow definitely, 'is more of your devilry! I was coming to visit you to ask anyway. Why, when she is not in your line at all, have you been spending time with my sister-in-law?'

Sir Damon raised two hands, palms forward, in a placating manner, and said, 'I admit I *did* have a self-serving,' Georgette gasped, and Damon's eye turned to her, 'but *utterly innocent* purpose when I began to spend time with Miss Fortune.'

Georgette's fists bunched, and Onslow was amused. 'You had some *purpose* for my sister?' Georgette said venomously, 'And so you *used* her?'

Damon was rather surprised by the direct attack from the reputedly serene marchioness. Seeking the words to explain himself had one eyebrow raised and another do a quizzical ripple on the baronet's brow and Georgette found her ire diverted in fascination. 'I have no such purpose now,' he said contritely, touching his heart. His histrionics reignited Georgette's ire, but her husband interrupted.

'Yet, you have spent time with her. Something I have just been made aware of,' said Onslow dangerously.

Damon's hands raised again, palms forward, 'I assure you, Lucian, I have been *consistently* unpleasant to her.' He smiled at them both, seeming to expect gratitude. '*Really.*'

'Now I know,' said the Marchioness of Onslow, menacingly, but under her breath so as not to attract attention, 'why you are called the Demon King. You sought to fascinate her by keeping her at a distance and pursued her at the same time. You fiend! If I were a man, I would call you out.'

Onslow had been entranced by his wife's sudden rage, and had completely forgotten any but her in the process of watching it, but her last comment called him to order. 'I do not have a gauntlet about me to slap on your face, Regis, but consider yourself called out.'

'Lucian, I...' protested Georgette, afraid.

Damon Regis continued, his voice as placating as before. 'Really, Miss Fortune's heart has not been damaged by me. She has always known I had an ulterior motive.'

'Which is?'

'*That* I cannot say, and it is not important anymore, for I have given it up.'

'You say she knew, and that her heart is not engaged. Yet for all you were unpleasant to her, she still spent time with you.'

'Yes. I *could* explain why, but that would be to betray confidences that were given to me on the understanding, I believe, that they would not be repeated.' Georgette looked at him hard. 'Yes, I know it is strange that she gives me her confidence when *you*, as her sister, are left wondering what ails her. Am I correct?' Georgette looked up at him. 'And you are wondering what this means? I came by this knowledge, which I cannot reveal, by the happenstance of Miss Fortune not caring a fig for me.' He looked over at Onslow, 'But now that I do *have* that information, I feel duty bound to help her.' Onslow frowned. 'For who else may?'

Georgette had her turn to frown. 'But why *should* you? I do not understand you, sir. You say you are not interested in my sister...'

'I am not. Young females have never interested me.'

Georgette glanced at Onslow at this. Her husband gave a reluctant nod. 'Then...'

'It just happened this way. I accidentally, by dint of pursuing a scheme of my own, found out the depth of sadness in a young lady who is quite lost at the moment.' The marchioness' eye drifted towards Jocasta once more, as she skipped in the dance, apparently carefree.

'Is it as bad as that?'

When the marchioness turned back, Regis held her eye and said seriously, 'Yes.' He regarded them both. 'But I *do* see that my spending much more time with Miss Fortune will arouse the speculation that none of us want. And so, I propose to become ...' he paused dramatically, 'a *Family Friend*.'

'But I don't like you,' said Onslow, flippantly.

'Yes, just like that, old friend. Just treat me as you always have, but I will be nearer you more frequently. I need an excuse to take Miss Fortune out, to help her. It is not remarked when Justin takes her out, for she is part of the family to whom he is most close.'

Georgette looked at her husband and read something in his eyes. 'We are not firmly engaged tomorrow. Come to dinner, *Family Friend*.' Regis swept her a low bow, then clasped her gloved hand briefly. 'I am trusting you because my husband does,' she hissed at him. He nodded, and then departed before Jocasta and Justin returned to their side.

'Was that King?' asked Faulkes.

Jocasta's eyes, Georgette noticed, did not follow the baronet's departure. She did not know if this was a good thing or a bad. She must have a care for Jocasta's heart, which could not take another blow, she thought. If Regis was wrong, and Jocasta became entangled with him, she would try to protect her sister at all costs.

Later, in bed, Georgette lay against her husband's chest and said, 'I am not sure about this, Lucian darling. Young girls get such notions in their heads...'

'They do. I have heard tell of a young lady who fell in love after exchanging just one look with a gentleman, afterwards refused all offers and returned to her country castle to pine.' He grasped her more firmly as he teased her about the love she had kept hidden so long.

'She did not pine,' said Georgette. 'She was much too sensible to go into a decline. No physicians were called at all.'

Onslow laughed, 'I'm glad the tale had a happy ending. But you think Jocasta is in danger of being like that?'

'Yes, I fear just that. I do not want her hurt by becoming close to someone who says he does not care for her in that way.'

'He says *she* does not care for *him,* and that only *he* can help her. It is unusual, but it may well be true. Certainly, *something* troubles Jocasta. I was not much interested in her, I confess, but there is a sadness in her that has disturbed me, because she has tried to hide it. And I know that it has disturbed you.'

'Yes, I was sure that getting her away from the house with Paxton and Portia in it would do the trick — not to mention Papa — but she is only a little better. However, Regis is too dangerous, I think. It would be much better if he were a deal uglier.'

'I shall suggest it to him. Perhaps some duelling scars would do it.' Georgette giggled. Onslow sighed. 'I am not entirely easy, either. But for Damon Regis, as well as for Jocasta.'

'Whatever do you mean?' Georgette was surprised enough to raise her head and look up at him.

'The Demon King is entering into a dangerous game. And I know enough of Regis' honour to know that *he* knows it. If, in this process of helping her, the young lady should fall for him, I am sure he will accept the consequences — however much he may not wish to. And he would never let her know.'

'You *mean*-?'

'He would marry, and feign love for an entire lifetime. It would, after all, be his responsibility.'

'It will not come to *that*, surely. If Jocasta does not prefer any of her court at present, and I cannot see that she does, we must tell her that she need not fear that this is her last season. She may come to us again next year, whatever Papa intends.'

'I knew it! I'll be knee-deep in Fortune sisters for the foreseeable future.'

'I promise you it will not be so! Jocasta is a special case—' but she felt her husband's chest rumble in amusement. 'You—!' she gave him a light buff with a fist and snuggled in more firmly. 'But would Sir Damon really do what you said, merely for honour?'

'I believe he would,' said Onslow.

'How do you know?'

'I suppose,' said Onslow, considering, 'it is because it is what I would do if I were so foolish as to be caught in such a trap. He's risking something to help your sister, you know.'

'Men are such complicated creatures,' sighed Georgette, subsiding, and Onslow laughed, getting back to the serious pursuit of kissing her.

So now Sir Damon Regis meant to ignore her! Well, he had refuted his purpose after all, thought Jocasta, viciously attacking a pillow, attempting to tame it into submission. As she had danced with Sir Justin, numbed by his kindness, she had noted the Demon King's back as he conversed with Onslow and Georgette. Something in his eye on their last drive had alerted her. Had it been *pity?* As she approached her party once more, Jocasta had been ready to rebuff any offer of a dance from him, but he had vanished quickly.

There was no increase in *kindness* at least, but to ignore her entirely ... he was a true *demon*. It did not matter. His plan was dead, he had said. There was no reason for them to meet again.

But his rudeness was not to be borne.

Her head rose and thudded the pillow again. It was some time before she was able to sleep.

CHAPTER 7

Tutelage Begins

S ir Justin Faulkes, who had come to breakfast after riding with all three Fortune sisters, Lord Paxton and Onslow, was held back from his meat by Onslow shouldering him into the study. This was a magnificent apartment, lined with books, with two handsome desks in the centre of the room (for marquis and marchioness), and enough space, thought Faulkes, to drive a gig around them. Against the wall was a further desk, where the marquis' secretary, Mark Proctor, was engaged with correspondence.

'Are you trying to deny me breakfast once more, Lucian?' asked Faulkes with irritation. 'I do think you are—'

'I *should* deny you breakfast. Before your household completely loses the way of serving it. Why do you eat mine?'

'I—'

'Mark! You're here!' said the marquis, as though surprised.

The young man stood up, smiling cheerily. 'Not anymore, my lord,' he said, and left the room.

'Anyway, *that's* not it,' said the marquis. 'Want to tell you we will be seeing a deal more of Regis around here.' Onslow sighed, 'Though why I am telling you, I have no idea. It is not as though you live here.'

'Regis? You don't mean to say—'

'I don't mean to say anything, and neither should you, if asked. You *might* spend a little more time with him yourself.'

'What—?'

'Just do not reprimand him for spending time with Jocasta.'

'I have already done so.'

'And didn't inform *me*? I only heard in the last two days that he was doing any such thing.'

'I didn't inform you because he said that he meant no harm to Miss Fortune.'

'*King*? When you know what ructions he causes even when he means no harm? How could you not tell me?'

'If you didn't talk to him for six months after a dashed horse race,' said Faulkes, and Onslow grinned, 'I could only imagine what you would do if you knew he was driving your sister-in-law. I was keeping an eye on the situation.'

'Well, you have done an ill job. A man of your address should have gotten Jocasta to confide, not he.'

'I beg your pardon?'

'Never mind. We'll miss breakfast if we don't hurry, for the girls are ravenous after a ride.' He pushed the baronet *out* through the study door in the same way as he had pushed him *in*. 'They are tiny, but they eat a prodigious amount.'

'Georgette will explain all to me later,' goaded Faulkes.

'Don't speak of it before Jocasta!'

Sir Justin gave him a scoffing look and they went to eat.

The famous rift between Sir Damon Regis and the Marquis of Onslow that Sir Justin Faulkes had referred to, had been somewhat of a comedy for the knowing ones in the *ton*. Two years ago, after the fabled carriage race, the marquis had given Regis, his erstwhile friend, the cut direct at a ball; after that, Regis had arisen from a gaming table at White's only because Onslow had joined it, saying he did not play with poor sports. Their intimates knew that this was posturing in both cases, and never doubted that the rivalry was exaggerated, but rumours spread, of course.

Now, it appeared, all was mended. Sir Damon and the marquis and marchioness were seen often together, obviously enjoying each other's company. The baronet hosted the Onslow party, plus Sir Justin Faulkes, in his opera box, and to supper afterwards. The Onslows included the two baronets in a party to Vauxhall Gardens. Both baronets danced at least once with Miss Fortune, (if they could get a slot before she was fully engaged) and both took her riding or walking in the park separately. There was nothing in this, decided the *Beau Monde*. Regis paid attention to a married lady, Mrs Norton (which raised some talk, since her husband was known to keep two mistresses) and spent more than was usual with the plain Lady Sumner — but since everyone knew this was just to discuss horseflesh (her ladyship being known as an expert judge) no words were spared on this intimacy, even by her dissolute husband. No, Regis' interest in ladies was dull work, the World was much more interested in a wager he had made with Lord Alvanley, betting his skill with an archer's bow against Alvanley's nominee, the brilliant Mr Beresford.

A drunken incident with the Earl of Grandiston (on furlough from the war in the Peninsula) where the two had stopped their carriages on London Bridge and engaged in a leaping contest over the roofs of the mercantile buildings that lined that landmark, gave high entertainment when whispered of in drawing rooms throughout the fashionable world. They held up traffic for a half-hour, it was said, and caused the Watch to be called. It was declared a draw.

It was rumoured, too, that Mrs Norton's husband, who was seen sporting a sling, had had a dawn meeting with Sir Damon Regis, and had become the victim of his deadly aim with a pistol. The jocularity with which the two greeted each other, when next they met, gave lie to this *on dit,* but some canny ones doubted still. More ructions around Regis, but as ever, he carried it off with style.

Around this time, Sir Damon was walking somewhat ahead of Sir Justin and Georgette. 'Did you really,' asked Jocasta Fortune, with unbecoming relish, 'shoot Mr Norton?'

Miss Fortune had been frostily cold for a few days after the Carmichaels' Rout, but she had since returned to a state of mere indifference. This comment was the most interested she had allowed herself to appear. But Regis quashed her, coolly. 'This is rather too direct, Miss Fortune.'

Jocasta swung her parasol, unconcerned. 'It is the latest *on dit.*' She turned and looked at him pertly. She was wearing a grass green bonnet, the colour of her parasol, with yellow ribbons, and trimmed with silken flowers tucked under the brim, resting among her blonde curls.

'You look as though you might be *flirting* with me, Miss Fortune.'

Jocasta looked away, her face a little sad. 'I was playing my tricks, I suppose. That is what my brother George calls them. My tricks. I am not always aware of it.'

Regis was conscious of being another who slapped down her spirits. What had she done but tease him a little? However, to allow such an energy to continue between them was to invite the very consequences he sought to avoid.

'It is your charm, not your tricks. It is only that, between us, charm is not an issue.'

'I suspect you mean my charm, as you call it, is shallow.' He began to speak, but she continued. 'It is, I know. It means no more than the charm gentlemen use upon me. Only, I do not know any other way to go on. How should I be, Sir Damon?' she asked, seriously.

Regis kicked a stone in his path in self-disgust. 'I have told you before, you comport yourself as might any young lady of quality, who has the attention given to her that you do. You have nothing to reproach yourself with, except that you do not seem to enjoy it anymore.'

Coming towards them was the pairing that always made Jocasta stiffen. Portia Fortune, looking relaxed and pretty in a fawn pelisse and bonnet, was on the arm of her beloved, the fair Lord Paxton. They were smiling at each other, and were almost upon their party before Portia saw her sisters. 'Jocasta! Georgette! Isn't it a fine day for a walk?'

'Yes!' said Jocasta brightly. 'Do you go to Almacks this evening, Portia?'

'No. There is a concert that Paxton and I wish to attend. A virtuoso from Italy, Pasquale Giordano, is playing, and we do not wish to miss it. Have you heard of him?'

'No,' said Jocasta, baldly - causing Regis to utter a short laugh.

Georgette and Faulkes came forward and chatted to Paxton and Portia, and Regis stood apart, seeing all. Miss Fortune's younger sister was deliriously happy to be with her swain, and could hardly contain it. Paxton was similarly happy, but seeing Jocasta Fortune made him pucker up, ashamed. He stood stiffly, looking sometimes distant, and sometimes piteously, at Jocasta. What a clod, thought Regis. If he had enough address to carry it off, Jocasta Fortune would not now be trembling. Regis moved rather nearer her than he usually permitted himself, and saw that the marchioness had done the same, but they were probably only adding to her humiliation. He at least should not be kind. But it was hard. This was a peculiar fate to have to cope with, and Jocasta Fortune was doing her utmost.

He was not known to be unpleasant in company, but Regis did his best, in imitation of the Beau at his deadliest. He yawned, holding a hand to his mouth, as Jocasta, in response to an inquiry from Portia, described her toilette for this evening.

'I fear we are boring you, sir,' said Jocasta sharply.

'Oh no! I assure you,' he drawled.

'It is somewhat chilly, ladies,' said Paxton, a trifle desperately. 'We should not keep you back.'

'I'll ride with you tomorrow, Jocasta!' said Portia. 'Goodbye, Georgie!'

Paxton, damn his hide, blushed and bowed, and the happy pair took themselves off.

'Where are your manners, King?' chided Faulkes.

'I do not suffer such dull dogs.' He bowed at the marchioness, 'I do not refer to your sister, of course.'

Georgette, noting that Regis' unpleasantness to Paxton seemed to have had a heartening effect on Jocasta, that her own sympathy did *not* produce, was quick to catch on — and interrupted before Faulkes could berate him again. 'You should not say so, sir, but I cannot but agree. Five minutes in Paxton's presence is enough.'

'He means well, and he can be dashed interesting when talking about art, for example,' argued Faulkes. Georgette's elbow was in his ribs and Regis rolled his eyes; head turned from Miss Fortune. Faulkes made a late connection to his brain, 'but I'm glad he doesn't ride with us often. Fellow has the worst seat in England.'

They walked on, Regis and Jocasta taking the lead once more.

'I do not yearn for him, you know,' said Jocasta to Regis as soon as they were out of earshot of the others.

'You are a silly child, but I do not think you quite such a ninny as that!' Regis answered with one eyebrow flying comically.

Jocasta laughed. 'He *is* dull, isn't he? Though I am glad that Portia does not find him so.' She looked up at Regis, 'It is just that I find it so awkward.'

'I am aware. You give it away entirely.'

Jocasta gasped at this reprimand, for such it was. 'Georgette says that my heart has not been damaged, but merely my pride.' Jocasta said, twirling her sunshade distractedly, 'Only, I seem to have been entirely made of pride, for once it was shattered there does not seem to be much left of me at all.'

Regis looked down at her, and at her tiny wrist on the parasol, at the downcast eyes with long lashes resting on her cheek. It was difficult not to wish to protect her little person, as one would a child. But he must not fall victim to her fairy magic. He knew that was not what she needed from him.

'Last Season,' he said to her brusquely, 'what did you do with yourself? What did you enjoy?'

'I did much the same as this Season. I shopped for clothes, danced at Almacks, attended the theatre. Why?'

'Have you lost interest in your finery?'

'Not ... entirely. It is just that to be admired for the trappings...'

'Give that up. When you dress, just look your best. Regard yourself in the mirror and be grateful that you do not suffer from unruly hair like Lady Sumner, or spots like poor Miss Ross. *I* do not lament that I am taller that Mr York, or slimmer that the Regent, however *shallow* that may be. We have all the duty to give others the best sight of us they can see.' Jocasta appeared to be listening, but her eyes fixed rather critically onto his carelessly tied cravat. 'Being admired by Mr York for your fine eyes, or fairy appearance, is certainly not something you should be congratulated upon — for it is no more your fault than Miss Ross' spots are hers. But as the parable says, we each have been given our share of talents and must make the best use of the coin we have received. This, Miss Ross knows, hence her wonderfully coiffured hair.'

'Her hair is glorious,' smiled Jocasta. She became thoughtful once more. 'I smile when I am complimented, but it makes me uneasy. Perhaps I am giving encouragement to young men whose admiration for me will only cause them pain.'

'As Paxton did to you?'

'Perhaps.'

'That is not your affair,' said Damon shortly. Then he remembered her particularly winning smiles and thought again. 'Are there any, in the gentlemen who pay court to you, any whom you *definitely* do not like, or are not attracted to?'

'I do not especially feel attracted to any,' she said, mildly reviewing, 'but with Sir Piers Brandreth and Mr Carson I actually feel slightly repulsed, but I do not know how to stop them.'

'You have that right - in Carson's case, at least. I know no ill of Brandreth, but that *you* do not like him is enough. Next time,' he instructed, 'you may dance one dance with each for politeness' sake if you are not engaged — but *never* two. That is a cruelty to those you have no interest in. You must feign deafness for most of their remarks, and give a half-smile, such as this one,' he demonstrated a distant half-smile that looked like a sneer, and Jocasta, who had been paying close attention, laughed. 'Show me!' he ordered, unpleasantly. She attempted it — but it looked far too winning in the attempt, Regis thought. He drew down his expressive eyebrows. 'Not at all,' he said severely. She raised her brows a trifle haughtily, and curled her lip again, sliding her eyes away quickly. 'Precisely! Practise it tonight.'

Jocasta could not help but laugh.

Regis fell back, and joined the marchioness, and Faulkes took Jocasta's arm. Regis said, 'I'm going to tell Justin to stop dancing with Miss Fortune at every party. But Colonel Bellamy is a different problem. It may be impolite for me to make such a demand.'

'Must they desist indeed?'

'Trust me. It distresses her — and for a good reason.'

Georgette resolved to think what this reason might be at her leisure, but she was already impressed by the effect Regis' dealing with Paxton had wrought on the nervous Jocasta, so she went along with it, her sharp brain thinking. 'I have only to suggest that my papa has taken note, and will surely call on him soon, to stop the colonel's gallantry in but an instant.'

The demonic eyebrows swept up in an appreciative dance. 'I knew I would like you, my lady.'

'Call me Georgette. You are, after all, a *Family Friend*.'

CHAPTER 8

New Arrivals

Bowling along the Great North Road, but within only two hours of London, was a handsome travelling coach bearing the gilded Enderby crest, and housing a pretty, dark-haired maiden, in a yellow silk bonnet. A young man rode on a magnificent steed beside the crested carriage, when the width of the road permitted, occasionally managing a few words with the passenger, when obstructions or crossroads necessitated a halt. Another, older coach rode behind, and housed two middle aged persons, plainly dressed, with the aspect of upper servants. These two shared a pork pie and kept up a comfortable, if infrequent, conversation, mostly affectionately complaining about the dispositions of their respective young employers.

Both carriages were laden with strapped-on baggage, as was a following cart, so it was evident that the party was a late entry to the London Season.

It came on to drizzle, and the coach stopped again. The yellow bonnet appeared through the window. 'Do get in, Tom!'

The young man appeared to dispute this, but it was not long before he dismounted, the groom seated by the coachman jumped down from the box and got on the horse, and the gentleman entered the carriage.

'Just when I was comfortable!' sighed the sturdy maid in the carriage behind, and bustled out of her seat and towards the crested equipage.

The second servant, a thin man with a long face, sighed too.

'Oh, Jane, must you?' said the yellow-bonneted female when the maid stepped in. 'It is only Tom.'

'Yes, I *must*, miss. What would be said if you appeared in London in a closed carriage with His Grace? Or any gentleman for that matter?'

'Well, we shall be crushed,' complained the young man. 'My legs need space to stretch out.'

The maid contented herself with ignoring this, and settled down opposite her mistress, to look out of the window and feign deafness for the rest of the journey.

'We have missed so much of the Season already!' said the girl. 'If it hadn't been for my carriage breaking down, I should not have had to wait for all your stupid delays.'

'A duke has a great many responsibilities,' the young man replied, a little portentously. 'I could not leave just because you desired it. You might have hired a chaise and charged it to Regis.'

'I do not like to hang off his arm at every turn,' the girl replied. 'He annoys me too much.'

'He has been very good to you since your papa...' the duke seemed to think better of this sentence, then added, 'He visits often, and even sent his Aunt Agnes to stay with you.'

'You call that being *good* to me? He might have sent a less tiresome person. All she does all day is complain, then say she is *grateful* for the roof over her head and my *magnanimity*, and all sorts of unpleasant things like that. Thank goodness she broke her leg, and I am to go to the Ushers instead. Mrs Usher is a dear.'

'The address is a little out of the way.'

'*I* shall make it fashionable!' the young lady declared.

The duke laughed. 'How? You are not an heiress—'

'I *am*!'

'You cannot call Crumley Park something to crow about. But I suppose it keeps you.' He coughed. 'You interrupted. You are not *enough* of an heiress to set the town on fire, and you are only moderately pretty.' He saw that she looked a little chastened, and was a bit ashamed. 'Never mind,' he added hearteningly, 'I shall dance with you at balls, and pretend to admire you, and bring you into fashion.'

'*You?*'

'I assure you — *my* notice can *make* a young lady. I am known as a leader of fashion.'

She gave a grunt of derision. 'It is being a duke, I suppose. Every young lady in our district seemed smitten after—' but the young girl hesitated. She could not say *after your papa died*, for she knew how affected he had been and still was, even though it was two years ago, '—after you became Enderby. Even being a *viscount* did not bring you such adulation. No, *that* face required you to be a *duke* to be accounted handsome.'

72

The maid chimed in in a very intrusive way, 'He were very pretty as a boy, Miss Cecilia!'

'He was,' said Cecilia. 'But his blond curls have sadly dulled to an indeterminate brown and now he is just … just ordinary.'

The young man stiffened. 'You, alone of all the world, refer to me as ordinary.'

'Well, *you* said I was only moderately pretty!' She did not appear much annoyed by this however, and continued. 'But you *shall* dance with me at balls and seem amused by me.'

'Ah, so *now* you acknowledge that I *can* bring you into fashion!' He said it smugly.

'No. We shall do so to annoy *Damon*. What *right* had he to kick up such a fuss when he found us together playing spillikins in the drawing room? If Aunt Agnes was lying in bed, how *was* I to be chaperoned?'

'I'd just stepped out to get the tea, too!' said Jane the maid, interrupting again. 'Sir Damon *did* dress me down. But he were quite right, Miss Cecilia, I should not have left you alone with a gentleman. I should have called a footman to fetch the tea.'

'But it was *Tom*. What on earth did he think—?'

'*You* added fuel to the fire by talking to me so affectionately and smiling at me. You never do so usually.'

'Serve him right for harbouring such ridiculous ideas!'

'But not me! It made him as mad as fire and he accused me of all sorts of things afterwards. Playing with your affections and so on.'

'How could he think I would have become such a zany in the four months since he visited as to have affections for *you*? Whatever the rumours about Damon, I always thought he was *sane*.'

'Or me! Why should *I*, suddenly, with all the beauties that surround me in London, be interested in *you*?' He paused. 'But why *don't* you want to marry me, Miss Montgomery? Every other unmarried lady does.'

'Because I *know* you,' she answered shortly. 'Besides, I know just what kind of man I shall marry. He will not be a callow boy such as you, but a man. And he shall be handsome and tall, with kind eyes.'

The duke sat up, interested. 'You are obviously thinking of someone in particular. I must know him, for you have never been more than five miles from Crumley Park.'

'I have been to Evescombe. And that is quite twelve miles. *And* Bath for that week with Aunt Agnes.'

'I forgot. But who is the handsome man with kind eyes that I do not know about?'

'I met him at Enderby, so he must have been a friend of your father's. Betty the pig had just escaped again, and I was trying to catch her before she quite destroyed the ornamental hedges just at our boundary. The duke would have been livid. So, I was herding her with my apron, you know, but Betty turned and saw me and ran straight at me. Suddenly I was plucked up into the air, and the gentleman protected me. Unfortunately, Betty then nudged him over, and we landed in a heap.'

Enderby laughed. 'Betty would never have hurt you!'

'Yes, but the gentleman did not know that. I scrambled up and caught her rope, and then he quite saw that she behaved herself with me. But he rang me a peal about running amok in private grounds, quite as though I were a child.

'How long ago was it?'

'Six years ago, I was fully thirteen.'

'A complete child. And I suppose you were wearing that horrible faded pink gown you always had in the garden, as well as the dreadful brown apron.'

'Well, it was convenient for visiting the pigs.'

'You must have looked a fright.'

'I suppose so. But he was kind, and after he had finished giving me a dressing-down he smiled, and gave me a sugarplum.'

'Who was he?'

'He didn't introduce himself. I suspect he thought I was the gardener's daughter or something.' She looked at the duke. 'Do you know who he is? Tall, with brown hair and kind eyes?'

'No, but he sounds too old for you if he was a friend of my father's.'

'He was quite young. In his twenties, I think.'

'And now he will be *thirty*. It is disgusting to think about.'

'But I *want* a mature husband. Someone I can depend on.' She sighed. 'It is not really him, but that *sort* of man I wish for. I suspect *he* must already be married.'

The duke sighed, too. 'You are the silliest girl. That is probably why Regis fears for you. But I think I understand him.' He looked shamefaced. 'Regis had words with me in London two years ago about giving young ladies false hope. Was I not supposed to dance, then? I do not seek a wife yet. To be shackled for life doesn't bear thinking of...' He sniffed. 'Then he caught me at a place that a friend had rather dragged me to when I had imbibed too much...' he blushed when Cecilia looked at him enquiringly, 'and once in Vauxhall I was with a ... *lady* ... I may understand him, he thinks me a rackety sort of fellow,

I suppose. After Papa—' he looked at Cecilia Montgomery's grey eyes. 'That winter I went to the dogs a little.'

Cecilia frowned. She did not quite understand the confession, but she disregarded it anyway. 'Well, we shall pay him back for his stupid suspicions. You will make him worry anew.'

'I don't know, Cissie! Regis is dangerous. Everyone in Town knows it. And I don't want to be the talk of the polite world.'

'You won't be! We shall just act so before *him*. We shall be discreet in public. Trust me to find the ways.'

'But I don't know what he will do.'

'I know he left with some scheme in mind. After being angry he knew he had dealt with me in a very ill-judged manner, and he left for London, thinking I was to follow in a week only. Which I would have done, if not for the carriage problem.' She narrowed her eyes. 'No, he was already planning some more subtle way to achieve his goal. I wonder what it may be?' she looked over at her companion. 'He won't hurt you, don't worry. He likes you.'

'But he disapproves of me, damn his hide!'

'Your Grace!' chided Jane, and he grinned.

'You do too, Jane. But I shall not brook it from Regis. *Let us* make him worry!'

'You two up to tricks again,' the maid lamented, 'like when one of you distracted me, while the other escaped to be a little kitchen thief.'

The Duke of Enderby exchanged a grin with Miss Montgomery. 'We never failed.'

'Let us see what the Demon King has planned for us, and pay him back in his own kind.'

They shook on it, and the old maid sighed, shaking her head.

How it was possible to feel alone in a place as bristling with people as Enderby House was difficult to know. The duke walked through a sea of persons, all at the disposal of his little finger. He remembered how his father used to greet them all boisterously, some even by name, but he was shyer by nature, though he tried to hide it. Back then, the house would be filled, soon after their arrival, with his father's many friends who would also greet his son affectionately. His uncle and aunt would be there, too, as well as his ancient, but affectionate, grandmama, who resided most of the year here. It was two years since Uncle Jack was gone to Scotland to live in his wife's family home, and he now spent the Season in Edinburgh society. He was seldom in London. The duke's grandmama had followed her eldest son to the grave, and now the house had only himself and a thousand (it seemed) servants. At home in the country, he knew the servants better, for many of them had raised him when his father was away from home. He did not feel alone at the Enderby estate. And then, there was always Crumley Park to ride over to, and get into mischief with Cecilia.

He had run riot there, as Cecilia had at Enderby, and from this distance in time the young duke suspected that her papa, Baron Montgomery, had a vague notion they might make a match of it someday. He seemed to have given up this notion when he found the viscount, aged eighteen, chasing fourteen-year-old Cecilia around with a leafy tree branch — which he whipped her with whenever he caught her. This was because she had made fun of the new lilac-grey waistcoat which had just arrived from his London tailor. The baron was not much impressed by the reason for his assault, but he was resigned.

'We should not,' sighed Baron Montgomery, grasping his collar-back, to stop him chasing Cecilia, 'have let you two grow up like pups from the same pack.'

Now, the duke had dropped off Cecilia at the Ushers, and stood in the drawing room as his secretary, John Fordham, handed him a stack of cards of invitation. He looked through them dully.

'Is there anything amiss, Your Grace?'

In Enderby there was not a servant that did not use his title ironically. "Dinner is served, *Your Grace*," would say Porter the butler, with all the insouciance of one who had upended him as a boy, to empty his pockets of his father's guineas. These had been purloined (advanced from his next allowance, the young boy had told himself) in the hope of visiting the fair that he had been forbidden. Before others, the servants at Enderby were deeply respectful, but behind closed doors their eyes chided him as ever. He found now that he preferred that to the proud dignity of his London household, Enderby House. He answered now, 'Nothing at all. I shall decide on these tomorrow.'

'Do you go out this evening, Your Grace?'

'No. Or wait, I think the Ushers plan to take Miss Cecilia to Almacks. Have vouchers been delivered?'

'I believe so, Your Grace.'

'Tell Baxter I shall dine early and go there then. It doesn't do to be late.'

He left the room whistling, and the secretary raised his eyebrows at such a change of mood.

Only a week ago, Sir Justin Faulkes had surprised Colonel Bellamy, who had his eyes riveted to the dancefloor.

'Still?' said Faulkes, with some sympathy. He had spent rather more time with Bellamy in the Season, and had found him to be less black than he had once thought. The colonel had just harboured a longing for Georgette Fortune all the years he had been making his vast fortune in India, a woman he had only met once. Over some drinks, Faulkes had even been able to commiserate with the colonel, admitting to his own old predilection for Georgette, two full years before the House Party at Castle Fortune, where Bellamy and he had first met.

'She makes a magnificent marchioness,' Bellamy remarked, his eye on the married couple who were waltzing with each other.

'She does.'

'It is getting easier. Being in her presence, seeing her so happy, helps, you know.'

'I know.'

'I sometimes wish that when I had returned home, she had not been so true to my remembrance of her. If she had been less kind, less pretty, less amusing, then I could have thought myself mistaken.' He looked at Faulkes. 'I cannot rid myself of the notion that had I not been called away that evening, she might now be Mrs Bellamy. We were so easy together that night, all those years ago.'

'It may be so, but best not to think of it.' Faulkes smiled. 'You might have made her a fine husband, but things happen as Heaven decides. Look at them. Could you have made her quite that happy?'

Bellamy looked and sighed. 'Miss White arrives in town this week. Shall I court her in earnest?'

'Rather, look for other diversions for the present, or consider taking up religious contemplation. No one with a lost heart should woo any lady.'

'None or many. I shall opt for the latter, I think.' Bellamy smiled easily, and moved away.

That evening Jocasta, in a dress of two shades of pale green gauze, saw Regis as he stood talking, as was usual lately, to Georgette and Onslow. Her partner, young Lord Jeffries, was leading her back, but she saw the baronet's eye was not on her. A pretty, dark-haired girl was dragging a young fair-haired man behind her by the sleeve, and she saw Regis' terrible frown cross his face, before he composed himself for the greeting.

'The Duke of Enderby is back in town, I see...' said her dance companion, and Jocasta realised that *here* was Regis' purpose for her.

'When did you arrive, Cecilia?' Regis was asking the young girl impolitely, after giving His Grace the Duke of Enderby the merest nod.

'This afternoon, only.'

'Should you not have rested after the journey?' he asked, but Jocasta did not deduce compassion in his tone.

'Well, I knew Tom was coming to Almacks this evening,' the pretty and pert young thing was saying, quite evidently unfazed by his disapproval, 'and I have so longed to attend. Thankfully, I had already met Lady Jersey in Bath last year with Aunt Agnes, so vouchers awaited me at Mrs Usher's.'

Jocasta's beau was bowing to her, reminding her of the cotillion she had promised him later, and he was gone. Georgette was gossiping with Lady Sarah Alderly, and Onslow's attention had also been claimed by a neighbouring friend, so Jocasta deliberately moved beside Regis. He looked down at her, distracted. 'Miss Fortune, this is Miss Cecilia Montgomery, a young friend of mine, recently arrived in London.'

Jocasta looked at Miss Montgomery, she had pretty, brown eyes, darker hair and a sunny, but defiant smile, but decided to evaluate her person and her character with Regis later. For now, she had another purpose. Regis had made no attempt to introduce Miss Montgomery's companion. Jocasta turned her large blue eyes on "Tom" and said, in a gently enquiring voice. 'I do not think I know you, sir.'

Enderby, who since the moment that Jocasta had joined them had been spellbound, said dreamily, 'You look like a woodland nymph!'

'Tom!' cried Miss Montgomery.

The squeak Jocasta gave at the same time was covered by this scold from Miss Montgomery. Regis had jerked her elbow.

'Oh, I beg your pardon!' the young man said, blushing, 'I'm Enderby, you know.'

'His Grace the Duke of Enderby, Miss Jocasta Fortune,' said Regis, resigned.

'Should you care to dance, Miss Fortune?' the duke ventured.

'Well, I *am* engaged to dance with Colonel Bellamy, but he is a little late.'

'The set is forming, Miss Fortune. Let us go,' said the pleasant-faced young duke, roguishly. 'The gentleman deserves his punishment.'

'Shall we?' said Jocasta confidingly, and laid a hand on Enderby's proffered arm, tripping to the dancefloor.

Regis and Miss Montgomery were left, looking similarly disgusted (for their own particular reasons) to watch the pair go.

Colonel Bellamy arrived and greeted the Onslows. 'Where is Miss Fortune?' he asked. Onslow gestured to the floor, where Enderby and his sister-in-law were standing opposite one another in the set. Bellamy was at his most waggish. 'It never does to be late for the belle of the ballroom.' Regis introduced Miss Montgomery, and the colonel gallantly asked if she fancied making up the last set.

She agreed, but Regis heard her say, in a manner that betrayed her youth, 'I am only today in town, Colonel Bellamy, or you should not have found me without a previous engagement.'

'I am quite sure it is true,' said Bellamy respectfully, leading her into the set. 'It is my good fortune.'

Georgette, with leisure to notice them, suddenly remembered her task for this evening. She would take Bellamy aside later, even if it set Lucian's eyes alight. It was her sisterly duty. And her history with Bellamy was *months* ago.

<hr />

No one in the ballroom would have noticed the look that drew Colonel Bellamy to the side of the Marchioness of Onslow. She had hardly to raise an eyebrow, when their gazes crossed, for the colonel to know he was summoned. There was a little throng around her, but he easily inserted himself beside her and gazed ahead at the ballroom, asking quietly, 'What can I do for you, my lady?'

'Colonel, I am delighted to have such a quick wit as you to deal with, since we may not have much time.'

'Before Onslow arrives? I thought you did not have a love of the clandestine?'

'You are a wag sir. There is nothing *clandestine* ... but you tease me. This regards my father.'

'The baron?' Bellamy was nearly surprised enough to turn towards her, but he held himself.

'I thought you should know, sir, that my father has been informed of the attention you pay my sister.'

'I beg your pardon. You *know*—'

'Of *course,* I do. And you are exceedingly kind, sir. But I thought that I should warn you of an impending visit...'

'I dance with Miss Fortune no more that Faulkes or Regis—'

'Quite! However, Papa understands that they do so because they are friends with Onslow, and often in our house. And he expects—' here she adopted a deep booming voice, *"nothing from that direction"* she laughed, and Bellamy gave a shaken laugh with her. '—but *you...*' her voice trailed away.

'I see.' Bellamy's tone was a trifle panicked. 'I do not wish to upset Miss Fortune, however. She may feel slighted if my friendly attentions were to cease—'

'I do not say stop, sir. Occasionally, it is quite permissible. And do not worry about Jocasta's sensibilities. I shall talk to her on the matter. If my father were to mistake your intentions, she, too, would be put under parental pressure.'

'I see.' He sighed. 'I thank you for informing me. Perhaps I should visit the baron directly, or talk to your brother...'

'*Really*, you should *not*,' Georgette was a little panicked herself at this. 'It is better to turn it off as easily as possible.'

'Yes,' said Bellamy. 'Is that all, my lady?' he added rather sadly.

'I think it ought to be,' said Georgette, wryly, regarding her husband approaching with a martial light in his eyes.

Bellamy bowed slightly, and moved off, and Georgette looked up at Onslow.

'What did *he* want?' he said nastily. 'To give you another *note*?'

'Yes. I am to run off with him to India on the morrow.'

'He can go, but I'll lock you in your room.' He looked less angry and more resigned. 'What are you about?'

'How do you know it was not he who approached *me*?'

'Because I told him not to.' Onslow's voice was back to nasty.

Georgette shook her head, hoping it was untrue, but suspecting it was not. 'I just asked him to dance less with Jocasta. It is Regis' instructions.'

'Very well. Have I to talk to Justin?'

'Regis has already done so. He will decrease his attentions, but not so much. Regis needs him as cover for his own time with Jocasta.'

'I'm beginning to understand the baron's disposition. Each of your sisters is a trial in her own special way. It must grate on the spirits of even the most even-tempered of gentlemen to have ten such daughters. I've only had Jocasta stay for a month and ridden with Portia on a few occasions and already my temper is fraying.'

'Poor *dear,*' said Georgette in mock sympathy, 'But you said you would climb mountains for me.'

'A mountain of Fortune sisters is more than any man can weather coolly.'

'Katerina won't be much trouble, apart from being reluctant to meet people. But just *wait* until Leonora comes to town,' she warned darkly. She smiled at his groan and said in a brighter voice, 'I promise not to invite the twins to stay with us.'

'I will not be afraid,' said Onslow with a show of stoicism. 'Leonora is a long way off. Let us handle Jocasta first.'

'Now, *that* is the fighting spirit I know and love.'

CHAPTER 9

Quarrelling Couples

On the next morning, two carriages held similarly angry couples, driving in St James Park at the fashionable hour.

'*You are a complete buffoon!*' said Miss Montgomery, (*looking charming today in a chip straw hat and sunny yellow pelisse with fawn satin ribbon trim. Alas, her expression was not so sunny*). Her companion looked sheepish.

'You are a meddling minx,' said Regis to Jocasta Fortune, his brows at their most horrific, while she played unconcernedly with her parasol.

'*You collapsed all our plans at the sight of the first pretty face!*' One little satin-slippered foot kicked the duke's elegant hessian boots.

'You knew I did not want to introduce you, so you were as pushing as a female can be. *Fine* manners!'

'Well, we might be able to fix it,' said the Duke of Enderby in an apologetic voice, and with a pleading tone, 'due to my reputation as a rake.'

'I was determined to be of *use* to you. It *was* your original purpose, after all,' Jocasta Fortune said, unapologetic.

'You? A rake?' Miss Montgomery snorted.

'I no longer wish you to be of use to me, I thought I made that clear. You are not fit to ... I had not judged your situation aright.'

'I have the reputation of a slayer of female hearts,' said Enderby, somewhat proudly, 'I can easily worry Regis by leading you astray at the same time as I pursue Miss Fortune.' He added in a dreamier voice, 'I say, did you see how lovely she was? Apparently, she was in town last year with another of her sisters but somehow our paths did not cross.'

'Not fit?' said Jocasta, showing her teeth. 'I do not understand you sir.'

'She seems like a nice girl,' remarked Miss Montgomery in a fair-minded way, 'but if you really like her, she will be mightily confused by your pursuit of me.'

'Stop puckering up. It does not become you after your fast behaviour of last night. Do not encourage Enderby. You are no more able to cope with his inconstancy than Cecilia.'

'I keep telling you it is no such thing,' said the Duke of Enderby, sagely. 'There are so many unmarried females whose mothers I know, and cannot therefore escape, who surround me. You two will be lost in the throng.'

'Am I now under your protection, like Miss Montgomery?' purred Jocasta. 'And what matters if a duke be inconstant, after all, if only he marries me.'

'Do you know how insufferable you sound?' said Miss Montgomery, relieving her temper by kicking him again. 'But I suppose it might still work. Regis was not pleased to see us together.'

'Jocasta Fortune!' said Regis severely. 'I have a good mind to take my whip to you!'

⁂

Dropping off Jocasta Fortune at Onslow House, Regis encountered Faulkes, whom he invited back for a glass or two.

Leaning back in a chair in his sitting room, the baronet looked morosely into his wine glass and said, 'How many of my devilish plans have gone astray, Justin?'

'There has been many a dashed kick-up surrounding you, King, but you have the reputation of pulling it off at the last.'

'This one seems doomed to be my downfall,' Regis sighed, slugging his wine with a distinct lack of finesse. 'It was insane in the first place; I see that now. But my instincts have served me—' He sighed once more, and Faulkes looked at him hazily — for it had taken three silent glasses for Regis to begin talking. 'She is not at all what I first thought.'

'Are we talking of Miss Fortune? You do not mean you have *fallen* for her?'

Regis let out a 'Phshaw!' He shook his head. 'That would be one solution. It would be fine if that *were* the case, I could just protect her, and stop her falling into some awful scrape. But can you see me married to a featherbrained fairy?'

'That isn't a fitting descrip—' the other baronet began with customary politeness, but then alcohol impelled him to the truth. 'No, I can't. But what scrape can she possibly fall into with Onslow and her sister to look out for her?' Faulkes slugged his wine, giving into Regis' mood. 'And she looks to me to be a success this Season. She never lacks a partner, is sought after everywhere. Very pretty girl. Not my type, of course.'

'She is not a success at all,' said Regis, 'That is what is driving me mad.'

'Onslow said she has confided in you. Is there some problem that I can help resolve?'

'If it were something practical, do you not think I would have dealt with it and been on my way?'

'Whenever you speak of Jocasta Fortune, you speak in riddles.'

'And now she is enmeshed with Enderby.'

'The duke? That is a good thing, surely. It is not as though he were a sixty-year-old lecher like the Duke of Southwaite. He's a handsome young man.'

'A handsome, fickle, young cad who has come into his honours too early, with not a guiding hand about him. He might play with her affections, without even understanding what he does. And I fear he may even ... it doesn't bear thinking of.'

'Here, Damon, I've never heard that Enderby is that kind of ... you should be careful what you say.'

'Too much is forgiven a duke,' said Regis baldly. He drank some more. 'Forget I said anything. He may not be dishonourable, but he is wild and unschooled, too much flattered. Dangerous. Even if he did offer, can you imagine those two wed? It would be a shipwreck, right in front of our eyes. And it would be all my fault.'

Faulkes was having difficulty following this. 'Why *your* fault?'

'Because I conceived a Devilish Plan, and I made the grave error of telling Jocasta Fortune.'

***

Jocasta was not quite sure *why* she had approached the young Duke of Enderby. Was it really to be of use to Regis — or to annoy him? The wonderful thing about her relations with Regis had been their mutual lack of interest, so it was disturbing now to find herself trying to get a reaction from him. His devilish scheme was for her to attract a duke, to save the lady he was protecting. She had pretended indifference at this, but really, it had rankled that *she* was to be thrown under the horses, so that another might not be injured. His explanation that she had her family's protection was ill-informed, of course. So, she had decided to give him what he had originally wanted, even though he had forbidden her to. No, *because* he had forbidden her to.

Enderby was a pleasant-faced boy, with an enthusiastic disposition, and a fund of compliments for her. That her dancing with the duke upset Regis was a bonus. He should *feel* the results of his evil plan.

She did not really blame the baronet, had known he had a use for her, but suddenly, she was angry. Angry that he had cared so little as to make such a plan, and angrier that she feared that now that he knew her a little, he, too, was *being kind*. He did not say so, but this was her fear. If she could make him annoyed with her, well, then they might be able to return to their old relations.

Even as she thought this, she knew it was illogical. But that annoyance might cancel out his pity, somehow seemed possible.

***

Regis did not see Jocasta again until an evening at Almacks, where he watched her dance with the Duke of Enderby with apparent enjoyment. As they left the floor, Jocasta met Regis' eye, and then turned to smile at her partner. Little minx! If she were anyone else, he might have thought that she had done so for flirtatious purposes, but he made no such mistake.

'May I take you to supper, Miss Fortune?' Enderby enquired hopefully, as she joined the Onslow party.

'Indeed, you may, Your Grace,' said the vivacious fairy version of Jocasta Fortune, gazing up at him with dewy eyes.

The young duke gulped and said, bowing low over her hand, 'Until later, then.'

Enderby left, and as another set was being formed for a cotillion, Regis saw him head in the direction of Cecilia. She, however, was being led out by Colonel Bellamy, and Regis grinned. What the devil was Enderby playing at? Did he really think he could flirt so obviously with two girls on the same evening with no repercussions? Dukes, on the whole, face too few repercussions, Regis thought. Time to teach him some. He would take Cecilia to supper himself and bring her together with Miss Fortune and Enderby. See how he would bear that.

Jocasta was chatting with her sister and Onslow, and Regis, unwilling to enter her new game, did not speak, just watched as Cecilia tripped around the floor with Bellamy. He saw the colonel look over at their party several times. Justin had told him the story of the house party at Castle Fortune. It seemed that Bellamy was having difficulty accepting his fate, for his eye was not on the younger sister, but the elder. Cecilia said something to the colonel, and it made him laugh. Regis was glad of it. Bellamy, now, might be the very thing for Cecilia.

He was a grand match, and a little older of course, but ... Regis caught himself becoming a matchmaking mama. But Cecilia should be taken care of. And if young Enderby was to be routed, Bellamy might just be the right diversion.

Regis took delight in appearing at Cecilia's side before supper, and taking her arm to lead her away before her young dancing partner had been able to ask her. As they moved off, Cecilia said, 'What have you to scold me for now, Damon?'

'Scold? Why would I?'

'I have no notion, but it is what you do when you seek me out these days.'

'Unfair. I am only here for the pleasure of your company, scamp.'

She made a dismissive sound before she noticed they were approaching the elegantly clad back of Tom, who was chatting to another. She was soon aware that it was Jocasta Fortune, and Regis saw Cecilia's mouth pinch up. His devilish scheme was working.

'Ah, Enderby, Miss Fortune, shall we find a place at the table?'

Enderby flushed. At least the young cub had some shame. 'Cissie!' he said, 'Regis!'

Regis shepherded the two ladies to a seat while Enderby ordered plates from a lackey.

'You are well acquainted with His Grace, I see, Miss Montgomery,' said Jocasta, with just a trifle more than polite manners. She was playing this scene much as he would have wished, were he still of a mind to use her.

'We are very close,' emphasised Cecilia with a sweet smile. 'We have known each other since childhood.'

'I see,' Jocasta said. 'Then I am quite the odd one out, I fear. For you are also *particularly* acquainted with Sir Damon, too.'

'Well,' said Cecilia, 'forcibly acquainted merely. But I have known him for a long time. He was a great friend of my father, though somewhat younger.'

'But you, Miss Fortune,' said Enderby gallantly, after a swift, annoyed glance at Cecilia, 'must not imagine yourself an outsider. The brevity of an acquaintance does not define the power of the connection.'

Regis looked to see how Cecilia took this, and saw that a faint line of annoyance appeared between her brows, and he wondered at it. He wanted her annoyed, but had expected a stronger, or a different, reaction, knowing Cecilia. There was something to ponder here, but Regis saved that for later. Enderby, seeking to appease Jocasta's feelings, had been betrayed into a distancing of Cecilia. This should show Cecilia how fickle he was, but something was wrong with the whole scenario. Cecilia shot a look at Regis, and then turned to Jocasta with a smile.

'I'm sure, Your Grace, that our new acquaintance must be favoured by us all. And such a pretty one too!' she laid a hand on Enderby's arm. 'But you do not forget old friends, do you, Tom?' She looked into Enderby's eyes as he turned into her, and sent him a look with such affection that the young man blinked. He looked down. For a second Enderby's face seemed contorted, but then he looked into Cecilia's innocent face and smiled, laying a hand on hers and saying, 'How could I, my dear Cissie?' He followed this up with a rather defiant look at Regis, who returned it coldly.

Jocasta, in her best social manner, began to chat to Miss Montgomery of ballroom matters. 'I saw you dance with Colonel Bellamy, Miss Montgomery. He is charming, is he not?'

'He is. I believe he is a friend of your family?'

'Yes, indeed. Though it is scarce a half year since we were acquainted. He knew my sister Georgette before that, I believe.'

'The marchioness is universally admired,' said Enderby.

'Yes. Georgie is a marvel. I realised, only after she left, how important she had been at Castle Fortune. To all of us.' Regis looked at Jocasta's little face, her eyes somewhat winsome. As he knew she would, she turned them onto his face and their gaze locked. This was the kind of confiding she divulged only before him, and in her eyes, he saw her surprise that she had revealed herself so much, in this more public situation. Her eyes changed, and he saw she blamed him for it. He caught himself smiling down at her, acknowledging her reproof with his amusement. This would never do. They both pulled back a little.

However, in theory, he considered later, this had been a good thing. Cecilia's eyes softened towards Jocasta, and Enderby was entranced at her openness. This last might be a bad effect, for Regis now had no more wish for Enderby to lead Jocasta Fortune astray than he had for him to capture Cecilia's affections. The young scamp was not right for either of them. Perhaps once he was older, and had achieved some maturity, and some sense ... but Regis doubted even that. His position might arrest his development: the admiration of his rank, the compliments and attention he was bound to receive, would probably pave an oily path to even more selfish indulgences.

It was a shame, for Tom had been an attractive young child, easily affectionate, and full of devilry of the sort that Regis (himself a demon) had approved of. But, as in his own case, devilry did not make for life as an attentive husband.

CHAPTER 10

Parental Interference

Mrs Usher, a friendly and amusing society wife, left the young Duke of Enderby with Cecilia in the small parlour. This was not strictly *de rigueur* for a chaperone, but she had known them both since childhood and had a different opinion on the matter than the warning that Regis had whispered in her ear. As far as Fleur Usher was concerned, Enderby would never harm Cecilia, and if, as the baronet had suggested, his feelings towards her had changed (though Mrs Usher had seen little but friendly scorn between them) then so much the better.

'I wish,' said Enderby, 'that you would leave off kicking my leg, Cissie. You always seem to hit it on the same spot, and a Season with you will probably lame me.' He raised his leg now and put it on the sofa, looking at her piteously.

Cecilia knelt before it and touched it tenderly. 'Oh, does it hurt?' she asked sweetly, then slapped it, adding, 'well you deserved it! Is it that you cannot think whenever you are near to Miss Fortune? You forgot our pact to make Regis worry!'

'Ouch!' said Enderby. 'You take advantage of the fact that now I am a man, and I can no longer hit you back!'

'Yes! Thank Harrow for your training. But no need to feel aggrieved, you hit me enough in the first of your youth for me to feel the need to pay you back now.' She put her back against the sofa seat. 'Do you really not wish to help me anymore?'

'I *do*. But it is so distracting when Miss Fortune is present.' He grinned sheepishly. 'I find myself very drawn to her.'

'There is no need to *tell* me so, you make it perfectly obvious,' she said sulkily. Then she turned, knocking into his other knee with her shoulder so that he gave a protest again. 'But there is something strange about last night at supper. Obviously, Damon brought us together to display your philandering ways, but it was not just *you* who seemed to be taken with Miss Fortune, was it?'

Enderby pulled himself upright and looked at her suspicious eyes. 'Do you think that Damon is more than a friend to Miss Fortune? You think him a suitor?' His voice was shocked — and anxious too. For all his rank, Regis made him feel like a callow youth, and he was not at all sure of himself as the baronet's rival.

'I do not know. Only the connection between them sometimes seemed strong, they looked like they shared some thoughts that they did *not* share with us. It was not flirtatious, precisely, but something ...' She looked ahead again and grasped her knees. 'Damon and Miss Fortune ... I shall have to think of how that I can use this to my advantage.'

Enderby sank back on the sofa arm. 'You exhaust me! I'm sure your brain is as full of trickery as the Demon King's.' As she turned back to him, he waved a dismissive hand, 'No, no, don't explain it to me. Just tell me what you want me to do when it is time. I can step up my affection for you in his presence, but not when Miss Fortune is near, I beg of you. She might misunderstand.'

'We can't have *that,* I suppose!' said Cecilia, with deadly sarcasm.

'Anyway, as diverting as the enterprise of *Worrying Damon* is, should you not pay some attention to your own debut?'

'Ah, find a husband you mean? Well, I must say there are a number of interesting gentlemen who danced with me last night.'

'I didn't see anyone interesting. Old Boring Boston was your best bet.'

As Lord Boston was fifty-eight years old and inclined to corpulence, this could only be taken as another insult, so without looking round, and with amazing accuracy, Cecilia hit him in the same spot on his shin. 'Lord Jeffries is amusing, and Colonel Bellamy is very handsome.'

'Bellamy is too old for you!' groaned Enderby.

'Perhaps ten years difference only. It is not excessive. And he is so very charming.'

'He was looking at the Marchioness of Onslow the whole time he was dancing with you,' scoffed Tom. 'I hear he was disappointed in that direction.'

'He *was not*! He spoke to me the whole time. He was excessively charming and attentive.'

Enderby gave off a dismissive grunt, then moved his leg before the little fist hit him.

'Shall we go for a drive this afternoon?'

'No, for I am to attend the dressmaker with Mrs Usher. I feel that my riding habits are too shabby now that I see the ladies in town. Such a great deal of military frogging on display. I should at *least* be in fashion.'

Enderby supposed so, and took his leave, affecting a limp as he crossed the room.

'Huh!' said Cecilia, unmoved by his histrionics. 'Just as well I'm not in kicking distance. Oh, and Tom, if we are with those two again, please remember that you are devoted to *my* beauty, too.'

'Eh?' he said, as though contemplating this impossibility. Seeing her dreadful glare, he added appeasing, 'I'll throw you my best flirtatious smile. Just as though you really *are* pretty.'

She sighed resignedly. 'Just look at me and do your best. You have no clue how to flirt.'

'Unlike you,' he said, at the door. 'You indulge in the most shocking behaviour, smiling like that at Jeffries. Damon's right. You are not safe to be let out.'

He shut the door before the cushion hit him and went off, whistling.

Cecilia sat back to seriously consider what her observations of last night might mean for her plans.

⚜

It had not escaped Sir Damon Regis' notice that watching over Jocasta Fortune had somehow become his premier occupation in life. The urge to confide in her excellent, intelligent, and sensitive sister (thus abnegating the responsibility) was sometimes overwhelming, especially as the marchioness queried him both in word and expression. But he understood that the things he knew about Miss Fortune were told in confidence. Implied, if not stated. And Damon Regis was a man of his word.

He watched Miss Fortune now giving the handsome, young, Lord Jeffries a run for his money. Regis realised that if Sally Jersey or even Dorothea de Lieven, for example (two of the patronesses of Almacks) were to discover where his eyes habitually landed, he would be considered *épris* in the direction of Miss Fortune. Presumed jealous of her court. Actually, he had little interest in the flirtations of the vivacious version of Jocasta Fortune, and certainly had no feelings of jealousy. He was fixated on the deeper things, not noted by others, in these busy balls or social gatherings. The smile that fell from her face after her companion turned away, the determined straightening of her spine, afterwards, in a brave attempt to continue her performance. It all broke his heart. He realised that his own scheming brain was at a loss. How to set Jocasta Fortune up in her own self-esteem, when she believed in no one's compliments anymore, was a conundrum. He watched as the flattery around her was received with a smile, but was discarded immediately. He needed to set her back on her path of youthful innocence, of simple enjoyment, so that he could walk away, and begin to pay attention to his own affairs.

The one hovering figure who did make his blood boil was Enderby.

Mrs Norton, whom he often spent time with at balls, but never now in private, was intelligent enough to know that she was being used as a smokescreen to keep matchmaking mamas away, perhaps. But Damon was entertaining, and besides, his attentions boosted her morale since all the World knew that her husband kept other women.

'Who is it that catches your eye so, Damon? I am never quite quick enough to see.'

'My attention could hardly waver from your eyes, Maria.'

'Yes, yes, my dear, but tell me all. Are you entranced by some new beauty? Or have you a new demonic scheme in mind?'

Damon looked down at her. She was a bright and beautiful woman, still under thirty years old, who was one of the sad casualties of a society marriage. He liked her bravery and her humour in the face of what must be humiliation. He decided to confide just a little. 'I find myself in the place of guardian to young Miss Montgomery, and I wish to keep her from young Enderby's clutches.'

She laughed. 'How absurd! His Grace is a poodle, not a wolf! Take it from one who knows, Damon.'

But it had already circulated in the clubs. While the duke danced with many young ladies, it was obvious that most of each evening was spent between two. Miss Cecilia Montgomery and Miss Jocasta Fortune. Bets were laid on who might be the next Duchess of Enderby. Miss Julia White, newly returned to town, and last year's favourite, was now relegated as an outside runner.

Regis noted that The Marquis of Onslow had stepped in front of the worst of Jocasta's suitors, in his icily polite way, but he allowed Enderby full rein. Nowadays, Miss Fortune, who was beautiful but only one step from impoverished, still attracted *some* of the fortune hunting riffraff. For Jocasta's sister Georgette had married a marquis, and Portia was to marry an earl's son. To be into a family connected to such status, a leech might hope for boons.

So, of course, in theory, Enderby was a catch. It was just that Regis knew more of him. He could no more drop a hint in the Fortune family's ear about Enderby's dissipations than he could about Jocasta. It was against his honour to do so. He had known him as a child. But he gritted his teeth when he danced by.

George Fortune, brother of Georgette, Jocasta and Portia, was tall, athletic and handsome with an abundant mane of hair controlled by pomade. For those young ladies in the ballroom at Almacks who had not actually *met* him, he seemed like a magnificent god. The whispered words from their mamas, speaking of ruinous habits, might easily be disregarded when one looked at his form and thrillingly arrogant expression. He played idly with a fob, he struck a heroic pose, and young girls sighed. Those who knew Jocasta or Portia Fortune, or who had spoken to Amethyst Bailey (his neighbour) might discern, that all *within* was not as magnificent as his outward form. This might be deduced from the rolling eyes of the sisters, or the terrified look of repulsion from Miss Bailey.

One Miss Spooner, for example, being introduced to him by a patroness, blushed and stuttered with excitement. George Fortune had looked down upon her from his great height with an immobile face, and turned to his father, the baron, who was at his side. His voice, though it dropped a little, was still quite audible to Miss Spooner when he asked 'Portion?' and his father answered, with a shrug, 'Respectable.' Miss Spooner, shocked, could not believe what she was hearing. Mrs Drummond-Burrell, the patroness making the introduction, seemed not to have heard, but recommended Mr George

Fortune to her as a partner for her first waltz. Young girls around sighed at her good fortune, but Miss Spooner went off, fingertips just on his arm, with a sinking heart. He addressed just two remarks at her.

'Your mother must know Mrs Drummond-Burrell.'

Miss Spooner did not respond. When the steps of the dance brought him back to her, he said, 'I see you have a great number of teeth.' Miss Spooner recoiled and closed her lips firmly, wondering how she could ever have seen that cold face as handsome. She could not wait to leave the floor.

Her mother had said to her upon her return, 'Your first waltz, Catherine, and with such a *distinguished* partner!' Catherine Spooner only shuddered.

George Fortune went on to dance with the newly arrived Julia White, and they looked quite wonderful together. Her blonde beauty a foil to his dark, as his stature was a foil for her delicate loveliness.

Damon Regis said to Justin Faulkes, 'Fortune and Miss White make a fine-looking pair.'

'They deserve each other,' said Faulkes in a flat tone.

Regis knew Fortune as a puffed-up blockhead, but was surprised at the normally kind Faulkes' implied stricture on the fair Miss White.

'You have taken the lady in aversion?' He frowned. 'Ah, there was something with Onslow and her, was there not?' When Faulkes did not answer, Regis looked on as Julia White returned to her mother's side. 'I see that those with the taste in fairy princesses have evenly divided themselves between Miss Fortune and Miss White. It seems Miss White no longer takes all the attention.'

'I think that Miss Jocasta Fortune looks rather more poised this Season. She is even prettier than last. And her manner is more vivacious than Miss White's. Lord Jeffries, for one, seems entertained by her company more.'

Regis watched as Jocasta laughed up at the handsome, playful, young man. And then at her solemn face when the gentleman turned away. He glanced over at Justin, in case he noticed, but his friend's eye seemed to have been diverted elsewhere. Was he alone, thought Regis, destined to be the only one who recognised her sadness? He saw her brother approach, saw her blush and look down, and wondered what unpleasant thing he had had to say to her.

Baron Fortune had been wandering Almacks, for the distinct purpose of keeping an eye on Jocasta's progress. He had watched her dance partners and came to no firm conclusions. *'That won't do, not at all,'* he said loudly when Jocasta danced with Lord Bertram, rake and fortune hunter. *'I'll drop a word in his ear that there will be nothing for him to look at there.'*

This booming monologue caught the attention of neighbouring guests, and though the remark had been her papa's usual audible thoughts, and not addressed to her at all, Georgette pulled on his sleeve and said in an under voice, 'Pray do not, Papa, Lord Bertram is only dancing with a pretty girl, that's all.'

'Well, who *is* her principal suitor, my lady?' He regarded her from his great height with derision. 'You undertook her chaperonage, Georgette, it is for you to assure that she makes a match. And soon, my girl. I cannot long delay. What have you done, I say, since you took on the responsibility?' Georgette turned her head away and rolled her eyes. He looked around again. 'I had high hopes for that Bellamy chap. He looked like he had an interest in *you* at one time—' again his booming voice made Georgette shudder, attracting the interest of several neighbouring guests, 'but that did not take, either. *He* might have been more open-handed in financial matters.' Since this implied that her papa had reapplied to her husband for funds, Georgette's stomach squirmed. At least Onslow had evidently resisted. 'But Bellamy has not been seen with her much these days. Hedged off again!'

Georgette, while finding her father ridiculous, was still embarrassed. She longed for Onslow to reappear from the card room and save her.

But the baron continued to watch Jocasta all evening. He had heard the young Duke of Enderby had been showing an interest, but His Grace was not present this evening, so whatever encouraging words the baron had wished to share with him, could not be delivered. Even Sir Justin Faulkes, who the baron had kept a slight glimmer of hope for, seemed to have ceased dancing with the girl. There were rattles enough around her, and she never sat out a dance, but he could see no dedicated candidates for marriage.

Another evening, he had tried on young Lord Jeffries. 'An estate in Kent, haven't you, Jeffries?'

'Well sir, my father has.'

'About time you had a wife, surely?'

'No sir, I don't intend to wed until I am thirty, Baron,' said Jeffries, scared but stoic. 'My father insists on it, you know. Says I'm not responsible, as yet.'

The baron walked away, running a hand through his grey thatch of hair, destroying his valet's artistry. *'No bloody hope there. Thirty, indeed! I had five children before I was thirty. Young men today have no ... Spindly legs anyway. Didn't like his spindly legs.'*

The Honourable Mr Linton Carswell, who had been nearby, loped over to the recovering Jeffries to say, 'Dreadful old chap that. I was caught at a house party with him for a week, you know.' Carswell slapped Jeffries on the shoulder. 'Near escape that, Spindles.'

'You set that name about, Foggy, and I'll...'

Carswell walked off, grinning.

He had his just desserts, for his mother, Lady Eloise, collared him in the passing.

'I have not seen you dance much this evening, Linton dear,' she said in the soft voice that instantly made him feel guilty. As usual, his mother's elegant, if a trifle shocking gown (of palest blue sarcenet over only a sheer muslin shift) seemed at odds with her gentle disposition. '*Do* dance with at least *one* unmarried lady, dear...' when the panic crossed his face, she laid a soothing hand on his arm. 'Just for practice, Foggy dear.' She looked a little conscious. 'Linton, I know you are acquainted with the Fortunes, but do not frequent that set, I beg. Miss Fortune is so very pretty, but I do not think your papa or I could bear to have Baron George Fortune as an in-law. We are not strong enough.'

'No fear of that, Mama!' said Foggy, a little too forcefully. 'Not the marrying kind.'

His mother sighed, 'That is just what your father once said to his friends, I hear. But these things happen...'

By female agency, he thought, shaken, for it was his mama who had brought his shy papa to the point, he'd been told. He blinked his large eyes, pulled what served as his chin further beneath his cravat, and escaped as quickly as he could.

Meanwhile, Baron Fortune's listlessly wandering eye hit upon something. Onslow's friend, wasn't it? The Corinthian whose sportsmanship was legendary. The man with the devilish reputation. Demon King he was called, and the baron was reminded why, looking at his haughty, arresting face, with the eyebrows drawn in a dramatic 'v'. The baronet's attention was somewhere to the baron's left. Could it be? Was the person that Sir Damon Regis was regarding in so concentrated a manner none other than his own Jocasta? Baron Fortune did a quick calculation. Was the man solvent? Regis dressed magnificently, and his stable was legendary, but the baron knew this meant very little. Many men lived dodging the duns. He had done so himself for many years. No, he had to look into Regis more thoroughly. He vaguely remembered seeing the baronet squire Jocasta in the park. As he was Onslow's friend, the baron had dismissed it. Also, his daughter's demeanour during the walk had left her papa with the impression that he was a dull companion. She had not seemed to be flirting with Regis at all.

But Regis' expression was more than idle admiration. It did not look like admiration at all, it was more dangerous than that. The baron hoped by the deity that Regis was as rich as he looked. The face could be fierce and cruel. His reputation was as a ruthless devil. But the baron naturally took no heed of this, felt no fear in sending his fragile little fairy to such a man. What happened after marriage was not his affair at all. His only goal was *settlements.*

CHAPTER 11

The Beginning of Partiality

Georgette had recommended, idly, that Jocasta accept Regis' latest offer of a drive out that morning, and so she did.

'The duke was absent last evening at Almacks,' Regis began, after some silent time where his companion made no effort to engage with him.

'Yes,' said Jocasta, 'I missed him most dreadfully.'

He slid his gaze to her pert profile. 'You have begun to wish to anger me, Miss Fortune. Why?'

'Permit me some amusements in this dull Season, sir.'

'You're starting to behave like Cecilia.'

'Miss Montgomery?'

'Yes. And I warn you, one of her kind is quite sufficient.'

Jocasta Fortune surprised him by giving a giggle that was quite genuine. 'I like to see her make you uncomfortable. She is the mistress in annoying you.'

'I have been glad to accept your *lack* of interest in me, Miss Fortune. But don't be an irritant if you still wish to use me as your escape.'

'No, Sir Damon,' she apologised. Then: 'But I have no idea why the duke should bother you. After all, you show no interest in my other dance partners.'

'Why should I? But Enderby is dangerous.'

Jocasta seemed to conjure up the duke's pleasant young face. 'I do not see how. And others, like Lord Bertram, or Mr Trusk, have a worse reputation, and you do not care at all.'

'*I* did not introduce you to Bertram or Trusk. I *did* with Enderby, so of course it is my concern.'

'Your evil scheme. You conceived it, I do not *at all* understand why you object to me carrying it out.'

'Yes, you do.'

'Do *not*,' Jocasta became heated, 'be one other who is *concerned* for me. You know—'

'I am now bored, Miss Fortune,' said Regis, sounding it. 'Be assured that I have no unusual concern for you. But stop encouraging Enderby unless you wish to see my wrath. It is a matter that touches my honour.'

'I would believe you honourable had you not conceived of the scheme in the first place. I shall do as I wish.'

'Try to disobey me and see what you will suffer.' His brows drew down in that terrible "V" once more.

'Ho! A threat,' Jocasta scoffed, with spirit. But she looked a little concerned.

'A promise.'

She suddenly became aware of their position, pulled up before a building overlooking the park.

'Why did you bring me here?' Jocasta said, somewhat suspiciously.

'It is the start of your education,' he said, and gestured so that the tiger on the back stand jumped down and took the reins. He got down and held out a hand for her to do the same.

She looked around, but then the maid who Georgette had allocated to her at Onslow House stepped out from the doorway. Chaperoned, Jocasta jumped down, intrigued. Inside the house there seemed to be few attendants. It was not tricked out elegantly, as one might think a house of this address would be, but had rough, unfinished walls in the hall and along the staircase. She climbed a number of flights after the quick, sure figure of Damon Regis, the maid following. He took her to a room with huge, shuttered windows facing the park, and he folded them back so that she could see the view.

'Do you find the prospect pleasing?'

'Who could not?' Jocasta said, entranced by the vista below her. From here, if one ignored the street directly below, the park looked as though it belonged to nature not to man. Tall tree canopies blocked the view of the carriage paths that she knew existed, and the human traffic seemed light.

'Then begin.' Looking about her, Jocasta saw that the room, with bare boards and a skylight of windows that gave it a peculiar light, was an artist's studio. It was a large open space, with only a number of pillars supporting the roof above. There was the smell of linseed oil, some easels and rags, rough earthenware jars of brushes and palette knifes, paint supplies here and there. A sofa piled with drapes, an old stuffed chair, some wooden ones also dotted around the barn-like space.

'Your studio?'

'I told you I used to paint, indeed when I was just a little older than you, I defied my father and travelled Europe to pursue my artistic studies. I have not painted for some time, but this place belongs to a friend, and is divided up into studios for artists. He let me borrow it for the afternoon.' Regis brought a leather pouch out from behind a chair, and took from it a tablet of sketch paper and some charcoal. She looked at it as he held it out to her, touched. 'Today you are free of anyone's concern. *Drawing* has not hurt you. The joy you took in it cannot have deserted you.'

She removed her kid gloves, laying them aside, and accepted the offering. 'Portia is the true artist,' she said, in a small uncertain voice.

'Did you compare yourself to your sister last year?'

She met his eye. 'Of course, I knew that she was more gifted — but I enjoyed drawing for its own sake. Just an occupation to be immersed in—'

'Exactly. I used to paint, and so I know the feeling. Why should *now* be different?' he held her shoulders briefly, and her gaze along with them. It was that complete attention he sometimes gave her, when he was not being flippantly rude — the energy that he conveyed to her in these moments held Jocasta spellbound. 'Just *be here* and draw!'

She looked down at the tablet, so that he could not see how much he had moved her. 'And what will *you* do while I am thus employed?'

'I shall read. I came equipped. Do not hurry. This outing will give me a chance to enjoy a quiet time, something that I do not always allow myself.' He gestured the maid onto the end of the sofa with the least clutter, and she sat down on the edge.

Jocasta looked at the window seat in the embrasure, with a dusty hassock upon it, and shook it out before she sat down, taking off her bonnet immediately. She looked around and saw Sir Damon drop to the floor, using a pillar to support his back, drawing a book from his capacious pocket. He paid her no attention, so she began to sketch, roughly at first, becoming engrossed in the unusual view of the park this place afforded.

As he read his book, Regis stole looks at her in her little nest by the window. Her knees pulled up to support the sketchbook, her eyes moving from paper to the view beneath. At first, she was a trifle tight and hesitant with her strokes, but he saw her relax and become engrossed. Her body became pliant and free, her eyes lit by concentration and delight.

He was reminded of how he met Isabel in a Spanish square, each of them drawing feverishly, sitting at pillars on different sides of the plaza, capturing faces from the marketplace. She looked intense and beautiful, and met his eye across the distance, in a manner that thrilled his youthful heart. They had gravitated towards each other, and had shared their sketches under the watchful eye of her attendant. It transpired that Isabel was collecting the faces of suffering (supplied by the poorest souls they had seen that day) for a study for a painting of the early Christian martyrs, while he was searching for beauty, wherever he could find it. 'Your drawing is so _alive_, señor!' she said to him with a vibrant look on her face.

'May I—' he had begun, mesmerised by that face.

'Do not say it. You may not paint me unless you let me paint you, first.'

He raised an eyebrow. 'As a martyr?'

'Not that, I think — as a pitiless Roman general, perhaps,' she laughed back at him.

Now, he looked again at Jocasta, who had a charcoal smudge on her nose, and he smiled to himself at her engagement with her pursuit. His eyes closed, and he began to drop off.

It was some time before Jocasta looked around again, suddenly aware that she had not heard the turn of a page for an age. The maid's head was drooped, eyes closed, and snoring gently while still upright upon the sofa. Regis was sprawled against the pillar, one long limb stretched out, also asleep, his book fallen on his lap.

Jocasta, who had progressed with her landscape, turned another page. Damon Regis' forehead was contracted, and once she had drawn some reference strokes for eye, nose and mouth positions, she began with the furrow between his eyes and the dramatic sweep of the brows. Then came the long eyelashes that lay on his high cheekbones, and, finally, his strong face in its entirety. The collar that brushed his cheek, his carelessly tied cravat, the strong column of his neck. Her fingers flew over the page, afraid he would awaken before she could finish. She sat a while, remembering other fascinating lines that his expressive brows had made, the range of fantastic shapes that animated his face. At the side of the sketch, she drew these lines from memory. The plaintive scrolls that sometimes almost met in the middle of his forehead, the flying brow of derision or amusement, that dreadful demonic frown. His eyebrows in repose, a frame for those strangely coloured eyes. She imagined mixing paint that would describe them.

The light had begun to change, and Jocasta, suddenly aware of the time, jumped down and knelt beside him and touched his shoulder, shaking it gently.

'Sir Damon!' she said softly. He opened his eyes and found her face so close to his that he took a breath. Their eyes locked for three seconds; Jocasta found herself unable to move. He levered himself forward and she drew away so suddenly that she fell backwards, putting her hands behind her to stop herself falling. He had risen, and held out his hand to help. Jocasta found herself unable to take it, and got up on her own, saying, 'I fear we are dreadfully late.'

The maid awoke with a jolt and stood, terrified of rebuke.

Regis looked at the sky, 'It would seem so.' He dispatched the maid to tell the tiger he needed the phaeton, retrieved her sketchbook and bonnet, and they hurried downstairs. The tiger came bowling around from the mews in but a few minutes, and Jocasta pulled herself up into the vehicle without assistance. The maid was directed to walk back. As Regis drove off, Tiger back in place, Jocasta was busy with her bonnet strings. 'Might I be allowed to see your sketch?' She opened the book to the unfinished landscape.

'Did you enjoy it?' he asked, briefly taking his eyes from the horses.

'I did. The time flew by.' She smiled at him, still a little embarrassed. However, she adopted a railing tone. 'But you did not say what you thought of my sketch, as yet.'

'It looked very accomplished. But that was not really the intention, was it? It was finding something that is genuinely yours—'

'Yes,' she said dreamily. 'Finding a little piece of myself that I love, a bit of the pleasure I had lost.'

'You have not lost yourself at all.' He saw her little smile, and was touched, but said stoutly, 'What next? Music? And do not tell me Portia is better—'

'She is, of course. But I enjoyed ... I *will* enjoy my flawed playing on my own.'

'Good. You must report to me how you feel. Perhaps, one day, I shall have the privilege of hearing you.'

'I doubt it, Sir Damon. I only play at family affairs, never in public.'

'It must have been hard, comparing yourself to your artistic sister.'

She laughed. 'Not really, for I had other, much *less* artistic sisters to compare myself to. Georgette, for example, can neither draw nor play.' She looked so naughty when she said so that he was drawn to smile in response.

'What is *her* gift then?'

Jocasta looked off, considering. Finally, she said, 'Warmth. Georgette's gift is warmth. I did not notice it until she left us and found she had taken it with her. I see her more clearly now. She is particularly good with people. She is a *true* person.'

'Yes, I have noticed.' He looked down again, seeing that the sightly depressed look had returned. '*You* seem to share the gift of attracting others to you, if your success in town this season is anything to go by.'

She was cold again. 'Oh, but that is not warmth, I am a mere pretender.'

'Your enjoyment today was not pretence. And as for the ballroom, I have watched you. You are never unkind. That is rare in popular young ladies.'

'You *watch* me?'

He bit his lip. Something between them was becoming unstable, he did not wish there to be any misunderstanding. 'Well, I am often nearby, with your brother-in-law, after all.'

'You are bound to see me, I suppose.' She looked askance. 'But thank you, Sir Damon, for saying as much. I should not like to do more damage.'

'Tonight,' he instructed, 'play something when you go home. But play it for yourself alone. Try to reacquaint yourself with your love of music. There is no competition.'

'What is your favourite piece, sir?'

'I do not know. My gloominess inclines me to nocturnes.'

'I shall find the gloomiest of nocturnes to practise, then.'

He frowned horribly. 'No. I have changed my mind — find me something uplifting.'

'Yes,' said Jocasta with the most natural smile he had yet seen from her, 'we must repair *your* spirits, too. I will find something in *A major*. It is a very cheering key, I find.'

He thought, *my spirits?* But then he considered that she might be somewhat insightful. His spirits were not low, he thought, but he did not live in the joy he was preaching to Miss Fortune about. That had ended when he left Spain. 'Then, let us both strive to live *A major* kinds of lives, Miss Fortune.'

'What a happy notion, Sir Damon. I shall search for things that cheer me each day.' She looked at him. 'But only if you promise to do the same.'

One ironic eyebrow flew. 'You think my spirits lowered?'

'I do not know you. But sometimes, you look quite terribly fierce. Then, at others, quite as disinterested in life as I.'

'Ah, so you watch *me*, Miss Fortune.' He looked down archly at her, and saw her confusion.

'Well,' she recovered herself, 'I am often nearby you, after all.'

'Yes,' he replied. What was he about? His remark was the beginning of flirtation. It was bad enough that he was driving with her at this late hour. How could he keep the necessary distance if his blasted mouth betrayed him? Why had it? He remembered the little face so close to his as she woke him, remembered his own held breath and the large pale blue eyes that innocently invited him to fall into ... what, precisely, he did not know. But he was a man, and she was a very pretty young thing. He must be careful.

He was reflecting on this still, when he returned Jocasta to her sister, noting the marchioness' assessing, disapproving glance. There were reasons that the rules of society existed. These reasons included the effect a young, pretty female could have on the male, whether it was sensible or not.

He must, he concluded once more, be *much* more careful.

'George!' Baron Fortune said to his son at breakfast the next day, 'What is Regis' position in life?'

Portia Fortune, eating a mouthful of egg, choked.

'Regis? You mean the Demon King?' asked George Fortune lazily. 'He always seems well-breeched. Wins at the tables a good deal, pays his gaming debts quickly. I do not know more. Why talk of him? Does he owe you, Pa?'

'No. Saw him looking at Jocasta.'

'*Interesting,*' said George Fortune, speculatively. 'But I shouldn't think so, mind. Why should he ...?'

Portia coughed. 'I think that he is just a friend of Onslow, you know.'

'Should pay him a visit, at least,' concluded her papa, ignoring her as usual.

Portia swallowed with difficulty. 'I've heard that Sir Damon pays attention to a number of married ladies,' she said desperately. 'I shouldn't go, if I were you, Papa.'

'I'll see what more I can discover on the financial matter. Don't think she's in his style, Pa.'

'He can't go about *looking* at a girl without explaining himself,' grumbled the baron. 'I'll have a word.'

'Onslow might be annoyed if you approach—' uttered Portia, desperately.

'If he's short of the liquid, it won't do, Pa, she might do better. Seems unlikely, but I heard Enderby's been paying attention.'

'See him, too,' said the baron.

'Papa! George!' squeaked Portia, but these two gentlemen left the table, apparently deaf to the female voice.

Portia got her pelisse and bonnet in a trice. The Onslow party and she had ridden together before breakfast, but *where* had Jocasta said she would be this morning?

In the end, Portia burst into the breakfast room to find Sir Justin Faulkes, Onslow and her two sisters still at table. 'Disaster!' she squealed as they looked up.

Onslow stood, 'Portia, tell me what—'

'No, *family* disast—' she stopped. 'Sisters, can we talk?'

Georgette got up at once and even Jocasta looked mildly concerned. Portia's character contained the histrionic, so she maintained her calm as they all made their way to the smallest salon, Portia shedding her bonnet and pelisse as they went.

'Papa will visit both Enderby and Regis today!'

They did not need to ask for what purpose.

'*No!*' said Jocasta, appalled.

'I tried to stop him, but—'

'—He did not listen,' said Georgette, sighing, 'You need not say so.'

'Oh, Jocasta!' cried Portia, grasping Jocasta's hand. 'He may scare off Enderby. Who knows what dreadful things he might say? And we thought that looked *so* promising.'

Jocasta pulled her hands away and clutched them together. *We*. Portia and Paxton, discussing the prospects of her marriage, hoping to be rid of the embarrassment of her. Jocasta hardly heard her sisters deciding what to do for the best. Georgette had a footman call in Onslow and Faulkes.

'Lucian, please find Papa and keep him occupied,' she was saying.

'Good notion, Georgie,' Portia said. 'Perhaps Onslow could persuade Papa—'

Jocasta was pacing, hardly hearing. Suddenly she turned to her elder sister. 'Georgie, I must go—'

'Jocasta!'

'I'll take my maid—' she reassured, running from the room.

He would be in the park, surely. After breakfast some days, he tooled his team and... She ran around to the mews and to have a gig hitched; a harried maid followed her. She drove to the park with only a semblance of control, the maid gripping the side of the gig in trepidation, not at fear of the speed, which could not be much in the busy London streets, but at the rash mood of her young mistress.

Jocasta had driven the avenue twice before she saw the familiar, red-trimmed wheels of Regis' phaeton. He was looking ahead, and did not see her until she pulled the gig into a perilous position close to his approaching pair. He pulled up, as she straightened her horse, manoeuvring herself opposite to the other driver.

'Miss Fortune?'

'Take me up, Regis,' she fairly ordered the baronet.

He looked down from his high perch, then around at the park. There had been no one in earshot, he concluded. 'Very well. Take your time and affect some fright.'

'How—?' she said, distracted.

'Put your hand to your head.'

She did so, and Regis passed his reins to the tiger who had dismounted from his stand behind, then he jumped down and approached the gig.

'Help your mistress from the carriage,' he told the maid. Jocasta appeared to be gently supported by the maid and baronet to Regis' equipage, and was tenderly aided to the passenger seat. The tiger handed Regis the reins, and with a swift word of instruction, that slight individual went to return the maid home and the gig to Onslow's stable.

It was, after all, perfectly acceptable for him to drive Miss Fortune, as he often had in the past, and deliver her home afterwards. But her evident agitation, should anyone see it, could give rise to talk of the worst kind. Seeing her face now, he regretted sending her maid off, but all he could think was that she needed him, and not an audience.

'What has occurred?' he barked. He watched as her hands were tightly grasping at the wool of the dove grey pelisse, her eyes on his face, her cheeks flushed. *'Speak!'*

'Take us off this avenue, Sir Damon,' she pleaded, her voice trembling.

He was loath to do so, since they were alone, but he understood her need to confide some new problem. She seemed unable to feign her usual relaxed demeanour — and how not to make this situation one to be talked of was more than he could, at the moment, imagine. He suddenly spotted Enderby and Cecilia Montgomery walking the avenue, with an accompanying maid of a certain age and resigned expression. Jane. He pulled up.

'No!' whispered a desperate Jocasta.

'Hand to your temple. Head down,' he whispered, and then to Cecilia, who was regarding him resentfully, 'Is Mrs Usher nearby?'

'Do not scold me Damon, Mrs Usher is just around the—' began a defiant Cecilia.

'Enderby, take Cecilia to her hostess directly.'

'Um, eh. Of course—' Enderby said, then moved his gaze to Jocasta. 'Miss Fortune, are you indisposed—?'

'Jane, get in!' ordered Regis.

'Yes sir,' said the maid stoutly, and did so, on Miss Fortune's side. Jane began to search a plain corduroy reticule for supplies, and soon held out a handkerchief, swiftly dampened by *eau de cologne*, to Jocasta.

Regis drove off, leaving the young pair gazing after the phaeton, and he took a smaller path towards a rose garden display, and pulled the horses up before he achieved its end, effectively blocking the way.

'Jane,' he ordered to the stoic maid, 'take the bench seat by the hedge.' Jane gave him an old-fashioned look, but after a lumbering dismount, did so. Soon Jocasta and he were alone, and unobserved by any but the respectfully distanced maid.

'Now, what on earth has upset your spirits?' His voice was cool, but at least he no longer barked.

Jocasta made some stuttering noises before she could get it out, 'I have to tell you, Sir Damon, that my papa ... oh, sir, my papa ... He means ... he means—'

'Calm yourself, Jocasta. At once!' His voice was flat, not angry. But that he had used her given name seemed to mean an acceptance of the imposition she was placing on him.

Jocasta, shocked out of her upset, took a sustaining breath. 'He will visit you. Onslow has been sent to stop him, but it cannot be halted. He will come to you ... even on another day ... he might say such things—' She grasped his sleeve. 'Oh sir, will you deny yourself to him?' She put a hand to her temple genuinely now, looking down, shaking her head. 'It is of no use, he may then talk to you at Almacks, or at some other function where he may be overheard, and say ... and say ... Only, *pray* do not heed him, sir.' Her eyes were flying about with her thoughts. 'It might be better if you admitted him to your home after all, in case he should publicly accost you ...'

'Jocasta,' he said, using her name for the second time. 'Why are you in such a taking ...? Calm yourself, I pray.'

'But Portia said he will go to you and Enderby today ... I had to come to warn you, to beg you not to ...'

'He will visit Enderby today also?' He remembered that she had not evinced a desire to speak to the duke when they had just met. 'If you

122

wish to intercede with His Grace also, you had best be in better charge of yourself.' He said it in the chiding tone that calmed her.

Her hands were shaking, her eyes alternated by looking at him with searing intensity, then looking down, compulsively grasping at the skirts of her pelisse. 'Enderby ... why should I see Enderby?' she asked, confused.

'Why—?' Damon Regis looked at her shaken figure. She had run to him with the compunction for action caused by the news that her father might visit him. She had no clear idea of why she had done so, he was sure. It was embarrassing, no doubt, to hear her father issue broad hints at her suitors, to discuss money in public as he was wont to do. Only his ancient lineage and his reputation for eccentricity made the *ton* tolerate him. He had heard the baron do such a thing to Jeffries recently, and to Mr York. Why was she so *particularly* concerned—? 'You do not wish to warn Enderby,' he asked, but he was really asking himself. 'Then why come to me—?'

Jocasta looked confused and for a second, it was as though those enormous eyes sought his for an answer. She blushed, stammered, then began. 'I supposed Enderby, being a duke, must be inured to such approaches. Although,' she attempted a laugh, 'they might not normally be as outrageous as my papa's.' She invited his laugh in return, shakily smiling. But Regis did not respond.

'So, you came to *me*—? Do you think *me* less able to deal with the baron's suppositions than young Enderby?'

This was so obviously preposterous that Jocasta could not think of what she might reply. Why *was* she here? Why had she felt it so imperative to ...? On the drive she had had only her aim in view. See him, warn him. Apologise. These made some of her scattered thoughts. She could not bear it if he thought that *she* thought... Now she scraped her inspiration to come up with some reasonable explanation of her disordered state, of her mission. Since she had little idea of her own motives, she had to work hard. 'The thing is, on this occasion Papa has been given a wrong impression about us. And it seemed so important that you do not think—'

'What? That you allowed him to think me your suitor? You must know that I, of all people, would not think so.'

She sighed a little, somewhat relieved, but still in great agitation. Suddenly, she brightened up. 'Oh, sir! You do not happen to have large debts, do you?' She hung on his arm and looked up at him so hopefully that he was amused.

'No,' he said.

'Oh, *such* a pity!' she mourned.

And now he did laugh. 'What a self-centred little cat—'

'Oh, but—' and then she too laughed. 'Yes, I am, am I not? I wish you in horrendous debt merely to save myself the embarrassment of my papa speaking to you of marriage.'

'Are you calmer, Miss Fortune?' Jocasta noted his reversion to formality, but smiled up at him in that brave way that, had she but known it, made his heart hurt. 'I shall not care what your papa may say to me, I promise you. I find your father amusing when he seeks out your other suitors, so the heavens are punishing me for that, perhaps, if I am sought out myself.'

'Who has he—?' Jocasta shook her head, so that the ornamental cherries on the band of her bonnet danced. 'No, do not tell me. It is better that I do not know. Take me home, pray.'

***

The baronet called the maid, and Jane's sturdy form once again squashed Jocasta's still trembling body close to his. He had a great deal to think about. A great deal. It may be that the outcome that he had risked was coming to pass. He glanced down. Perhaps it was not that. She seemed recovered, if a little embarrassed. He hunted for some flippant words. 'Which of your court has defected to Miss White's party now that she has returned? I missed the ballroom this week.'***

'Oh, quite a few,' she admitted, but blasé. 'She is much prettier than me, after all, as well as being an heiress. Oooooh, that last sounded cattish! She does seem like a charming person, and so much more poised than I am. I do not know why gentlemen wish to see us as competitors, though.'

'Because you both look like you might have only just escaped Oberon's lair.'

She giggled. 'I sometimes wish I'd been born a Valkyrie instead.'

No, he thought, looking down at her, do not wish to change. Be a fairy after all. It suits you. He wondered why he thought that, and of course, he could not say so.

That evening, at the Staffords' Ball, he danced with the favoured dark-haired beauty, a Miss Holland. She reached his nose in height and she was a charming conversationalist. But he found, when the figures of the dance put her in his grasp, that there was a deal too much of her. He had accustomed himself to fit to a smaller thing, whose topknot still tucked cosily beneath his chin, who tripped noiselessly about him in a way that cheered him. He made the decision to dance with the similar fairy figure of Julia White, her hair a lighter colour of blond, her face a vision of loveliness, and watched as she too tripped through the steps. But her hand was not as warm, her eyes were not closed off, but winsome. But those other eyes, larger than Miss White's, always seemed to hide beneath her guarded gaze some sudden hints of mischief, or a second of open trust. He took Miss White back to her mama, grim.

'Well!' said Cecilia Montgomery, once Jane had recounted her mission with Regis, 'so Damon, who *constantly* preaches the proprieties to me, acts to preserve *Miss Fortune's* reputation and leaves *me* to stroll with a rake!'

'What rake?' asked Enderby, confused.

'*You!*' replied Cecilia, in disgust.

'Oh, righto!'

'The young lady was distressed, and seemed to need to confide in him,' placated Jane from the corner of Mrs Usher's second salon, where she sat mending linen.

'How often has he warned me off Tom?' said Cecilia, still incensed. 'And he *abandoned* me with him in the park.'

'Well, you told him Mrs Usher was just around the corner, and so she was, therefore—' offered Enderby, reasonably, peeling an orange.

'I *might* have been lying. He knows I *frequently* lie to him, and *then* where would my reputation have been?'

Enderby sat up. 'Here, I say! It is just Regis who thinks of me so badly. I expect no one else would have turned a hair to see me accompany my countryside neighbour in the park for a short walk.'

'If Damon knows of your lecherous ways, others will too.'

'Here, steady there! I don't have lech—'

'You must have, or why would Damon have taken such a disgust of you—?'

'I already explained that.'

'*And* I have seen you flirt shockingly in the ballroom, smiling and trying to be charming. You really are a danger to unmarried ladies — and *still* he doesn't protect me from you—'

'I'm not a danger to unmarried ladies!' the duke protested, discarding the orange. Then reflectively, 'Actually, you haven't been in town enough to realise it, but even the *married* ones...' Enderby caught himself, then a thought occurred. 'Wasn't the object of all this to make Damon *stop* being so overprotective?' asked Tom. 'Why are you complaining?'

'You don't *understand*!' said Cecilia, throwing herself on a sofa.

'Spoilt!' exclaimed Jane from the corner.

'I *beg* your pardon?' asked Cecilia in an imperious tone, looking over her shoulder at Jane.

The maid looked up placidly. 'My work is spoilt. I shall have to take out some stitches.'

Cecilia gave her a narrow look, but turned around again. She sat back, but Jane's reproof had had an effect, and she was calmer. 'I wonder,' she said musingly, 'what distressed Miss Fortune—?'

'And why ever,' added Enderby, an orange segment poised before his mouth, 'did she choose the *Demon King* as a confidant?'

'*Exactly*!'

CHAPTER 12

The Practice of Obfuscation

Georgette caught her sister's return, and saw that she was agitated. She put off the pelisse she had just donned, and gestured her into her private sitting room. 'Where were you, Jocasta dear?' Jocasta was silent. Georgette raised her brows. 'Shall I ask the maid?'

'Georgie!' protested Jocasta, rather desperately.

'You know I would not,' Georgette laughed, pulling one of her curls.

'I ... I went to the park hoping to intercede before Papa—'

'I can see the impulse, but—'

'You are correct. Once I was there, I did not have the proper words—'

Georgette took her sister's hand. 'It must have been frightfully embarrassing!' but her eyebrows did a little dance, and Jocasta grinned.

'Frightfully! I do not know *what* I was thinking, Georgie...'

Georgette laughed a little. 'What did the duke say? Did you make him understand?'

Jocasta blushed and withdrew her hand. 'I did not see the duke — that is, I did — but I did not speak to him...'

'Ah, then,' said Georgette, sitting back a little, 'it was Sir Damon you wished to speak to?'

Jocasta blushed, hung her head, and then smiled a smile that Georgette had seen a little too often this Season. 'Well, after all, Enderby is a duke and must be simply beleaguered by matchmaking parents, but in the case of Sir Damon, there exists *no* such intention towards me and I felt it would be particularly awkward—' she attempted another laugh, 'almost as though he were to approach Sir Justin on the same mission.'

'He has already—'

Jocasta jumped. 'Oh *no*!'

'Would he have lost such an opportunity?' she retook Jocasta's hands in hers. 'But of course, you must know that such gentlemen as Sir Justin or Sir Damon have known Papa in the past and are equal to any situation.'

'I did not think—'

'No, you were distressed. Since you feared for your friend...'

'Sir Damon is not precisely a friend—' said Jocasta, covered in confusion.

'Well, he is our *family friend*. I suppose that you have spent a good deal of time in his company and feel particularly—'

'No, I assure you. When we go driving or such things, he never says a kind word to me. We are quite unpleasant to each other.' She paused. 'Most of the time.'

'Then, why *do* you agree to spend time with him? If it is on our account, I assure you, you need not be polite.'

'No, it is not that. I suppose we *are* close, but only in the way that one might be with an annoying brother.'

'He treats you like *George?*'

'*Of course not!* No one could be as foul as George.' Jocasta considered, her head on one side. 'More like Frederick Bailey being annoying to Amethyst.'

'Ah, I see,' Georgette looked askance again, 'but we know Frederick's affection underneath.'

'No. It is not *precisely* the same. Sir Damon has no affection for me at all. Or I for him. We have made that clear repeatedly.'

'Repeatedly,' muttered the marchioness, almost to herself.

'Yes.' Jocasta screwed her eyes up in concentration. How to explain some, if not all, of the strange relation she had to Regis? She felt she must venture something to Georgie now that she had acted so impulsively today. 'Sir Damon and I started with a mutual *use* for each other.'

'I *beg* your pardo—' exclaimed Georgette, remembering the words of Regis that had induced her ire.

'Nothing really disreputable. He wished me to ... to help a friend of his, and I wished him to ... render me a service, too.' She could not go further than this, or her misery might be discovered.

'I see,' said Georgette, forgoing to probe further.

'But now he has given up his own project and only seeks to help *me* and so...'

'And so, you are grateful, and do not wish him insulted by Papa. It is quite understandable.'

Jocasta took a deep breath. 'Yes, that is it, Georgie. You mustn't mind about Sir Damon, you really must not...'

As her sister left, Georgette, who had not previously been overly concerned about Regis, was now thoroughly frightened.

***

She was not the only one.

Regis had dealt with Baron Fortune easily enough that evening at the small party given by the Booth family (only about a hundred guests or so and a drawing room cleared to permit dancing) as the baron stood watching Jocasta being squired by Enderby. Regis claimed Baron Fortune's attention, and looking at the couple on the floor, said, 'Well, Baron, you must be thrilled at the success of Miss Jocasta this season.' He smiled into the baron's eyes. 'She has so many suitors and is at present dancing with the most eligible man in England.'

'Enderby, yes!' said the baron smugly. 'It would be a great thing, a *great* thing.' He then did his usual audible thought ramble, speaking to himself in a voice that could be heard by every neighbouring soul. '*But you never know with Jocasta. Stubborn as a mule. Sister Katerina's the same, but in a different way — she doesn't like men much. But no saying that Jocasta might scare young Enderby off.*' Then he looked back at the baronet. 'Anyway, Regis, I've heard that *you*— Wanted to talk to you about—'

'*Me?* With a *schoolgirl*?' he slapped the baron's shoulder and laughed. 'I know you are in jest.' His hand fell twice more and Regis moved off, saying to himself, 'That's a good one!'

'*Knew it would come to nothing,*' muttered the baron, in an echoing tone. '*Bloody Regis. But I would not have liked to deal with him on the settlements in any case, he's a deal too knowing...*' A neighbouring young lady, whom the baron's eye had landed on (without his awareness) trembled, lest politeness required a reply.

Regis, though, did not feel *knowing* at all. He lay in bed, staring at the ceiling, fearing that the worst was upon him. Perhaps not, perhaps he could still escape unscathed. He may be mistaken. It could be that her state today was nothing to do with affection, but with a new form of humiliation. She was tender to this feeling at the moment. That could explain it. Her enormous eyes filled with tears, her shaking limbs. He had known the urge to take her in his arms, to comfort her and tell her not to be silly. But he could not be such a figure to her. She was much too vulnerable now. If only she was not such a pretty, lost, little thing he would not now be fighting off this urge to be her only protector. Really — was he soon to be auditioning for the role of papa, brother and lover all in one?

He had been aware lately that the charms of her delicate face and frame, (which he had seen at first as the kind of shallow prettiness that better men than he had succumbed to, only to find themselves married to very dull wives indeed) had begun to affect him physically. Where at first, he had been cavalier about handing her down from the coach, or even lifting her over some rough ground, now he kept his hands to himself as much as possible. It had been almost impossible to stop kissing away her tears today. He had wanted to gather her in his arms and take her hurt away. But where might that leave them? He could offer for her, and once she got over being astounded, she might either laugh him off with outright derision, or accept him with the heart that she was so sure she did not possess. While he ... he was more and more convinced that Jocasta's heart was as big as the sea, and that once she gave it, her lover might be overwhelmed by it.

But he should not accept that emerging heart. That she now excited his male desire was not enough for him to make her a good husband. She should be treasured by someone who would not require as much as he from a wife.

He had once loved a woman in Spain, the Isabel he had remembered that day in the studio with Jocasta. Isabel had been wild and wanton, intelligent and artistic, sophisticated and charming in company. They talked of books and art and made love in an ancient bed, fit for ten men to sleep in. But she had needed more than him, or less than him, he had never quite understood. Isabel had sent him away, saying that he was close to taming her, to making her no more than a wife, and he had seen that that *had* been what he had wanted all along. To keep her at his side, to stop watching others smile at her, or blatantly show their desire for her. He was, at that time, considered a hellion, but he seemed bridled beside that magnificent woman. And he *might* have been seeking to tame her, just as she said, when replying to his plea to be his wife.

He had returned home and been reputed a demon and a libertine, but his rebellions were empty. His parents both dead, no one important was even left to disapprove. Yet he had continued until this Season had given him his new occupation. Haunting ballrooms to watch over Jocasta Fortune.

Now, in the end, if he offered for this little one, after his desire for Jocasta was fulfilled, what would be left if they married? Perhaps he would continue to feel affection, but she might descry his soul's yearning for more. Something like the passion he had known with Isabel — but to Jocasta it would look like the passion of Paxton and Portia, the passion she had not been able to offer. The very thing that had made her doubt herself so completely. He must not do that to her unless her heart was really in danger from him. Unless they had gone too far already.

Jocasta had shaken herself. She had to think what she had been about, but an evening afraid of Papa's mission had not helped. She had seen him approach Enderby, and had observed the young man's blushes and evident stammers until the figure of Miss Montgomery had appeared, rescuing the duke by leading him to a dance, in an unladylike way. Jocasta, narrowly observing, had noted that another man seemed to have appeared to claim Miss Montgomery, but she affected not to notice, and saved Enderby instead. Now Miss Montgomery, whom Jocasta had genuinely liked for her spirit, had heard her papa's vulgarity. Normally, she was inured to Papa and his ways, but this Season had upset her sensibilities, and she was feeling things more deeply. It was lowering to think that she was probably figuring as a female fortune hunter by the time Papa had made the rounds of the ballrooms, as Regis had already suggested he had. Last year, Papa's ways had seemed an irritating embarrassment merely, now they seemed poisonous.

Georgette had said once, 'Mama treated his mutterings as though he were like Mrs Potts from the village.' Jocasta knew she referred to an old lady of feeble mind.

'That was all her charity, I think. But it can be amusing, in those times it is not directed at you,' Portia had said, rather guiltily.

'As when he muttered after Mr Baxter, who had just disparaged Georgette's looks, *"Why he's talking about my gel when his has teeth like a horse, I don't know,"'* had added Jocasta. Yes, they had some affection for Papa, led by their mama's example. But there was no doubt filial piety was difficult.

Now, Jocasta was more completely humiliated, as she watched Regis approach Papa. The steps of the dance did not allow her to see the whole thing, and her pale complexion caused Enderby to claim her attention as he said, 'Are you quite well, Miss Fortune?' and she had to answer. Her head turned back to her papa, and she saw that Regis was wandering away, looking nonchalant. She let out a sigh of relief.

Later, when she joined the Onslow party once more, he had leaned over to say in a lowered tone, 'Don't worry. Your papa will not approach me on the issue again.'

Jocasta strove for a light laugh, in case of eyes turned in their direction. 'What did you say?'

'Attack is the best means of defence. I said you looked charming with Enderby.'

'Thus throwing the duke and I beneath the horses!' complained Jocasta.

The baronet grinned. 'But *I* escaped unscathed.'

'*You—!*' she began an insult, but looked away, for someone from a neighbouring group had seemed interested in their closeness.

'Is that not what you wished?' There was something low and dangerous in his voice, and her breath stilled, as she stood at his side, unable to risk looking at him. His tone changed, and she heard something like embarrassment, as well as the attempt at lightness in his voice, as he said, 'Enderby can handle it, too, never fear. It is as you said, he has been encroached upon almost since birth. He has learnt to cope with it.'

Later, Jocasta lay in bed, full of self-doubt. After her behaviour today, her reckless drive to the park, her shaken panic, she could no longer think of her feelings for Regis as indifference. On top of that, there was whatever-else-it-was that had sent a wave of heat through her frame as she stood next to Regis during those few minutes at the Booths' party, or the time when she had been close to him in the studio, frozen in place by new awareness of his proximity.

She tried to consider his voice at the ball. That — *Is that not what you wished?* — had been a challenge. It was a challenge he regretted immediately, she felt. But what did it all *mean*? He was not a kind man to her, full of neither the admiration, nor that empty sympathy, she felt from others. He was asking more of her every day. Not for *him*, not at all. He wanted her to be herself — a person she had forgotten — a person who, even in her previous state of self-satisfaction, could never be someone interesting enough to befriend him, the legendary Demon King. But she felt his unique approach to her, realised that he, too, was no longer indifferent. He had some impulse to be of use to her, some feeling of responsibility, perhaps. She reflected on how this could have occurred. It was the fault of her confiding in him the misery she had not been able to reveal to others. She had, by this means, induced him to more intimacy than he had desired: made him, in fact, her mentor. Because, whatever his demonic reputation, Regis was an adult who offered her childishness a helping hand.

Before dinner this evening, she had sat at the piano and played first a nocturne, and then a piece in A major: a Bach piano concerto. She had found the music in Onslow's library, where generations of Onslows had kept their favourite pieces. She stumbled as she practised, but the passages she managed had an exhilarating effect on the spirits. She would play it for him, she thought, and make him smile.

No, she was no longer indifferent to Regis, or he to her. Could they, perhaps, be friends? But the gap was too much. She knew that he wished only to right her, as a father might lift a fallen child, so that they might continue to run. Then, he would disappear from her sight, she was sure.

She chided herself harshly. Today's behaviour could have caused talk, and she suddenly realised that this could have placed *Regis* in trouble. She saw again all he had done to protect her today. Leaving Miss Montgomery alone, with only the companion that he most feared beside her, using the maid he trusted as Jocasta's protection, stopping her tears with his harsh words. She saw how ridiculous her mission had been. Even if she feared the humiliation of Papa's approach to him, a scribbled note, delivered by a footman, would have been more helpful than today's histrionics. She had behaved, incredibly, more like her sister Portia.

Humiliation, her constant companion, overtook her again. He was kind, truly kind, though he would never admit so. She would never again cause his behaviour to be questioned by the *Beau Monde,* not on her account. She would con her lessons well, recover her equilibrium, and free him from the worry for her, free him to walk away from the burden she had, through her own selfish foolishness, placed on him.

CHAPTER 13

A Spirit of Independence

Jocasta did not respond to Georgette's gentle probing into the state of her emotions. Georgette began to grasp that what Jocasta feared most was that her heart be known. She had been masking her feelings of jealousy and upset at Paxton's defection very well, but there had been more to it. She could not stomach sympathy, for it made the mask a failure. Suddenly Georgette saw it. Was *this* what Regis knew? It behooved her sister, therefore, not to pry too much, to wait, perhaps vainly, for Jocasta to come to her.

Her residency at Onslow House had furthered their intimacy. Jocasta, never seeming concerned for such things before, told Georgette that she admired her way with the servants, and that she envied her warmth with new acquaintances. 'How do you do it, Georgie? I never really noticed it before.'

Georgette had been prepared to turn the compliment off lightly, but something in the serious look in Jocasta's eyes had made her reply, 'I think, you know, that I just ask a little, then listen a lot.'

'That will be my watchword, Georgie! I wish to be someone much more like you.'

'Silly!' smiled Georgette, pulling one of Jocasta's curls again. 'You should simply be yourself. That is quite enough.'

'Sir Damon has helped me with that,' Jocasta blushed. 'I told him, you know, that this Season was not quite as amusing as last.'

'Yes?' encouraged Georgette, loath to stop this beginning of confidence.

'And he said that I should remember what *I* liked to do, rather than be distracted by what I *thought* I should do. The simple pleasures, you know.'

'I did not think that society's Demon King was so wise. And you must not worry about what Papa requires of you, Jocasta, or rush yourself. For whatever he says, Onslow and I will invite you next year, with Katerina.' Georgette inwardly winced at her husband's reaction, but continued in the same tone, 'If Onslow bears the expense, Papa will not forbid it.'

'*Thank* you! But Georgie,' added Jocasta with a hint of her old wickedness, 'only think of Katerina having to attend *balls*! *How* she will hate it!'

Both sisters giggled before Georgette said, 'Well, we shall have to help her enjoy it, in our way.' She paused and then ventured, 'But about the wise baronet ... it does not seem that you wish to spend time with him now. Has he offered you any insult?'

Jocasta laughed at this, and it seemed genuine. 'He is not sufficiently interested in me to offer the insult you suggest.' She looked away for a second, then regarded Georgette straight in the eye with her own large blue ones. 'It is just that our business together is concluded.'

The next evening it seemed so indeed. Jocasta, now used to moving off from Sir Damon, came up to him in a hallway where she and Amethyst Bailey were seeking a withdrawing room. This time, he nodded distantly and passed her. She knew her behaviour deserved it, but her heart contracted.

Amethyst, twittering on about her sister Maria's return from her wedding trip, was many steps ahead before she realised that Jocasta was no longer at her side. She called to her, and Jocasta found the will to move, at last.

He seemed angry with her, when all she had sought was to relieve him of his burden. But she saw now that she had done so amiss. Her sudden change of behaviour was cold and heartless. But knowing that she might cause rumours just by being with him, and perhaps unable to govern herself as she had in the park, she had meant to save him. And then, too, their old relations of indifference were now spoilt, they both knew it. How was she to *be* around him now? She had taken recourse in her social manner, but that had turned out to be flirtatious by default, and she was desperately trying to change this. She used Georgette as her template, and it had been useful. But with Sir Damon she could no longer be the bleakly honest girl she had once been, or the newly sensitive girl she was being among her court in the ballroom. At the opera, she had realised that with Sir Damon — who had been the only place where she had entrusted her honesty at the first — she must now disguise her feelings.

What her feelings were, she had no clear idea. But the pain in her chest told her that they were profound.

She gave the knife another twist, remembering, even as she agreed to visit Lady Maria Bucknell with Amethyst on the morrow. He had looked so cold. Should she try to explain that she had only behaved so for his sake? But no. She knew instinctively that *he* was worried about *her* feelings after her behaviour in the park. He feared them. She did not wish to begin some new conversation that might trap him further. She did not know what she might say to him if probed. He knew too much about her.

He wished to cooperate with Miss Fortune's spirit of independence, and knew it was time to avoid her, as she was him, but in the next week it began to annoy him. He continued the morning rides with the viscount's party, for the company of his old rival Onslow and his beautiful wife, plus his good friend Faulkes, made it a happy group. But Jocasta's insistence on distance was becoming a bore. She sought to avoid even the briefest of conversational remarks, rode away if his horse approached hers, and sought the shelter of Faulkes or her sister. He was not often pushed away like this; rejection was new to him. So, one morning, after the marchioness' usual invitation to breakfast, he finally accepted, aware that Jocasta had not heard.

The Onslows went up to change, and Justin and he held a desultory conversation and read the journals, while waiting for their arrival. The door of the library was ajar, and Regis looked up, happening to see Jocasta come downstairs. She went into one of the salons, and soon he could hear the strains of music played on the pianoforte. He moved from the room, and Faulkes did not look up, supposing he was going somewhere to relieve himself. In fact, he walked to the door where the music came from, and stood watching Jocasta Fortune as she played. It was a lively piece, and she faltered a few times and restarted a chord, but her little face was engrossed as she practised, a slight smile on her lips. She was wearing a pink gown, made up to the neck and trimmed with white lace, which edged the long sleeves too. The sunlight shot through the tall window and made her blonde curls gleam. Her whole frame was lit up. She looked utterly charming.

Suddenly aware of another presence, Jocasta turned her head, her fingers faltering on the keyboard, her gaze a little shocked, a little serious.

'Sounds awful,' Regis said, laconically.

And then, and then, was the moment that was his undoing, for Jocasta smiled in amusement and relief, a bright, beautiful, genuine smile, her eyes glowing up at him.

'Oh, lord,' he muttered under his breath, looking at her.

'Breakfast is served,' intoned the butler from behind.

Regis moved off to the breakfast table, glad to be with others, and with difficulty exchanged insults with Onslow over breakfast.

Faulkes, departing with him afterwards, said, 'What ails you?'

'Lost a bet,' Regis answered shortly.

'Ah!' said Faulkes in sympathy.

What was to be done? Nothing, definitely nothing. This would wear off. All the arguments against a union with Jocasta Fortune remained the same. She was a flibberty-gibbet, a little girl of eighteen only, who had no serious interests in common with him (an old man of thirty-one), no sensible thoughts and, by his observation, was not even in need of him any longer.

He had been distant with her in that corridor to pay her back a little. See how *she* liked it. But when the next day came, he realised that there was more to it. He was provoking her to come to him, to offer him some explanation. It was only when she did not come, that he knew himself.

She continued, in the following days, to avoid him. He purposefully did not ride with the Onslows for the next two days, but he was engaged to go to a play with them the next night, and after Miss Fortune turned her back on him at Almacks, when he had been wishful to say a casual word only, he wrathfully decided *not* to avoid it after all. Onslow himself had asked if he had given Jocasta any hard words, for even the marquis noted her studious avoidance of him. He had, of course, but her evident amusement at his words, evinced by the smile that had almost brought him to his knees, was not the cause of her avoiding him. Why, exactly, she now sought to evade him, he did not wish to think about seriously. If her heart were in danger ... but no, he would not choose to think so, quite yet.

Again, the rules of propriety, so often denounced by him, were right. *This* was what happened when you spent too long with someone of the opposite sex. Especially if she had needed you, and looked to you, and was, moreover, perfectly gorgeously lovely. No matter if you knew that only poisonous boredom awaited any such union in the future, for the moment all you could think about was seeing her smile at you, or holding her close. It was mad. But he had overcome this kind of madness before. Isabel had almost slain him, but he had overcome. And Jocasta was not that perfect woman, but a little fairy, merely. It should be easy.

He began to flirt more with Mrs Norton, aware of Jocasta's occasional glance. He danced twice with Miss White, starting a new *on dit* when he took her to supper.

'I want a word, Damon,' said young Enderby to him, after he had done so.

'Mmm?' said Regis, indifferent.

'Are you taking an interest in Miss White just to spite me?'

'I thought,' said Regis, uncaring, 'that you favoured Miss Fortune?'

'I do, of course, but she let Jeffries take her to supper, and I was going to take Miss White. First you pursue Miss Fortune, and now Miss White.'

'First you pursue Cecilia, and then Miss Fortune — and now Miss White,' answered Regis, bored.

'I haven't pursued Cecilia,' said the duke, as though Regis was insane. Regis looked at him. 'That is,' said Enderby blushing, and trying to recover from his slip, 'I have of course, but I am just ... just trifling with her.'

'I *beg* your pardon?'

The duke blanched and took a step back. 'That is ... you cannot tell me what to do, King!' He left, after this bluster, and Regis saw Cecilia Montgomery regarding them from a hundred yards away. He saw the rake Lord Bertram at her side, and frowned. Then he concluded that Cecilia was not rich enough for the fortune hunter's blood, and he turned away. But he thought of Enderby's words. He had sounded frank, before he had recollected himself. If Regis had considered the duke's secondary remark about *trifling* to be true then he would have dragged him from the ballroom by his collar and dealt with him soundly. No, something was behind all this, and Enderby had not the wit to carry it off.

Then he understood. Cecilia, annoyed by his strictures, was playing off her tricks again, and had enlisted her friend's help. Regis had been too precipitate in dealing with her, he knew it. And clumsy. Only, there had been another young girl in Regis' life, from a neighbouring estate, whose heart had been broken by a rake. She had ended her life in a river, probably by her own will. He had wished to avoid any such tragedy with Cecilia. Once he had thought of young Tom as harmless, but Town and flattery had changed him, and Regis had witnessed when he had, soon after his father's death, succumbed to the temptations.

Regis' eyes sought Jocasta as by homing instinct. He wanted to be assured that his work with her was truly done. She was with Lord Jeffries, that charming, curly-haired scamp, right now. But he saw not just the flirtatious Jocasta, but something else. She appeared to be listening with true attention, appeared to be laughing at some story Jeffries told, with genuine warmth. Her smile did not drop as he turned away. She seemed to be engaged with people once more. This was good, surely? But her smiles bestowed on others caused a rip at him. Though he knew this was only an illusion, it would be better to give her no attention at all.

He happened to see, though, that Jocasta's glance snagged on someone more than once, and he was unable to stop himself following her, as she moved towards the figure.

A young man was standing alone beside a column, regarding the dancers. Jocasta stood on the other side of the column, and addressed him, also looking out at the throng. Regis felt himself move towards the place where she was, standing several steps behind the pair, eavesdropping in the most vulgar way imaginable.

She appeared to have greeted the gentleman already, for the young buck gave her a stiffened bow. 'I wished to approach you, Lord Bryant,' Regis heard her say, her voice both nervous and gentle, 'to make an apology to you.'

'Apology? I do not think,' said the young man, flushed, but not looking at her, 'that you owe me any apology, Miss Fortune.'

'I think I do, My Lord. Last Season, I fear I was very young and inexperienced, but that is no excuse for my behaviour towards you.' She took a breath to steady herself and continued, 'I believe I was so vulgar as to *flirt*, and then be unresponsive, to some of those who requested my company.'

'Please, Miss Fortune,' said Bryant, even redder, but in a cold tone, 'there is really no need.'

Jocasta was trembling, Damon saw, but she continued, nevertheless. 'But I think there is. My thoughtless behaviour caused you pain, I think...' she broke off, looking at his flush of humiliation, '... or at least, angered you. I am truly sorry.' He was silent, but he turned towards her, seeking her eyes. She smiled at him faintly and added, 'I was served back my own sauce, as I am sure you have heard from your friend Mr Carswell, who was present at our house party.'

The young man looked at her with a serious face, and to his credit, a hint of concern was discernible. Jocasta continued.

'It was good for me, I have been told, for it made me more noticing of the feelings of others. Anyway, sir, you have every right to be angry with me, but pray don't let the behaviour of a shallow child, such as I was, affect you.' He tilted his head, as though to warn off her sympathy. 'I speak because I seldom see you smile this Season, and dance less. I would hate to think you distrustful of the world because of one selfish young girl.' As he flushed again, it seemed to be for another reason, and Jocasta, thought Regis, guessed her new mistake. 'I am still too flighty and shallow for such a serious young man, but I truly hope, Lord Bryant, that you meet a woman worthy of you. I shall not trouble you again.'

Seeing the young buck's look as he followed her with his eyes, Regis feared she had done more harm than good. She had reanimated the feeling that had disguised itself as hate. But, like Bryant, he could not help but admire the bravery of the little figure as she left.

CHAPTER 14

The Beau Monde Wonders

'Has it occurred to anyone,' asked Lord Alvanley of his cronies at Whites, 'that no explosions have yet been heard, or ridiculous bets been laid recently?'

An eyebrow greeted this, and George Brummell said, 'Ah, how did I miss it? I am really letting age overcome me. What on earth has the Demon King been about? Is he deceased?'

'Stanhope wanted to goad him to a wager of skill, tooling his carriage with two wheels only on the raised pavement on Albemarle Street, his bays against King's greys. He'd organised the street cleared at great expense, but Regis denied him,' Pierrepoint said, idly throwing down a card.

'Regis admired those bays. Even said they were better matched than his team — and he *refused* the wager?' Sir Henry Midmay said, astounded. He moved some hair from before his eyes to better see the cards, for all the hair he had (which was but a valiant remainder) was brushed forward aggressively in attempt to ape Beau Brummell's rather more fastidiously arranged style.

'He did, and one from Alvanley to set two archers against him, with my lord's *hunting box* as a prize if King won,' Pierrepoint added.

Alvanley grinned. 'I was sure, while under the influence of brandy at least, that even if Crichton couldn't take him, Harrington might.'

'What did King say?' drawled the Beau.

'He said,' uttered Pierrepoint, 'that it sounded like a bore. I am glad he has not my profession.'

'No. A diplomat Regis is not,' said Alvanley, with a shrug. 'What on earth is he up to? He has not even been frequenting his clubs with any frequency.'

'*Where* is the man who shocked a nation by running off to Venice with a countess in the middle of Lady Cowper's ball?' lamented George Brummell. 'I was vastly entertained by her husband's wrath.'

'The Demon King barely escaped ostracism for that one. I was surprised he was admitted to society again,' mused Pierrepoint.

'He came back the next season — it seemed the romance palled quickly,' remarked Midway, never taking his eyes from the cards.

'There was never a romance,' said Alvanley, dismissively. 'That fateful evening the countess, I heard, had just been permitted to come out from her husband's confinement of her — for she had just recovered from two broken limbs, inflicted by the hand of the noble earl.' Alvanley's tone held derision and disgust.

'The prince, though not approving, understood Regis' motive,' added the often-silent figure of St John Peyton. 'He was not a demon for taking the countess to her sister in Venice.'

'So, everyone, knowing this, chose to forget?' asked young Charles Booth, awed.

'Not *everyone* knew, but when the regent greeted Regis as though nothing was amiss, the world followed,' said Alvanley.

'Sometimes, not often, society behaves with dignity,' remarked the Beau.

'*I* still remember the race last year in Hyde Park in Harlequin costume,' grinned Midway, returning the mood to the ridiculous.

'Yes, I remember that Peterson had somehow displeased the Demon King,' said Brummell.

'I saw that race. I never knew why Peterson looked ridiculous wearing the costume, while the demon did not,' Midway reminisced.

'Ah, he has good legs for stockings,' laughed Pierrepoint.

'Nonsense!' said Brummell, 'Merely, Regis has an air!'

'Yes, but you are right, Alvanley. Nothing much this Season from the Demon King at all. It is as though he were becoming a respectable citizen.'

'He *did* do the London Bridge wager with Grandiston. That was sufficiently mad,' offered Booth.

'Risking life and limb and compensating the poor vendors for damage to their roofs. That was inspired!' Midway granted.

'Inspired by a couple of bottles of Chambertin, I fear,' said Alvanley.

'And Grandiston is back to his regiment in Portugal now,' said Charles Booth, sadly. 'He told me it had refreshed him to risk himself on *ordinary stupidities.*'

The Beau granted this a 'Ha!'

'The Demon King knows a military man's need for distraction. That is probably why he accepted the wager,' said Pierrepoint.

'Regis as benevolent! *That* is an idea to ponder,' laughed Midway.

'Oh, I don't know. He has always had the spark of an angel in his black heart. You know the new girl Mrs Usher is putting out?' said Alvanley.

'Montgomery's daughter? Yes — pretty little thing. Enderby seems taken with her,' Midway replied.

'Oh, I don't know that! They have been friends since childhood, I believe.' It was young Booth who interrupted, but a flying eyebrow silenced him.

'Well, Regis has been looking out for her, I hear. Warned off Bertram and a few of the others.'

'No need for that. She is not rich enough to tempt Bertram. She has a small estate, merely. Comfortably off, but not enough to fund Bertram's excesses,' remarked Pierrepoint.

'However that may be, Regis is warning off the riffraff, like a guardian. Don't know if the girl knows, but I heard from Gascoigne that the Demon King paid off Montgomery's gaming debts, for he tried to pay Gascoigne his due share, but the viscount refused,' concluded Midway.

'Yes. Gascoigne is not such a one as to dun a poor orphan girl for her father's folly,' said the innocent Mr Booth.

'But some *did* take the Demon King's money, wherever it came from. Hence that girl is at least comfortable,' concluded Midway.

'Don't, I pray you!' pleaded Brummell theatrically. 'If I hear any more mawkish sentimentality, I shall take a dislike to one who has shown a modicum of originality in this sea of dreariness that is called fashionable life.' The Beau shook his head, as though a thought occurred. 'Oh *no!*'

'Eh?' Alvanley looked surprised by the Beau's showing signs of animation.

'My dratted memory! Why did I have to remember something so disheartening? Were not you present, Booth, two Seasons ago at the table when Van Meering lost his shirt?' asked Brummell.

'When he wagered his entire estate against the King's last hand? I *was*. It was horribly thrilling for my first time in Town. I could not believe that such a bet could be placed.'

'Has anyone noticed,' sighed the Beau, 'that Van Meering is still *living* there?'

'He has stopped going to town as much and I wasn't his intimate so … Good Lord, does that mean Regis refused to *collect*?' said Midway.

A long sigh escaped the Exquisite One. 'And *I* thought he refused my advice on the fitting of his coats because of penury caused by hearty dissipation — not out of saintly mercy for a fool.' Flicking open an enamelled snuff box with his fingernail, the Beau took a pinch with a frown, as though resorting to medicine.

'You must be crushed, George. How will you ever forgive him?' Alvanley laughed.

The Beau waved a startlingly white handkerchief beneath his nose. 'I do so only because of his immaculate linen.'

Georgette joined Amethyst Bailey and Jocasta at Lady Bucknell's abode. This was not Bucknell House, where the Dowager Lady Bucknell, that hard-edged friend of Viscountess Swanson, was installed — but instead, a pretty, new townhouse in a fashionable close.

Jocasta had never been able to understand the gentle Maria's decision to wed the grim-looking Bucknell, eight years her senior and of a joyless disposition, she felt. She was afraid to think that Maria might now regret it.

However, it was a radiant Maria who came forward to meet them, now dressed in a handsome claret silk rather than maidenly muslin, looking very fashionable. Her swain stood beside her, still stiff, thought Jocasta, but after a bow to the guests his eyes rested on his wife — and overarching pride could be the only words used to describe his expression. His hair was different too, thought Jocasta. A few locks fell on his forehead, and she saw him strive to replace his severe style with his hand. Jocasta, with a blush, thought that his hair might have been rumpled, some time before they entered, by someone's exploring fingers.

Bucknell placed a cushion behind his wife as she began to sit, and she gave him the warmest of smiles over her shoulder. This made Bucknell, Jocasta was astounded and amused to see, blush — and he moved from the room with a word of apology to them, citing business, but really leaving them to a comfortable gossip.

'Well, Maria dear,' said Georgette for all of them, 'we need not ask you if you are happy, for it is perfectly obvious.'

'I fear,' said Jocasta, as Maria blushed, 'that you are destined to be that most unfashionable thing — a happy couple!'

'Oh, indeed Maria, you look so well,' said the buxom Amethyst happily, adding, 'but is Bucknell not frightening? I feared that you, who are so gentle, might find his manner repressive to your spirits.'

'My lord is so very wonderful!' this was said in Maria's sweet gentle voice, and shyly. 'His manner is a little stiff in society, perhaps, and his face may seem grave. But *he* is much gentler than I, I assure you, my dear sister. I cannot now remember what my dream of a husband might be, but it could *never* have been so good, so kind, so strong as my lord.' She put her hand to her mouth, looking guilty. 'I should not say so lest I become a braggart, and I would not, or only before all of *you*, my dears.'

It took very few questions from the bubbly Amethyst (now reassured) for Maria — normally shyly reserved — to wax long and lyrical about her husband. How he had seen to her every comfort on her wedding trip, procured only the best rooms at inns, had, on one occasion, driven five miles to an apothecary only because she had coughed once, how she could not look at anything in a shop or the linen drapers but that he would insist on purchasing it for her, how he would not let her pay a visit to his mother, lest that dame upset her. 'Indeed,' said Maria, 'I quite pity Her Ladyship. She asks that we join her at Bucknell House, and my lord will not hear of it.'

'It is just as well you have him, Maria,' said Jocasta, suddenly seeing it, 'for you are just the sort of girl who might be bullied by her mother-in-law 'til kingdom comes.'

'Jocasta!' sighed Georgette, vaguely reproving. Then she smiled. 'Not but what she is right, Maria. I have no mother-in-law, but if I did, and she had the temperament of old Lady Bucknell, I should be inured to her bad temper, after so long with Papa. Jocasta, too. But with your dear parents, I fear that you and Amethyst need someone to protect you against bad temper, for you have never had to deal with it!'

'Yes!' said Jocasta. 'We must all meet *Mr Dickson's* parents before we let him run away with Amethyst.' She said this frivolously, having observed that rather skinny young man dance with Amethyst at most of the Almacks assemblies.

'Oh, my dear sister!' cried Maria. 'Have you a suitor?'

'Perhaps...' Amethyst blushed. 'Mr Dickson has danced with me many times now. James is a friend of his, and he told me that he had wondered to Mr Dickson if he had not got the headache, listening to his sister's incessant chatter—'

'Oh James! Is he *trying* to scare your suitor away?' Maria allowed herself to be a trifle annoyed.

'Well, Mr Dickson is so silent that I did not think of him as a suitor, however much he has danced with me. For he *says* nothing at all. But I am grateful to James really, for apparently Mr Dickson replied that he had no headache at all, and on the contrary he liked to hear me chatter, as his own home is deathly quiet.' Amethyst blinked, and the others blinked back. She should capture this silent young man, thought Jocasta, for one who could bear with Amethyst's chatter for long was a find indeed.

'But do you *like* him, Amethyst?' asked Georgette, as amazed as everyone else.

'Since James told me so, I have observed him more closely, and I think I like him very much indeed. He is not precisely handsome, but I like his face. He has nice eyes. And I do not always feel the need to talk quite as much if I am with him, for his silence calms me.'

'How, though, if he is so shy—' worried Maria, 'how will he ever...?'

Amethyst blushed. 'I believe James is taking him to visit Papa tomorrow.' She looked around at the three faces surrounding her. 'It may not be ... I cannot be sure ...'

'Well,' said Georgette practically, 'it is very encouraging, but perhaps we should not think of it quite yet.'

'Oh, yes!' said Maria Bucknell. 'And you, Jocasta, have you enjoyed your Season?'

'Oh,' sighed Amethyst, 'Jocasta is once more a favourite in the ballroom. I am so jealous of her many suitors.'

Jocasta was glad she thus avoided Maria's question, for she would not have known how to answer it honestly.

Bucknell returned, and this signalled their departure. His excuse was thin, he had brought his wife a shawl against the chill. He exchanged a fleeting, charged glance at Maria, as he placed it gently around her shoulders.

As they looked back, Jocasta saw that their hands entwined, just visible behind Maria's skirts. He still stood stiffly, as ever, but Jocasta was not deceived.

'Well, if that does not prove,' said Georgette in the carriage home, 'that there is indeed a glove to fit every hand, I do not know what would.'

All three, surprised at the happiness they had witnessed in a place where they had hoped, at best, for contentment, looked at each other and giggled their way home.

⚜

Despite her good intentions, the next morning Regis, in his riding attire, was in the drawing room, ready to join them on their daily ride. The full Onslow party now regularly included Portia, very occasionally Paxton, the Onslows themselves, plus Jocasta and the two baronets. She was shocked that he was here, so shocked that she hardly gave Paxton, regrettably set to hold back the other riders by the pace of his safe canter, a glance.

Portia had been trying to claim her attention, but only managed to do so once they were all safely in the park and she could move forward to walk her horse abreast her.

Portia's face was full of the dreaded sympathy, but at least it had a different origin this time. 'I saw Papa with Enderby — did the duke say anything to you afterwards, Jocasta?' she asked, concerned.

Jocasta looked at her sister's face, and for the first time recognised some affection in her concern. However, she did not clearly remember if the conversations she had had with Enderby last night were before or after his talk with Papa. She thought back, and realised that he had led her out for a dance *after* his encounter with Papa, and had been his usual attentive self. She had been distracted, watching the baron with Regis. 'He was as usual,' she now said to Portia, indifferently.

'I saw Regis approach Papa first, had you warned him, too?' asked Portia worried.

'I mentioned it to him, and he found it amusing. He said to me afterwards that he told Papa how well I looked dancing with Enderby — taking the wind from Papa's sails completely.'

'That's a relief. One does not know how dangerous Sir Damon might be if he were to make an enemy of Papa. And men of his age can handle any social situation better than someone like the duke.'

'Indeed,' agreed Jocasta.

'I'm glad Sir Damon did not take offence. How absurd of Papa to think that he—' then Portia hesitated, 'but I suppose you *have* been seen a great deal in his company, even before you moved in with Georgette. And yet you two never seemed particularly thrilled at the thought of your drives. He did not appear to be as enthusiastic as Mr York, for example. Why *do* you—?'

There was much in all of this to make Jocasta angry, but Portia's concern seemed genuine, so Jocasta did not tell her to mind her own business, as she might have done in the past. Instead, she said, 'Well, do not say so to Paxton, but the first drive was in the nature of a — a wager.'

'Oh,' said Portia, 'but how did you discover it?'

'He told me. Only because he could see I was quite afraid of him. We laughed about it, and then we decided to win the bet for him, and endured each other's company. It suited me too, for Mr York's attentions are so marked, and I am not yet decided on my course. Papa would soon have pressured me to—'

'I know, I know,' sympathised Portia. 'Now I can see how horrid it would have been to be here as an *unattached* Fortune sister. How *all* our elder sisters must have suffered the embarrassment of Papa's intrusion into even their *slightest* male acquaintances during their Seasons! I had not thought of it before, but it must have been so.'

'Mmm,' answered Jocasta. 'Can we turn the topic now? It is bad enough experiencing last night, I do not wish to relive it.'

'Of course,' her younger sister said apologetically, 'you are quite right.' She looked again at Jocasta's bland face, 'But Jocasta, why does Sir Damon *still* drive you?'

Jocasta only hesitated for a second before answering carelessly, 'He and Sir Justin share the burden of teaching me to drive a high perched phaeton. It is a different skill to driving Papa's gig you know.'

'I wish *I* could try.' As Regis approached, Portia turned to him. 'Sir Damon, Jocasta has been telling me that you are teaching her to drive a phaeton, might you spare some time to take me up once?'

'No one drives my horses.' Regis replied flatly.

'But Jocasta said—' protested Portia, betrayed into rudeness.

'Ah,' said Regis, shooting his glance in a blushing Jocasta's direction, 'but I instruct her by words and example only. She may not take the reins.'

'Well, what a hoax!' said Portia. 'I assure you, there is no one better at driving our gig than Jocasta. Unless it be Leonora, nowadays.'

'Another sister?'

'Yes. Only fifteen.'

She found Sir Damon was looking bored, and she made an excuse to join her plodding swain.

'You are always horribly supercilious when Portia is near.'

'I find her irritating.'

Heaven would say that Jocasta should be annoyed about this rudeness about her sister, but she found that she was not. 'And me?' Jocasta wished it back as soon as she said it.

'Infuriating, these days,' he drawled.

'And before?'

One eyebrow gave a comical curl. 'Not irritating, nor infuriating, but merely uninteresting.'

'I fear I am no more interesting now.'

'You are correct: just more annoying.'

Jocasta bucked up at this insult. 'I *always* found *you* annoying — but that comforted me, then.'

'And now?'

'Somewhat similar,' she said, matching his flippant tone, 'but your annoyingness is more challenging. As you wish it to be.'

'I do?'

'You do. It may not seem so after yesterday, but I *am* improving, you know. I practised piano last evening.'

'*A major?*'

'Yes,' she smiled. 'I'll play it for you once I have learnt it well.'

'Ah, musical recitals!' he said with distaste. 'I cannot bear the sort of strangulated performances of young ladies.'

She ignored his rudeness and merely pleaded, 'Just fifteen minutes — on a visit to Onslow House, perhaps.'

He sighed, then asked, 'Do you really wish to learn to drive a phaeton?'

'Yes. But not as *you* do! Sir Justin or Onslow will teach me if I ask.'

'My style,' he admitted, 'is not for young ladies.'

'Nor for anyone who values a whole skin, gender regardless.'

He laughed. 'Shall we drive this afternoon?'

'No. I think we have plans. Georgette and I...'

Regis merely smiled and rode on.

CHAPTER 15

Friendship and its Foibles

For the next two weeks, Regis was constantly denied the company of Miss Jocasta Fortune. She had no dance for him when he casually enquired. She was not available to drive, her hand never seemed to be on his arm at any of the group visits to the theatre, or Vauxhall, or on walks in the park. She found other arms than his — but still, in their occasional exchanged words, there seemed no distance in her manner. Rather, Miss Jocasta Fortune claimed a friendly, easy tone around him, which he did not find comforting at all.

'What have you been doing with yourself, Miss Fortune, since last I saw you?' he asked finally, as they were seated at the back of Onslow's box at the opera — the rest of the party engaged in chatter.

'Oh, I have been driving, and riding, and sketching, and practising my music, you know, as well as taking some of your other advice.'

'What advice, pray?'

'Well, I have refused more than one dance to certain gentlemen, and have gently rejected them, as you suggested. It has had a melancholy effect on my social status.' But her tone was arch.

'Oh, yes?'

'Indeed. I had to sit a dance out a few days ago. My first since my come-out.'

'How *very* dreadful for you,' he drawled.

'It really was. It hasn't occurred again, thank goodness, but my morale was in decline.' She sighed histrionically, then smiled at him.

So, *this* was the flirtatious Miss Fortune of the ballroom. He saw that she realised it herself, but there was a gap between them now, that could only be filled with this nonsense, perhaps. 'I see.' His tone was bland.

She said, in a more serious tone, 'I am trying not to take on board my father's preoccupations so much. Sometimes, gentlemen simply want to dance, not to set up home with me.' She laughed again. 'There is sufficient enjoyment in this for both, I feel. I am beginning to quite like parties again.' *So, you can stop worrying about me.*

'I can see that there is a sparkle in your eye that I did not see before. I'm glad, Miss Fortune.'

'So am I, and I am grateful, Demon King. I will always be grateful that you would not allow that habit of self-pity I had gotten myself into. I was *even* happy to dance with Lord Paxton last week!'

He raised his brows.

'Well, perhaps *happy* is the wrong word,' she giggled and looked wickedly confiding, 'I still find him deadly dull. But I mean, it was easier to be polite. The situation no longer feels like a weight on me. Just by turning my attention to what I truly enjoy, as you suggested, I was able to see how trivial my worries have been.' She seemed to become aware of the time they had been talking. She had an afterthought. 'I think, you know, that the Duke of Enderby is harmless. Don't torture Miss Montgomery over him anymore.' She smiled a friendly smile, and moved away, to take a seat near Georgette.

It seemed, somehow, like a goodbye.

Regis supposed he was relieved. Though there was a kind of a hesitancy about their exchange, he believed that she was different from the sad little thing he had felt burdened by. Her eyes were clearer. There was something there that acknowledged the strange intimacy of their relationship, and that was honest, at least. Who they were to each other was not quite definable by the proprieties. It might be called friendship, to be prosaic — but they had never been friends, not really. And certainly not lovers. The elder brother she should have had, he thought. Perhaps he had been that. Scolding her, but wishing the best for her happiness. That might best describe it. A little like his feelings for Cecilia. She annoyed him, and yet he felt responsible for the promise he had made to her papa. He would not let Cecilia go astray if he could help it.

But he had never had to fight the urge to take Cecilia in his arms, and he knew it.

When the Duke of Enderby loped along to Mrs Usher's these days, it was mostly to find Cecilia Montgomery missing. He never thought to make an appointment, of course, and he never came at the designated hours of morning callers. When he had done so, after the first few days of Cecilia's arrival, he had had to sit with any number of other men — all making small talk laced with idiotic compliments addressed to a flirtatious Cecilia. So, he had taken to coming after the hours for callers, or before the time when the ladies might change for dinner, and that had allowed him to lounge about with Cissie, just hearing what was going on, or making new plans to annoy Regis.

But now when he came, it was much less likely that he could see her. He complained to Mrs Usher after he had missed her the last time. 'Well, Tom, this is her Season, you know. Its purpose is social engagement, a young lady's come out and so forth. Did you expect her to be just waiting any time you stop by, as it was in the country?'

'No, no! It's just that...'

Mrs Usher rolled her eyes. 'Then why don't you make an appointment like any other young man? If Cecilia knew you were coming, I'm sure she would be happy to spare you an hour or so for a walk or a drive.' Enderby recoiled. 'Shall I tell her you are coming tomorrow? When? In the morning? We have a rendezvous in the afternoon, I'm afraid. And if you do not want Cecilia to be driving with Mr Wray, or Sir Timothy Walton, then you had best tell us beforehand.'

But there was something wrong with this. Make an appointment to see Cecilia? It placed him in the same category as ... Arrange an assignation like Wray or Walton? It gave him the shivers.

Mrs Usher was looking at him sarcastically. He had to deal with that impertinence.

'No need, I suppose I'll catch up with her sometime.' He shrugged airily. 'Don't tell her I called. She might be sorry she missed me.'

'I don't think she *would*,' said Mrs Usher, sweetly reassuring.

He looked at her sourly, and turned to go.

'Your Grace!' she called as he reached the door. 'We're at Almacks this evening.'

'Mmm,' said Enderby, not turning, and left.

He had spotted Cissie at a ball the night before, and he had meant to ask her to dance, but what with one thing and another, including Miss Fortune's allowing him to take her to supper, he never had. He had felt guilty at one point when he had noticed Mrs Usher head to the card room, and meant to go find Cecilia, but when he looked it was to see her with a group of young people, who had obviously just danced a set together, and had decided to continue the encounter with conversation. That made him let go of the guilt, and he had been called away by a friend and not even spoken to Cecilia the whole night.

He was glad she was enjoying herself. And so was he — enormously. But there had been a few sticky moments last night, with a match-making mama with a bullish temperament, then with a Miss Roberts whom he had failed to join for an appointed dance, and who had actually cried at him in the supper room, where she had been accompanied by her irate brother. He had wanted to tell Cecilia how Miss Fortune had helped the girl, and how he had dealt with the brother. And how when Regis appeared, Miss Fortune had disappeared, almost as though there was some sort of rift between them. All this, plus the stirring tale of how his valet, Dorkin (that prince among discreet servants) had tripped on a carpet edge and thrown chocolate on him.

Only to Cecilia could he describe his own heroic attempts not to laugh, and Dorkin's exquisitely stiffened face.

That night at Almacks was to cause the furthering of the acquaintance between Miss Montgomery and Miss Fortune, who had only met a few times previously in the company of Regis or Enderby. They otherwise were lucky if they had the chance to nod to each other in the crowded ballrooms where they were most likely both present, since Mrs Usher was not an intimate of anyone in the Onslow party, excepting Regis. However, happening to find themselves in the same set, they smiled and nodded to each other, and were about to pay each other no further attention when Cecilia was called upon, by the steps, to twirl beneath Jocasta's partner's raised arm.

The gentleman smiled down at her briefly, and it caused Miss Montgomery to lose her step for a moment, which amused him. He was handsome, tall, and of good figure, an elegant man in his thirties, and Cecilia trembled as he righted her and helped her back into place for the next partner to approach her. At the end of the dance, her own escort sought to return her to Mrs Usher, but Cecilia curtsied and left him, hurrying off after Jocasta. She paused for a moment as Jocasta's dance partner re-entered the Onslow party, but once she saw him disappear (moving off after a few words) she touched Jocasta's shoulder.

Jocasta turned, and then said, 'Oh, no!' in a voice that would have been insulting if Cecilia had not realised that Miss Fortune was looking over her shoulder, not at her.

Cecilia called her attention, 'Miss Fortune, might I ask you something?'

Jocasta looked at her for the first time. 'Yes,' she hissed, 'if *you* will help *me*.' She turned back to her sister in a rush. 'Georgie, this is Miss Montgomery. We are going—'

The marchioness, splendid tonight in a pink silk gown with a crystal encrusted bodice, looked like a girl when *she* glanced over Cecilia's shoulder, too, and said, 'Yes, yes, go! I'll delay him.'

As Jocasta Fortune pulled her away, Cecilia looked over her shoulder to see who they were running from. A magnificent figure of a man looked in their direction, frowning, and Cecilia asked her companion, 'Who was that?'

'Oh, my brother George! Is he following us?'

'The crowd has covered us.'

'Oh, thank goodness!' said Jocasta, taking refuge behind a large square pillar, and leaning up against it as though exhausted.

'You don't want to see him? I have always thought that I should be so glad to have an elder brother.'

'That is because you haven't met George.' Jocasta laughed. 'I should not say so, I know. Please forget I did.'

'Of course.' But Cecilia was intrigued. 'I suppose he is perhaps a tad over-protective? He does look so much like a hero.'

'George has ten sisters. I do not suppose he has protected any one of us. He left poor Marguerite in the river once, though he knew she could not swim. If Katerina had not come along ...' She saw that Cecilia was round-eyed and added, 'well, I shouldn't tell tales of George, but now that I am in Town, he wants to know everyone I speak to and—'

'I know just what you mean,' sympathised Cecilia, but crossly. 'Regis does *just* that sort of thing to me: always warning me of some gentleman's reputation, just because I danced a *boulanger* with him.'

'Oh, that's not George! He just wants—' Jocasta blushed. 'Oh, it is too shameful to tell you, so perhaps you should just tell me what it was you wanted...'

'Oh yes!' Cecilia looked down for a second in embarrassment. 'It might seem ridiculous, and perhaps intrusive, but might you tell me the name of the gentleman you danced with just now?'

The Duke of Enderby, meanwhile, had witnessed Cecilia accosting Miss Fortune and had, with some difficulty, followed them. He knew no reason, other than mischief, that Cissie would wish to speak to his angel, so now that he caught them, he said, 'Cissie, what are you about?'

'Oh, pipe down, Tom, do!' This halted Jocasta in mid-curtsy to the duke, and since Miss Montgomery had thrown formality out of the window, she giggled as Enderby returned this insult with a terrible frown. 'Miss Fortune was just going to tell me something important.'

'The sets are forming,' said Enderby, attempting to regain his dignity, 'I was about to ask Miss Fortune...'

'Sssh!' said Cecilia, looking at Jocasta, her eyebrows prodding for a response.

Jocasta refocused. 'You mean, Sir Justin Faulkes?'

'What is it about Faulkes?' interrupted Enderby.

'I was just dancing with him, and Miss Montgomery wished to know who he was.' She turned to Cecilia with a confiding smile. 'He is a close friend of my sister and the marquis.'

'Is he not, then, your suitor?'

'Goodness, no! Just a family friend.' Jocasta looked into Cecilia's hopeful eyes. 'Do you, perhaps, wish me to make an introduction?' she asked archly.

'Yes! No!' said Cecilia, flustered. 'I am not ready. And he is gone now anyway.'

'What is this about—' interjected the duke. 'Why on earth do you want to see Faulkes?'

'Well,' said Jocasta as though the duke had not spoken, 'he is always with us. If you join me again, I'll make the introduction.'

'Oh, *will* you?' sighed Cecilia. '*Thank you!* He won't remember, but we have previously met.'

'Cecilia! Why-?' Enderby's frustrated voice was loud enough to turn a few nearby heads and caused Cecilia to make a hushing motion with her hand.

'Ssh! It was *him*, Tom! The man with the kind eyes...'

'You don't mean the pig story?' cried Enderby. 'That was Sir Justin Faulkes? Well, I never!'

'The pig story? Oh, do tell!' cried Jocasta.

'Let us take that bench if you're going to tell tales,' said Enderby practically, aware of the eyes upon them.

'But there are already two gentlemen...'

'Doesn't matter,' he said, leading the way. He nodded his head at the men. 'Might I seat the ladies?'

'Your Grace!' one of them, a middle-aged man in a rather inelegant coat stood up, as though to attention, and bowed stiffly but deeply. Enderby nodded. The other rose hastily and they melted away.

'Not well done, Tom,' started Cecilia. 'Coming it on too strong with "Your Dukeness" behaviour.'

He shrugged at the taunt. 'Got us the bench, didn't it?'

But Jocasta interrupted. 'I really want to hear the pig story ...'

It was a full twenty minutes before Mrs Usher eventually found them, by which time the pig story had naturally led onto another of Betty the pig's adventures, then onto a tale of Tom getting chased into a tree by a wild boar, which Enderby topped by telling how often Cecilia had toppled from Juniper's back since she began to try to copy the journal illustration of the feat of an equestrienne at Astley's Amphitheatre.

This reminded Cecilia that she had not yet visited this establishment, Jocasta said she had always been meaning to go, too, and so the young people made an arrangement to go on Thursday of next week, supposing the ladies were permitted.

Mrs Usher approached, annoyed at Cecilia's disappearance, and was prepared to scold her, but the trio on the bench were giggling so much that she ended by only giving a cursory reminder to Cecilia that she should inform her chaperone where she was, at all times. Cecilia apologised without much remorse, and Mrs Usher sighed and took her off, first inviting Jocasta Fortune to call at her home at any time. 'For she does not have a deal of *female* friends call, you know.'

Jocasta realised, with a jolt, that *she* did not either — or only the Baileys whom they had known forever. So, she smiled, and promised to do so, and even engaged to go for a walk tomorrow morning in the park with Miss Montgomery.

CHAPTER 16

The Triangular Conundrum

Gentlemen paying calls on the Onslows, and at the Ushers, were disappointed the next morning, to find only the house owners in residence, and not their prey at all. Misses Fortune and Montgomery were walking in the park together. Mr York, in the phaeton he had hoped to persuade Miss Fortune to ride in this morning, spotted them. However, Miss Fortune must not have noticed him, for the two girls took a side path that was too narrow to allow for carriages.

'I am quite glad to escape the morning calls today,' said Jocasta, 'I sometimes find them oppressive.'

'Do you? I think it is quite thrilling! Seeing gentlemen in the drawing room is a quite different thing than in the ballroom. One can really observe them.' Jocasta did not look convinced. 'Perhaps it is because you are in your second season, and it has become something of a bore, but I only ever had Tom — Enderby, you know — as a visitor at home in the country, for I do not count Damon, who only comes to lecture me .'

'Your parents do not accompany you, Miss Montgomery?'

'No, my parents are both dead.'

'I'm so sorry!'

'Don't be. I am mistress in my own house, with only a cumbersome companion-chaperone whom Damon foisted on me.'

Jocasta was not shocked by Miss Montgomery's heartless description of her chaperone, in fact the honesty attracted her. 'Sir Damon is a guardian of sorts to you?'

'Self-appointed, in consequence of my father being his mentor or some such thing. My guardian is, in fact, a fusty old lawyer who is quite happy to let Damon rule the roost. Anyway, I have known him forever, and he interferes in my life dreadfully.'

'I am surrounded with interference myself, Miss Montgomery,' Jocasta sighed.

'*Do* call me Cecilia. Should you like it if we become friends?'

A female friend was something Jocasta had never had. Someone who did not seek anything of her, and who chose to be with her for more than familiarity and proximity (like her sisters or the Bailey girls) — and despite herself, she was thrilled. 'Oh, yes! Do let us!' She paused and giggled a little. 'I overheard something that will likely make our friendship seem a little peculiar in town.'

'Why on earth—?'

'I should not say so!'

'It is the first test of our friendship, Jocasta!' declared Cecilia, solemnly.

'Well,' said Jocasta, inclining towards her new friend, 'it is too silly, but I overheard Sir Justin Faulkes tell Lord Onslow that they were placing bets in the gentlemen's clubs about whether the Duke of Enderby would choose you, or I, by the end of the Season.'

'How ridiculous! Our friendship shall confound them all!' Cecilia pulled Jocasta to a bench. 'I shall tell you my secret, Jocasta.' Jocasta listened avidly. 'Tom is *not* my suitor at all. We only said so to annoy Damon.'

Jocasta was confused. 'Did you wish to make the baronet jealous?'

'*Jealous*? *Damon*? No! I shudder at the thought. It is just that he found us rolling on the floor at home trying to find our spillikins pieces, and reacted like a medieval monk, telling me to keep away from him and so on.'

'But why? If the duke is just—'

'He thinks that Tom has not had enough governance since his father died, and that he has become a dangerous rake because he has been flattered too much.'

'How silly!' Jocasta laughed, thinking of the young duke's inept courtship of herself. He was nothing like that other rake's — Lord Bertram's — smooth and insinuating presence. 'So, Sir Damon got it all wrong? And therefore, his stupid demonic plan was all for nought?'

'Whatever do you mean?'

But Jocasta had remembered that the plan was confidential. 'Oh, merely that I understand how you hate interference. One wants to do one's duty to the family, but hideous interference that is based on mindless suspicions is dreadful!'

'I know! Do you speak of your brother?'

Jocasta nodded.

'Will you tell me something of your family now, Jocasta? I feel that today we should solidify our friendship, and know something of our respective situations.'

Jocasta told her of the draughty Castle Fortune, her ten sisters, five of whom were already married, and her sister Portia engaged to Lord Paxton, and of her father and George's determination to have her wed soon.

Jocasta had not elaborated on her father and brother's tactics, but Cecilia divined a little of it by her tone.

'I am glad to tell you about Tom in case you misunderstood. The deception was meant to be all for Damon, not for discourse in the clubs.'

Jocasta nodded sagely. 'Ladies have the reputation for gossip, but I have learnt that gentlemen seem to be worse.'

'Putting wagers on us! Disgusting behaviour.' She turned to Jocasta impishly. 'Although I suppose it *does* make us rather famous! We must be somewhat distinguished among this year's turnout.'

Jocasta found herself giggling in agreement. Then she sobered a little. 'But don't you find it a bit oppressive?'

'No, why should I?' Jocasta looked down. 'But perhaps we are differently situated. I have no real need to marry. I am happy at home, you know, and there is no one to pressure me.'

'Sir Damon?'

'Oh, he does not put pressure on me *to* marry, just who *not* to marry, as though I were an idiot.'

'I see. Does he, perhaps, wish to marry you himself?'

Cecilia laughed. 'Me — with *Regis*?' It was so infectious that Jocasta joined in. 'I am not attracted to demons.' She turned avid eyes on her friend. 'But do tell me more about Sir Justin. He is so *terribly* handsome, is he not?'

'I suppose,' said Jocasta, who could not remember considering it, 'that he is.'

'He must be an athlete, too, with such a fine figure.'

'Well, he is an exceptionally good rider.'

'Oh, I would love to see him on a horse! And can he drive?'

'He is teaching my sister how to drive four horses soon.'

'Ooooh! I just *knew* he would be a wonderful whip.'

Jocasta laughed into Cecilia's dreaming face, 'And I understand he is a man of *extremely* large fortune!'

'Really? But I do not care for such things. But don't you think, Jocasta, that he has truly kind eyes?'

This was too much. Those eyes were among the things that had wounded *her* most. 'Yes,' she answered colourlessly, 'he has.'

Jocasta got up from the bench, and they walked on, the topic turned to their views on London society in general. Cecilia's outright enjoyment reminded Jocasta of herself last year, and she was able to partake a little of her joy, in so remembering.

After the visit to Astley's Amphitheatre had been noted, it was soon the talk of the town that the Duke of Enderby, who had appeared to be wooing Miss Fortune and Miss Montgomery equally, was now squiring them *together*. Even for a duke, this was a feat indeed.

He took up not just one, but two, young ladies in his phaeton the next morning (and the gentlemen quipped that this was a very delightful squeeze indeed), was to be seen at the ballroom benches seated between the two, took both the Onslows and the Ushers to share his opera box.

'Someone should really tell young Enderby,' drawled the Beau to his cronies at Whites, 'that it is bad form to let one's wife meet one's mistress.'

'Ah...' sighed Alvanley, 'modern manners! Shall he take two wives, like a Turkish potentate?'

Regis, also present, gritted his teeth. He did not really know how to feel, precisely. The young girl that he had wished to protect, befriending the pretty tool he had meant to use to protect her, were both now in the presence of the very danger that he had sought to protect them from. Seldom had one of his schemes gone more badly astray. He did not like that Cecilia Montgomery was a subject of wagers, or that the innocent he had brought into this was, too. He had created a bumble-broth, and now he was undecided whether to stir it, or leave it.

In the intervening time, he had watched from afar. For a start, Cecilia Montgomery had arrived in London from her quiet life in the country as up to snuff as it was possible to be. Approached by some questionable gentlemen, Regis had at first interceded, but very soon saw how Cecilia spotted the most sophisticated of charmers at a glance, and that she had her own, quite ruthless, way of dealing with them. She feigned boredom. The change from naughty, vivacious young gadabout to yawning, cold-eyed princess was quick, startling — and unmistakably a slap-down. Present at one such occasion, Regis had asked her, 'Filbert thinks himself such a killer with the ladies, how did you spot him?'

'Were you going to warn him off, Demon?' Cecilia laughed. 'I assure you I am perfectly capable of telling friend from foe.'

'It would seem so,' admitted Regis. 'Only, with such a sheltered background, I am fascinated at the origin of such skill.'

Cecilia thought about it. 'I suppose I simply compare every gentleman to Tom, you know. If they do not have honest eyes, like he, then I do not wish to know them.'

Regis was beginning to feel that his devilish scheme had been unnecessary in the first place. Watching young Enderby this closely was to be reminded of who he really was, a precocious young pup: too flattered perhaps, but with very little harm in him. The duke's half-admission of romantic disinterest in Cecilia had let Damon see it all as his own overreaction, and he divined Cecilia's attempt at revenge. The young duke's evening adventures, which had so worried Damon, were a youth's experiment, and it was not a path he now trod. Goodness knew, Regis himself had experimented with worse, and for longer.

Enderby's constant contact with Miss Fortune was another thing. Regis could not descry the duke's intentions, and the duke's interest had led that young lady to be speculated upon. Regis had overheard her father the baron — who ought to be protecting Jocasta's good name — say to Onslow. 'Good news, marquis, the odds have changed at Whites and my Jocasta is now the favourite to capture the duke!'

Regis resolved to have the bet taken from the books, by threat, if necessary.

A faint look of disgust had crossed Onslow's face at his father-in-law's *good news*, and he had merely inclined his head a quarter of an inch. The three young people had arrived at their party, and the baron continued, his great voice booming, 'Here they come! Welcome, Your Grace. Welcome, my boy. I trust my little Jocasta has been entertaining you well?' he looked over to Miss Montgomery and sniffed, saying to himself but loudly, '*though I don't know what* she's *doing here.*'

The Duke of Enderby, Jocasta, and the whole party stiffened, but Cecilia, after a blink, let out an unladylike guffaw.

'Oh, I beg your pardon, sir. But you are so funny, you know!'

The baron recoiled.

Regis, set to intervene, felt himself relax. Onslow offered his hand towards Cecilia.

'You must be Miss Montgomery, the new friend that my sister-in-law has told me of. I'm charmed to meet you.'

'And you, my lord marquis!' Cecilia smiled up at him prettily.

'*Putting yourself forward,*' boomed the baron's audible thoughts.

Cecilia laughed once more. The baron found himself with the pretty minx before him, grinning impishly. 'You are such a card, Baron!' She held out her hand, which he reluctantly took. She curtsied and said brightly, 'I am so happy to meet my dear friend's papa.'

The baron, flummoxed, stepped back and lowered his great eyebrows at her terrifyingly, but she just giggled.

'*Encroaching!*' he said, as he turned, and melted away — to the continuing sound of Miss Montgomery's amusement.

Georgette, arriving from the ballroom floor in the middle of this interchange, was mightily amused.

'Your friend,' she said to Regis of Miss Montgomery, 'is the first person to find the perfect method for dealing with my papa. *Why* did none of us just laugh in his face?'

'I apologise for her rudeness—' began Regis.

'Oh, do not, Family Friend, or I should have to apologise for Papa's rudeness, and that would be an everlasting task. Miss Montgomery is quite delightful.'

'But, I think, a handful,' laughed Onslow.

'Oh, undoubtedly. A little like my youngest sister Leonora. By the way,' Georgette said, under her breath, 'What precisely is going on with the three of them?'

Regis looked from the young duke's attention on Jocasta, Jocasta's concern for Cecilia, and Cecilia's laughing response, and shook his head. 'I have no idea. Nothing too dangerous, I think.'

'You are right. They seem, whatever the gossips say, like three children playing together: it appears to be restoring Jocasta's spirits.'

'That is good, then,' answered Damon.

But he was not convinced that Jocasta's spirits were entirely free of pain. He had seen a vast improvement in her, before the severing of their more intimate relations, and from a distance he now saw that she was brighter upon occasion, but sometimes, when their eyes crossed and met accidentally, and briefly, he still saw a wound there. And he could not convince himself that it was not he who was the one responsible for it.

Then too, there was the situation of her dreadful father and bullying brother. He had known a severe need to dash George Fortune's head against a wall when he found that he placed a bet on his own sister in Whites. How could she cope with this situation? And just who might the baron sell her off to if Enderby failed to offer? She was accustomed to obeying him, that was the trouble. She would try to avoid an evil fate, but in the end she would obey. He could trust Onslow and her sister to keep her safe this Season, but the weeks were running out. He had tried to get Mr York in conversation, as one of the most determined of her suitors. But while he was a respectable, probably honourable, man, he was a bore — and had the old unrealistic vision of a fairy princess in his head. If York were to woo her successfully, Jocasta may try to live up to his expectations of her — and that might destroy her true spirit.

Why could no one else see the danger she was in? He had tried to discuss it with Faulkes, but he could see within three sentences that his interest was open to misinterpretation, so he had not continued.

But it was all, he knew, none of his business. He did not even know why he kept close to the Onslows still, when he should keep away. He was in the grip of a desire to be near her, to look at her, to touch her — as he had once done so carelessly, and now could not. This was a base male reaction to her prettiness, he was sure. It had had little effect on him at first, but he had grown warm towards her, and then the warmth had become a spark when she had smiled at him over the piano. That genuine, joyous smile haunted him. He wanted her always to smile like that — and only with him.

But time would take care of this insanity, this illusion. She remained a mate who was not right for him by any logical standards. Isabel had been his equal, in interests, in passion, in intelligence. Jocasta Fortune was just a sad, faux-vivacious little rabbit, and he would never approach her seriously, unless his honour demanded it. Unless, that is, that he had already wounded her.

Perhaps this was why he watched her in the ballroom, at the opera, in the park. He had to know that she was genuinely well. That he had not affected her heart.

He was convinced that, with her new-found friendship with Cecilia, she seemed brighter than ever.

Why, seeing this way out for himself, did it not make him happy?

CHAPTER 17

Miss Montgomery's Idol

A t Almacks the next night, the odd threesome once again sat a whole dance out together on a bench.

Enderby was refusing to let either young lady drive his four greys, on any account.

'Especially not you, Cissie!'

'You have always said I was a good whip!' said Miss Montgomery, in high dudgeon.

'Of a pair, yes! Not of a team…'

'That is what all gentlemen say, and I find it most unfair,' Jocasta joined in. 'If they will not let us drive in the first place, how do you *know* that we can't drive a team? It's absurd!'

'It requires strength, you know.' Enderby shrugged and looked superior. 'I'm sorry ladies, but it is a *male* skill—'

He got no further, for two voices were raised against him, and in order to not to start a ballroom scandal, he quickly caved in. 'Alright then, I will buy another team that you can practice on, but never my greys!'

Cecilia was about to protest, but Jocasta acknowledged his judgement. 'He's right, you know, Cecilia!'

'No, he's not!' replied Cecilia, 'He's just copying the Demon King.' She mimicked Regis' deep voice, '*Nobody drives my cattle!* Oh! Jocasta, it's him!' she added about the faraway, but approaching, figure.

'Who?' asked the duke, looking round.

'Oooh! He's so handsome, I'm shaking...' Cecilia turned to her friend.

'Wha—?' Enderby was still at a loss.

'It is perfectly alright, my dear Cecilia,' said Jocasta comfortingly. 'We shall do it all just as we have planned—' she grasped her friend's trembling hand and held it beneath her skirts.

'Planned?' enquired the duke.

But the ladies were locked in their own drama. Cecilia said, squeaking, 'But now he's here, I will freeze up, I know I will. Oh, how elegantly dressed he is! I think his coat even better than Mr Allison's, don't you?'

The duke was still looking for who they were talking of, then hit on it, '*Faulkes?*'

'Do not regard him anymore,' said Jocasta urgently, 'but look at me and laugh, as though I said something funny.'

Cecilia did so, although her laugh sounded a little high pitched. 'And Tom,' Cecilia said, finally noticing him — but talking in Jocasta's direction, 'You are to say *nothing!* If you ruin anything...'

'But it's *Faulkes!*' Enderby said, disgusted.

'*Tom!*' said two young ladies at once. The duke was too surprised and delighted at Jocasta calling him so to be able to utter another sound.

Jocasta was surprised at herself too, for she glanced over at him, blushing, then back to her task, said in a bright conversational tone to Cecilia, 'Did he *really*?'

'Miss Fortune!' said the suave tones of Sir Justin Faulkes.

She turned to him, delighted. 'Sir Justin! I have not yet seen you this evening.'

'I was a trifle late, but now I am here to claim the waltz you promised me.' He bowed jocularly, and nodded to the silent duke. 'Your Grace.'

'Oh,' said Jocasta, as though recalling her manners, 'Sir Justin, let me present my friend to you, Miss Cecilia Montgomery. She is a neighbour of the duke's you know! Miss Montgomery, Sir Justin Faulkes.'

Faulkes bowed from the waist a little and said, turning his grey eyes to hold Cecilia's, 'Charmed.'

Cecilia had turned mute, but a sound issued from her throat, which caused a scoff from Enderby's direction. Cecilia smiled on, however, and Faulkes returned his attention to Jocasta saying, 'Shall we?'

'I rather twisted my ankle on the last dance, and I believe I shall sit for a while longer, Sir Justin. I am so sorry.'

'Not at all.' Justin's eyes looked briefly at the Duke of Enderby, who made no move to take the other young lady to the floor, and said politely, 'Are you engaged, Miss Montgomery? Would you care to—?'

'Yes,' said Cecilia, finding her voice and interrupting him. She rose. Faulkes turned his glance to the duke, and after a reproving hint from those pale grey eyes, Enderby felt impelled to say, 'In a moment, I shall go and find the marchioness.'

Faulkes nodded, and took Miss Montgomery off to the dancing throng.

Seeing Cecilia's besotted eyes looking up at Faulkes, Enderby said with disgust, 'Well, of all the little madams! You two schemed over Faulkes? *You* told an untruth!' This was said in the manner that he spoke to Cecilia, rather than the worshipful tones he usually adopted with Jocasta, but she only laughed.

'Is it not shocking? But my intentions were pure.'

'She'll come to fiddlestick's end there ...' Enderby said sulkily, still too casual. '*You* don't think Faulkes is so very handsome, do you? She went on as though he was a Greek god or some such.'

'You are *jealous*!' Jocasta said, wonderingly.

'Over Cissie?' he said incredulously. Then he added, 'Miss Fortune, I understood that Cecilia already told you that—'

'No! Not of Cecilia, but of how handsome she sees Sir Justin as,' comforted Jocasta, in a friendly way, 'But many young ladies find *you* very good looking indeed, you know.'

Why this handsome compliment from his princess did not cheer him, he could not have said. But he looked at her rather resentfully and gathered his dignity to say, 'I shall fetch your sister to you.'

'Only if she is not engaged. I can quite easily sit here for the waltz.' He had gotten up and she looked up at him teasingly, bent over and grasped her ankle, saying mournfully, 'the pain, you know.'

He stood, enthralled at this new, teasing intimacy. Then he recollected himself as her hand made a quick dismissing gesture, and turned to find the Onslow group.

'Marchioness, excuse me,' he said. Georgette turned, smiling, from her sister, Miss Portia Fortune. Also in the chatting group were three males, young Paxton, the marquis and Regis.

'Yes, Your Grace?'

'Miss Fortune is on a bench just behind and I thought I should come for you...' Georgette's eyebrows enquired. 'She has twisted her ankle a little...'

Something moved past him, but he held his arm out to escort the marchioness in due form. They moved off through the crush of people, and Georgette remarked, looking at the changing expressions on Enderby's face, 'I thought she was to dance with Sir Justin?' The duke's mouth moved, but he said no words. 'Is she playing off her tricks?'

'Well,' he began, looking down into Jocasta's sister's laughing eyes, he found he could tell her. 'She wanted Sir Justin to dance with Cissie, that is, Miss Montgomery...'

'Oh, girls' tricks! I did *just* the same for my sister Cassie when Mr Hudson was engaged to dance with me and...' she appeared to see something ahead and turned her warm brown eyes on the duke again, 'Actually, I could do with some air, Your Grace. Would it be too shocking to take a married lady to the doors of the terrace? Jocasta can repent on her own for a moment — she is in clear view of Onslow.'

The duke thought that the Fortune sisters were just too lovely, in their differing ways, and veered towards the terrace doors nearest them.

'A trifle crowded,' said the marchioness, 'might we go further…?'

Georgette was, in fact, playing her own tricks. She had not liked the avoidance tactic that Jocasta had adopted to Regis. She was unsure of what had happened between them, but as she had seen Regis move towards the bench so swiftly, she had a strange, and perhaps misguided, inclination to force the case. It was time to know what was afoot, what dangers were ahead. She should, perhaps, be supporting Jocasta's avoidance of the Demon King, but she was now very sure that Regis meant her no harm. And that he did, in fact, understand her sister rather better than she did herself. If Jocasta's heart was engaged, trust Regis to find it out, and act accordingly. The ultimate sacrifice that Onslow had spoken of? Georgette thought it was not so simple. Studied avoidance did not indicate no feelings, quite the opposite. So much for Jocasta. But Georgette had witnessed the incident where Regis had finally been the one who ignored her sister. He was too much of a gentleman, she considered, to offer this insult if he were not hurt himself, or perhaps trying to teach her a lesson. Georgette suspected the former.

This was, at least, something that could not be resolved without talking, and Georgette wanted to give him this opportunity.

Regis had reached Jocasta's side with surprising speed. He said, urgently, 'Miss Fortune, are you injured?'

There was something in his tone that caused another young lady, sitting at the opposite end of the bench, to move away. She looked over her shoulder at him, a trifle longingly, as he took a seat beside Miss Fortune.

Jocasta, taken off guard by his tone, and the concerned look in his eyes, said, 'Oh, no. My ankle is really fine now,' she lifted her leg and let him see her move her little satin-clad foot in circles. 'I just thought it would be better to rest for this dance.'

He smiled, relieved, and said in his more usual tone, 'I thought, perhaps, that you were sitting here because of the diminution of your court. Could you not find a partner?'

'I assure you,' she defended herself, 'I was engaged to Sir Justin...' then looking into his strange yellow green eyes, 'You are teasing me.'

'I cannot believe that both Justin and Enderby abandoned you to your fate. Your popularity has definitely slipped.'

'It is simply that Sir Justin bore off Cecilia, and then the baronet's eyes scolded the duke that it would not be appropriate to be long alone with me.' She shook her head. 'Silly really, for Georgette would have soon noticed that Sir Justin was dancing with someone else, and would have come to find me in a trice.'

'Justin was quite right though; you should not sit alone with any gentleman.'

'*You* are here!' she laughed at him. She looked giddy, and a little embarrassed, too.

He too, felt giddy, but he said with insouciance, 'But I, my dear, am a Family Friend.'

She laughed then, that warm, genuine laugh he had heard once before, and he laughed with her this time, *per force*. Her eyes dropped suddenly, but he said, 'I'm sorry I behaved so foolishly the other day...'

'Giving me the cut?' she laughed shakily, 'I suppose I deserved it.'

'Well, I do not think you should avoid me so *very* thoroughly,' he said, one eyebrow flying.

She laughed again, then became a little serious, looking at her hands. 'It is just that my foolish behaviour that day in the park ... I began to see that I had not just risked my own reputation, but *yours*! I am determined I shall not do so again.' She looked around. 'Indeed, you should go!'

He looked too. 'No one is paying us the least attention since I am Onslow's shadow this Season. They will not think that such an old hand as I could be favoured by the Town's beauty.'

'You are not old!' Jocasta burst out. This was amusing and startling at once. That had not been his meaning, but she had evidently been thinking about it.

He gazed through the throng at the dancers, catching sight of a smitten Cecilia in the arms of Faulkes. 'Have you any injury at all, Miss Fortune?' She looked sheepish. 'Minx!' he reprimanded. Then he said gently, 'I am touched that you feared for my reputation, which has, I might add, been in tatters for years,' she gave a delightful gurgle at that, 'but there is really no need. Do not avoid me quite so assiduously, or I might fear that you harbour a *tendre* for me.' He said it teasingly, but she stiffened up.

'That is as likely as *Cecilia* doing so,' she said, derisively. 'It is only young ladies who are not *acquainted* with you who harbour any feelings for you whatsoever — in this, you are just like my brother George,' she added, for good measure.

He stood up. 'Let me return you to your party, Miss Fortune, while I recover from that undoubted facer.' She took his arm and moved off.

'A facer? Is that boxing cant?'

'Ask your brother,' he replied, unpleasantly.

But he saw that Jocasta was cheered at the return to their old relations. He was glad, for her relief, but also his own. However, he must not let these exchanges turn to flirtation. He knew they were on the brink of it, and that way all tonight's good work would be undone.

When Georgette returned to her husband's side, it was to see Jocasta safely restored to them, speaking to their father. She moved to hear the baron say to Jocasta, 'Just arrived. Have you danced with the duke this evening? Saw him with Miss White the other night, Jocasta. If you do not reel him in quickly, he will be off your hook, my girl, don't mistake.'

Jocasta looked up, blushing miserably, only to meet the eye of the approaching Enderby. Those words had stopped his step for a moment, but he still came forward and smiled down her blushes, saying, 'Our dance, I think, Miss Fortune?' Glad that her partner Fredrick Bailey was late again, Jocasta nodded. The baron lost his composure for a moment before saying, with bluff cheer, 'Go ahead, Your Grace!'

As they moved to the floor, Jocasta heard Fredrick Bailey behind her, who must have just reached the Onslows, say casually, 'Thought I was to dance with Jocasta, must have been wrong.'

'If you are not going to marry her, Bailey, what do you want to waste her time for?' her father was saying in his booming tone. Some ladies held their hands to their faces to hide a smile as Jocasta passed, and she squeezed her hand on Enderby's arm, saying, 'Thank you so much, Tom! Oh, excuse me, I mean, Your Grace!'

'Not at all. And do call me Tom, I like to hear it from you.'

'I'm sorry ...'

'About your papa? I should not worry. Heard a lot of such things.'

'Surely not *quite* like my papa,' Jocasta tried to laugh. If she had not spent so much time lately with Enderby, who Cecilia treated with a sort of affectionate derision, she might have affected not to know he had heard, but they were now closer than that.

'Never been referred to as a fish — true,' said the duke, to make her laugh.

She gurgled. 'I have never really considered it, before,' added Jocasta naively, 'but being a duke must be quite difficult sometimes, too.'

'It is!' he moved to her place in the set and whispered, 'May I use *your* given name?'

She blushed a little. 'How *can* I object since I have taken such a liberty already. It is just that Cecilia always calls you so—'

'Yes, and if it means that I can call you by your name, I'm very pleased.' He smiled down at her, and Jocasta thought that he was getting rather better at flirting. But the set had formed, and so they could only smile at each other and say friendly words when the steps drew them close.

There was something about their looks to each other that caused attention, however, and Regis overheard a discussion about a proposed change of bet by Peirrepoint and another crony, and frowned. He touched Pierrepoint's shoulder and said, 'A lady's name, gentlemen.'

'Oh quite, Your Demonic Majesty!' laughed Peirrepoint. 'We shall be mum.'

Regis' brows scowled, and Pierrepoint shuddered histrionically, but said, 'Apologies, Your Royal Devilry.'

'Watch your mouth. Prinny is near!' said Pierrepoint's friend.'

'Oh, when Regis returned to White's, the regent enquired about his court in hell.'

His crony laughed, bowed at the baronet ironically, and Regis moved off.

Enderby was not the fiend he had mistaken him for, Regis knew it, so he need not worry for her any longer. In fact, he was not worried at *all* anymore. But he should tell her to rein in that look she was giving the duke. It was probably just some joke they were sharing, but it was a confiding, amused look such that she had once given him, and Regis knew what it could do to a man. Regis himself, being experienced, could control himself — but encouraging a young buck like Enderby was dangerous. He looked over at Onslow and his wife, who were chatting to friends. Should they not be paying attention? What if the duke lured her onto the terrace or into an anteroom while they were busy laughing? He may begin with innocent intentions, but if Jocasta smiled up at the duke *that* way, and Enderby had taken her somewhere retired, then who could say what that young buck might be led to do...?

'Why are your brows down, King?' Justin Faulkes tapped him on the shoulder, and he almost jumped.

'Merely, balls are becoming a bore.' He watched in relief as the duke led Jocasta back to the Onslows, and he headed there, too.

Faulkes followed. 'You sound like Methuselah. Good God!' he said, arrested, 'Who is *that*?'

Regis looked over towards the door. The last late arrivals had entered. Several people stared at the handsome couple in the doorway. The woman was tallish, slender — but with curves so exaggerated beneath the sheer layers of her gown that she embodied the name woman. Her full breasts were barely covered by her light, exquisite, red gown — golden ribbons clasped beneath, and trailing to the ground to match those woven through her thick black wavy hair, falling with some black ringlets over one shoulder. It was a style of another age given a new twist by the high, top knot. A Roman goddess whose abundant locks could not be tamed by mere ribbon. One of her sleeves had fallen from a shoulder in a way that looked accidental, but that Regis knew was not. The top silk gauze overdress was split open and trimmed by Italianate woven edging in gorgeous shades. This allowed the petticoat to be seen, a simple muslin layer which barely hid a short slip and long limbs. Her lips were full and turned up at the corners in a way that looked not merry, but sensual, her long lidded tawny eyes were almost yellow, the exact same shade as Regis', and were framed by dark lashes.

'Who *is* she?' murmured Faulkes, ignoring the lady's handsome companion entirely, 'I declare that must be every man's sensual dream in the flesh. Is she Spanish, you think?'

'Her name is Doña Isabel Maria de Zuleta, and she is Spanish.' Regis' voice was particularly flat and informative, but he stood stock still for a moment before he deliberately turned his back and walked towards the Onslows.

.

It was always nice to have The Duke of Enderby at your gaming table, many gentlemen thought. Especially at White's, where the staked tended to be high. He was very young for his great position, moreover, he had just that sort of youthful bravado — and enough money to back it up — that delighted more seasoned gamesters. However, the Beau publicly adjured him to leave a table, saying he could no longer conscience winning from him — *"It is too much like torturing a puppy,"* the Beau had said, waving him away. The dash of humiliation was a warning from his hero, and did the trick, the duke still played recklessly, but never more than three hands on any night, so one had to be fortunate to secure a game before he left.

As he sat at a little-occupied (as the evening was still young) table, the Beau, in passing, remarked faintly to his friend Pierrepoint, 'Watch the vultures gather...' as the table became fully inhabited in a few moments.

The other laughed, and they took their place at the table in the Bow Window, where due precedence was given.

Sir Damon Regis meandered over to exchange greetings with the Beau's table.

'You have disappointed me this season, royal demon. There was never any point in placing wagers on your sporting events, but there was, at least, the entertaining fall of the arrogant and bumptious who thought to challenge you,' sighed the Beau. 'Have you no good news for me? Has not Dumont challenged you to stand on your head for an hour?'

'I have no idea; my valet reads my correspondence.'

'Well, I'm done with you then, Regis, for you have no wit to offer in mitigation.'

'Do you seek to come to blows with me, George? Now there is a challenge I would take on...'

The Beau shuddered. 'Heaven forbid.' Then, following the direction of Regis' restive eye he said, 'Do I bore you? Whom do you regard — ah, the young duke! Don't worry, he isn't ruining himself.'

'I'm glad to hear it,' said Regis, but he sounded bored.

George Brummell was not deceived. 'He is a friend of yours, is he not?'

'I have known him as a child, certainly.' Regis sighed. 'I am a little unsettled this evening. I think I will seek another spot, lest I spoil the decorum of your creation, George.' He waved a hand, encompassing the whole club.

'Manners *have* improved under my intolerant eye, it is true,' admitted Brummell, lazily.

Sir Damon Regis smiled, and wandered off.

Meanwhile, the inhabitants of the duke's table were not all gamesters. One gentleman, Mr Wray, had quite other business with the duke. That young man, older than Enderby by four years, with brown curls brushed forward in a fashionable cut, and an open, pleasant face, played with his cards a little and listened to the chatter of the players for some time, before he ventured, 'You are a neighbour of Miss Montgomery, I understand, Enderby?'

'That's right,' said Enderby casually, but he looked askance at Wray.

'You spend a great deal of time in her company.'

'Do I? I suppose I do, but not as much as in the country. We're friends, you know.'

'Ah! Not so much ... forgive me, I do not want to intrude, but have I it right that you do *not* seek to woo Miss Montgomery?'

'Woo?' Enderby jumped, dropped a card, then laughed to conceal his reaction. Why, he was thinking, do people always say *I do not want to intrude* just before they do precisely that? Around the table several other interested eyes were on him, awaiting his response. He did not quite have the nerve to say *it is none of your damn business and why on earth are you interested?* so instead he laughed and said, 'Woo Cissie Montgomery? You have that wrong.'

'Ah!' said Wray again, looking down at his cards and smiling.

Enderby found the smile suspicious.

'Interest there yourself, Wray?' muttered Lord Bertram.

The young man blushed.

'Are we to wish you well soon, Wray?' laughed another player.

'Gentlemen!' said Enderby in what the old maid Jane would have described as his "duke-voice" 'That lady's name is not a subject for discussion in this place.'

Mr Wray blushed again and muttered an apology, and the duke's bad temper survived only the rest of the hand, and caused him to leave the table straight afterwards before Lord Bertram had even made his next month's lodgings.

The Onslows went into supper as a group that included the duke, Regis and Faulkes. Regis was not particularly surprised to see Cecilia join them, and watched as she whispered a giggling tale into Jocasta's ear. It seemed to be good news, for they grasped hands in girlish glee, and Enderby's attempts to flirt with Jocasta were falling on deaf ears. Regis caught Onslow noting the direction of his gaze, his blue eyes concerned. So, he began a conversation (about a bet on the books at Whites concerning which of two gentlemen's mistresses might give birth first) in a low voice with Faulkes.

His eye went back to Jocasta and Cecilia, though, in time to watch a silent pantomime with hand signals from the latter to the former, which Jocasta seemed to understand perfectly. The party moved off to find a table suitable for them all, and as usual Enderby's nod dislocated the only two people on a table big enough to accommodate the Onslow party.

'Seriously!' muttered Cecilia as she moved past Enderby. Jocasta held back Georgette a moment, and Regis saw at once, but with disbelief, what the ladies were doing. With a smug smile, Cecilia was seated by Sir Justin Faulkes, who had been directed there by Jocasta. *Faulkes?* Cecilia was giving the baronet a smitten look that Regis had seen her wear on the earlier occasion on the ballroom floor. Faulkes chatted amiably to her, and with hardly a flicker of his eye did he seem to recognise her condition, but Regis knew he did. Justin tried to pay attention to others at the table, but Cecilia recalled his lost attention with the look of a wounded puppy, and Regis concluded that his hoyden of a ward was a severe trial to even Justin's experienced social aplomb. Under other circumstances, Faulkes might feign indifference, or even move off to distance himself, but good manners would permit neither at such a party. Like Cecilia or no, Justin had been forced into a corner by her persistence.

Regis got up and tapped Justin's shoulder. 'I'd like a word with my ward, Justin, could we exchange seats for the moment?' Cecilia regarded him wrathfully, but before she could berate him, he seated himself, saying under his breath, 'Stop it!'

She blushed but said, 'Since when am I your ward?'

'Something of the sort, and you know it!' he returned. 'Don't make Faulkes embarrassed, or yourself ridiculous,' he hissed.

Cecilia got up abruptly and the table's occupants all looked. She managed with some dignity, 'My gown has been smudged, I must go and—'

'I'll come with you!' said Jocasta.

'Yes, do, Jocasta. The nearest withdrawing room is behind that pillar.' Georgette indicated the direction.

The girls left, but met Lord Paxton with his friend, The Honourable Mr Linton Carswell, on their way. Jocasta watched as Paxton stiffened up. She therefore became a board herself, and only muttered their names before drawing Cecilia onward.

Jocasta had some difficulty in assuaging Cecilia's wrath, but she did so as best she could. When Cecilia required reassurance that Sir Justin had been admiring of her, Jocasta did not think it prudent to lie.

'Sir Justin is always most polite,' she said judiciously.

'You do you not think he favours me, then?' Cecilia's attack was direct.

'I am not really sure. You are so very pretty that he *may* do, Cecilia, but he did not, I think, betray any special partiality.'

'Oh, I know!' said Cecilia honestly. 'I like how direct you are, my friend. But I shall not give up quite yet. Perhaps, though, I should try to be more aloof — and entice him in this way.'

Jocasta was not sure how long Cecilia's vibrant personality could sustain aloofness, but she nodded her assent. They returned to their supper party, but among the crowd they saw two exotic creatures standing next to their table. They stopped a little way off.

'Could that be—?' said Cecilia.

'The lady is incredibly beautiful. And the man is so handsome. Somehow, they do not look English ... Who do you think they are?'

'See how she is regarding the Demon ...?' said Cecilia, excited. 'I *think* that must be Damon's lost love.'

'From a far country—' said Jocasta to herself.

'Let us go forward behind the pillar and listen to what is being said,' whispered Cecilia.

This was very rude behaviour, but so closely in line with Jocasta's present desire, that she gave in to Cecilia's pulling arm.

The foreign man was speaking. 'I am happy to make your acquaintance. My sister and I are newly in London from Madrid.'

'It must still be difficult to travel in Europe in these times,' replied Georgette pleasantly.

'I am a diplomat, and so it is easier for me than others, and with the emperor gone...' the man said pleasantly. 'As Sir Damon says, we were friends in my city. We have so few friends in London, I hope you will forgive this intrusion.'

Jocasta, as though in a dream, was regarding the face of the beautiful woman, whose gaze Regis had met for only the briefest of moments. It was beginning to be embarrassing, that unfaltering gaze on the baronet, it was beginning to draw attention, certainly of everyone at the table, but also of neighbouring supper parties — and Regis' usually mobile face was stiffening.

The woman spoke suddenly, her voice melodious and deep, her accent fascinating, though her English was fluent. '*We* must come to *you*, Sir Damon? You do not approach us as friends, though I am sure you saw us in the ballroom.' Their party all looked at Regis in shock, but though the woman had not troubled to lower her tone, a quick glance around the neighbours assured Jocasta that no one at surrounding tables had heard. Only she and Cecilia, besides those at the table, were placed to hear all.

Damon's eye flickered over to the woman. '*Are* you sure?' he said coldly. 'Then what must be your conclusion?'

The lady's companion bridled. '*Damon—!*' he began angrily.

'Manuel!' Regis said, directly looking him in the eye.

The Spaniard sighed, 'Pooh! My sister and you — the same bullish temperament! It has not changed,' he remarked, shrugging.

The woman gave a crack of laughter, and her smile was genuine and beautiful. 'We were always the same, in so many ways, were we not, Damon?'

This was not ballroom chatter, and everyone looked uncomfortable. Jocasta saw Regis look down, and noticed a white edge to his mouth, and his brows were drawn in a way that indicated more rage than she had seen him display. He had himself in hand, but not for long, she thought. Suddenly, she was aware of Georgette's eye on her, and she grasped Cecilia's wrist and moved forward from behind the pillar.

'Oh, there he is, dearest Cecilia!' she twittered while Cecilia looked blank. The whole table turned to look at her, for her voice was louder than usual, as well as considerably gayer. 'Sir Damon! It is our dance, I think.'

He jerked himself out of his rage and stood once more, saying, 'Is it?' Jocasta gave a slight frown at his lack of aplomb. 'Ah, yes, Miss Fortune, forgive me.'

'Oh,' said Jocasta prettily, seeming to have seen the Spaniards at the last minute. 'I beg your pardon; I seem to have interrupted.'

'Marqués de Casa Prado and his sister, Doña Isabel Maria de Zuleta, let me introduce my sister, Miss Fortune,' said Georgette, much quicker than Regis.

'Oh, Doña Isabel, I am so pleased to meet you. Your gown is so exquisite!' smiled Jocasta. She turned then and held out an imperious little hand to the marqués, and the Spanish nobleman held it and kissed above it, an inch only.

'I am charmed, Miss Fortune.' He looked up, his dark eyes warm and roguish. 'Has it been told to you that you resemble a fairy princess?'

'No, indeed!' lied Jocasta, with a smile that made Cecilia snigger. 'How kind of you!'

'We must go, Miss Fortune,' said Regis, 'the sets are forming.'

'Oh, yes, do let us,' said Jocasta, sounding much more enthused than usual. 'We should join Lord Jeffries' set. Miss Frampton will be *delirious* with rage that you dance with me, and not her.'

'Your sister is close to Sir Damon, it would seem,' they heard Doña Isabel say, as they left.

And Onslow's most acerbic voice answered for Georgette, 'Yes, he is a Family Friend.'

'Are you,' Damon enquired, looking down at Jocasta's little frowning face, 'by any chance, rescuing me, Miss Fortune?'

'Am I presumptuous?' Jocasta asked, a little embarrassed. 'Only, that lady's manners are not very English. Perhaps she does not know that it was rude to pass such remarks in a ballroom in England.'

'Or in Madrid, but she would still do so. She says what she thinks at all times.'

'One must suppose, then, that she is extraordinarily rich,' said Jocasta tartly.

He guffawed. '*That* explains all toleration of eccentricity exactly.'

They had achieved the edge of the ballroom, but Jocasta's hand grasped his arm to hold him back. 'I like people who are direct, but *not* in a crowded ballroom where everyone can hear. *She* might leave England soon, but *you* will have to deal with the chatter about all the remarks that are overheard.'

'Don't worry, I can bear it.' He laughed a little, but it was not a happy sound. 'But for tonight, after I return you to your sister, I shall leave.'

'She looks just like the sort of woman who will lie in wait for you.' She frowned. 'I have a better idea. After the dance, or even now if you like, you can send a servant to Georgie saying that I am unwell and might she come attend me. We can all leave together.'

'That is not necessary. And it might disturb the marchioness' evening.'

'Do you want to see that lady again?'

'Not here, no.'

'Then nothing could be simpler. Georgette loves to help.'

'You do not ask why Doña Isabel is so rude.'

'It is her nature, I think. Like Papa. But Cecilia told me that she is your old lover.' He pulled back a little, but her voice soothed. 'You need some time to consider before you speak with her.' She said, more formally, 'Sir Damon, I feel unwell and no longer wish to dance. Could you take me to a bench and call for my sister?'

He sighed, looking down at her. 'I will only say thank you.'

'It makes a change that I rescue you, when all along it has been you who helped me.'

He was touched, but strove not to show it. He took her to a bench and sent one lackey for Onslow's coach and another for the marchioness.

꧁ ⚜ ꧂

Earlier, as they moved away from Jocasta Fortune and her companion, Foggy Carswell had grinned. As witness to all that had occurred at the Castle Fortune house party, he had a fair idea of his friend's feelings. ' *Still* terrified of her?' he said. 'Not but what it is your just deserts.'

'I know, I know.' Paxton shook his head. 'It is just so very awkward.'

'Yes,' said Carswell, 'It must be. It is not like you can just avoid her since she will be your sister-in-law.' He laughed, gloating somewhat. 'I thought it was just me who stuttered around young ladies.'

'You always seem pleased to dance with the marchioness,' protested Paxton.

'You forget...' began the vague young man.

'Ah, yes! She's married now.'

'I wish m'mother didn't make me come to these things,' said Foggy, miserably. 'She says it is practice for supporting my sister Christiana when she comes out, but that's an age yet. I have to learn to talk to girls and so on...'

'Lady Eloise must realise that it will take her son longer to learn than others,' said Paxton, gloating in return. 'Not your strong suit,' he added, putting a hand on Foggy's slight shoulders.

'Yes, well, seeing you blabber before Miss Fortune makes it at least *entertaining* this evening.'

'Some friend! And there is another sister coming,' said Paxton, drearily. 'I don't know if she will be in support of Portia or of Jocasta, so I'm—'

'*Another sister?*' said Foggy Carswell, suddenly completely at attention, full-blown panic in his voice. 'Not the little 'uns?'

Paxton looked at his friend strangely. 'No. An elder sister and her husband.'

'Ah!' said Foggy Carswell, a hand to his heart in relief.

'Whatever ails you, Foggy?' said Paxton, suspicious.

'Just a nightmare I keep having. About falling white clouds.'

'Eh?'

'Out of trees,' added Carswell, helpfully.

'Did you hit the brandy this evening?' enquired Paxton.

'Wish I had!'

CHAPTER 18

Another Fortune Sister

The next morning, as the Onslows, Faulkes, Jocasta and Regis were gathered for a quick cup of chocolate before their ride, a pair of unexpected visitors were announced.

'Cassie!' cried Georgette, moving forward to take her sister in her arms. Her husband, Mr Hudson, stood back, and Onslow shook his hand warmly.

'Where is your luggage?' the marquis enquired.

'Oh, we will not stay here, never fear,' boomed Cassandra Fortune, still pretty after her three years of marriage, although slightly thicker at the waist. 'We thank you for the invitation, but baby is *much* too loud to foist upon this household, though I relish foisting him on Papa's.' She looked around the company. 'I should not say so, but I understand that you are all well acquainted and have met my papa, and may guess why I do so. I know that you are going off on a ride, for Portia has told me your habit, and that Jocasta is staying here. You shall not delay for us, my dears, I have only come to escape breakfast at Misery Hall. Papa spent all of last night's dinner berating me and I am exhausted already giving him back his just deserts.'

'But you did, my dear! Quite marvellous with the old gentleman, my wife!'

'Oh, she was always the best of us at dealing with Papa!' said Jocasta.

'Indeed — although you have a rival in Sir Damon Regis' ward.' Georgette's hand indicated Regis and Cassie moved forward.

'Regis, is it?' she said thrusting out her hand in her frank manner, 'Happy to meet you. Heard about you in town, of course, but we have never met. I like a man with a scandalous life.'

'I have met your husband, though, Mrs Hudson. At Whites. Nice to see you once more, Hudson.'

'Didn't think you'd remember. Put a wager on you for the Southampton race a few years ago, you know. Didn't win much of course. Always short odds on you.'

Cassie looked to the side. 'Sir Justin Faulkes, ain't it? Remember you. I always thought you'd offer for Geor—' She was stopped by a nip from the marchioness.

Jocasta turned her swivelling eye on Faulkes, amazed at this new piece of information. 'Sir Justin and Georgette?'

'Oh, mum's the word, don't worry,' laughed Cassie.

'Mrs Hudson, how lovely to see you again. As you can see, I am *still* devoted to your sister.'

'Ah!' said Regis, significantly.

'Yes, my dear Cassandra,' said Onslow wearily. 'You must know that he used to be a friend of *mine*, and now just hangs about languishing after my wife.'

'I think I should have a turn up with a fellow who did so to the dearly beloved,' laughed Hudson.

'Ah, but Onslow is so vain as to consider me no threat at all,' said Sir Justin, lightly.

'True,' said the marquis.

'Yes, well, all of you should go off on your ride and we shall poke around the place a little before breakfast. If that is alright with you, Onslow?'

'I shall have my butler give you the tour.'

'Cassie, shall I stay with you?' asked Jocasta.

'No, don't. I know it must be a treat for you being able to ride something other than our Bessie.'

'Won't you ride, Cassie? Onslow could mount both of you,' said Georgette.

'Do not boast of your stables, or I shall be jealous. No, I will not ride.'

'Can't,' said her husband with pride. 'Interesting condition, you know.'

'Oh, Cassie!' cried Georgette, beaming. 'Well, we shall talk our heads off over breakfast and hear all your news.'

'Don't mind Cassie,' said Jocasta to Regis as they left the room, 'She is sometimes as blunt as my papa, but she is a kind soul really.'

'Of course, I shall not mind her,' he said 'I am, remember, a Family Friend.'

When Georgette laughed suddenly, Jocasta grabbed at Sir Damon's arm. 'Why do you all say that constantly? It is as though you have a joke I do not know.'

'We do!' said Damon, demoniacally.

On the ride, Jocasta and Regis found themselves walking their horses side by side on a narrow path in the park.

'She is exceptionally beautiful, that woman,' Jocasta said, suddenly.

'Yes,' he answered, not pretending to misunderstand.

'And cultured.'

'Mmm.'

'And passionate, like Portia. She does not seek to rein in her feelings. She is very ... certain of herself.'

'You seem to have taken a great deal from the briefest of encounters.'

'Cecilia and I were listening and watching for a while.'

'Not very ladylike of either of you,' he remarked, but blandly.

'I should think you would have given up hope for that, in either of us, by now,' said Jocasta wryly.

He laughed. 'You have rather better manners than Cecilia.'

'I should not have, if I had her position in life.'

'Mistress of your own home?' he ventured. 'That will happen soon, I quite expect it. You have many suitors to choose from.'

'Yes, though I should not say so. It should be simple, I suppose. Amethyst Bailey was expressing, earlier in the Season, how fortunate I was to be able to have so many admirers. And I suppose so, but it does not feel quite like that.'

'I should like to ask an impertinent question, Miss Fortune.' She nodded her consent. 'How many offers have you had this Season?' She was silent. 'I promise not to tell your papa,' he quipped.

'Five.' He gasped. 'But they are not all *serious*. However, if Papa were to find out, he would be furious that I am not now affianced.'

'Not serious — how can that be?'

'Well, I should not tell you who. But I will say that one gentleman was over fifty and a widower. We could not share a thought together — so why he should want a silly young thing such as I, is quite beyond me.'

It was certainly not beyond Regis, and he looked grim. 'McFarlane?'

'I cannot say. But if he were to tell Papa ... I am glad they do not seem to be acquainted, or he might guess how easy it would be to ... but I may be wrong. *Has* that gentleman a fortune of note?' she asked of Regis innocently, confirming his guess.

'He is very wealthy indeed.' Jocasta blanched and he was sorry to have said as much. 'I think that he is pursuing the Matthews girl now.'

'Oh, thank goodness!' Jocasta looked guilty. 'For me, I mean. But Miss Matthews seems to have a kind mama who would not allow such a match, surely?'

'It is to be hoped so.' He looked down at her. The offers, instead of making her proud, seemed to weigh on her. She was doing her best to rise above all this. He should mention something to the marchioness. She would ensure that the little thing could not be pressured. But Baron Fortune was still her papa. He had the right to plan his child's future. Regis' blood ran cold at the thought.

'Enough about me,' said Jocasta. 'It is my turn to ask an impertinent question. Did you love her very much, that magnificent lady?'

He paused before he answered. 'I did.'

'I see.' Jocasta was keeping her voice detached. 'And why did it end?'

'A second impertinent question.' He saw her look away. 'I asked her to marry me, but she said she did not care to be a wife.'

'But she later married—'

'Yes, to Don Alberto de Zuleta. The next year.' His voice was bleak, and it pierced her.

They were silent for a little, then Jocasta said. 'I expect she wanted another sort of husband.'

He looked hurt for a second, but answered sardonically, 'Apparently so.'

'Perhaps because she loved you too much.'

His eyes burned into hers, avidly. 'What do you mean?'

'It is something a friend of mine said last Season. She did not want to marry the man she loved the most, and took another offer instead.'

'But why?' he asked, raw.

'Because she wanted a *compliant* husband.' Jocasta looked into his burning eyes. 'I don't expect that you would make a very compliant husband.'

He closed his eyes and laughed shortly. 'I don't suppose I would.' There was a long pause before he looked at her more normally. Then he added. 'It fits something she once said ...' his eyes were miles away, but then he focused and held her gaze. 'I must thank you, Miss Fortune. You may have unravelled a puzzle that has taken me too long to solve.'

Jocasta was stung a little, but she did not know why. This woman was dangerous, but whether to Regis, or to herself only, she was afraid to contemplate.

'Let us canter. There is space enough now,' she said, and dug her heel in.

They did so, but when she looked back, Regis' smile to himself wounded her.

After breakfast, during which Cassie had chatted thunderously, the other sisters were happy to know of her domestic contentment. It was to Jocasta, a little like that morning with Bucknell and Maria — a strange pairing. Mr Hudson was not particularly handsome, and it would be difficult for Jocasta to support his heartiness for too long — it was well meaning, but exhausting. They were, however, mutually engrossed by talk of their baby's antics, which they regarded as awe inspiring. 'The little fellow belched in appreciation after his first solid food,' recounted Mr Hudson, 'just as his papa does, don't ye know?'

This genius act made Jocasta smile, and she observed that special look between Onslow and Georgette that she saw indicated their mutual amusement.

The Hudsons were just as satisfied with their lot as the Bucknells had been, and indeed as the Onslows were, and, thinking about it, as Paxton and Portia were. Jocasta wondered briefly whether she would ever be so happily smug herself. It seemed unlikely, for her Season was fast closing in, and she had not met a man who admired her and set her heart aflame in return.

After breakfast, Georgette and Onslow politely undertook to accompany her sister back to Papa's house, and required Jocasta to visit the circulating library for the latest novel. Jocasta took her maid and did so, cutting through the park, glad of Georgette's excuse to save her from Papa's interrogation and lamentations, at least for today.

Traversing the path, she saw a familiar figure walking towards her in the distance. But Regis did not see her, as he was mesmerised by his dark-haired companion, who looked up at him with similar intensity. He must, Jocasta concluded, have gone straight from their ride to her residence.

Jocasta herself had explained the beautiful woman's possible motive to him — now he understood. Now, since she was a widow, finally the lovers could be together. For Jocasta knew, with every fibre of her being, that the dark-haired beauty wanted the Demon King all for herself. Their reconciliation was happening right now. That great love that Regis had once told her of, was being reignited in the carriage path in Hyde Park. Jocasta started looking for some crossing lane that she could take so that she need not see this anymore. She fought to catch a breath, for her lungs had ceased to function, and still the pair got ever closer. How could she bear to pass them? They were still some way off, the exotic beauty's arm through his in an annoyingly intimate fashion — where, oh where, could she escape to?

At that moment, Jocasta's eye was caught by a carriage beyond them. Behind the couple, quite far along the carriage road, Jocasta saw Enderby on the box seat of a rig with handsome red and yellow wheels that she had not seen before. He was driving two magnificent blacks — but in tandem. She looked over at Regis once more, and he was now looking at her — so there was to be no escape. Her eyes went back to the figure of Tom, though, when she heard a shout. Enderby had lost control of his leader, and was frantically trying to control the horse.

Jocasta watched in horror as he inadvertently touched the horse with the lash of the whip.

The great beast, enraged, leaped forward, pulling the wheeler with him. Jocasta stopped dead; her maid gave a shriek. Tom, unbalanced then righted, seemed to be lost, panicking.

She saw Regis turn and run towards the horses. Without her will, she ran as well, past his companion without a glance, shouting she knew not what. She was almost upon him; Regis had grasped one rein and another gentleman was trying to grasp the other side. Jocasta jumped in front of the horse, which was still a little way from her, making soothing sounds and large, flowing gestures. She sought to get the beast's attention, then change his state. Regis and the other young buck were dragged by the horse, Enderby pulling on the reins in a manner that might cause damage to the delicate mouths of his horses. There was nothing else for it, however, in such a populated area. As the horse slowed down somewhat, Regis called 'Miss Fortune, *move—!*' and she looked at him, stepping back before the horse was upon her. One strong arm thrust her to the bushes, where she toppled inelegantly. She watched aghast as the rein slipped through Regis' hand and he was thrown to the ground, the second panicked beast bashing open his head with his front hoof, and even as Regis rolled away, catching him again on his body with the back hoof. The horses calmed: the other gentleman, on the other side of the leader, had fared better. A groom got down from the back and went to the leader's head. Enderby dropped the reins, shocked.

Jocasta crawled to Regis' unconscious figure as a crowd gathered. 'Tom,' she said, looking at the duke briefly, 'You must get down. Let the groom deal with the horses and take Sir Damon home.' She looked around and saw Viscountess Swanson's carriage nearby, halted to regard the spectacle. 'No, help me get him up. You sir!' she ordered the other heroic gentleman, 'Help the duke carry Sir Damon to that carriage.'

Jocasta was vaguely aware of the dark Spanish beauty suddenly bursting into life, flying towards them. But she had no time for that now. Too much blood was staining the gloved hand that held his head wound, amongst his dark hair. His eyes were closed, and he was on the edge of consciousness.

As the gentlemen lifted his prone figure, Jocasta got up, then pushed through the crowd as the gentlemen followed her figure obediently. Viscountess Swanson's bonnet poked through the window of the carriage. 'Take him home, my lady!' Jocasta ordered. 'Sir Damon is unconscious.'

The viscountess looked down her nose at Jocasta, but that diminutive young lady was opening the door rudely, and directing Enderby and the other gentleman to dispose of the baronet within. They, thinking they had gained permission, did so: the young stranger saying, 'Excuse me, my lady.'

The viscountess sufficed herself with a withering look at Jocasta, but merely said 'Mount Street!' knocking on the roof of her carriage with the long-handled parasol that was, in truth, her walking stick.

Jocasta said to the young and handsome gentleman who had taken the reins on the other side, 'Thank you, sir, I am sorry not to know you, but please, could you tell my maid over there,' she gestured with her hand, 'to fetch a physician to 14 Mount Street as fast as possible?'

'The name is Benedict Fenton, miss. And I go immediately.'

'Are you alright, Jocasta? I'm so sor—' said a feeble voice.

Jocasta, seeing at last that Enderby was shaken and trembling, said gently, 'Tom, would you walk me to Mount Street?' and she took his arm in a comfortable way, grasping it a little as though for support, but really to reassure him. This woke him up.

'Of course,' he said. 'Let us go.'

He was still flushed and humiliated, as Jocasta saw. 'You do not mind if I lean upon you a little, Tom? Only my legs are a little shaken.'

'Of course!' he said again, but bucking up a little to be of service. After some steps he said, 'I should be flayed. My groom told me they were too strong for me in that formation, but I would not heed him.'

'Well, one must try every new thing, Tom. I quite see how you had to try, for how else are you to learn?'

He looked a little comforted by this, but still said, as a self-scourge, 'But not in the park.'

'True!' said Jocasta, forcing a jocular tone, 'not in the park.' As he still trembled, she added, 'I believe my dress is muddy. If it cannot be cleaned, you shall have to buy me a new one, you know.' She was teasing him for his comfort, and he smiled a little.

'Righto! Happy to...'

They walked silently then, both wrapped in other thoughts. When she felt, as though by telepathy of the body, that Tom was berating himself too much, she gave his arm a squeeze to recall him. He looked down once, and said wryly, 'You must think me a dashed fool.'

'It was an accident, Tom. It might have happened to anyone.'

'Only to someone arrogant and vain as I, wanting to show off my skills.'

There was a limit to how much comfort she could offer, however, when her every nerve was concerned about Regis. He had looked so pale as she knelt before him. Would he regain his senses? Could he *die*? She shuddered again as she recalled the hooves striking him. Surely the one to the head was a glancing blow, but why was there so much blood? It had been enough to render him unconscious, she believed, when he was finally placed in the carriage.

Feeling the shudder, the duke said, 'You are shocked, Jocasta. Perhaps I should take you home and bring you word on Regis later.'

'I am going to Mount Street,' answered Jocasta, as coldly as he had ever heard her speak. It took them only five minutes to reach Park Lane and from there they could see Mount Street Gardens. Jocasta fought off the urge to run.

It turned out, when Enderby enquired, that Regis was no longer in the gentlemen's rooms in Mount Street, but had moved back into his town house on the departure of his tenants. It was only two streets off, and so Jocasta said they should forgo the cab and walk on.

They were met in the impressive vestibule by a butler whose manner showed less finesse and more military-like bluntness.

'You cannot see him, Your Grace, the doctor will arrive directly.'

'We will wait,' said the duke, after a squeeze from Jocasta's fingers.

The butler nodded with bad grace, and did not bother to show them to a room, but left them to themselves in the large, square hall. The duke led the shaking Jocasta to a chair against the wall.

'Shall I have them fetch you something?'

Jocasta looked around. It was evident that the household was in an uproar, with maids carrying linen and bathing water running upstairs, footmen on errands walking faster than decorum would permit, and the butler issuing orders like a general on a battlefront. She knew she was an imposition — a glance from the butler showed her so. But she could not go until she had some word. She would not.

'No, Tom, let us not disturb them. Let us just wait.'

'Dash it!' he said after some moments. 'I should tell Cissie!'

Jocasta's eyes were on the staircase since this was as close to Regis as she was allowed. How was he? She had heard a crunch of bone, she shivered as she remembered, and his body beneath the horse was etched on her brain. His head was struck, she thought, but only a glancing blow, surely? He would not *die?* No, no, no! He could not. As though her will was enough, she screwed up her eyes in concentration as she stared at the steps.

'I said,' pursued Tom once more, touching her shoulder lightly, 'I should tell Cissie. She would want to be here.'

'Wha—?' said Jocasta, dazed. 'Of course, you should, Tom. Go and find her.'

'I could send a note...'

'No, for how could she bear to hear of this from a note? You go. And on your way, tell my sister what has occurred, and to come for me here as soon as she may.'

'Perhaps you should not stay. The doctor is not even here yet...'

But at this moment, that individual appeared. He was quickly ushered upstairs, and Tom, looking at Jocasta's pinched and pale face, said, 'I should not leave you...'

'There are plenty of staff here. Do not worry, Tom, I shall leave after the doctor has dealt with him and I hear his condition.'

The duke looked down, worried. 'Are you—?' he began.

'For goodness' sake, Tom. Just go!'

He started, but then he exchanged a glance with the butler, who had caught this exchange, as well as the strain in Jocasta's voice, and the butler nodded. The duke gave up. With a final squeeze on Jocasta's shoulder, he left.

The butler sent a maid to ask the young lady if she wished some refreshment, or to go to one of the salons to wait for news, but Jocasta nodded her away and the butler watched as she sat, still and frozen, staring up the stairs.

Fifteen excruciating minutes later, the gruff doctor came downstairs, issuing orders to a servant, who Jocasta thought must be the valet, a step behind him. She rushed to the bottom of the stairs.

'Doctor! How is the baronet?

The doctor's gruff tones softened somewhat as he met her at the bottom step. He was not a particularly tall man, but he felt so beside this tiny woodland creature in fashionable clothes who gazed up at him. 'The baronet has some broken ribs—'

'Oh! Is this dangerous?'

'Not if those that should look after him will stop him moving around. He's a fine specimen!'

'It is the head that's bothering me,' said a gloomy Scottish voice to his side. Jocasta met the lugubrious eyes of the valet in panic.

'Oh!' she said.

The doctor patted her shoulder with a little too much force. 'Don't listen to Mr McKay. The blow was not severe, I think. I stitched it up, and now we have only to wait until he wakes again.'

'If he wakes!' said the depressing voice to the side. Jocasta gave a squeak. 'And who are you, miss?' he added, rudely.

'I am Miss Fortune — and I saw the accident. There were two hoof blows, I … I saw them!' To Jocasta's annoyance, her voice shook as she said so.

'It seems you are in shock, Miss Fortune,' the doctor soothed. 'I shall give you some drops and you'll be right as rain after you've slept.'

'Aye, go home now, Miss Fortune,' said the dour Scottish valet. 'If you tell me your direction, I'll have someone send you the news.' This seemed to conjure *bereavement* news, and Jocasta backed up to her chair and sat down again, grasping the seat, as though she might be forcibly removed. The valet sighed. 'Ach, suit yerself. I've no time to be bothered with you.'

'Someone needs to see you home,' said the doctor. 'His head injury will be better directly. You ought to go home and rest yourself, Miss Fortune. I will prescribe a draught to calm you.'

'I must stay until he awakes.' She looked at the doctor's expression of pity and exasperation. 'But do not worry, my friend has gone for my sister, the Marchioness of Onslow. Our family are great friends of the baronet, you know.'

'Ach,' said the valet with his now customary rudeness, 'do as you will. I'll be with my master.'

CHAPTER 19

A Distressing Breach of Etiquette

The doctor had finished his tortuous business at long last, and Regis had been only semi-conscious during the process. He felt more awake now, his valet had seen him with open eyes, and left again, too, at Regis' insistence. Now Regis was able, finally, to close his eyes to ease his aching head — without adding to Mr McKay's panic. He heard the door open and frowned a little, but did not open his eyes, hoping whatever servant hovered there would depart when they saw him asleep. But the sound was wrong. The rustle of clothes was not such as ... he opened his eyes to see Jocasta Fortune's concerned face, still wearing the silken bonnet he had admired earlier, a foot from his own. He sat up reflexively, bumping his forehead on hers in his panic, underneath the poke of her hat.

'Ow!' she said, holding her head.

'Miss Fortune! You should not be here!'

'Oh, I know. I *tried* to wait for Georgette, but it was twenty minutes, so in the end I have stolen in to see you. Is your head very sore, sir?'

Since he was in the middle of a wince, he could hardly deny it. 'It is now! This is crazy! You must go at once...'

'I will. Only the doctor would tell me nothing, making light of it because I am a female, but I *saw* it. I saw that hoof strike you twice. Once here—' She had removed her gloves, and Damon was utterly stunned when a frantic little hand touched his broken ribs, and he felt the warmth through his shirt, 'and here!' She touched his bandaged head, the fingers between his curls. Their eyes met, there was a beat that neither could break, stronger than the time in the studio. She jumped back, removing her warm fingers. 'Oh, excuse me. But are your senses not disordered? Will there be any lasting damage? I had to see for myself, I *could* not wait any longer. It is all my fault.'

Damon's thoughts were reeling, but something was paramount. 'It is *your* senses that have become disordered, Miss Fortune. You must leave the room immediately.'

'Oh, I will! I just needed—' The door began to open. Regis later gave thanks for the un-oiled squeak.

To the baronet's horror, but intense amusement, Miss Jocasta Fortune disappeared beneath his bed.

'Ah, Mr McKay. I think I want some ... posset.' He heard a faint squeak beneath the bed, but it was apparent that his valet had not.

That individual had raised his brows a little at the unusual request, but said, 'Aye sir! I am here to tell you that the Marquis and Marchioness of Onslow have arrived, and enquired about you, before they take Miss Fortune home.'

'Miss Fortune?' enquired Regis, amazed.

'The wee lass who saw yer stupid heroics and would not leave until she had news of you. A nuisance, like most females.'

'Ah, she is here? She must have been shocked to see the accident.' Mr McKay turned to bow himself out, but Damon said, 'Have them come up!'

Mr McKay allowed himself to enquire, 'Are you sure you are well enough, sir?'

'Yes, yes, old friend. Send them up and let us not be disturbed. I have something particular to tell the marquis.'

'Sir.' Mr McKay was at his most bland (and therefore disapproving) and he left the room.

Damon heard a noise and looked over the bed, with considerable pain caused to his ribs, and regarded the dismembered head that poked out and said, '*Posset???*' She looked disgusted as she squirmed out and got up, brushing herself off. 'Couldn't you think of something more likely than *posset?*' She shook that off, and looked panicked. 'I know they will save me, but now that I think of it, what *will* Onslow make of this situation sir?' Jocasta shook her head. 'I shall be in such trouble.'

'You should have thought of that before you entered a gentleman's chamber.' Jocasta shot him a glance of dislike. 'Go into the dressing room there. Mr McKay might come back in with them.'

Looking as though she wished to reply, Jocasta nevertheless stole through the dressing room door, so that she could not be seen. After a silent moment she said from the doorway, which she had left an inch ajar, 'At least your senses are not disordered.'

'It is a pity yours *are*.'

'Must you repeat yourself?' said Jocasta resentfully. 'I was only concerned.'

'And now you have landed us in more trouble.' He winced, adjusting his position.

'You are heartless.'

'You were worried about me so recently, too.'

'And now I have seen that you are just the same as ever, I'm not worried at all.'

'You are a very foolish girl. Onslow may demand the ultimate price for this. He has every right.'

She did not pretend to misunderstand. 'I would not marry you even if I had to go home now, with my reputation in tatters — so do not fear for yourself. Your reunion with your lover is safe from me.'

Damon ignored her last remark, enjoying himself despite the pain, and said, 'This was probably your plan all along.'

She jerked her head from behind the door and gave him a fierce look. '*You—!*'

'Your bonnet's crooked,' he informed her. She blushed deliciously, righting it, and his face almost displayed his inner grin. But he frowned at her horribly with his eyebrows.

She frowned back. 'You don't frighten me!'

'But Onslow does. They are coming.' Jocasta ducked back in her hiding place, and he regarded the entrance of the Onslows.

'Regis! How are you?' said Onslow.

'I feel,' answered the Demon King, at his most urbane, 'as though I were just kicked by a horse. Twice.'

'It is kind of you to see us, we shall not stay long. But it is good to know you are in your senses and that there is no further problem that rest will not solve, Mr McKay tells me.'

Regis sighed. 'It is not quite correct to say that there is no further problem, which is why I asked you up here, Onslow.'

'Yes? Anything in my power, Damon, you know that.'

'You may not feel that in a moment.' He rested back, wincing once more as a pain coursed through his head. 'Come out!' he called.

Jocasta emerged from behind the door, like a child who had been caught stealing sweetmeats in the pantry. She looked at her shoes. 'It is not what you think, Onslow.'

Jocasta! cried the marchioness, 'What—?'

Onslow looked at his sister-in-law with interest. 'I hardly think you dangerous at this moment, Damon, whatever your reputation. But I think I am owed an explication.'

'It is my fault!' cried Jocasta. 'They would not tell me clearly how Sir Damon was, and I had to see for myself. I hoped you would come sooner so that they would let me in, but in the end I *could* not wait. I saw the horse's hooves strike, you see, and—'

'Oh, yes, I understand,' said Georgette consolingly, drawing Jocasta to her. 'It must have been the shock.'

'But how did you manage to get in here unseen? At least — I trust it was unseen,' added Onslow.

'Yes. I asked if there was a room where I could—' Jocasta blushed, as all eyes were upon her.

Her horror of having spoken of it reared up, but then Georgette, understanding, said, 'But surely they offered a room below?'

'Oh, yes they did,' said Jocasta, glad to be understood. 'But I told the maid that I was afraid to be disturbed, and wondered if there was another room above, and she sent me to the room opposite this one ...' she looked at Regis. 'Once your mother's room, I believe, sir.'

'Very enterprising of you, I'm sure, Jocasta, but it does leave us in something of a pickle,' Onslow drawled.

'Not enterprising, just a stupid impulse!' cried Jocasta.

Georgette's voice was amazed. 'But you are seldom impulsive, Jocasta ... lately you have been unlike yourself.'

Regis interrupted. 'Onslow, send off any servants hovering outside on errands, will you? We have only to get Miss Fortune to descend the stairs and all will be well.'

'No!' said Georgette. 'Let us get her into your mother's room, where she was taken, then I will affect to have found her there and ask a maid to attend to a ... a torn ruffle.' She bent at Jocasta's feet and pulled at a ribbon adornment on the bottom of her dress. 'I am sorry, love, if this is a favourite...' she yanked and sure enough the ruffle came away about six inches.

'Georgie!' complained Jocasta.

Onslow stood with the door ajar and nodded to the pair. 'My dress!' whispered Jocasta as she passed the bed.

'Serves you right,' uttered the baronet, unfeelingly.

She contented herself with a look, and left with her sister.

Onslow came back and regarded Regis as he closed his eyes briefly against pain. 'We avoided the worst. But nevertheless, Damon,' Onslow said, wryly, 'it has now become apparent that we might have something to discuss.'

Regis opened his eyes and met Onslow's directly. 'Yes, Lucian, but for God's sake don't ... let me deal with it. Let her think that we escaped today with no suspicion. As we did. It is just that now we know ...' Onslow and he exchanged a wry look. 'Miss Fortune is too easily damaged — if she were to think any of this was a consequence of today—'

'Then...?' interrupted the marquis, his blue eyes piercing.

'I'm telling you not to worry. I'll handle Jocasta Fortune.'

In the bedchamber of Regis' deceased mama, with the screen set by the maid so that one could relieve oneself behind, Georgette located the bell pull and rang. In but a minute a little maid arrived, and Georgette informed her that she had noticed that her sister's dress had caught, probably on a carriage door or some such, and needed some stitches. The maid ran for supplies and sometime later returned and pinned and stitched the rosette in place. 'It needs a piece beneath to be secure, your ladyship,' the little maid confessed. 'You had best send it to your dressmaker for a proper repair.'

'This will do splendidly for now, Alice. We thank you very much. And I hope that your mother recovers quickly.' She held out her hand and dropped some shillings into the maid's, very discreetly.

As they wandered down to the hall, where Onslow was already waiting, Jocasta thought of the easy way that Georgette had chatted with the maid, putting her at her ease and eliciting the history of her family home in the country. It was like her, Jocasta thought. Georgette was interested in people. She watched as the marchioness thanked the butler for the help his excellent staff had given with Jocasta's gown, and all three got into Onslow's crested carriage.

It was then, with only James the coachman to hear, that the peal was rung over Jocasta Fortune's head.

⁂

Earlier that morning, while Jocasta had been still at breakfast, Sir Damon Regis had been admitted into the salon of the Marqués de Casa Prado, not surprised to find the brother absent and Doña Isabel quite alone. She stood to greet him, and they gazed at each other across the room. 'I was going to use your English manners, and refuse you,' she remarked, but her eyes never left his.

'I am glad you did not.'

'*Damon*—!' she rushed towards him, but he stepped back, and she stopped, her breast heaving.

'Might we walk in the park, Doña Isabel?' he said, pleasantly.

'So formal, from one who once breathed my name in my ear. More English manners?' she said, disdainfully. But beneath he heard some sadness.

'I am, after all, English.'

'You did not behave so once, when we were everything to each other.' Her eyes were aflame and she looked beautiful, so alive that the room seemed aglow.

'And then we were not,' he said, dryly. 'Untying that "knot" almost cost me my life.'

'That is more like you. A man of feeling, an open man.'

'Nevertheless, my lady, I am going for a walk. If I might escort you, it would be an honour.'

'Ah, the return of the English gentleman. So cold.' He picked up his long coat in a gesture of leave taking. She laughed, challenging him. 'Are you afraid to be with me here alone, afraid of what you might do? Well, I do not care for those cold English walks where nothing is talked of but the weather.'

'I want to talk to you, Isabel,' he said gravely, but the smile that tinged his lips drew her. 'I want to say things that should not be overheard. But I do not wish to do so in a room alone with you.'

They regarded each other for a moment, her eyes hot, and his steady.

'I shall go,' she said, finally, 'but you might regret it. You never know what I might do in public. Will you risk the scandal?'

'You need ask? I have not changed *that* much.'

She laughed, and summoned a maid for her pelisse.

Walking in the park, she accepted the support of his arm. She turned heads in her elaborately frogged scarlet pelisse and elegant bonnet. The bonnet framed those dark curls, a few of which lay unfashionably, but gloriously, over one shoulder, highlighting that exotic beauty. The pelisse hugged her upper curves. She could still, for those gentlemen whose jaws dropped as they passed, even in the middle of the English winter, summon up classical paintings of wild, scantily dressed, wanton women lazing under the blazing sun. Her eyes were turned towards her walking companion, however. Even when a Mr Stevens tripped over, while attempting to tip his hat and gain her attention, she failed to notice. Several other young bucks did, however, and he would be roasted for some time to come.

'I missed you,' she breathed at Regis, looking up into his eyes.

'That sounds like a pleasant, nostalgic emotion. *I* was cutting up a ruinous ruckus so as *not* to miss you.'

'Oh, Damon!' she grasped his arm tighter, but he did not change his step or acknowledge her. 'You think I have no right to recall our old relations?'

Then he did look down. 'Not at all. Until recently, I believed that I could never again recall those times without pain, Isabel. I came today to tell you how grateful I am for all those precious memories.'

Her eyes clouded. 'Recently ...?' she mused. Her voice was a little sharper when she asked, 'How did you rid yourself of that pain, pray?'

'Someone explained it to me. The reason you left.' He smiled down at her faintly. 'I could not give up that question, even after I strove to give up my love.'

'Explained me to you?' her tone was not derisive, but wondering.

He nodded. 'You wanted a more compliant husband.'

'Ah!' she said. 'I suppose that is true ... I did not think of marriage with you. You could have eaten me whole. You *were* eating me. My desire for you would have changed me into *compliant* myself.' He said nothing, just shook his head sadly, looking at the ground. 'Who explained me? Not that little nymph from last night?' She gave a harsh laugh. 'She was quite beautiful, my dear, but surely a passing fancy? A flighty beauty with no extra intelligence that I could gather, or any of that passion for life that you used to crave so much.' He did not answer, yet his eyes crinkled in laughter. 'Her firefly glimmer can never be a match for such a brilliant sun as *you*.' She waited, and he still made no response, but with his eyes still smiling. She uttered, in a voice that would have drawn attention if there had been amblers near enough, 'Why, Damon, *why?*'

'You know, Isabel, for all I thought we breathed one breath, for all you set my soul on fire with admiration and desire, I never felt needed by you.'

They walked on while she absorbed these words, which fell into her, harshly. She tried to make light of it. 'And so, now you are full of charitable concern and a desire to relieve the plight of waifs and strays?'

'Just one waif. It is an occupation I began by accident, but it started to take up my days.'

'You pity her?'

'Not precisely. I find it my imperative to shield her from harm. I don't think I can help it.'

'You do not love her, then. That little girl could never be your equal.'

'*Love* her? That is a strange thought—' he heard Enderby call Jocasta's name, saw her ahead and met her eye, and then spun around to face the oncoming horses...

In the carriage ride home from Regis' house, Jocasta, in a manner most unlike her, accepted the strictures of Onslow and Georgette, knowing that his stern tone and her slight hysteria came from concern and affection.

Georgette stopped at one point, looking at her sister's expression. 'Why ever are you smiling, Jocasta?'

'I promise I shall not make you worry again, Georgie,' said Jocasta, trying to suppress her smile. 'It just occurred to me how very fond I am of you.' Georgette's mouth opened, unable to respond. Jocasta looked to the blond-headed marquis and smiled at him, briefly clutching his coat sleeve. 'And of you, sir.'

The frown disappeared from Onslow's face and he threw himself back against the squabs, hands in the air. 'And *this* is why I cannot speak to women. You see to her, Georgette.'

'I know it all,' said Jocasta. 'If my behaviour had caused a scandal today, then I could have risked not just my reputation, but the reputation of my unmarried sisters. I did not think of it. I only thought of the sound of crunching bone ...' Georgette shivered. 'But I will *never* do such a thing again.' Jocasta tapped Onslow, who was looking out of the carriage window, on the knee. 'I promise, my lord.'

As Jocasta got out of the carriage and ran to the house, Onslow handed his wife down. She was still in shock, and their eyes met as she said, 'She is very fond of me. And of you.'

'Yes,' agreed Onslow, with a sigh, 'and she has crept up on us, too. I suspect we are very fond of her, also.'

'I'm so glad we all escaped today with no harm done,' sighed Georgette.

Onslow did not inform her of his conversation with Damon. He was not sure yet what Regis was up to. But that the Demon King was putting Jocasta's interests before his own, that he knew.

❧ ⚜ ❧

It had taken the duke some time to find Cecilia. Thanks to the servants at her residence, he finally located her, with Mrs Usher, at a modiste's on the outskirts of the fashionable area, getting fitted for some more evening gowns.

She clutched at Tom as he told her, and Mrs Usher sent her off with the maid who had accompanied them, saying she would return home on her own.

As Jocasta had done before, Cecilia burst into Damon's room over the objections of Mr McKay, but since the maid trailed after her, there was no break in etiquette. The relief she felt on seeing him, pale and alive, naturally caused her to vent her anger and tell him off, asking what he had thought he was about, thinking he was a hero. 'You should have just let the beasts run away with him. It would have served Tom right.'

The duke, who had followed in behind the maid, gulped. 'I might have died if Damon and the young Fenton chap had not helped. Th … thank you, Regis.'

'I was only trying to get out of the way,' said Damon, bored. 'You should thank Miss Fortune. She calmed the horses from the front and almost got injured for it.'

'I didn't see …' said the duke, appalled. 'Dashed sorry, King.'

'Could have happened to anyone. Take this little minx away and I shall count us as even. She's giving me a headache.'

They left, and went to see Jocasta directly. They were denied, but Georgette greeted them sweetly and told them her sister was a trifle shocked, but well — and she would convey the duke's belated thanks and her friend's concern. She suggested they go driving after breakfast on the morrow, and it was agreed upon.

But the next morning they had to go driving alone, for Jocasta had a visitor, and the butler suggested they return in a half hour.

CHAPTER 20

Jocasta vs the Spanish Beauty

J ocasta stood as the butler announced the caller. She straightened her spine a little, as though she could add an inch to her stature, but she would need more than that to equal the height and magnificent figure of Doña Isabel Maria de Zuleta. Jocasta welcomed her stiffly, and gestured the guest to a seat, but the woman moved around the room first, laying gentle, elegant fingers on some porcelain figures, looking at the paintings on the wall.

'I thought,' the lady said as she walked, with only the slightest of accents, 'that you might wish to know how the patient is.'

Something in the older woman's manner was beginning to annoy Jocasta, so there was no inflection in her voice as she uttered the merest, 'Yes?'

'He is in pain, but insulting me royally, so he is improving.' She laughed then. 'I heard he is called the Demon King in London. It is so strange. When *I* knew him, he was not so devilish.' Jocasta looked at her blandly. 'Well,' she said, arching a brow, 'perhaps a *little* devilish.' She looked to share her laugh, but Jocasta almost shook with rage. She did well in banking it down, however, just looking back at that lady with a slight smile. After a second Doña Isabel began again. 'I was most impressed by *your* bravery, Miss Fortune. You sped past me so swiftly, before I could move.'

'I was concerned for the horses.'

'And for Sir Damon, I'll wager. You seem *muy intima* with him.'

'I am a friend of the Duke of Enderby, who was driving the carriage.'

'Ah, I see. And to Damon?' Again, that show of intimacy: this time, by the use of his name without his title.

'He is a friend of my family. I believe he has known my brother-in-law the marquis since they were at school.'

The woman had taken a seat, not where Jocasta had indicated, but on the sofa beside her. Jocasta felt stifled, and the woman's dark eyes captured hers. 'I suppose you have gathered that your Demon King was once my love.' This, from someone she had briefly seen twice before, was too much.

'I do not pry into the affairs of others, my lady.'

'Ah, we are different, I think. Although we Spaniards may be brought up strictly enough, we open our hearts more quickly, and express our emotions. I find the English a little cold, as I told Damon.'

'Ah,' Jocasta said in a manner set to reflect the woman's belief.

'And he said that: *it is not that the English are cold, they just conceal their passion*.' She smiled at Jocasta. 'I must say, *you* did not conceal yourself yesterday. Your passionate heart was on display.' Jocasta stiffened more. 'I admired you greatly.' Jocasta met her eyes and saw no sarcasm there, but it still did not make her warm to this person. When the woman did not receive an answering smile, she began another turn around the room. 'I suppose you must be wondering why I left him, all those years ago? Damon told me yesterday that he had believed then that we breathed one breath.' Jocasta's body trembled, and she grasped the seat briefly, before controlling herself. Thankfully, Doña Isabel seemed riveted by a figurine. 'And so did I, but when I found that he wished to marry me, I knew I could not. He was too strong. His love was overwhelming. I love to paint, to follow my passions for art and music, to say and think what I like — be my own true self. It is not easy. I made my family accept it, I forged myself in a world that wanted me to sit at home with a needle. *I* did that.' She looked back at Jocasta, and for the first time, Jocasta showed her some understanding as she met her eye. What woman of spirit would not be roused by those words? Then a slight frown appeared on the lovely face of Isabel, as she continued to reminisce. 'But his love, his great love ... It would have changed me, made me someone else, someone less than I wished to be .'

Jocasta stood at this, and rang the bell. She was three feet from the lady and faced her squarely. 'Suddenly, I am sorry for you. You are more than a match for Sir Damon Regis in intelligence, in spirit, in your interests and in your quite astounding beauty.' Isabel held Jocasta's eye with that intense gaze, almost holding her breath at the gravity of the little one's demeanour. 'You have known him *how* many years? And yet, you do not know him at all.' The beauty looked struck, the breath she had been holding escaped. She remained there, as though still locked in a look with Jocasta, but Jocasta had turned away. A maid came in, and Jocasta's eyes swivelled to look at the servant, and said, 'See my guest out.' The little fairy turned back to smile pleasantly at the still beauty, who searched her face. 'My apologies, Doña Isabel, but I have some friends who await me,' said Jocasta. 'Thank you for your visit, and do have a pleasant morning.'

Jocasta sat again and lowered her eyes. There was a moment's silence before she heard the lady say, in her rich, warm voice, 'Yes. As you English say, I wish you a pleasant day.'

Jocasta was shaken, astounded at herself. Could she really have said those impertinent words to Sir Damon's love? Could she? But her voice had been steady, and at the time when she had spoken, her conviction firm. She did not feel so now. This woman was older, more intelligent, more beautiful, more sophisticated, truer to herself, and more expressive of her feelings than Jocasta could ever be. And yet, moved by rage at her behaviour, her careless crossing of many polite boundaries, Jocasta had spoken to her thus. Jocasta had been infuriated, and something more, she knew. Where could there be a female who did not envy that woman? It was lowering to be jealous of another's attributes, and this was a feeling that Jocasta was not prone to. She had sisters with a variety of attributes and talents, many of which superseded her own. It would have been too exhausting in life to have been jealous of them all. Most of the Fortune sisters did not give themselves the trouble. But she had been jealous of Doña Isabel.

Jealous because Regis had told her once how much he had loved that beautiful creature?

While she was still trying to recover herself, her papa was announced.

'Ha! Thought I'd find you here. Just saw your sister in town, so I hurried here to talk to you without Georgette's damned interference. You would think she would listen to her father, even if she is married. But nowadays, she has taken to wearing all those fine clothes and walks around with that silly smile she hardly drops. Why does she have to keep smiling?'

'I believe she is happy in her marriage, Papa.'

'Well, no need to keep smiling about it. It is six months since she was wed. Which reminds me, there is only a month or so of the Season left. You are surrounded by young bucks whenever I see you, there must have been some offers. Spit it out, my girl.'

The Duke of Enderby and Miss Montgomery were announced at this happy moment.

'Ah, we are engaged to walk, are we not, Your Grace, Miss Montgomery? I shall not keep you long. Papa, I shall speak of this with you at another time.'

'What? Oh, Enderby's here. Yes, yes, you go along, my dear,' said the baron, smiling his heartiest smile at the duke. His eyes took on the figure of Miss Montgomery. *'You here?'* he said, disappointed, in that mumbling voice that denoted his inner cogitations.

'And I,' said Cecilia laughing up at him, 'am glad to see you again, too, Baron.'

'*Glad to see me, minx?*' muttered the baron to himself. '*You should take yourself off if you are not wanted. After him yourself, are you? Yes, I thought so.*'

Cecilia, with added wickedness, said, grasping at the duke's arm for show, 'Let us go, Tom. The baron says we should take ourselves off.' A maid awaited all three in the hall with Enderby's hat and gloves and Jocasta's spencer and bonnet.

They could hear the baron mutter, '*That girl! If she were a daughter of mine, I'd—*'

Cecilia was laughing, but Jocasta dragged her out before she could find out her imagined fate.

***

Three days later, blond-headed Lord Onslow spotted Sir Damon Regis in the entrance to Mrs Ashton's ballroom and moved to intercept him.

'What on earth are you doing walking around?' he asked Regis. 'Get back to bed immediately!'

'If I have to submit to Mr McKay's ministrations for another day, without any diversion, murder will be committed.'

'You did not previously call the ballroom a *diversion*.'

'Yes ...' Regis mused, 'this Season *has* been different.'

'It is not the ballroom that has been diverting you, but my sister-in-law,' said Onslow, somewhat grimly.

'Only because her family have been particularly insensitive to her situation.'

A sardonic eyebrow from Onslow acknowledged a hit. 'Still, cause any trouble and don't think I won't call you out,' said Onslow, thudding one hand on Regis' shoulder.

'Certain death for you,' answered his friend blandly.

'Oh, I don't know,' said Onslow with more spirit than hope, 'I remain the only man who has pinked you in a match.'

'I was crazy that Season, hardly myself,' Regis let his eyebrow fly up in a wry scroll, 'and don't think I'm unaware that you knocked the button off the foil deliberately, just so that Seaward couldn't challenge a wounded man.'

'He *did* deserve to die, but *you* did not deserve to be his killer. Not until you recovered your senses, at least. You had lost your head.'

'No — merely my heart, which usually governs my head truly.' Regis changed his tone to a more jocular one. 'Anyway, we may be evenly matched, but don't deceive yourself that you could ever win against me with foils again.'

'Oh, if you angered me, I might,' Onslow said, a little steel in his tone.

'How might I do that?' said Regis, interested.

'If you were to wound Miss Fortune, and in that manner, my wife.' Onslow's voice was silkily dangerous.

'Spare me. I'm here this evening merely to be entertained.'

'Having now seen the *Isabel*, whose name you breathed so frequently in your cups,' mused Onslow, 'I can better understand your loss.'

'Magnificent, isn't she?' said Regis, but heartily.

'Yes, and here tonight.'

'*I* am looking for someone shorter and slighter.'

'Ah, well, you might want to witness the Battle of the Fairies.' Regis' eyebrows asked the question. 'By happenstance, Julia White's frightful mother and Georgette were talking to the same person. The two girls are thus united, and their courts naturally followed.'

'This, I *must* see.'

'You will get buffeted in the ribs by the crush if you go into the ballroom properly. Go home.'

'I shall not get buffeted. My charisma shall part the crowd like Moses with the Red Sea.'

'Very well then! To the left.' Onslow tried to steer Regis to the wall as protection on one side, but Regis was right. The sight of the pair together was striking, the blond handsomeness of one, and the vital, dark demonic masculinity of the other, parted the crowd indeed. As they approached the Onslow party, Regis stood back before Jocasta could spot him, and watched the interplay of the combined courtiers of the two fairy queens.

The marchioness joined them, and with an arched brow at her husband, said confidentially, 'I may be biased, but *I* think Jocasta has it by a nose.'

Onslow was delighted. 'By a nose, you say? From whence have you this gamester's parlance, my lady?'

'If you think I do not have ears to hear you and Justin when you discuss racing for an hour together, you underestimate me, marquis.'

Onslow sent her a look and they exchanged that secret glance that Regis had noted so often before, when Justin Faulkes came upon them. 'I have to say, once you see the beauties together, you really do notice the differences.'

242

Regis thought so too. It would not be long until the next set formed, and no doubt this break for discussion would end by both ladies being claimed for the floor. But meanwhile he, too, had noted the differences. Miss White was more poised, and her beauty more refined. Jocasta, however, had the truest eyes. It seemed, when she talked to her beaus, that there was no less of her old ballroom vivacity in her manner, but a deal more sincerity. She had begun, in the last weeks, to give her admirers a special glance of attention, one that she had previously given only to him. It seemed to have, on those fellows not too self-interested to notice, a remarkable effect. Their eyes became dreamy under her gaze, their answering looks devotional. Regis, who had watched Jocasta be vivacious among her throng of admirers since the start of the Season, with no effect to his spirits at all, felt suddenly annoyed. He had told her that the young men deserved her listening ear, but she did not have to take it so to heart. Soon she might send one of them that smile: not the pretty flirtatious smile that they had seen before, but that gorgeous, genuine smile that had almost brought him to his knees over the lid of a piano. It lit gunpowder in a cannon as he knew.

The young Duke of Enderby moved towards that throng, and though it was obvious to Regis that he was heading towards Jocasta, his attention was purloined by Miss White. 'Your Grace!' she said sweetly. 'How lovely to see you here this even—'

Jocasta, suddenly noticing Enderby's back, did some purloining of her own, without, thought Regis, any notion of doing so. 'Oh, Tom, is it you? Where is Cecilia? Has she arrived?'

Miss White's cheeks flamed, though Jocasta was unaware of it. This claim of intimacy was unwarranted. Jocasta did, however, become aware of the starts of some gentlemen beside her and said, in pretty apology, 'Excuse me! Your Grace, I *meant* to say.'

Since Enderby greeted this with a complicit smile and wandered over to her, saying, 'Ballroom manners, please Jocasta. I *mean*, Miss Fortune,' this was greeted with jocularity all around, as it was meant to be. Though there were some among her court who gave the duke an unpleasant look. Those intelligent enough to realise, understood this exchange as a sort of familial intimacy, not a flirtatious one, and relaxed.

At this moment, Regis noted two things. One, the arrival on the outskirts of the group around Miss White of the imposing figure of the Fortune brother, George. He had undoubtedly heard this interaction between his sister and Enderby, and certainly did not have the discernment to distinguish the nuances of the exchange of first names so jocularly. He smiled unpleasantly, and was making his smug way to Jocasta, no doubt to help the pairing along. If it *had* been a romance, thought Regis, the intrusion of her clodpole brother would undoubtedly have ruined it in a second. Regis saw that Colonel Bellamy, noting the same thing as he, meant to head George Fortune off by claiming Jocasta for the next dance. Knowing that this kind move would lower her spirits immediately, Regis reached her first, from behind.

'I am sorry, gentlemen,' he said suavely, but with that dangerous energy that recalled his nickname, 'but Miss Fortune is pledged to me for this dance.'

'Regis!' Jocasta hissed, her eyes flashing just as dangerously as his, ' *What* are you doing out of the sickroom? Onslow — did you know?' She turned in fury to the marquis, making up the rear. He, never having seen his sister-in-law in a rage, was mightily amused, as well as shocked.

'I told him not to...' the marquis managed weakly, giving her an apologetic blue-eyed gaze, but Jocasta had turned her flaming eyes for a second onto Regis. '*Stay still!*' Only Lord Jeffries had been close enough to hear Jocasta's lowered voice before, but everyone in the company had seen the change in her demeanour. Obviously, for all the Demon King's smug certainty in claiming a dance, the lady was at outs with him. Jocasta raised her voice a little. 'Gentlemen, could you move back a trifle, Sir Damon has newly broken ribs.' *And was insane enough to come into a crowded ballroom*, it was obvious she wished to add.

'What on *earth* are you doing here Damon?' said another piercing voice to one side. Now a dark-haired little fury stood before the baronet.

'Cecilia!' cried Jocasta. 'Thank goodness!'

'*Look* at this crush, Damon! You are mad to come here,' seethed Cecilia Montgomery, with less care about her volume than Jocasta.

'He is. We have to get him out of here at once.' Jocasta had angled herself in front of Regis' body, her back to him protectively, and Regis looked down at her blonde curls with a wry smile. 'Cecilia, you stay at his other side. Tom, you take my place here and walk in front. I'll go to the right.' She stood on Regis' right-hand side, then turned to the marquis. '—and Onslow, you behind! We must get him out of this crush uninjured.'

'But Miss Fortune,' said Damon Regis, placating, 'I am quite alright—'

Jocasta jerked his sleeve and pulled him around until he faced the exit. 'Right Tom, straight ahead!'

'And be as duke-ish as you like!' commanded Cecilia.

'It looks,' said Colonel Bellamy to Georgette, who watched, laughing, as the small procession with its reluctant centrepiece moved off, 'like a military escort for a prisoner.'

'Yes, I fear that the Demon King, as you all call him, had become a captive of two fierce females.'

'And his crime?'

'Being out of bed before his wounds have healed.'

'Well, sister,' said a voice from Georgette's side, 'It seems that Jocasta has a *duke* wrapped around her little finger. I thought she was delaying too long, but it seems she was holding out for a prize that clearly surpasses your own.'

Seeing the marchioness make little fists at her side to contain herself, Colonel Bellamy rode to the rescue with a slight smile to her, 'Let us to the card room, Fortune, unless you await Miss White?'

'I await no woman.' George Fortune raised his head, for he had seen Miss White accept the hand of another for the next set. He added, with a sneer, 'But I don't think *you* show any promise in *that* direction, Bellamy.'

Georgette could only be glad, for the sake of embarrassment, that although George's voice and sentiments were equally obnoxious, he had not the baron's, nor her sister Cassie's, volume. Small mercies should always be appreciated.

'Should I go after them, Justin?' said Georgette, as Faulkes and she watched the prisoner and his escort achieve the tall doors of the ballroom. 'Chaperoning is much more work than I expected.'

'Leave it to Onslow, and let *us* to the floor,' said Faulkes gaily.

'What a lovely idea!' said Georgette, accepting his escorting arm. But she was thinking. Regis' shock when verbally attacked by her sister had been swiftly followed by a certain look in his eye. His eyes had followed Jocasta's every commanding move as she rallied her troops. Her sister, too enthralled by her need to save the baronet from further harm, had not noticed at all. Georgette knew she must not run ahead of herself. But it seemed, it really seemed, that the look was one of amusement and something else. Something that Georgette might call doting fondness.

CHAPTER 21

Visiting the Invalid

It was not long before the Onslow party declared themselves bored with the ball, and took the carriage back to Onslow House.

Certain looks had already been exchanged between the Onslows, but Georgette sought some clarification from her sister.

'Did you all see Sir Damon off without incident?'

'Yes. He was foolish beyond permission to come to such a crowded place, but I believe it is the fault of too much cosseting by his valet, and a fear of being bored. He has asked Cecilia and I to call tomorrow, for I believe he does not want his gentlemen friends to see him in his weakened condition.'

'Ah, yes! The threat to his manhood!' said Onslow feigning sadness.

'Gentlemen worry about the silliest things, I find. George is just so. When he broke his ankle, he would not permit the Bailey brothers to enter Castle Fortune, do you remember, Georgie?'

'Vaguely. But I supposed that he had fallen out with them again. Frederick Bailey only just tolerates George's humours.'

'Well, on that occasion, I heard George say to Papa that he would not let Fredrick or James Bailey crow over his wound.'

'As if they would!'

'Perhaps it is a case of your brother judging others on his own behaviour.' The marquis looked at Georgette. 'Forgive me, I should not speak so of your family.'

'Well,' said Jocasta, laughing, 'it is your family now, too, and the rest of us say much worse about George.'

'Isn't it strange?' muttered Georgette, 'that even when one knows who he is, one cannot deny how handsome he is.'

'Some of my friends have complimented me on his good looks, and even when I tell them he has a dark heart, they are *still* admiring!'

'Oh, a handsome man with a dark heart is many young ladies' dream figure,' said Onslow, 'for which I lay blame on the circulating libraries. That is why Regis has always been so popular among young females. Thankfully, the Demon King has no truck with them whatsoever, and so their hearts remain unbroken.'

'And in the case of George, thankfully we can depend upon him to open his mouth and disgust at least half of the female population.'

They laughed. Jocasta was becoming daily more comfortable with Onslow. He had been her tall, handsome, and somewhat intimidating brother-in-law, but lately his private jokes with Georgette often included her. Sir Justin Faulkes, too, no longer seemed a just too-kind reminder of her humiliation, but another teasing friend. Jocasta was able to appreciate Georgette better, too. She was aware that her sister had sought to save her from her predicament in Papa's house, then tried to divert her mind from the Portia and Paxton situation, with a much less heavy hand than others. Moreover, that she had done so at a time that could almost be considered her honeymoon. Too many times had Jocasta surprised the couple with the marquis' arm around her sister's shoulder, or saw a secret hand clasp, for her not to know she was intruding on their sweetest time. Yet neither Georgette, nor Onslow, had ever made her feel awkward or unaccepted, and Jocasta had begun to be if not happy, then certainly at peace, in their home. Georgette and she, who had lived so many years together with the others in their castle home, had spent more time together in London than in many years at Castle Fortune. Georgette had shopped with her, planned some of her wardrobe, joked around the dinner and breakfast tables with her, rode with her, driven with her, and protected her from the unpleasantness of others — such as the Viscountess Swanson, or their own male relatives. Jocasta had not been able to confide everything, but she had come to think that Georgie would understand even that. Her sister, in the past, had kept her secret love for Onslow locked in her heart for over two years, because she could not share her pain. And Jocasta could not share hers, as yet, either. For Georgette, as she now understood, would be in pain herself at the thought of Jocasta's suffering, like she really did have a sister — a relationship more like the affectionate Bailey sisters, Amethyst and Maria.

When they left the carriage, Georgie said to her, casually, 'I have a mind to visit Regis with you tomorrow.' She looked at her husband. 'But not you, Lucian.'

'Good!' said the marquis, callously.

'Leave some laudanum on the side table, Mr McKay.'

Mr McKay cast his deprecating eye over his master's prone form, stretched out on the yellow brocade sofa in the large salon, with a rug over his knees, and one arm dramatically trailing the floor.

'Laudanum? Whenever have ye ever let anyone give ye laudanum, apart from when your arm was almost blown off in Portugal?' Mr McKay's tone lacked either the servility or disinterest of a servant, but Regis did not seem to mind. 'I told that stupid nurse ye widnae have it. Are ye in so much pain? The sawbones said ye could puncture a lung if ye're not careful.'

'I do not wish to *take* the laudanum, old friend, just to—'

A noise of arrival was heard in the hall, indubitably of ladies from the chatter, and Mr McKay finished for the baronet, '—you just want to *display* the laudanum, ye rascal.'

The baronet's yellow eyes sparkled up at him as the ladies were announced.

There was a pause as they stopped on the threshold and beheld the touching scene, before the baronet said, 'Help me up, Mr McKay.'

The servant gave his arm as the baronet sat up, only a manly bite to his bottom lip giving away the pain this manoeuvre evidently cost him. Seeing it, Mr McKay made a derisive sound, but a glare from Regis held him in check.

'Damon! Is it very painful?' Cecilia rushed forward. 'Not but what it serves you right for coming to the ball last night. I suppose you must have been dreadfully jarred by the crowd on your way in. How has he been, Mr McKay?'

'He needs to rest, Miss Cecilia, without knocking himself about on the back of a horse or the like, as he threatened this morning. Rest is the only remedy for ribs.'

'And his head!' exclaimed Jocasta. 'Does it still hurt, sir? He had a lump the size of a billiard ball on it.'

'How do you know?' asked Cecilia interestedly.

Jocasta's eyes went from Cecilia's to Regis', who looked back with two scrolling eyebrows — his amused look, Jocasta knew.

'I, uh, Sir Damon told me, since I had seen the hoof hit his head, you know.'

No, thought the interested Georgette, you must have *touched* him. She regarded Regis' wicked amusement with a scolding look of her own. But he missed it, for his eyes were on Jocasta's blushes. More and more, Georgette was inclined to trust him. But why did he not speak of his intentions last night? It was obvious that Jocasta, while perhaps unaware of it herself, was head-over-heels. Did he mean to live up to his honour, or be devilish, still?

Jocasta's attention was claimed by Cecilia for a moment, and Georgette watched as Regis' yellow green eyes went from challenging amusement to gentle fondness. He must have become aware of her gaze, for his turned to herself and gave her, to Georgette's amazement, smiling reassurance.

Both younger girls indulged in conversation with the patient, largely consisting of terse orders, which the baronet meekly accepted.

'You will not go out in company for at least another fortnight, or until the bones have started to knit together. I asked the apothecary who brought Tom's tonic how long you should stay still, and he said at least two weeks, if not more.'

252

'You must know that I am famous for my ability to heal, Cecilia. My sporting wounds have always healed quickly.'

'You,' said Jocasta, cruelly, 'are not a young man anymore, and must do as you are bid.'

'Yes, Miss Fortune.' Regis inclined his head sarcastically. 'I shall do my level best to protect my agèd bones.'

'You may laugh, Damon, but if anything were to happen to you, *I* should have no one in the world, except for Aunt Agnes, and you cannot say she is a comfort.' Cecilia's self-interest amused and touched him, since it was more of an acknowledgement of his position in her life than Miss Montgomery was wont to admit.

Presently, the duke called at the house to take the two youngest ladies for a drive, but Georgette and Jocasta opted to stay behind, as the baronet had requested a piece on the piano to aid his diversion.

'Oh, you wish a ballad, perhaps, to entertain you,' ventured the marchioness, 'or—'

'*Something in A major!*' Both the baronet and Jocasta said at once, and then laughed. Georgette looked at them, quite oblivious to the rest of the world for that second, before Jocasta stood and headed to the piano at one side of the room.

'It may *sound awful,*' said Jocasta with spirit, quoting Regis to himself, 'but it is a little better than the last time you heard it.' She sighed, 'But I don't have my music, and I don't think I can remember it aright.'

'I had someone look it out for you, in the hope that you, or someone, might play it for me.' His eye found the marchioness, who shook her ringlets while Jocasta laughed.

'You would not want to hear my sister play, I assure you.'

'How ungenerous of you!' declared Regis.

'Oh, no,' said Georgette with a smile, 'she is quite right. I have no musical skill at all, and can only enjoy the skill of others.'

Georgette was about to sit beside Jocasta, to turn the pages, but she suddenly chose to sit at the window side of the piano bench, so as not to block the baronet's view.

It was an uplifting melody, and Georgette observed Regis watching her sister. His eyes seemed to caress her animated face, and at the joyous smile she gave him at the end of her piece, she saw him catch a breath. Georgette, who was no good at stratagems at all, felt the need to at least *try* at this very promising occasion.

'I *must* visit Madam Godot's about the figured silk I'm wearing to the reception at Buckingham House — I quite forgot!' she said mendaciously. 'You stay Jocasta, I'll send in the maid, and you may play a little more for Sir Damon. He must be mightily bored. I shall return in the carriage in two hours at the most. Will that suit you, sir?' she added, favouring the baronet with an innocent stare. 'If you become too tired, Jocasta may read a book in the library, perhaps, until I return.'

Regis inclined his head, his eye equally innocent. 'You must fulfil your commission, my dear marchioness.'

Jocasta was a little perturbed, but she met the baronet's look before he laid back against the sofa back, closing his eyes. 'Could you play it again, Miss Fortune, before I call for refreshments? Perhaps you will play it better this time.'

She did not give this sally any attention but merely said, 'The same piece? I could search for another.'

'No, the same piece. I find it cheering.'

She took the chance to look at him properly, since his eyes were closed, and she noted even from this distance, that pain had given him pallor. Her sister Cassie, who had ridden with them this morning, had said, when she heard of their plan to visit the invalid, 'I have heard it said that broken ribs inflict as much pain on the sufferer as God has seen fit to burden women with during childbirth. But I *very* much doubt it.' Now Jocasta, seeing his strong face so pale, did believe it. He had not praised her play directly, but she wished to lift his spirits, and was glad to play again a piece she had, at least, practised.

An appreciative silence of two seconds reigned after she lifted her hands from the keys. Then she looked over at him as he said, without opening his eyes. 'Could you ring?'

He dispatched a footman for refreshments and Jocasta moved, a little nervously, to sit opposite him on a handsome, spindle legged chair. His eyes had remained closed, but he opened them suddenly to look into hers. 'Might you dispose this cursed pillow for me?'

She moved to do so, though the maid had risen from her corner to act, and then sat back down again in a second. Regis sat up, grasping Jocasta's arm for support while she placed the pillow behind his back. She felt much too close to the warmth of his body, too conscious of him. 'Hold!' he said — as she, shaken a little by the strangely languid atmosphere, began to pull away. 'There is something on your cuff.' Strong, gentle fingers held her hand in place while his thumb moved over the muslin ruffle on the inside of her delicate wrist. She looked upon it, dazed, as the thumb gently caressed, once, twice, three times. Her back blocked the maid's view, but Jocasta's cheeks burned, nevertheless. The marchioness' servant, who felt her young mistress had been static too long, coughed to make her presence felt. In a dream, Jocasta took away her released hand, moved back and sat down opposite him, just as a servant arrived with a tray. She sat on the edge of the chair, sipping her drink with her eyes lowered.

'It has improved,' Regis said casually.

'I beg your pardon?'

'The piece. It sounded a *little* better.' He was disparaging her in a teasing voice.

'I shall never play for you again!' said Jocasta, glad to be angry once more.

'Yes, you will.' Regis said it with insolent certainty. She glared at him, but his lazy smile and the wicked, narrowed eyes shook her. *Why* was he —? If this was flirting, Jocasta had never been flirted with before. *This* was unbearable, dreadful. *Demonic!* She looked away immediately, and peeked through her lashes to check. His lip curled, his eyes were still narrowed and wicked. She jumped up, scaring the maid in the corner. 'I must go, Sir Damon. I have remembered an appointment.'

'Really?' the awful man said, with no attempt at *politesse*. 'Well, then. If you must, Miss Fortune.'

'Do not rise sir! Pray do not.'

'I shan't.'

'Goodbye!'

She was in the hallway with little remembrance of how she got there, and the maid joined her in retrieving her bonnet and spencer. They left precipitously.

When the Marchioness of Onslow was announced a half-hour later, she looked at the baronet, who stood before the fire, with her brows raised. 'I trust you made good use of your time, Sir Damon?' she said, briskly.

'She ran off,' he said with a shrug. The marchioness looked her reprimand. 'If I had done as I presume you wished, she would have refused to see me again.'

'Why ever—?' demanded Georgette.

'She might have attributed the offer to the dreaded pity. Or to an *honourable necessity* caused by her visit to my chamber. So, I have begun softly.'

Georgette put her head to one side. 'Ah, so you complimented her? Or thanked her gallantly, perhaps? I imagine that you are practised in the flirtatious arts.'

'Neither. I do not usually give myself the trouble. The direct approach usually suffices. But in this case ... I am not such a sluggard as to use a mere compliment. At that rate, I should need more months to speak my piece.'

Georgette gave him a dreadful frown of her own. 'What did you *do*, sir?'

'Only a *very* little,' Regis' wicked eyes teased her. 'She was attended at all times, remember.'

Georgette's eyebrows rose. 'And yet she bolted?'

'I have introduced the idea in her head, never fear.'

Georgette shook her head at him. 'You are devilish indeed. I only hope you are not too clever for your own purpose.' She frowned. 'Is there anything I can do?'

'She's afraid. Best leave it to me to take the ribbons.'

'My sister is not a team, sir!'

'Should you care for some ratafia, Lady Onslow?'

'I should not!' She looked at him, assessing. 'You had better take care. I only trust you because Onslow does. And because ...' she thought of the look in his eye as he watched her younger sister.

'Don't worry, my lady, I have always known how to point my leaders.'

CHAPTER 22

Confusion and Rage

There had been a ball that night that had to be attended.

Jocasta met many people there, and supposed she may have talked some sense. Cecilia and Tom were there, and both remarked on her lack of attention. Tom complained to her when Sir Justin Faulkes carried off Cecilia for a waltz.

'She is becoming a deal too fashionable,' he had said, watching the froth of Cecilia's muslin gown disappear in the throng.

'Indeed! She has refused two offers already!' said Jocasta thoughtlessly.

The duke stood to attention. 'Offers? *Cecilia?*'

Jocasta had been called to her senses. 'I should not have said so, Tom. I do not expect she wished it known. I am a little dull tonight.'

'No ... I won't say,' said the duke at once. 'Of course.' There had been silence and Jocasta had not had the wit to fill it. Eventually he said, 'Not *Faulkes*?'

'No, no. I cannot really say any more, Tom!'

'No. But who would want to marry Cecilia? It seems very strange...'

'You sound just like my brother George,' said Jocasta, disgusted. 'He can never imagine what any man might want with his sisters.'

'Speaking of which, your papa is almost upon us. Thankfully, his height makes it easy to catch him. Do not look up. Let us head to supper early.'

'You are a true friend, Tom,' had said Jocasta, rushing off with him.

This, and an interlude with her sister Cassandra, was all she could remember.

Cassandra, at her side at one point, had been greeted by Maria, Lady Bucknell, who introduced her upright husband.

'It has been an age, Maria. You look as though marriage agrees with you. It is wonderful to meet you, my lord,' Cassie held out a decided hand to Bucknell, who found himself taking it. 'You are not what I would have expected for Maria, it is true, but my sister Georgette assures me you are gentler than you appear!'

Jocasta groaned, and Maria looked pained. But unexpectedly, Bucknell came to the rescue. 'And my wife assures me that your *forthrightness* hides a warm heart.'

Mr Hudson, upon whom Cassie's frankness never appeared to have any effect, laughed heartily at this. 'Quite right, quite right, my lord. We will be friends all together, I am sure.'

It occurred to Jocasta that Cassie had the manners of her papa and George, but as Bucknell had said, a much purer intention.

'I always thought,' Cassie had said to her in the coach, 'that London life would be just the ticket for you, Jocasta. But you seemed a little lacklustre this evening.'

'I have something of a head, I'm afraid,' she had replied.

'Syrup of prunes!' said Mr Hudson with crashing bluntness. 'Pain in the canister is always caused by an irregular constitution, I say!'

Cassie laughed loudly. 'It is the only medicine he recognises. I daresay I could have Scarlet Fever and my husband would request the apothecary to send syrup of prunes.'

But secretly, Cassie squeezed her hand. Her sisters were more affectionate at heart than Jocasta had ever imagined. Upon reflection, Jocasta considered that it must be the left-over influence from their dear, deceased mama.

Now it was a new day. At least she could be sure not to see the Demon King. She would not visit again today, as Cecilia had already suggested last night — citing a need to keep Regis entertained, lest he disobey his physician.

'You may visit on the morrow and I shall try to go with Georgette during the week,' said Jocasta, vaguely. 'For we may count on Onslow and Sir Justin to take their turns. They will be much more amusing to Sir Damon than mere females.'

'I suppose...' said Cecilia, looking at her strangely. Only yesterday, Jocasta had been as concerned as she. 'By any chance ... was Damon cross-tempered after I left? Did he say something unpleasant?'

'Oh, he disparaged my playing, only,' said Jocasta, brightly. 'I do not mind it — you know he thinks his bad manners amusing.'

'I shall punish him for it, never fear!' said Cecilia with relish.

Now, coming back from the morning ride, Jocasta dressed for the day with a new feeling of freedom. She had blown off yesterday's events, and was now set to enjoy her breakfast and the morning calls. Her morning dress of pink-striped muslin suited her very well. Her arms were bare, but it was a mild day. She regarded her offending wrist (which even now betrayed her by a wave of heat) and by some sudden impulse took up a scrap of pink ribbon and tied it, like a bandage around, so that she could not see her pulse. The maid who tended her adjusted it to a bow, saying, 'That is such a pretty touch, miss, you have such an eye for lovely things.' It had not been what she meant by it, but never mind, Jocasta tripped down the stairs for breakfast with a light heart.

Sir Damon Regis stood at the foot of the stairs, beholding her blandly. She stopped for a moment in shock, one hand on the banister rail, and his gaze dropped to the ribbon at her wrist. The eyes that met hers smiled wickedly. Her colour rose, but she came down the stairs and passed him without a glance.

'Not even a greeting, Jocasta? How cruel!' he murmured, but she continued to the breakfast table without reply.

It was a strangely charged, but not as jocular, breakfast table. Georgette looked concerned at Jocasta's coldness, Onslow was therefore concerned by Georgette, and even Sir Justin Faulkes, who had been strangely perturbed on the ride, was not his usual amusing, self. Only Regis seemed relaxed, thanking the Onslows for their diverting invitation, at an hour when he could be sure the streets were quiet. 'For I have promised Miss Montgomery and Miss Fortune that I shall not allow myself to be buffeted by crowds!' he said with a general smile.

Then he turned to Jocasta, 'And see how obedient I am being, Miss Fo rtune!'

Jocasta shot him the coldest of looks, while Faulkes looked a shocked enquiry at Onslow, who nodded.

'Cassie means to go home tomorrow,' said Georgette to her sister. 'Did she tell you?'

'She did. Papa and George have finally defeated her. She says she is quite sorry for Portia.'

'I asked Portia how she coped with such horrible proximity daily, and she says she only sees them occasionally. They are frequently from home.'

'She will miss Cassandra, though. For she was always able to draw Papa's fire, usually by asking him to explain himself when he is rude.'

Onslow laughed. 'I think her husband has his own simple ways of drawing off the fire, too. He is a gentleman who is most impervious to a snub!'

'Yes, a simple, good man, I thought,' remarked Faulkes.

'Of all the people able to deal with Papa, I think Jocasta's friend Miss Carmichael is the *most* accomplished,' offered Georgette.

'Really?' laughed Regis. 'It doesn't surprise me!'

Onslow noted that his friend, Faulkes, had looked conscious at the mention of Jocasta's friend and his colour heightened. He saw his intelligent wife notice too, so there was no doubt that later she would ask the questions that gentlemen friends found it difficult to broach. What *might* he have done in the days before Georgette? On-slow thought now. Suggested an outing to a gin house and hope that alcohol might open his friend's mouth — then stew over any hints that fell from Justin's loosened lips. His marchioness' way was more direct.

He saw his friend Faulkes observe the suave smiles that Regis was directing at his furious little sister-in-law, and wondered at the look on Justin's face.

'You should go, Sir Damon, before the world awakes and the streets are full once more,' said Jocasta tightly.

'I am at your command, Miss Fortune. I'll leave at once, but only if you say you will visit this afternoon to help me pass a pleasant half hour of my enforced confinement.'

'I am sure that Cecilia comes today.'

'But she does not play. You must come and play for me again, you know.' His smile was sure and affectionate, and it made Jocasta blush with fury and embarrassment. 'You'll bring her, marchioness, won't you?' he said to Georgette.

'Certainly, my friend. At two, then!'

He bowed himself out, and a furious Jocasta turned to her sister. *'Georgie!'*

Georgette hardly looked at her, but her eyes followed the departure of the other baronet, who had waved himself out casually. 'I must just catch Justin!' She ran out after him, leaving Jocasta suffocated by her resentment. She could not wait! She was in the grip of that new, horrible impulsiveness again, and she knew it. She took some turns around the now empty room. What did the awful man mean by it? All those smiles and claims of obedience, as though her orders meant anything to him at all, his shocking display of affection — and within her own family circle! No one had seemed to react, moreover. What did Georgette and Onslow mean by *that*? Was it visible only to herself? Was she truly a candidate for Bedlam, imagining things? But no, his remark about her ribbon! She now pulled it off and threw it, furiously, in the grate. It had betrayed her! Dreadful scrap of silk.

She ordered her pelisse and bonnet and called for her maid. Going to find her one friend in London was useless, for how could she explain herself, or Regis' devilry, to Cecilia? She could not go alone, and she would not wait for Georgette, who seemed, suddenly, untrustworthy. If it had not been that Georgie had left her alone at the baronet's house yesterday, Jocasta would not now be uncomfortable. She wanted to drive with Regis in the park so that she could find a quiet path and just shout at him, demanding his motives, and telling him how offended he made her — but she could not. Her whole being wanted to rap down his door *now*, and scream at him, but she could not.

Her promise of making no more ruinous scenes she would keep.

There was only one other option.

Meanwhile, Georgette had caught up with Sir Justin and dragged the baronet, without compunction, into a salon.

'I'm flattered, of course, marchioness,' Faulkes said, with insouciance, 'but I believe your husband is still in the house.'

'Stop it, Justin, and just tell me, for I will nip at you until you do ...'

Justin sat and crossed his legs, 'I have no idea what—'

'Justin!'

'It is nought...' he looked at her concerned eyes as she had now joined him on the sofa. 'Just ... Miss Montgomery! I believe I have made a misstep ... it is not like me ...'

'Cecilia? Jocasta's friend?'

'Yes. I danced with her last evening, and I should not.'

'Why not?'

'This is ... I sound like a coxcomb, but ...'

'I have noticed that she admires you.'

He met her eyes more easily. 'Yes, I thought so, and therefore I avoided ...! A young girl's *tendre* ... well, it is a dangerous thing.'

'Then how came you to waltz with her last evening, if you were avoiding her? Do you perhaps...'

'Heavens, no! She is a child! But because she is Jocasta's friend we are often together and she ... well, last night she demanded that I waltz with her.'

'She's a minx! Regis has his hands full there.'

'I know ... but situated as we are, and in front of others, it would have been churlish to decline.'

'I see. Because we are all so intimate these days. It was difficult for you. But there is nothing in that, surely? She did not confess her feelings during a waltz.'

'Not precisely. She told me an amusing pig story.'

'Pardon?'

'It seems we met when she was a child. And I could tell that I have become some sort of memory to her ...' He sighed. 'I passed it off lightly, but she was upset, I saw.'

'Perhaps she imagined that the memory should have made you incline to her! I'm afraid we ladies are apt to create fairy tales in our heads...'

'I cannot decide if I have done her ill. Perhaps I have given her hope by agreeing to the dance when I already *knew*...! I feel like a cad, and as if something else is now required of me...' At Georgette's guffaw, he sighed. 'Lucian would understand.'

'Gentlemen's honour! You and Regis and Lucian!' she held the baronet's hands. 'On no account are you to do *anything*, Justin — do you hear me?' He frowned down. 'Listen to me. It is a young girl's crush only and it would be fatal for Cecilia to have a reluctant husband.' He did not raise his eyes and she shook at his captured hands. 'Do you hear me?'

He looked up, laughing. 'Get your claws off me! I promise not to be precipitate. But it is Almacks tonight. I do not think I should go...'

'You shall go, and be jolly in the company, and never notice her at all. That is the best way. Pass it off, Justin. I'm sure you know how!'

He looked then. 'But she is a child alone. I've thought about it — and it changes things.'

'She has Regis and Enderby — she is hardly alone. And she is too sensible to refine too much on a waltz!'

The marquis walked in, 'Georgette, I am going to ...' he looked at his wife clasping the hands of another man, while the culprits looked up at him with no sense of shame apparent. 'Take your hands...' he began dangerously, but a glance showed him that his wife was the one who had possessed herself of Faulkes' hands.

'I'm going!' announced Faulkes and sauntered off, putting a hand consolingly on the marquis' shoulder as he passed. 'Good thing you came in just then, Lucian! Who knows *what* might have happened?'

'Justin!' Georgette called after him, 'You must mind me!' He nodded over his shoulder and was gone.

'Well!' said Onslow as Georgette tripped towards him, 'You inconstant woman!'

'I, sir, have an appointment with Cassandra!' she laughed at him.

He captured her on her way past and wrapped his arms around her, dropping his chin on her shoulder. 'Wait a moment!' he said in a piteous tone, 'I need the reassurance!'

She wrapped her own arms about him, hugging him soundly. She laid a cheek on his other shoulder, knowing he was only partially joking. 'You are silly!' she crooned, and he sighed, content.

Jocasta wondered when, or if, the two inches of skin at her wrist might cease to burn. After that visit to Regis yesterday, she had walked out of the baronet's house and had taken some turns of corners before her maid asked, 'Where are you wishful to go, Miss Jocasta? Only we are...'

Jocasta had stopped. They were once more in front of Regis' house. 'How...?' she wondered. 'Ah,' she said to the maid, 'I am a trifle distracted. I meant to take the road to—' There was no need to explain, she reminded herself. With more attention she took the route home.

What had he meant by it? She remembered those wicked, narrowed eyes... Previously, she had been treated by him with cool indifference, sometimes irritation, and once, almost fatally, by compassion. This last had kept her angry for days. She had pushed him away and ignored him until the carriage accident. She could still hardly think about the crack to his head and crunch of his bones without a shudder. She had exposed herself by bursting into his chamber. And even earlier, her running to him in the park that day: it was shameful. Was this change in him some response to her betrayal of feelings that even she had been unaware of?

This behaviour of his was not the flirtatious compliments of cheerful Lord Jeffries, or the serious devoted looks of Mr Mark York. This was the behaviour of a rake, she thought, the look from his eye wicked and teasing and inviting her to ... *what*? If another man had given her such a look, had behaved in such a knowing fashion, had taken such a liberty, she would have known what to do. Ignore him disdainfully and instantly let her protector, The Marquis of Onslow, know of his shameful behaviour.

But it was Regis. The wickedness that he was famed for, she had never seen, or only in jest. He had become, without her knowledge, her most trusted friend. Did her past behaviour make her seem loose to him? Is this why he had behaved so wickedly? For there was no disguising that he had acted with intention. To insult her? To punish her for risking his reputation by her impulsive behaviour? But no, he had been alarmed, but amused, she was sure, by her entrance into his chamber. Everything he had done for her, every lesson that she had taken to heart, had shown him to be a fount of wisdom, a man whose care of her, she now saw, was obvious. So, *what* was he now about? What did he mean by it?

Was she composing a melodrama for Covent Garden? A friend brushing some invisible dust from her wrist. That was all. She was making too much of it. But still, the tender skin throbbed and burned. It was *she* who was making a mountain from a mere molehill. She who was shaking while he, probably, had merely crossed his legs and supped more wine. She would stop these nonsensical thoughts now.

And so, she could, if only she could forget those mocking, wicked, eyes. He had *meant* it.

'Miss ...' had said a small voice by her side, 'you have overshot the door.'

Jocasta had not attempted an explanation, but had turned back to Onslow House and moved up the stairs in a daze.

Then had come the next day's breakfast, and she could no longer doubt his wickedness at all.

***

Cecilia, still eating pound cake at a rather late breakfast with Mrs Usher, was monstrously pleased with herself. 'Do you not think, madame, that Sir Justin Faulkes is the most elegant dancer?'

'He is ...' Mrs Usher cast a disparaging look at her pretty charge.

'And so very handsome!'

'Mmm,' muttered her hostess, discouraging.

'I never thought I should be called upon to waltz with him...'

'Nor I, indeed,' agreed Mrs Usher calmly. 'I must almost suppose you asked him yourself.'

As no reply came from the other side of the table, Mrs Usher lifted her eyes from the roll she had been selecting, to look at Cecilia. '*Tell* me you did not!'

'Well, I wanted to speak to him of our previous meeting when I was young, and the waltz is the only dance that allows one to converse.'

'*Cecilia!* That is outside of enough! You were lucky not to meet with the shocking rebuff you deserved.' Her charge blushed at the most serious tone she had heard from her easy-going chaperone. 'You knew that was not becoming of you! I hope no one else heard you—'

'Only Tom. He was crosser than you, but I ignored him.'

'Because he knows what shocking behaviour that is for a young lady. If a patroness were to hear of it, you would be refused admittance to Almacks.'

Cecilia, not used to authority, had flaming cheeks, but she was sensible enough to know that she had overstepped herself. 'I shall not do so again. But Sir Justin did not seem shocked at all. He agreed without hesitation.'

'And what else should he do when the female who behaves thus is a friend of one of his closest companions? He had no other option, even if your behaviour gave him disgust.'

Cecilia ate the rest of her breakfast in silence, but it rankled with her all morning. So, later, when Tom came to take her to visit with Regis, she displayed her sense of injustice.

'She said Sir Justin must have felt *disgust* at my behaviour. What language ... when he was perfectly pleasant to me, and even laughed at the story about Betty the pig, and said he remembered it well.'

'I told you last night it was fast behaviour, Cissie, but you would not listen. You trapped him, and he's too good-natured to give you the set-down you deserved!'

'I hate you, Tom!'

'Do so if you must. But just know this is not Crumley Park and you cannot behave as you please in London!'

He sounded more serious than usual, and Cecilia was a little chastened. She kept a sulky silence, hoping he might break it, but it was she who did, after three tense minutes. 'I *know* I must behave differently in London, Tom, and I have already promised Mrs Usher never to behave so again. Can we not forget it for the moment?'

'Yes, we can forget it,' Enderby sighed. He snapped the reins. 'It is just that this is only one thing. It is giving me dyspepsia to see you running around and always having to wonder what next you will do.'

'What business is it of yours?'

'So many fellows seem to be after you,' he said with an indecent amount of incredulity. He looked down at her and observed her smug head tilt. 'I cannot understand it at all.' She gave him a look of annoyance. 'But not every fellow knows how to toe the line, Cissie, and you are quite silly enough to find yourself in a scrape in no time.'

'You, of all people, must know that I can defend myself.'

'I have no doubt that a molester would come off the worst at your hands, Cissie, but not before your good name would be trampled. It makes my head hurt, as well as my stomach.'

'Pooh!' she scoffed. But she was remembering Mrs Usher's words. She was *certain* that Sir Justin had not ... *disgust?* Surely not! But she rethought some recent behaviour and realised she had been lucky. She *had* received some improper requests to seek a quieter spot, from two certain gentlemen. She realised, belatedly, that she was careless enough that if either had been someone she felt an inclination towards, she may very well have agreed. Perhaps her dominance at Crumley had had a bad effect on her adherence to the proprieties. She began to seriously regret the lack of a mother's guiding hand. She assumed too easily that she could handle any situation, she understood that now. In London, it was not what *happened*, necessarily, but what was *suspected* to have happened. She had heard enough *on dits* in the months she had been here to know how fast rumours spread.

But it would not do to let Tom think he was in the right. Just on principle.

CHAPTER 23

Cat Among the Pigeons

Having thrown the cat in amongst the pigeons again, Regis was feeling cheerful. He knew that Jocasta was seething to have it out with him, and she must even now be plotting an occasion, since, knowing her, she could hardly wait until tomorrow. To wait until this afternoon's visit with her sister, when an opportunity to chew him out would hardly be afforded her, would not suit either.

He was, still, in a good deal of pain from his ribs, but he found his new situation with Jocasta vastly entertaining. Keeping her cross with him was better than making her embarrassed and afraid by offering for her quite yet. If he did so right now, she would suspect him — she might withdraw entirely, and that would never do. He wished her to come to him on her own. He wished her to cease to worry if he were honourably offering for a woman to whom he had given expectations, and see, really see, that his feelings matched her own. For he, noticing the marchioness noticing him, had realised: he could not take his eyes off Jocasta, and he never wished to again.

His opinion of her had been formed, in part, by her appearance and in part by the social butterfly that she appeared to be among her admirers. But after he had been forced by his conscience to watch Jocasta, he had entered into the enterprise with increasing interest. For Jocasta's beauty and society manners hid her extreme sensitivity, her bravery, her kindness. In the midst of her own pain, she had been concerned not to give pain to others. His little beauty was not sure of herself yet, but she was changing under his gaze — for unlike others who used their hurt to embitter, Jocasta was using hers to become a better person. Invitations to sporting events, challenges to ridiculously dangerous wagers he had been happy to ignore this Season, as he had sought out the fascinating Jocasta Fortune. He had begun to realise that he was watching her for his own sake, just as much as hers.

He had a small concern. Jocasta certainly cared for him: all her out-of-character impulsive acts had shown him so. She had protected him like a lioness protects her cub. But did she love him as a man? Did she even know herself if she loved him?

But it did not matter, he thought, one dreadful eyebrow aloft. He would make her.

⚬⚬⚬

Jocasta's steps led to her papa's townhouse. As she mounted the steps and rang the bell, she had the awful presentiment that Papa might be at home — so when the butler opened the door she enquired, hissing, 'Is my father at home, Nisbet?'

'No, Miss Fortune, he left after breakfast, as usual.'

Jocasta swept past him. 'My sister?'

'In the morning room, miss.'

She did not wait to hand her maid her bonnet, but carried on to the morning room with what Nisbet considered unbecoming haste.

'Portia—!' she began. Portia was setting stitches, looking miserable, and the reason was perfectly understandable. For their brother George was warming his coattails at the fire nearby her, his smug expression denoting that he had been saying unpleasant things. Jocasta, so wound up by her mission, and full of intention, was thrown off for a moment. Portia looked up with supplicating eyes, and Jocasta snapped out of it. 'Did you forget?' she answered the look in Portia's eye, 'Georgette is already awaiting us at Madame Godot's.'

'Females and their fripperies,' said George with disgust. 'They exist only to cost money, Papa says.'

'Well, on this occasion it will be Onslow's money, George, so you need not regard it,' snipped Jocasta, uncharacteristically.

'Ah! Yes, Georgette must be waiting — I forgot,' said Portia, looking her gratitude. 'How silly of me. I shall go and fetch my pelisse.'

They escaped the house in a trice and exchanged a giggle at the bottom of the stairs.

'*Thank* you,' said Portia, heartfelt.

'No need. I came to make use of you on this occasion, Portia.'

'Whatever—?'

'You must go somewhere with me.'

This was Jocasta in commanding mode, a version Portia had not seen for some time. Somehow it cheered her, for since her engagement, her sister had been far too polite to her. 'Not to Georgette?' she enquired.

'No. And without telling falsehoods, I would prefer if Georgette did not know.'

Portia was pleased to conspire, in the spirit of sisterly reunion, but she was still a little shocked. 'Something you cannot tell *Georgie* about? I cannot be sure—'

'You owe me something, Portia...' Jocasta reminded her.

Portia blushed rosily, but said decisively, 'Of course I'll go. But hold! Robbie ... Lord Paxton ... is visiting this morning, I cannot—'

'Leave a message for him with Nisbet. I'll send the maid back—'

'He'll be here directly...!'

'Very well,' said Jocasta, thinking on her feet, 'we'll await him at the corner. He might come too, but only if you can seal his lips.'

'Robbie is an honourable, noble—'

'Yes, yes!' said Jocasta briskly. 'Don't go on so.'

Portia was concerned. Jocasta was evidently on edge, and had some object in view. It was unlike her sister to be impulsive, however, and Portia felt she owed her, indeed. If she could assuage a little of her guilt with this service, she would do so. However, in their past life when Jocasta had some mischief in view, she would look naughty. Now, she looked a little too grave.

As the two girls waited at the corner, a light chaise appeared and stopped rather abruptly.

'Portia!' cried the slender figure of Lord Paxton, emerging quickly. His tone annoyed Jocasta once more. It contained surprise, shock, reproval, and passion all at once. The pair were just as irritating as ever, thought Jocasta, but without rancour. Having a cup of tea constituted a drama with them — full of melting looks over the teacups — but they were her only hope, at the moment. Four of them, including the maid, squashed into Paxton's coach, Jocasta bringing up the rear since she had given the direction to the coachman.

The couple had conducted a whispered interchange, but ceased when Jocasta got in. 'Where are we going?' Paxton enquired after she was seated.

Jocasta looked at him, and then at the attendant maid, significantly. 'To visit a sick friend,' she said, and turned her face to indicate her determination to say no more.

They were admitted to a house by the casually miserable butler, and Jocasta said to Paxton, 'Go and pay your respects to Sir Damon, who was injured a few days ago.'

'Regis?' said Paxton, confused. 'This is Regis' house?'

Jocasta sighed. He was perfectly useless as a conspirator. 'I wish to speak to Portia, Lord Paxton. So, on you go!'

'But Regis — I hardly know him!'

'Paxton!' ordered Jocasta, on her last nerve.

Lord Paxton moved through the door the butler held for him, looking over his shoulder at Portia, as though for aid. Jocasta once more reflected that she was well out of that connection.

She had some whispered words with Portia. After Jocasta had laid out her request, Portia's eyes were wide with excitement and concern at the same time.

'This is not what you think, Portia. I *do* have to speak to Regis privately, but it concerns another — and not I.' She had thought of this excuse on the way. 'It is regarding my friend Cecilia Montgomery, but it is secret.'

'Miss Montgomery. Ah, Sir Damon is some sort of guardian ...'

'Precisely! It is a matter of some urgency, but Georgette was busy and so...'

'Of course. I shall do just as you say. Rely upon me!'

They both moved through to the salon where Jocasta had played only yesterday.

Paxton was standing stiffly opposite the baronet, who was looking bored. As ever, Jocasta was secretly pleased when Regis displayed his boredom with Paxton. As the ladies had walked in, the baronet said, 'Welcome!' and his eyes sought Jocasta's, amused.

Jocasta stayed at the door, the sight of his wicked knowingness igniting her temper again. Portia moved forward to enquire politely after his injuries.

He responded in kind, then looked up at the stiff little figure by the door.

'I have brought my sister to play for you,' Jocasta said, in a cold voice that rang across the room.

'As I see,' those eyes locked on hers.

'Portia, will you play now?' said Jocasta, in a strangely removed tone. 'Lord Paxton might assist you.'

All of this was abrupt enough to be rude, but Paxton, seeking enlightenment of his love, was surprised when she said, 'Of course!' and drew him away by his arm. They moved to the piano. Portia took off her bonnet and pelisse, as did Jocasta. A little maid laid them aside.

'Will you tell the butler we shall not require refreshments?' Jocasta said to her, dismissing another ear for her coming conversation. 'Sit, Sir Damon.'

He, amused, obeyed her order.

Portia had found some music on a side table, and selected a familiar sonata by Haydn — the confused Paxton standing beside her. She began, with a slight smile, to play. Jocasta joined Regis on the sofa where he had lain prone the day before. She did not look at him, but straight ahead at her sister, and after a moment he did the same. The two pairs were at least twenty feet apart, and he said quietly, apparently paying attention to the performer, 'Most enterprising, Jocasta! I wondered how you would manage to find occasion to berate me today — but I am surprised by your method.'

'You admit you deserve to be berated, at least,' said Jocasta, in a tight voice.

'I do, Jocasta.' His voice did not sound contrite, however, but warm and silky.

'Stop it!' she hissed at him. 'Do not call me by my name, and do not use that tone with me. I have no real notion what you are about, Sir Damon, but if I were to tell Lord Onslow, he would know how to deal with it.'

'What would he wish to deal with, precisely?' asked Sir Damon, crossing his legs — which cost him a groan.

'Hah!' barked Jocasta, 'Serves you right!'

'I am confused. You have been behaving as the chief of my medical attendants, the most concerned of all about my health — and now you gloat at my pain.' She was silent. 'I *might* have just punctured a lung, you know.'

'*You!*' she uttered, derisively. 'I did not act as though I were your medical attendant ... but as a fr ... an acquaintance of some time ... I could not *but* be concerned about your dangerous behaviour at the ball...'

'You feared for me — as you did when you paid that *shocking* visit to my bedchamber!' he reminded her, in the same wicked tone.

'But I saw the horse's hooves *hit* you!' she protested. When she stole a glance at him and saw the laugh in his eye, she added in a lowered, angry tone, 'You understood that very well. *Anyone* would have been anxious.' Her voice became resentful. 'But I knew you would wish to tease me with that, as though it was all my fault. It does not excuse your own behaviour since yesterday.'

'Ah, the pink ribbon!' he said reminiscently. 'Will you give it to me, my dear? As a keepsake?'

'I should rather choke you with it — but it is in the fire already!'

'So *violent* were the passions that went along with it, then. Such a pity...'

'So violent was my *disgust* at *your* behaviour! And you continue just now. Will you not *stop?*'

The piano had been at a quieter few bars, and this one last word rung out towards the couple there. Paxton looked up, alarmed, but Portia nudged him, and he turned a page. All that was to be seen from the sofa were two figures separated by a foot of space, the gentleman at his ease, the lady stiff. Paxton, who had been treated to Jocasta's stiffness, pitied the baronet a little.

'Tell me what I must *stop*, and I shall consider it,' offered Regis.

'The warm tone, the insidious remarks, the ... the...' her voice shook as she thought of his impudent thumb at her wrist.

'This?' his hand shot out and grasped hers.

'*Regis!*' Her voice was a vicious whisper, she tried to pull her hand away before the others could see, she could hardly bear his touch — but he moved the hand closer to him, turned it, and placed her palm on his heart. He held it there for a long five seconds, the heart below beating fast, before he dropped it. She would have called to Portia, but her breath was gone entirely.

'Did you not *feel* it, Jocasta? I am not pretending.' His tone was serious, hypnotic.

'I *hate* you!' she hissed under her breath.

'Why?'

'We cannot be friends again.' Her tone was serious now, too. She looked at him, and tears filled her eyes.

'Jocasta!' he said, sadly, '*Jocasta!*'

'*That* is what you have done.'

'Don't—'

'When you know how I *needed* you—' She pursed her lips tightly, as though to stop those words from escaping her.

'Jocasta…'

'How *could* you?'

She got up and moved to the fire. Portia, almost finished, noticed something in the back view of her sister that disturbed her. She finished her piece and stood up.

'You are quite right, Miss Fortune!' remarked Sir Damon in a conversational tone, as the performer came towards them. 'Your sister is *far* more talented than you.' Portia gasped, glaring at him. He smiled at her however, and merely added, 'It was a true pleasure to hear you play.' He requested her hand with a gesture of his own, then took it in an ancient, formal gesture and bowed over it, while Paxton looked on, annoyed.

Jocasta was stiff again, facing their host, saying, 'Do not look for a visit this afternoon, Sir Damon, I believe the marchioness is now otherwise engaged.'

'Ah, a pity!' His hand moved swiftly, and he captured Jocasta's hand from her side, without waiting for it to come to him. He made the same bow. 'I always enjoy her company.' He held Jocasta's hand between the two of his, and everyone was struck silent by it. 'Do you remember what I said about your sketching?' She stopped trying to pull her hand away at this, and met his eye. 'It has nothing to do with yesterday, but only to do with your feelings today. Can you not understand that this is the same?'

In one of the energetic, swift moves that defined him, he lifted her hand and kissed it. Paxton, stunned, felt it necessary to exclaim. '*Sir!*'

An eyebrow flew in Paxton's direction. 'You attend to your love, and I will to mine,' Regis said carelessly.

Jocasta pulled her hand away fiercely.

'Sister!' cried Portia, turning to Jocasta. '*What—?*

'Let us go!' said Jocasta, moving with her word. The three entered the carriage together, the maid instructed to walk home.

'Sir Damon — what does he mean by it?' said Portia, 'Are you betrothed?'

Jocasta's breath was coming swift and harsh. She was torn between knee-trembling physical reaction and blind fury. 'Do not, Portia, *please!*'

'You are shaking! We must tell Georgette.'

'Do not!'

'But Jocasta...' there was a dreadful silence before Portia tried again. 'I have heard tell he is a dangerous man. In one tale he ran off with a married countess in the middle of a ball!'

Jocasta laughed harshly. 'If he did so, there would have been a good reason for it.'

'How can you trust him so? You are too sensible for that. He used the word *love,* and he has not even offered for you, you say,' said Portia, distraught.

'He will,' said Jocasta, but disgusted. 'It is just the sort of stupid, honourable thing he *would* do.'

'I do not understand.'

'I have been thinking and thinking, and I have *just* understood what all of this is about. I see it clearly now. It is why Onslow and Georgette were so strange at breakfast, ignoring his behaviour entirely. It is all my fault!'

'*Your* fault?'

'I broke into his bedchamber, quite unattended, when he was injured.'

'*You—?*' Portia was shocked, but entertained.

'If Papa had found out, I would be married already. As it is, Onslow must have decided to let Sir Damon behave subtly, I believe,' she laughed, and looked at her still shaking, but now gloved, hand. '*This* is Regis' notion of subtle.'

'Are you sure?'

'He seeks to provoke me into believing he goes to his fate willingly.'

'His reputation is not so considerate,' said Paxton in a cynical, but concerned voice.

Jocasta rounded on him. 'That is because you do not know him. And would not understand him if you did.' Jocasta looked directly at the flushed cheeks of his lordship, and met his gaze as she said, with some little venom, 'If the wicked Demon King had ever led a young girl along, with compliments to her beauty and other distinguishing attentions, he is the sort of man who would take responsibility.' Paxton's colour deepened, as he heard her reproof of himself in this. 'Indeed, th is *dishonourable* man is at this very time trying to take responsibility, not for his *own* folly, but for *mine*.' A sob escaped her, and Portia held her hand. Jocasta dropped her head. 'I shall not let him!'

'Do you care for him, Jocasta?' asked Portia's small voice.

Jocasta pulled herself up a little, and grasped her reticule. 'That is beside the point.' She looked at Paxton's still humiliated face and continued. 'I have something more to say, my lord.' He looked afraid. 'Portia is *miserable* in that house with Papa and George. I know you think you understand, but you can have no notion just *how* miserable—'

Jocasta! cried Portia.

'I have heard the laudable reasons you have put forward for delaying your marriage. Your concern about her age, and giving Portia an opportunity to change her mind after she has socialised in London. But, as usual, my lord, you are doing what suits and protects your own feelings, without regard to another's.' Paxton reeled back and Jocasta continued ruthlessly. 'Portia has a much truer heart than mine, and it will never change. *You* should know that by this time. *Post the banns at once!* Put an end to her misery, and accompany her at *every* dinner in that *dreadful* house, although you be made miserable too. Take responsibility — for once!'

The carriage stopped before Onslow House. Jocasta jumped out, and the couple inside sat back, stunned.

CHAPTER 24

Love in Unexpected Places

That evening, Mrs Usher, sporting a very smart Turkish bonnet and striped silk gown, was aware that her charge, very prettily attired in blue figured muslin with a matching broad band in her hair, was not in her best spirits. Mrs Usher hoped that the advent of her friends Tom and Miss Fortune would lift her back to her usual spirited self, but one sight of Miss Fortune narrowed the possibility. For Miss Fortune, in white foam muslin trimmed with pointed *broderie anglais*, had a dazed, dull look in her usually sparking eye. Mrs Usher had regretted her words from this morning and, when tweaking the band in Cecilia's hair, had tried to apologise somewhat. 'I know that your intentions are pure Cecilia, but it is my duty to give you a hint if you are not to get yourself into dark waters.'

'I know ma'am, and I do appreciate it,' had said Cecilia flatly, and Mrs Usher had simply sighed.

She was determined to keep an eye on her charge tonight, for who knew what a girl in low spirits might do? She saw that Cecilia and Jocasta had sat out one of the dances on a bench, but did not see the duke join them. He was dancing with a Miss Holland, a pretty, black-haired young beauty newly arrived in town. It seemed that two young bucks, Lord Cunningham and Mr York, had come to claim Cecilia and her friend for the next set, so Mrs Usher relaxed. But when she looked back at the bench some minutes later, it was to find Cecilia seated alone, but with Cunningham standing to one side of the bench, in serious conversation with her. Cecilia's cheeks were flushed, and her hands grasped at themselves desperately. Mrs Usher broke off mid-sentence, and made a trip to her side immediately. Cecilia had moved off — Mrs Usher had not been quick enough. She saw her charge go in the direction of the withdrawal apartment, and Mrs Usher let her go, guarding the bench for her return.

The young gentleman who had spoken with her was only vaguely known to Mrs Usher. A friend of the Royal Duke of Clarence: not a recommendation in itself, but she had heard no ill of him. She had noted that Cunningham had danced with Cecilia on two previous occasions, but he had not paid her a morning call, or invited her for a drive, and so he had not featured as someone Mrs Usher needed to discover more about. Perhaps she should follow Cecilia to the ladies' withdrawing room, but she knew her charge. If Cecilia had been overset, her nature was that she would rather regain control of herself before she discussed the cause. Had that young buck made her an offer? Mrs Usher was not much impressed by him if so, for there was an order to these things, including the good manners of introducing himself to the chaperone, at least. Or Regis — it was well-known that Regis felt himself responsible for Miss Montgomery. That Cunningham had done neither suggested something to hide.

The set had finished, and the duke arrived at the bench directly, seeing Mrs Usher. 'Where is she?'

'Oh, Tom, good! Could you fetch Miss Fortune? I think Cecilia is upset, and might like her friend rather than me.'

'Where is she?' said the duke again, 'I'll go!'

'In the ladies' withdrawing room,' said Mrs Usher, significantly. 'Are you still going?'

'I'll find Jocasta.'

'You should not call her so!'

'I know ...' he said, but he had been looking around and now made a beeline to his prey.

Presently Jocasta led Cecilia back to her party, and with a word to Georgette, and the marchioness' good-natured promise in return, Mrs Usher went to find a friend in the card room.

Tom wandered off, since Cecilia would not talk to him at all. He was concerned, but it was useless to try to talk with her at a ball. It was not like her to be upset; she was the most fearless female he knew. But London could be deadly. He had begun to think that Cecilia was well able to cope, but now he was really worried. There were bounders enough around he knew, as well as females with sharp tongues. The thought that any of these had done or said enough to upset Cecilia Montgomery made it grave indeed. He did not much attend to his partner in the dance, but turned his head frequently to catch a glimpse of Cecilia. The upshot was, that some ten minutes later he saw her dash through the crowd in a way that was not precisely shocking, but did draw a little attention, as she headed towards the doors that opened to the terrace.

***

Cecilia's explanation to Jocasta that she had been made an unexpected offer by Lord Cunningham, and this had temporarily deprived of her usual even spirits, did not seem to cover her mood, Jocasta thought. On another day, Jocasta would probably have insisted on probing further. However, she was only just in charge of her own mood today, and could not think how to do so. ***

Jocasta and Cecilia had stayed in the withdrawing room a while longer, while maids fanned them and offered cool lemonade. Cecilia declared herself ready to re-join the fray, and looked it. Jocasta led her towards Georgette, who could be guaranteed to judge the situation and fill in with the care that Jocasta could not find within herself tonight.

However, as they approached the Onslow party, Jocasta saw Georgette spot Cecilia and frown. The marchioness covered it up quickly, however, and said amiably, 'How well blue becomes you, Miss Montgomery! You look charming this evening.'

Her tone was a little loud, and Sir Justin Faulkes, talking with Onslow, looked over his shoulder and acknowledged them with a faint smile. He made to move off, but Onslow stopped him, saying, 'Where are you going?'

'I mean to try my hand at getting a waltz with the lovely Miss Holland,' said Faulkes, suavely.

'You'll have no luck there! I asked for a dance from her while you were cavorting with my wife.'

'Onslow! Dangling after the latest beauty so soon...' cried Georgette, in mock shock.

'I know her father,' he scoffed.

'And still did not triumph!' said Faulkes, seemingly amused. 'I shall fare better — my address has always been superior to yours.'

'Wait, you cheat!' Onslow laughed. 'She hasn't had her first waltz yet. I'll bet you are taking Dorothea de Lieven with you to introduce you!'

'Yes,' laughed Faulkes, 'but it required a great deal of address to get the countess to agree to do it!'

Cecilia had been standing stock still, with clenched fists. It was too much. First, that dreadful proposal by a man who seemed to think she would be glad to take him only for his title, while more or less disparaging her charms. Now this from Faulkes, letting her know, indirectly, that she was nothing to him.

A tear fell from her cheek unbidden, and she put her head down. It was a moment's inattention on Jocasta's part, and on Georgette's, that saw the disappearance of Cecilia from their midst.

'Where is Miss Montgomery?'

'I don't know — I shall go and search for her,' said Jocasta at once.

'No, I will,' said Onslow. 'You girls should stay here, in case she returns.'

But it was the Duke of Enderby who found her. He had been facing her back as the set was finishing, and he saw small, clenched fists. She was either furious about something, or trying not to cry. Either thing had him in a panic. He turned to his closest companion in the gentlemen's line of the dance. 'Bellamy, could you escort my partner to her party as well as your own?'

Bellamy nodded, and Enderby patted his shoulder and set off at the quickest pace he could go, without drawing extra attention. She had been heading for the garden doors, he was certain of it, and he slipped through quickly, seeing a scrap of blue behind a pillar ten feet away, and found her there. She put a hand to his mouth to shush him, however, her large eyes glinting up at him in the gloom.

There were two gentlemen on the terrace, smoking cigarillos, some twenty feet from them at least, unaware of their presence. Their voices carried in the night, however, and the shorter man was saying to his companion. 'At least, since a female inherited, the entail is broken on Crumley Park ... it might not be such a bad bargain. You could do with it as you pleased.'

At the first word from the gentlemen, Enderby had made his move, but Cecilia grasped his arm and squeezed, her other hand over his mouth. He looked down at her and she shook her head, eyes pleading.

'You are nothing if not vulgar,' said the laconic voice of Lord Cunningham.

'So, it is a love match? You have more than one iron in the fire, Vernon.'

'The way you speak of ladies ...! But she is comely, and her estate is worth *something*.'

Only Cecilia's iron grip and her saucer eyes stopped Enderby.

'Take me away, Tom!' she whispered.

He breathed to defeat his temper, but was softened by her frailty. He led her down a garden path, lit only intermittently by mounted torches, and found a bench to sit on behind a tall hedge. He could barely contain his rage, but Cecilia's trembling muted his rage, and made him tender, too.

'You never said you'd marry that bounder?'

Cecilia dashed away a tear. 'Of course not, I refused him,' she said with spirit, but her voice became small and shaken as she continued, 'Only it is so difficult to do, Tom, you have no notion. Mrs Usher says to say "*We should not suit*" upon those occasions, but it seems so terribly insulting, and I ... I never find it easy. And he ... he said, he said he would not give me up.'

'I'll punish him for you, never fear. Don't take on so, Cissie. You are making me afraid. It is not like you.'

'Oh, it is not just that! Only today has been horrid. You know what Mrs Usher said, and you too, about Sir Justin — but I was so *sure* you were both wrong. I wanted to apologise to Sir Justin tonight, but I saw at once that everyone was right. I had put him into a dreadful situation, and I've embarrassed everyone... Oh, *Tom!*'

'You don't have a *tendre* for Faulkes, do you?' asked Enderby, tilting her chin.

'No!' she said, looking into his eyes, frankly. 'I saw at once it was all just a fantasy, but to be so mistaken is so *humiliating*!'

He put a strong arm around her shoulder. 'Don't be a goose! You've just fallen on low spirits because of a few silly things, and because you don't know how to go on.' He gave her shoulders a shake. 'Buck up now, for we must get back to the ballroom, Cissie. Lady Onslow will be looking for you, and we don't want to cause a furore.'

'No.' She sniffed.

'So, dry your eyes like a good girl, and then we'll be off.' He held her hand. 'But tomorrow, Cissie, I want a word with you.'

Cecilia was attempting to dry her eyes as instructed, by the use of Tom's enormous handkerchief, when some steps approached.

'Well!' said a reedy voice that tried for shock, but could not disguise some evil delight. 'I *suggest* you take Miss Montgomery back to her chaperone, my lord duke.' It was the repressive voice of Viscountess Swanson, her large pale face glowing horribly in the moonlight. 'I saw her leave the ballroom alone — but I never thought to see such a scene as *this*!'

'Shocking!' said her companion, the sharp-faced Mrs Hardy.

'I have been taking the air with my affianced wife, viscountess,' said Enderby haughtily, in what Cecilia referred to as his best duke-voice, 'but I *hardly* think it concerns you.'

Cecilia had jumped to her feet, dropping the revealing handkerchief behind the bench, her chin tilted. She stood still, frozen in place, but he placed her hand on his bent arm and led her away, deeper into the garden.

She let out a held breath. 'Oh Tom, *why* did you do that?'

'I couldn't bear it. Dreadful old bat. Won't have her speak to you so.'

'It will be all over town...'

Enderby stopped dead, grasping the hand on his arm and forcing Cecilia's halt, too. 'Let's just do it, Cissie,' he sighed.

Cecilia's head fairly whipped in his direction. '*What?*'

Enderby sat down on the grass just off the path, pulling her with him. 'I am *exhausted* trying to be a man about town. Or the target of girls or their mamas, with all their *significant* comments I pretend not to comprehend.' Cecilia looked at him. His voice dropped a little. 'And I *hate* the men around you now. You have always been only mine.' She gasped. 'And now some other man might claim you.' Their eyes met, hers wide and questioning. 'It just occurred to me recently that that is what young girls come to town for.'

'It *just* occurred to you?' said Cecilia, taunting.

'I always thought that, even if you or I were to be married, we could continue as we have before.'

'Of course we should,' said Cecilia. 'Why should we not?'

'But since you have been in town, I've suddenly realised that couldn't be. Would your husband permit it?'

'Why are you talking like this, Tom? I'm sure my husband would become *your* friend, too.'

'And we could do everything we do now?' he shook his head sadly. 'I don't think so. Damon is our friend, and even before he wanted to separate us, when we rode together and so on, he wouldn't let you practise the equestrian arts.'

'And I have nearly perfected standing upright on Juniper's back!' She laughed for the first time that evening.

'I *know!*' agreed the duke. 'You have only fallen on me twice this summer.'

'Your poor shoulder,' she said, patting it. They sat together on the grass like old companions, and as usual she sat on his coattails. It seemed to her right now that they were in the grounds of Crumley Park, not in the middle of London, and she could finally breathe.

'But a husband would want to protect you...' he continued.

'I suppose...'

'And then, if it were to be Wray or even Bellamy, they would take you to their homes. In Dorset, or even Yorkshire, or some such place — and though we might visit, it would all be different.'

'I didn't think of it!' cried Cecilia, in distress. 'I'm so used to seeing you all the time. But perhaps if I married a poorer man, like Mr Peters, he would be glad to live at Crumley.'

'Peters is after you, too?' He sounded disgusted, and Cecilia laughed again. 'Perhaps he *would* be glad. And he might even be my friend, but I should not like it,' said the duke, honestly. 'I could visit for breakfast, and a ride perhaps, but not breakfast and dinner both, and a picnic at the Forked Tree of Doom, in between.'

'No, and we could not tell our truths on the Mound of Honesty,' said Cecilia, somewhat sadly. 'But things must change, I suppose, we must grow up, Tom. It is what Damon has been trying to say to us.'

'I don't want them to change,' the duke said flatly. 'What if I were to have a wife? How would *you* be then?'

'Then we should be friends too, because I'll make sure you marry a nice girl like Jocasta.'

'Miss Fortune is still my angel. But you have quite ruined the regard she might have had for me by telling her all my failings,' he said gloomily. 'And even if I listen to you in my choice of wife, she would not want our visits to be the same, and I *do*. You, spending half an hour rolling on the floor with Solomon and Sheba for instance. I love to see how dishevelled you become — even when you arrive dressed smartly.'

'Mmm,' said Cecilia, suddenly concerned. 'Some ladies do not allow dogs indoors, even.'

Enderby held his head aloft. '*I* would be master in my own...'

'*You?*' scoffed Cecilia. 'Any woman worth her salt will have you do her bidding within a sennight.'

His head collapsed. 'You are probably right. I have been brought up to be respectful of women — except you. It doesn't bear thinking about.'

There was a silence for three minutes.

'But we *can't* be married,' said Cecilia. 'It is ridiculous! It would be like marrying my brother.'

'No, it wouldn't,' said Tom stoutly. 'I have been thinking about it. I meant to speak to you of it tomorrow. I know lots of men with sisters, and none of them want to spend as much time with their sisters as I do with you. None of them cut short their time in London just to go back to their sisters.'

Cecilia was quiet for a moment. 'I'm always so glad when you come home. It is so boring without you,' she admitted, her voice low and a little shaken. She turned her head to him then, only to find his face disturbingly close. 'You may not be my brother, Tom, but *however* could we be more than best friends?'

He kissed her swiftly on the lips. 'Here's how.' She was stunned into silence and he pulled his head away a little. 'Sorry. I did not want to do that before in case it changed us. In case you pulled away from me — in case it felt too awful.'

This last statement was in fact a question, and she answered it. 'It didn't feel awful. It felt nice.' Cecilia was looking into his eyes frankly, but shaking, nevertheless. 'But that is not enough for marriage, is it?' Her voice was small still, and shy. As unlike herself as could be.

He held her eye, blushing. 'I don't know. But I don't want another fellow doing it to you.'

She looked down. 'I didn't like Jocasta on your arm, either. Even though I liked *her*.'

He grasped her hands, bringing her eyes back to him. 'Can't we go on as before, only married? The worst part of my day is when I drive away, or see you off in the carriage. Then I must go back to being alone. That is when I am most lonely.'

'It is the same for me, you know,' she whispered. 'At night I feel so deserted.'

Tom leaned in a little. 'If we were married, we could hold hands all night.' He grasped hers now.

She touched his face. 'Or I could hug you when you were having one of your bad dreams.'

'And perhaps I could make a better job of kissing you.'

Cecilia, her lips still on fire, thought he had done a fine job already, but she could not say so. After a moment she ventured, eyes lowered, 'Do you remember when I fell asleep under the apple tree just before we came to London?'

'When you slid down onto my lap? I do. My legs went into a cramp.'

'How long was I there?'

'About half an hour, I think.'

She took a breath, deciding to confide. 'For most of that time, I was really awake.'

He held his own breath, amazed at her honesty, and risked some of his own. 'I think I knew that. I saw your eyelids flutter, but I knew you were thinking, like me, that if you woke up, then we must pull apart. For as adults, we have usually kept our distance, whatever Damon thought.'

'I know. But sometimes I wanted to be closer, as we were as children. Something everyone warned me *not* to do once you returned from Harrow and Oxford — and so I was rather ashamed of it. And then, that evening when you had too much wine with Stuart Sullivan, and came to my house to wish me goodnight ... McIntyre almost did not admit you! When you fell asleep on my shoulder, Jane almost had an apoplexy. But I shushed them because it was so pleasant for you to be there.'

'I wonder if McIntyre alerted Damon? If that was why...?'

'That — and your London behaviour,' she chided.

He blushed. 'I didn't enjoy it much. I like parties, and my club, but not ... not the other place Damon saw me at.' He held her hand and searched her eyes, finally seeing her understanding, and added, 'But we should visit London each year together.'

'But not for the whole Season,' she said, still shy.

'No.' He held her cheek. 'We ought to go back to the ball now. Being affianced excuses only so much bad behaviour.' He stood and pulled her up. She snaked her hand through his arm, and leaned into him, as they found the path again.

'Shall I have to move to Enderby?' she asked. 'What about my house? My people?'

'If I choose to have another house, why can I not?'

'And two full staff of servants and two stables so near to each other? It is zany.'

'A duke is expected to be a zany,' he said, patting her arm. 'We'll live at Enderby, but visit Crumley often.'

'What about McIntyre? Your Devlin is old now, but he would be upset at retiring. Only, McIntyre is my friend, and I don't want to leave him.'

'No need, we will have two butlers.'

'I foresee domestic ructions.'

'We'll talk to them all when we get home. Carson too. She has been looking forward to dressing my wife since mama died. But you'll wish to bring Jane.'

'I think Jane would be happy to learn from Carson. She really admired your mama's style.'

They talked continually, happily dispensing servants, hardly aware of an accepted proposal.

The duke, before they entered the ballroom, took her face in his hands. 'I warn you now that tomorrow I am going to kiss you properly. You might swoon, afterwards.'

She smiled at him, but blushed. 'Pshaw! I don't hold out much hope. But I'll bring a vinaigrette in case.'

Onslow was at the garden doors, frowning at them. 'I hear you are affianced.'

'Already?' said the duke, seeing some interested looks around them, as they stepped into the ballroom.

'Yes,' said the marquis dryly. 'My sister-in-law is crying in a withdrawing room.'

Enderby blushed. 'She *is* ...?' he said, appalled.

'He's teasing you for being a flirt,' said Cecilia comfortably. She looked squarely at the marquis. 'We are sorry, my lord. We had no notion ourselves.'

He raised his brows. 'It is often the way. I should wish you both happy. But you still must tell Regis, so I will delay that — as it may not happen.'

'Oh, leave Damon to me!' said the pert little miss. Then she looked somewhat flattened. 'Jocasta isn't *really* upset?'

'Here she comes!' said the marquis using the advantage of his height to see his sister-in-law's approach. 'Discover for yourselves.'

In a minute, Jocasta Fortune emerged through a press of people, who were standing near the garden doors in the unmannerly attempt to eavesdrop.

'Is it really true?' she said, with a shining face. 'Oh, how happy I am for you both!'

Jocasta's genuine joy dispelled any doubts, and the ladies hugged while the duke looked on, a trifle shamefaced. It had been some weeks since the dealings between Jocasta and he had been in any way lover-like, but he *had* flirted with her. The teasing look she gave him when she had finished her hug let him off the hook, however.

'Oh, Tom! *I* knew you liked her all along.'

The duke blushed. 'Well, I wish you had told me. It took her receiving a lot of annoying male attention before I had any notion of it at all.'

CHAPTER 25

Resolutions

The duke presented himself at the Demon King's townhouse after breakfast, quaking.

He found the baronet still at the table, in a bad mood due to a night of pain. He was doing justice to a plate of meat and eggs, however, and did not rise at Enderby's arrival, merely saying, 'I know why you have come.'

'You cannot!' protested Enderby.

'Justin called upon me last night after the ball.'

'Why should he?'

'He is afraid that Cecilia accepted you to protect her pride because he had been unkind.'

'Does Faulkes wish to marry her, then?' said the duke, troubled.

'No. But he thinks he should.'

'He can think again!' said the young man with energy.

'Oh, *really*?' Regis regarded him with amusement.

'Yes, he can. Cecilia shall marry no one but me.'

This was the most decided Regis had ever seen the young man, and he smiled inwardly. 'Are you not simply trying to save her face after she was upset, and you got caught by that Swanson woman?' Damon glared at him. 'Admirable, but not the only solution.'

'It is not just that.' He looked at Damon. 'I think, you know, that you were right all along, Regis. Cecilia and I were grown closer than friends. But we were so used to each other that we did not think of it.'

'Yes.'

'The thing is, Damon ... seeing her with other fellows — it was alright at first. Then, suddenly I imagined her married ... and I could not bear it. You probably don't understand me.'

'I think I understand that better than you could imagine,' Regis said, wryly.

'Perhaps I have loved her for a long time.'

'Mm.' A self-reflecting sardonic eyebrow was raised.

'What you were concerned about ... *those* things...' Enderby squared his shoulders, but only succeeded in looking absurdly young, 'I will be a faithful husband to Cecilia. You need not be concerned.'

'You had better be.'

Enderby took on the gist of this and smiled euphorically. 'Then you consent?'

'You need my consent?' said Regis, finally getting up, with a wince. 'You sounded surer of your purpose than I have ever heard you.'

'I am. It is just ... whatever you think, I know the care you have taken of Cecilia. And I know how she cares for you, though you might not think it. And I ... I respect you, Damon, and if you think me unfit for her ... well, I cannot promise to give her up, but I will wait to show you, until you realise ...'

'I was wrong, not right, Tom.' Regis sighed. 'I judged you on my own follies. You are not as unstable as I thought you. Just immature.'

'I ... no, you were right, Regis. I have been overindulged; I know it. Any hint you care to give me in that regard I promise I will respect.'

'Do not, I pray you, model your behaviour on mine.'

'I cannot think of a more honourable model,' said Enderby, but he blushed. 'I hate the overindulgence, in a way. It is why I like the estate at Enderby, rather than Enderby House here in London. At Enderby, the servants brought me up, as you know. And they are not all servile, even when they mouth respectful words. They let me know when they disapprove of me.'

'Old retainers are often so.'

'What I mean is ... I am not so arrogant as to behave so with Cecilia.'

'As if she would let you! I applaud your bravery in taking her on.'

'She is a handful! At this very moment I have bruises all over my shin where she has kicked me, only for saying the wrong thing.'

'You will have to learn to manage her. I will teach you a few tricks.'

'Shall you? My shins would thank you.' He smiled down at his shoes. 'But after last night ... I do not know. Perhaps we might be gentler with each other now.'

'I should hope so, for a time...' Regis grinned evilly, '... but the termagant will return.'

'I am ready for it.' Enderby grinned back. He saw Regis look concerned again, denoted by one scrolling eyebrow. 'I *will* be faithful to her, you know,' the duke reassured him.

'You are so sure of yourself?'

'Not quite that. It is just — I have never been able to bear it when Cecilia cries.'

Damon looked him in the eyes and dropped a hand on his shoulder.

'Let us have a brandy on it. It is morning, but I need some fortitude of my own.'

The duke, relieved of his terror, gratefully agreed.

'What fortitude do *you* need?'

'I also have a very tricky female problem.'

'*You?*' said Enderby shocked. 'But she's married—'

'Who is?'

'Mrs Norton.'

'Mrs Norton is merely a friend of mine.'

Another visitor was announced. An exotic vision was on the threshold, and the duke believed he finally understood. *This* female could constitute a very tricky problem — for any man alive. He knew instinctively that this sophisticated sort of problem was beyond his own skills.

Damon Regis saw his conclusion, and opened his mouth to clarify. However, he suddenly saw in it a way to further his latest devilish plan, so he held his peace.

'Isabel! Have you met the Duke of Enderby? Your Grace, Doña Isabel de Zeluta.'

'Ah, no!' she smiled at the duke, and despite himself the young man's insides melted as she took his hand, 'I am so pleased to have met you.' Her voice was open and frank, not the breathy tone he had hoped for, but its warmth still shook him. 'I suspect that all the ladies in town are at your feet.'

Regis looked on with amusement as Enderby swallowed audibly.

'No, no, no,' he babbled, 'for I am betrothed, you know. *Betrothed!*' he said rather fiercely, removing his hand from hers like a clockwork automaton. He excused himself quickly and left, almost as fearful as he had entered.

Doña Isabel laughed.

'Why did you torture the poor boy?' drawled Regis, a little amused.

'I do not seem to be able to torture *you* anymore, my friend, so I must keep in practice.' She smiled, but he knew she was hurt too.

Nevertheless, demon that he was, he decided to use her, if necessary, too.

'If Cecilia had not instantly told me of your engagement, Tom, you would be dead by now,' said Mrs Usher. They were still at a late breakfast, as was this home's casual custom. Tom took a seat and, with a grin at Cecilia's beaming face, stole a roll and gestured for a cup, which appeared promptly.

'Eggs?' he asked the maid, with puppy dog eyes. She left to be rebuked by Cook. Enderby turned to his hostess casually, 'Sorry, my dear Mrs Usher. If I had any idea of it myself, I should have followed form and declared my intentions, but I could not.'

'And it was my fault too,' offered Cecilia, sounding very happy, 'I ran away to the garden quite in the manner of a lunatic.'

'Poor Tom probably only offered out of pity,' said Mrs Usher, as punishment for last night's worry.

'Yes,' agreed Cecilia cheerfully, 'and I shall take shameless advantage of him.'

'Hey now!' objected the duke, '*Really—*'

'You clodpole, Tom, Mrs Usher told me earlier that she knew before either of us.'

'People keep saying that. They should have given us a hint.' He joked, but he looked at Cecilia rather shyly and she smiled into his eyes, reassuringly.

'I shall leave you alone, now, though I shouldn't,' said Mrs Usher comfortably. 'I congratulate you both. Don't do anything too shocking.'

'I won't!' assured the duke.

'I wasn't talking to you,' said Mrs Usher, and laughing, left the room.'

Tom put down his roll and moved towards Cecilia's seat in a predatory manner that made her giggle. He pulled her up, very straight-faced, and drew her towards the sofa. 'What are you about?' she laughed up at him.

'I promised,' he said, taking her face in his hands, 'that I would kiss you properly today.'

'You cannot,' she said, pulling away.

'Why?' he asked.

'I forgot the vinaigrette!'

He pulled her towards him, and stopped her impudence with his determined mouth. Cecilia gave herself up to being bested.

'By the way,' he said, much later, 'I saw that Spanish woman at Damon's earlier when I went to get his consent.'

'He gave it? *Truly?*'

'Of course. He admitted he was previously deceived about me, and that I am not such a bad fellow after all. But *then* he said that he himself had a tricky female problem. And at that moment she arrived — that beautiful woman who makes one think of classical paintings.'

'I expect you mean the shocking ones.'

'You are right there. Somehow, however lovely her gown, one always imagines it rem—'

'Tom!' But unlike many betrothed ladies, Cecilia giggled at this. Then she added, 'I wonder if Jocasta knows? About that lady?' she added, concerned.

'Why should she care?'

'I don't know. I just think she should be told. Let us go and see her now, Tom.'

'In a while, Cissie. Just a little while longer.' He grasped at her shoulders and she sighed against him. 'No one will have the right to berate us any longer when we are close. Isn't it just grand?'

'I told Jane last night,' Cecilia said of her maid. 'She wasn't surprised at all.'

'Only us, it seems!' He grinned down at her. 'And don't call me a clodpole any longer. My betrothed should call me only affectionate names.'

'Blockhead? Nodcock?'

Cecilia, finally relaxed, realised that this was the ache in her heart assuaged, and what she had wanted for a very, very long time. Tom was childish, and annoying — and completely belonged to her alone, at last.

Jocasta knew that she was not in her right mind. She had always had a temper, whatever her fair appearance suggested, but it had always been at her own bidding, and had not overcome her. When, on the occasion of the house party at Castle Fortune, she had met Paxton to reject him before he rejected her, she had been angry, but dignified. But since she had met the Demon King, her passions had thrice overwhelmed her. First, when she had heard that her father had meant to visit Regis and she had run to the park to warn him, the second occasion was bursting in to see him when he was injured, and the third occasion yesterday, when she had gone to him again, thinking that she was in charge of herself, just because she had the foresight to bring Portia.

She had been out of control, still. The things she had said to him and he to her were outrageous. The way he had grasped her hand twice, the word he had called her to Paxton. His *love*. It was her own fault, she saw it. It was useless, useless, to hide from herself anymore. All the things he seemed determined to do, the flirtation, the offer he was, no doubt, about to make — it was what she *wanted*. If she could but close her eyes and pretend that she had the right to accept him ... that he genuinely cared, well today would be a happy day, instead of a miserable one.

She loved him.

But she was not fit for him. She knew herself too well, as she knew him. He was making a game of all of this, only so that she would not guess how trapped he was. Trapped by the feelings she had let him see when she had not realised them herself. He was no fool. He had seen what she had not. That she loved him. And then all the time they had spent together, all the help he had given her in regaining some self-esteem, some authenticity and joy in her life, he would see all that as the reason she had given her heart to him. And though he had only meant her good, he would fear that he had led her on, like Lord Paxton before him — but he would pay the price by offering for her. Thinking of yesterday morning's breakfast, Georgette and Onslow had agreed with his decision.

She had taken her anger out on poor Paxton, but she did not regret it. Those words were too long unsaid between them, Regis had shown her that honesty came before politeness if one expected to live well. That truth was better than pretence.

Therefore, she would not let Regis pretend. She would save him from such a life, whatever his wicked plan for her.

She had gone to the ball last night and her friends had become engaged. It was strange, and yet obvious, that Tom and Cecilia were to end up together. She wished them well from her heart.

Today she must control herself. She was not well enough to do so, however. She would tell Georgette that she would go to bed with the headache, and strive to think what next to do to protect him. Her insanity even considered marrying someone else. Should she give Mr York some time to speak to her? She saw at once that she was no more ready to sacrifice this kind young man than she was to sacrifice Regis.

No, at the end of this Season she would return to the twins and Katerina at Castle Fortune, and bear her father's rage at her unsuccessful Seasons, as Georgette had done before her.

But before that, she knew she must overcome Regis' cunning.

CHAPTER 26

Regis and the Demonic Plan

Jocasta rode the next morning, and the company, consisting of the Onslows and Faulkes, tried to engage her in conversation. She remained largely silent, however, and worried glances were exchanged among the others. After she changed for breakfast, though, Jocasta found that the company had swollen, by one. Sir Damon Regis caught her eye with his wicked ones as she entered.

She paused, but was very upright when she said, moving into the room, 'Good! You are here.'

He looked surprised, as did the others, and everyone continued to regard her as she took her place calmly at the table. She drank some chocolate, in a collected manner.

Jocasta had dressed carefully for the possibility of this occasion. Her dress of pale primrose muslin was enlivened by a cherry red ribbon rose beneath her breast and by thinner trailing ribbons at her cuffs. Her hair was curled high, and the same-coloured ribbon was threaded through her topknot, and allowed to fall to one side of her face. She looked both charming and serious, and very self-possessed. There was a careful conversation around her over breakfast, which she took little part in, giving the impression of a woman who was biding her time.

'Let us to the salon,' Jocasta said, after they had eaten their fill.

Faulkes coughed, 'Ah — all of us?'

Jocasta turned around in the doorway to regard him. 'If you please, sir.'

A silent troop entered the salon, Jocasta having given the butler the gesture that meant they were not to be disturbed. Regis looked amused.

Jocasta stood framed in front of the large fireplace, her hands clasped before her in the manner of a governess about to give lessons. She regarded her pupils, who sat down before her, repressively.

'I thought for a long time yesterday about how to deal with this situation, but there seems no other way but frankness.'

Onslow's sense of the ridiculous could not but escape at this. 'In polite circles, that way lies disaster.'

Georgette frowned him down. 'What situation do you refer to, dearest?'

'Do not pretend to misunderstand, Georgette, I know you are part of the conspiracy.' The tiny figure looked around wrathfully. 'All of you!'

Sir Justin raised his hands. 'Acquit me at least, Miss Fortune. I have been involved in nothing.'

'Perhaps! But you are just as bad!' Sir Justin raised innocent eyes and looked aggrieved. Jocasta tilted her head and looked down her nose. 'Wanting to offer for Cecilia Montgomery just because of your honour!' He dropped his eyes, defeated.

'Miss Montgomery — *you?*' Onslow regarded Faulkes, astounded.

'Yes, dear,' said the marchioness, 'I'll explain later.'

Jocasta continued. 'The rest of you behaved disgracefully at breakfast that day, pretending to ignore Regis' ridiculous compliments to me as though they were the most natural thing in the world.'

'We did do that,' admitted Onslow to his marchioness, acting abashed. She stopped his wickedness with a look and returned her attention to her sister.

'What is it you wish to say to us, Jocasta dear?'

'That it is no use to continue, I shall not marry Sir Damon Regis *whatever* you say.'

'But I have not asked you,' said Regis calmly.

Jocasta blushed, but continued with determination. 'But you were about to.'

'How forward! I have a good mind not to propose after all.' Her blushes reached all the way to her bosom, but she held herself with that stiff spine still.

'If I was anticipating a genuine proposal, I should hold myself back in maidenly modesty,' she blushed, 'but as it is ...'

For all her show of fearless frankness, she looked adorably embarrassed. Regis let her off the hook. 'But you are correct, Jocasta. The next step would be to visit your father.'

Jocasta's bravery left her all at once at this horrible prospect, and she sat beside him on the brocade sofa, grasping at his sleeve. 'You would not, sir. *Tell* me you would not!'

'Tell me why you are so against it, my dear one,' he said, placing a hand over hers. She got up as though burned.

'Stop it, will you *stop* it?'

'I feel I am somewhat *de trop*,' remarked Faulkes, dropping his eyes.

'As do we all,' said the marquis, shaking his blond curls. 'Why are *we* here, Jocasta?'

She took her position in front of the fire again. 'Because you are assisting him, and now I wish you all to desist. *Please.*' She took a deep breath. 'From the first you might have misunderstood why Sir Damon spent time with me. He was helping me, he was helping me not in *admiration* of me, but precisely because he did *not* admire me.'

'I did not,' admitted Regis calmly, 'but that has changed, Jocasta.'

She barely glanced at him. 'Yes, that is what you would wish me to believe.' She squared those little shoulders again. 'I must tell you all now, what I have told no one but Sir Damon. And I could tell *him* only because he did not care for me at all, and it was such a *relief.*'

'A relief?' asked Sir Justin, surprised.

'Yes. After the engagement of Portia and Lord Paxton all of you pitied me so—'

'Not pity—' protested Onslow, more seriously.

'Then what?' she answered baldly, turning on him. 'Affection? You hardly knew me.' He looked shamefaced. 'And you were not alone. At every social occasion there would be you, Sir Justin, Colonel Bellamy, the Bailey brothers, as well as the rest of that family all being so very, very, *kind*.' Jocasta shuddered. 'It almost killed me.'

313

'You truly cared for Lord Paxton then—' said Faulkes, concerned.

'No, of *course* not!' she said, with evident disgust. 'Every day told me what a narrow escape I had had. We have not a thought between us. Sir Damon, who wanted me for his own purpose, understood at once. All that pity was just humiliating.'

'Of course!' said Georgette. 'I have guessed so recently, but I am sorry I did not see it sooner. To continue in society, you had to appear nonchalant—'

'Yes, and all that kindness reminded me of my humiliation at every moment.'

'*I* thought that removing you from that house—' began Georgette, sorrowfully.

'It did help a lot, Georgie,' Jocasta reassured her. 'Paxton is so full of useless, spineless guilt that he quakes when he meets me. I could not find a way of dealing with it until yesterday, when I finally told him what I thought of him.'

'*Did* you?' approved Regis. 'Good girl! It is about time.'

Jocasta regarded him from her now superior height. 'I escaped a connection with *one* man I do not share a thought with, and now you wish me to be tied to another such. Please stop, Sir Damon. Leave me some pride. I beg you — all of you.'

There was a short silence, which Regis broke. 'If it were just as you say, Jocasta, I would follow your wishes.' He stood and moved to her. 'But it is not quite so simple.' He looked at the others. 'It began the way Jocasta has described. I had a use for her, it is true, and so we spent time together, one using the other.'

'What was your plan, you fiend?' asked Georgette, cross again. 'I have forgotten to ask you. What use had you for my sister?'

314

'It does not matter telling you now,' said Jocasta, 'because Cecilia and Tom are to be wed. Sir Damon mistrusted the duke's intentions to Cecilia, he thought him a rake, and believed that he might come to admire me, and thus show his true colours to Cecilia.'

'And what of Jocasta in all of this?' said Georgette, now furious. 'If you thought the duke dangerous to Miss Montgomery, why would you introduce him to *my sister*?' She turned to her husband. 'Lucian — I take back my prohibition — you may call him out at your first opportunity,' she added, with relish.

'Yes, my love,' agreed Onslow.

'Ah, I understand,' mused Faulkes. 'It is because Enderby admired Miss White last year, and Jocasta, Miss Fortune, is the same kind of fairy-like creature...'

'Precisely,' said Regis. 'I only meant to introduce them, nothing sinister, I assure you, marchioness. But their arrival in town was delayed, and I thus spent more time with your sister to keep the acquaintance. I got to know Jocasta's mind, and I abandoned my plan.'

'But she *did* meet the duke,' protested Georgette.

'I got angry and introduced myself – precisely to annoy the Demon King,' explained Jocasta.

'Naughty!' Onslow remarked.

'Well,' said Jocasta, head tilted, 'Regis' presumption was not to be borne.'

'Quite right!' said Georgette.

'It began so, Jocasta,' interposed Regis, gently. 'But it is not so now.'

'That is what you wish to convince me of, Regis, because you are convinced, you are *all* convinced,' her eyes swept the company, 'that I have ... affection for you.'

'And you do not?' he said, his voice low, drawing ever closer to her.

She stepped back into the fire surround, and there was a great rattle as a fire implement fell in the grate behind her. 'Of course I do!' she admitted, unexpectedly.

Georgette held her breath and grasped her husband's hand. Faulkes forgot his manners and stared.

Jocasta pushed Regis away, one hand on his chest, and he stepped back. 'You have been, to me, a godsend,' she said, looking up at him. 'How could I fail to feel affection? You have brought me back to myself in so many ways. You have shown me how to be honest in my dealings with people so that I can begin to trust the world again.' She smiled up at him. 'I will never forget, Sir Damon.' She looked away again, to break the connection, and took a step to the side, looking at the others. 'He showed me how I could survive, at my very lowest point, and he did it all by being unpleasant — so that I would not, for a moment, mistake his influence for affection.'

'It is different now, Jocasta. *Trust me!*' Regis' voice was no longer suave, but urgent, and he grasped her wrist.

'How so?' she said, her eyebrows raised ironically. 'Am I the wife you always dreamed of? No — for we all know what *she* looks like. More beautiful, stronger, more brilliant and intelligent than I could ever be. Do not try to fool me, Sir Damon. It is beneath you.' He looked back at her, sad, and she continued, 'And it is not necessary to try to fool me, you know. Not at all. Though I admit I am sincerely attached to you, as a friend, I have been repulsed when you acted as a lover.'

He dropped her arm. *'Repulsed?'* he said.

'Yes!' she said, jutting out her chin. 'Take this wrist!' He looked down at the inner wrist she thrust before him. 'You had only to brush your thumb across it for it to burn most uncomfortably all day.'

Onslow looked at his wife, who suppressed a giggle. 'You repulse me,' he murmured.

'You too,' she whispered back.

Regis smiled down at Jocasta's belligerent little face, and Georgette saw it again, that warm, doting fondness. 'Mmm,' he said. 'And that repulsed you?'

'Yes!' she said rebelliously. 'And when you held my hand—!'

'I say, Regis—' began Sir Justin, somewhat shocked.

'That must have been worse still,' Regis commiserated, still smiling down into her face.

'Yes!' she agreed contentiously. 'I found it shocking and upsetting and my hand felt ... it was thoroughly unpleasant all day. It proves that I do not care for you in that way at all, so you need not be noble in the least.'

'I thought you knew me Jocasta. I am *not* noble in the least.'

'Well, then,' she said, victorious.

'If all of that was so *repulsive*, I have one last repulsive move for you.' In a step he was beside her, his hand was on her raised cheek, and he bent and kissed her swiftly, stepping back, as his friends cried, *'Regis!'*

The slap was delivered by the full force of her shock and fury. And the world stood still.

Suddenly, Regis dropped to one knee and a collective gasp echoed in the room. He possessed himself of a small hand and said, his voice rough and shaking, 'Jocasta — marry me and save my life!'

She looked down, dazed. The others rose, and moved to the door as one. Jocasta looked up, still held by Regis. 'Georgie — don't go! He is a demon! Who knows what he will do?' she said, desperately.

But Georgette, stopping for a second as the men slipped away, noticed that Jocasta had not pulled her hand away. 'I shall be within screaming distance, love.'

Regis kissed the little hand fervently, just as Georgette closed the door. He looked up. 'No answer?' He waited a beat then got up from his supplicant's position, retaining her little hand, and leading her to sit with him again.

'Save your life?' she managed at last, fearing mockery in his eye.

'My friend Isabel visited me,' He told her in a comforting voice, 'and she told me that on the evening when you shepherded me from the ballroom, she was present.'

'Yes?' said Jocasta, wondering why he was telling her this.

'We passed within a foot of her,' he informed her.

'Yes?' Jocasta was still confused.

'But the point is, *I* did not see her at all.' Something began to dawn on Jocasta's face, and her eyes shone at him. 'That beautiful, brilliant, desirable woman. I missed her entirely, because I could only look at my little general leading her troops to protect me.' He held her gaze and his eyes were so gentle and loving that she felt tears well in her own eyes. 'I do not know precisely when I came to love you, Jocasta, but do not doubt it.'

'Perhaps, perhaps it is just that thing that gentlemen sometimes admire about me...' she said blushing, lowering her eyes from his gaze.

'Your beauty? The fairy princess?' He saw her peep at him again and he laughed. 'Of course, I am a man, and since you *are* very beautiful, it had an effect on me almost from the first. But I was extremely strict with myself, and I would not allow it to influence me, for I know that beauty alone is not enough to make a marriage.'

'No,' sighed Jocasta, regretfully, 'and there is not much more to me than that.'

'I have heard you say so, so full of disillusionment with your admirers — and I always knew it was not true. From the beginning I admired you, or I should never have wished to help you.'

She tried to ignore the implied pity, and focused instead on the more interesting part. 'What was there to admire?'

'Your bravery, for a start. I never saw you as a fairy creature, but always as a girl full of courage and pluck, striving to keep your pain from affecting others. It was most admirable.'

'*Was* it?' her eyes looked up at him, hopeful.

'Yes. Some of your woes were imagined, of course—'

'Imagined?'

'Yes. A number of your admirers are sincerely attached to you. It was not *all* false. And as soon as you were more honest in your dealings with them, less worried about being vivacious, but instead paying *attention* to them — well, even more fell at your feet.'

'Nonsense!'

'No.' He looked a little wicked and leaned forward, as though confiding. 'I never minded the suitors of the vivacious fairy, but I *hated* the suitors of the kind and honest Jocasta.' He laughed at himself. 'It made me very jealous indeed.'

'You are just saying so to convince me...' she began.

'It became urgent to me to let you know my feelings, lest you let yourself love someone else.'

Her hand was still in his and he played with her fingers, causing her to feel dazed and dreamy.

'*No!*' she shook her head as though to wake up. 'You are trying to make me believe—'

'There was another thing the *magnificent woman* told me, Jocasta. She said that you informed her that she did not understand me at all.' He smiled, still holding her hand gently. 'What did you mean by that? Isabel would like to know, too, for she believed you — though she did not wish to.'

'It is only that she told me how you had parted, and what she feared from marriage with you.'

'Yes?' he prompted, his voice warm.

'She feared that she would be inhibited from being herself, that your love would control and confine her.' He looked his enquiry. 'That is *absurd*!' she said, definitely. 'Everything you do for a person, everything you want for another, is only to make them *more* themselves and not less. How could she not *know* that?'

He pulled her in a quick movement and clasped her to him. 'Oh, Jocasta!' he said into her hair. 'And you wonder why I love you!'

She pulled away. 'But you cannot! I am not fit for you! There is nothing worthy in me at all.'

He looked at her with his gold green eyes, gentle and caring. 'Can I tell you about how wonderful you are, Jocasta? And see if you *still* do not believe me? Early on I noticed what a pure heart you have.'

'No indeed! You are thinking of Georgette....'

'Not at all. If you were the shallow, selfish thing you always claim to be, how could you have forgiven Paxton and your sister so completely? How could you have held no bitter resentment at your sister for stealing your admirer—'

'I saw it happen!' cried Jocasta. 'Portia did not mean it at all! It was not planned. It was like ... like *spontaneous combustion*.'

He laughed. 'Where had you that expression?'

'Katerina found some old copies of the journal *Philosophical Transactions*, and bade me read of the strange death of ... never mind,' she said 'It was instantaneous for both of them. How *could* I have blamed Portia for that?'

'You could not. Because you are Jocasta.' He caressed her hair, his eyes full of appreciation.

'*No one* would have ...'

'*Most* people would have blamed their sister for their humiliation, but you didn't. Not even at the start, did you?'

'No...' she said, in a small voice, 'but I did blame Paxton somewhat ... you know I did.'

'No. You are annoyed with him because he is a buffoon. It is quite understandable.'

She laughed, despite her best intentions. 'I was so angry with *you* the other day that it spilt over to *him*, and I told him how ill he had behaved to me.'

'He needed to hear that, so that you might be friends again.'

'Do you think so?'

She was looking at him with that trust that she had given him from the first, asking him if she had behaved correctly. It had brought out the protector in him, but he needed to tell her more. 'You know, you have had just as profound an effect on my life as you say I have had upon yours.'

'Oh, how can you say so? Now I *know* you are being false.'

'First, you trusted me. It opened the heart that had been closed so long after Isabel. And your need of me drew me on, to open up, even more. Suddenly, I found myself laughing at your little face, inwardly crying about your brave attempts to carry on. Haunting ballrooms so that I could see how you were. When you played your *A major* piece that morning, and smiled at me so gorgeously, I thought I would drop to the floor right there. You had shattered all my defences.'

'Then?'

'Then. And soon afterwards your wisdom explained Isabel's defection to me. Suddenly, in a second, I was able to let ten years of pain escape my heart. When first I saw her again, I was only thinking of you.'

'Damon!' Jocasta could hardly believe it, but his glittering eyes and each word he spoke made her breathless with wonder.

'You are mine, Jocasta,' he said, holding her face in his hands. 'Do you understand? Mine. However long it takes you to believe me, I shall make you know it. Watching over you, loving you, is my only purpose on this earth, and what God created me for.' He smiled at her questioning face. 'You are transparent to me. I *know* how much you love me; you are incapable of hiding it. I have given up wondering how or why: it is a miracle beyond us both. But, my only love, do you believe me now?'

'Damon!' was all she could say before he bent to kiss her. She put a hand over her mouth however, then grasped his lapels as she hid her face on them. 'I cannot stand any more, my *darling.*'

'Ow! Mind my ribs.' He disposed her head against his shoulder instead. 'Is it still repulsive?'

'*Completely* ... how do people bear it?'

'You shall have to begin. For I warn you,' he said, unknowingly echoing another lover, 'I will kiss you again properly tomorrow.'

'You *could* not be so cruel.' She looked up at him urgently. 'I will be better for you!' she promised. 'I can read and learn —'

'You will do only what you like, watching *that* will be my greatest joy.' He hugged her closer, causing another wince.

'You are in pain.' She reached up and put her fingers through his hair. 'And your poor head. Is it mended?'

'No,' he lied. He took her hand back and put her fingers over the wound again. 'It needs to be soothed just like that.' He sighed as her fingers moved.

'Does that feel *repulsive*?'

'Very' he sighed, his head back against the sofa, his eyes closed. 'But I shall learn to bear it.'

CHAPTER 27

Epilogue

Georgette's dinner table was lively that evening. She had seen fit to invite His Grace, the Duke of Enderby, and his affianced wife, as well as Sir Justin Faulkes, her sister Portia and her betrothed Lord Paxton. They were at the table when Sir Damon Regis came in, smiling, taking the seat left vacant beside Jocasta.

'You here, Regis?' said Tom, surprised.

'Did you fare well?' asked Georgette of Regis, interestedly.

'Eventually so,' smiled Regis.

'What were you doing?' asked Jocasta. 'Why did I not know?'

Cecilia Montgomery frowned a little at this, but Regis only sent Jocasta a sideways glance, addressing his dinner.

'Visiting the baron,' he said, taking a bite of salmon *à la beurre citron*.

'You *didn't!*' said Jocasta in a panic, and Regis, mouth still full, nodded, grinning at her.

'How did it go?' asked Onslow, casually.

Regis swallowed. 'Better, once I'd told him that Tom was engaged.' Regis nodded at the round-eyed duke. 'Your timing was wonderful, Your Grace. I thank you.'

'Does that mean ... not you and *Jocasta!*' Cecilia regarded her friend, who smiled dreamily at her. 'Oh, you *poor* thing!' she commiserated.

'I *know*!' answered Jocasta, but beaming. 'I meant to tell you before dinner, but you were late.'

'I was fighting with Tom. He wants to decorate Crumley for Damon's Aunt Agnes to stay, but I think she should just go home.'

'Well!' said Tom when he'd found his voice. 'Congratulations! This is most ... surprising, Jocasta, Damon.'

'Not really,' said Onslow, arch. 'She tried for a duke, but when that failed...'

'Onslow! You shall pay for that!' promised Jocasta.

'That *is* what your papa thought,' Regis informed her cheerfully. 'He murmured a great deal about your lack of pulling it off.'

Jocasta shuddered. 'Tell me about it later!' she said, embarrassed.

'No, tell now, Sir Damon,' said Georgette. 'We are among friends.'

'Yes do!' said Cecilia. 'He's a very funny old stick, your papa. I have a great deal of affection for him.'

'You might take him!' said Portia. 'It is the most embarrassing thing to have your father hint at your betrothed for money all the time.'

'*You* must be richer than I thought, Damon, if you managed to agree settlement terms with Baron Fortune,' remarked Sir Justin, urbane.

'Probably. But pardon my rudeness, my darling,' he said, addressing Jocasta's troubled face. 'I have no intention of doing more than is respectable for your papa.'

'It takes fortitude,' remarked Onslow, wisely. He lifted his fork. 'You are, as yet, a novice at dealing with the baron's requests for remittance.'

'Mmm,' agreed Paxton, glumly.

'You poor dears!' said Georgette, feelingly. 'It is the ongoing price of wedding a Fortune girl.'

'He set upon Cassandra's husband, too, when he visited,' Portia informed them.

'Oh, dear! What did Mr Hudson do?' asked Jocasta.

'He feigned deafness,' giggled Portia.

'Given that we are having this vulgar conversation,' coughed Faulkes, 'how did you persuade the baron without franking him for life?'

'Well, he gave me a list of Jocasta's suitors,' said Sir Damon, cheerfully, 'and what he had calculated each one might offer in the way of settlements.' All three Fortune sisters hung their heads and covered their faces. Cecilia giggled. 'He told me that Jocasta, meaning he, could do better.'

'Well, that's true,' said Cecilia. 'I *still* can't believe it.'

There was a general nodding of heads in agreement, but Georgette continued, 'And he just surrendered?'

'I said he should take my respectable offer, for he could not be guaranteed another.'

Jocasta, a trifle affronted, said, 'Why not?'

'Because' said Regis, raising a terrible eyebrow, 'I told him I would shoot any other suitor he accepted — dead.'

There was a stunned silence, before the duke let out a guffaw! 'Good one, Damon!'

Regis raised his eyebrows in an amused manner, but it was Lord Paxton who said, admiringly, 'Laud!'

'Whatever made you agree to marry Damon?' asked Cecilia of her friend. 'He is dreadfully domineering, and always wants his own way.'

'Like you!' Damon shot back.

'The only advantage I can think of is that at last you may drive his horses,' continued the unrepentant one.

Jocasta's eyes lit up and she turned to Regis.

'Oh yes, the advantage of one's own horse and carriage,' said Georgette. 'It is certainly why *I* got married.'

Onslow gave her a wry look.

'Oh! May I, Damon?' asked Jocasta, looking up at him with particularly dewy eyes.

'Um...' Regis screwed up his eyes in consideration, his eyebrows doing an amusing dance, while his love held her breath. Then his eyes became cold, 'No.'

'You are correct,' Jocasta addressed her friend Cecilia, 'there is no advantage at all.'

'But...' Regis intoned, and Jocasta's head whipped back to him, hopefully, 'Lady Regis will, of course, have her own horses.'

'A team!' cried Cecilia.

Regis frowned her down. 'We shall begin with a phaeton and pair.'

'Fear not!' said Georgette, in a helpful tone. 'Later, his best friend will offer to teach you to drive a team, and he will completely give in.'

A noise from the marquis had Faulkes and Regis smiling, but Regis said, faux-stern, 'Such tricks will not work upon me.'

'As I said, I cannot understand why you have chosen him,' said Cecilia, sighing.

'*I* know why,' said Lord Onslow. 'Because she finds him...'

He, Faulkes and Georgette intoned the last word of the sentence, '*repulsive!*'

'A private joke!' said Portia, resigned, but the joy around the dinner table relaxed her enough to say, 'But Jocasta, I really want to thank you for yesterday.'

'*Hah!*' Jocasta met Paxton's eye directly, laughing, 'You have posted the banns, my lord.'

He smiled at her shyly, '*And* I went to dinner last night.'

'Lord Paxton!' said Jocasta, holding her glass up, 'I salute you!'

'*We* should post the banns,' said Tom to Cecilia. 'It would save us having to live apart when we get home.'

Cecilia looked uncharacteristically shy. 'Should we?'

'I have already posted our banns!' said Regis, as though in passing. 'Let us all stay in town for an extra week or so and get married here, together!'

Smiling looks around the table greeted this idea.

'Oh, let us!' agreed Jocasta. 'I cannot face going back to Castle Fortune, except on a visit to the girls.'

'It is the way of Fortune girls to go on their Season and never return,' Portia said. 'All except Georgette.'

'We should send for the twins and Katerina! They could stay here for the wedding. They will be so excited to come to London at last, although the Season will be over,' said Georgette. 'Papa will not put himself out to arrange it, but Great Aunt Hester would send them off in her carriage, if only to make him angry.'

'Of *course* they should stay,' sighed Onslow, long-suffering. 'But I'm warning you,' he gestured with his knife, 'Regis, Paxton, next Season the come-out of a Fortune girl shall not fall to me, but to one of you.'

'We might be travelling...' Paxton excused himself.

'For a whole year?' said Onslow.

'And my house is not as large as yours, Onslow,' said Regis smoothly. 'And my wife is not yet as wise as the marchioness, so...'

'I am not,' agreed Jocasta.

Onslow growled while his wife laughed.

'What shall we do on our wedding trip, Damon?' asked Jocasta.

'I shall paint you,' he decided. 'I feel like taking up my brushes again.'

Jocasta wrinkled her nose at this, as though displeased. 'Lord Paxton once said he wished to paint me barefoot, in a wooded dell, with a crown of flowers in my hair.'

'Miss Fortune!' pleaded Paxton, humiliated.

'Robert!' cried Portia, annoyed.

Georgette and Cecilia looked slightly bilious at the vision this conjured up.

'It is one of the reasons I didn't wish to marry him,' Jocasta confided to her love, who nodded his complete understanding.

'*Please*, I *beg* of you—' began Paxton.

His tormentor held up a little hand to her chest. 'That is the last of my ire, I swear, your lordship. I shall never say another word on the matter.'

'*Thank you!*' he breathed.

'*I,*' considered Regis, 'shall not paint a fairy, but instead paint my little general, with her determined bravery and her beautiful, kind eyes.'

There was nothing for Jocasta to do but blush.

'*Damon!*' cried Cecilia, finally understanding. 'I have never seen that look on your face. You really do *love* her!'

'And so, the Demon King has finally fallen! And we have all learnt the cruelty of kindness,' said Justin Faulkes. He stood, holding up his glass, looking around the assembled company. I feel,' he said, wryly, 'like the last unattached person in the world. But let us toast to marital bliss!'

They did so, and Georgette sighed her pleasure.

'Isn't it a lovely evening?' said Jocasta, and her smile was as wide and open as her sisters had ever seen it.

Damon looked, in contrast, wicked and intense, and kissed the hand he possessed.

Jocasta blushed once more. '*Repulsive!*' she teased, to cover her shaking, looking deep into his eyes.

'That is quite enough of that!' chided Georgette, to cover the table's embarrassment.

Lord Robert Paxton, newly relaxed in her presence, looked to see that Miss Jocasta Fortune (whom he had first perceived as perfect, then later as shallow and even cold) was capable of just as much passion as her darling sister, his Portia.

It just depended, he supposed, on who she was looking at.

Also By Alicia Cameron

Regency Romance

Angelique and the Pursuit of Destiny: getbook.at/Angelique
*Angelique was named by her French grandmother, but now lives as Ann,
ignored by her aristocratic relations. Can she find the courage to pursue
her Destiny, reluctantly aided by her suave cousin Ferdinand?*

Beth and the Mistaken Identity: getbook.at/Beth
*Beth has been cast off as lady's maid to the pert young Sophy Ludgate,
but is mistaken as a lady herself by a handsome marquis and his princess
sister. Desperate to save the coach fare to London, she goes along with
them, but they do not let her escape so easily.*

Clarissa and the Poor Relations: getbook.at/Clarissa

Clarissa Thorne and her three friends have to leave their cosy School for Young Ladies after the death of Clarissa's mama. all must be sent off as poor relations to their families. However, Clarissa suddenly inherits Ashcroft Manor, and persuades the ladies to make a bid for freedom. But can she escape their unpleasant families? The Earl of Grandiston might help.

Delphine and the Dangerous Arrangement: getbook.at/Delphine

Delphine Delacroix was brought up by her mother alone, a cold and unloving childhood. With her mother dead, she has become the richest young lady in England, and is taken under the wing of her three aunts, Not quite trusting them, Delphine enters a dangerous arrangement with the handsome Viscount Gascoigne - but will this lead to her downfall?

The Fentons Series (Regency)

Honoria and the Family Obligation, The Fentons 1 https://get-book.at/Honoria

Honoria Fenton has been informed that the famous Mr Allison is to come to her home. His purpose? To woo her. She cannot recall what he looks like, since he made her nervous when they met in Town. Her sister Serena is amused, but when Allison arrives, it seems that a mistake might cost all three there happiness.

Felicity and the Damaged Reputation, The Fentons 2

https://getbook.at/Felicity

On her way to London to take a post as governess, Felicity Oldfield is intercepted by xx, who asks her to impersonate his cousin for an hour. When, in an unexpected turn of events, Felicity is able to enjoy a London Season, this encounter damages her reputation.

Euphemia and the Unexpected Enchantment, The Fentons 3

https://getbook.at/Euphemia

Euphemia, plain and near forty, is on her way to live with her dear friend Felicity and her husband when she is diverted to the home of Baron x, a bear of a man as huge and loud as Euphemia is small and quiet. Everything in her timid life begins to change.

Ianthe and the Fighting Foxes: The Fentons 4 https://get-book.at/Ianthe

The Fighting Foxes, Lord Edward, his half-brother Curtis and Lady Fox, his stepmother, are awaiting the arrival from France of a poor relation, Miss Ianthe Eames. But when Ianthe turns up, nothing could be further from their idea of a supplicant. Richly dressed and in high good humour, Ianthe takes the Foxes by storm.

The Sisters of Castle Fortune Series (Regency)

Georgette and the Unrequited Love: Sisters of Castle Fortune 1

https://getbook.at/Georgette

Georgette Fortune, one of ten sisters, lives as a spinster in Castle Fortune. She refused all offers during her London Seasons, since she fell in love, at first glance with the dashing Lord Onslow. He hardly knew she existed, however, but now he has arrived at the castle for a house party, and Georgette is fearful of exposing her feelings. She tries to avoid him, but Onslow treats her as a friend, making Georgette's pain worse, even as he makes her laugh.

Jocasta and the Cruelty of Kindness: Sisters of Castle Fortune 2

https://getbook.at/Jocasta

At a house party in Castle Fortune, Jocasta's beau had fallen for her sister, Portia. Now Jocasta is back in London and has to suffer the pity of the friends and family that care for her. Only Sir Damon Regis treats her without pity, and she is strangely drawn to him because of it.

Katerina and the Reclusive Earl: Sisters of Castle Fortune 3

Katerina Fortune has only one desire, to avoid going on her London Season altogether. On the journey, she hears of a recluse, who dislikes people as much as she. Katerina escapes her father and drives to offer a convenient marriage to the earl, who refuses. But an accident necessitates her stay at his home, and they discover they have more in common than either could have believed.

Leonora and the Lion's Venture: Sisters of Castle Fortune 4

At the Castle Fortune house party three years ago, fourteen year-old Leonora fell out of a tree and into the arms of the the shy Mr Linton Carswell. From that minute on she decided to wed him and secretly prepared herself to be a good wife. Leonora's goals are known as the Lion's

Ventures to her sisters, but although the know she has a new venture, not even her twin Marguerite knows what it is precisely. But when the lovely twins arrive in London, they begin to realise her unlikely target. Foggy Carswell, not a marrying man, begins to suspect too and hides from his pursuer. But Leonora, the most determined of her sisters, is set on him. But when she sets him free at last, the tables finally turn.

Edwardian Inspirational Romance
(typewriters, bicycles, and leg-of-mutton sleeves!)

Francine and the Art of Transformation: getbook.at/FrancineT
Francine is fired as a lady's maid, but she is a woman who has planned for every eventuality. Meeting Miss Philpott, a timid, unemployed governess, Francine transforms her into the Fascinating Mathilde and offers her another, self directed life. Together, they help countless other women get control over their lives.

Francine and the Winter's Gift: getbook.at/FrancineW
Francine and Mathilde continue to save young girls from dreadful marriages, while seeing to their own romances. In Francine, Sir Hugo Portas, government minister, meets a woman he could never have imagined. Will society's rules stop their union, or can Francine even accept the shackles of being in a relationship?

About Author

Alicia Cameron lives between her homes in rural Scotland and rural France. She reads avidly, laughs a lot, and is newly addicted, unfortunately, to Korean Dramas ... for which she refuses treatment. Here is a link to get **Angelique and the Pursuit of Destiny** for FREE! https://BookHip.com/XSNQVM It puts you on the list to receive Alicia Cameron's book news and offers, occasionally. You can find the link on the first page of Alicia Cameron's website, too! It has news of new books and there is also an occasional Regency Blog.

All Alicia books are available on Amazon and as audiobooks on Audible. Some are available in several languages, German and Spanish especially.

You can find out more here :

The website https://aliciacameron.co.uk

Facebook https://www.facebook.com/aliciacameron.100

Twitter https://twitter.com/aliciaclarissa2

Bookbub https://www.bookbub.com/authors/alicia-cameron

The first chapter of the Fentons series to tempt you...

Honoria and the Family Obligation

The Fentons Book 1

Alicia Cameron

Getbook.at/Honoria

Blue Slippers

'He has arrived!' said Serena, kneeling on the window seat of their bedchamber. She made a pretty picture there with her sprigged muslin dress foaming around her and one silk stockinged foot still on the floor, but her sister Honoria was too frozen with fear to notice.

'Oh, no,' said Honoria, moving forward in a dull fashion to join her. Her elder brother Benedict had been sitting with one leg draped negligently over the arm of the only comfortable chair in the room and now rose languidly to join his younger sisters. After the season in London, Dickie had begun to ape the manners of Beau Brummel and his cronies, polite, but slightly bored with the world. At one and twenty, it seemed a trifle contrived, even allowing that his long limbs and handsome face put many a town beau to shame.

Serena's dark eyes danced wickedly, 'Here comes the conquest of your triumphant season, your soon-to-be-fiancé.'

Dickie grinned, rather more like their childhood companion, 'Your knight in shining armour. If *only* you could remember him.'

'It isn't funny.'

Serena laughed and turned back to the window as she heard the door of the carriage open and the steps let down by Timothy, the one and only footman that Fenton Manor could boast.

'Oh, how did it happen?' Honoria said for the fifteenth time that morning.

Someone in the crowd had said, 'Mr Allison is approaching. But he never dances!' In confusion, she had looked around, and saw the throng around her grow still and part as her hostess approached with a tall gentleman. With all eyes turned to her she stiffened in every sinew. She remembered the voice of Lady Carlisle introducing Mr Allison as a desirable partner, she remembered her mother thrusting her forward as she was frozen with timidity. She remembered his hand lead her to her first waltz of the season. She had turned to her mother for protection as his hand snaked around her waist and had seen that matron grip her hands together and glow with pride. This was Lady Fenton's shining moment, if not her daughter's. Word had it that Mr Allison had danced only thrice this season, each time with his married friends. Lost in the whirl of the dance, she had answered his remarks with single syllables, looking no higher than his chin. A dimpled chin, strong, she remembered vaguely. And though she had previously seen Mr. Allison at a distance, the very rich and therefore very interesting Mr Allison, with an estate grander than many a nobleman, she could not remember more than that he was held to be handsome. (As she told Serena this later, her sister remarked that rich men were very often held to be handsome, strangely related to the size of their purse.)

There was the waltz; there had been a visit to her father in the London house; her mother had informed her of Mr Allison's wishes and that she was to receive his addresses the next afternoon. He certainly visited the next afternoon, and Honoria had been suffered to serve him his tea and her hand had shaken so much that she had kept her eyes on the cup for the rest of the time. He had not proposed, which her mother thought of as a pity, but here she had been saved by Papa, who had thought that Mr Allison should visit them in the country where his daughter and he might be more at their leisure to know each other. 'For she is a little shy with new company and I should wish her perfectly comfortable before she receives your addresses,' Sir Ranalph had told him, as Honoria's mama had explained.

Serena, when told, had thought it a wonderful joke. To be practically engaged to someone you could not remember! She laughed because she trusted to good-natured Papa to save Honoria from the match if it should prove unwanted; her sister had only to say "no".

'Why on earth do you make such a tragedian of yourself, Orry,' had said Serena once Honoria had poured her story out, 'After poor Henrietta Madeley's sad marriage, Papa has always said that to marry with such parental compulsion is scandalously cruel.'

And Honoria had mopped up her tears and felt a good deal better, buoyed by Serena's strength of mind. To be sure, there was the embarrassment to be endured of giving disappointment, but she resolved to do it if Mr Allison's aura of grandeur continued to terrify her.

'And then,' her sister had continued merrily, 'the rich Mr Allison may just turn out to be as handsome as his purse and as good natured as Papa - and you will fall head over heels with him after all.'

The morning after, Honoria had gone for a walk before breakfast, in much better spirits. As she came up the steps to re-enter by the breakfast room, she carelessly caught her new French muslin (fifteen and sixpence the yard, Mama had told her) on the roses that grew on a column. If she took her time and did not pull, she may be able to rescue herself without damage to the dress. She could hear Mama and Papa chatting and gave it no mind until Mama's voice became serious.

'My dear Ranalph, will you not tell me?'

'Shall there be muffins this morning, my dear?' said Papa cheerfully.

'You did not finish your mutton last night and you are falsely cheerful this morning. Tell me, my love.'

'*You should apply for a position at Bow Street, my dear. Nothing escapes you.*' She heard the sound of an embrace.

'*Diversionary tactics, sir, are futile.*'

Honoria knew she should not be privy to this, but she was still detaching her dress, thorn by thorn. It was incumbent on her to make a noise, so that they might know she was there, but as she decided to do so, she was frozen by Papa's next words.

'*Mr Allison's visit will resolve all, I'm sure.*'

Honoria closed her mouth, automatically continuing to silently pluck her dress from the rose bush, anxious to be away.

'*Resolve what, dearest?*' Honoria could picture her mama on Papa's knee.

'*Well, there have been extra expenses – from the Brighton property.*' Honoria knew that this was where her uncle Wilbert lived, her father's younger brother. (Dickie had explained that he was a friend of the Prince Regent, which sounded so well to the girls, but Dickie had shaken his head loftily. '*You girls know nothing. Unless you are as rich as a Maharajah, it's ruinous to be part of that set.*')

Her father continued, '*Now, now. All is well. If things do not take with Mr Allison, we shall just have to cut our cloth a little, Madame.*' He breathed. '*But, Cynthia, I'm afraid another London Season is not to be thought of.*'

Honoria felt instant guilt. Her own season had been at a rather later age than that of her more prosperous friends, and she had not been able to understand why Serena and she could not have had it together, for they borrowed each other's clothes all the time. Serena's intrepid spirit would have buoyed hers too and made her laugh, and would have surely helped with her crippling timidity. But when she had seen how many dresses had been required - one day alone she had changed from morning gown to carriage dress to luncheon half dress, then riding habit and finally evening dress. And with so many of the same people at balls, one could not make do - Mama had insisted on twenty evening gowns as the bare minimum. However doughty with a needle the sisters might be, this was beyond their scope, and London dressmakers did not come cheap. Two such wardrobes were not to be paid for by the estate's income in one year. Honoria had accidentally seen the milliner's bill for her season and shuddered to think of it - her bonnets alone had been ruinously expensive. She had looked forward to her second season, where her wardrobe could be adapted at very little cost to give it a new look and Serena would also have her fill of new walking dresses and riding habits, bonnets and stockings. If she were in London with her sister, she might actually enjoy it.

'Poor Serena. What are her chances of a suitable match in this restricted neighbourhood?' Mama continued, 'And indeed, Honoria, if she does not like this match. Though how she could fail to like a charming, handsome man like Mr Allison is beyond me,' she finished.

'Do not forget rich,' teased her husband.

'When I think of the girls who tried to catch him all season! And then he came to us – specifically asked to be presented to her as a partner for the waltz, as dear Lady Carlisle informed me later - but she showed no triumph at all. And now, she will not give an opinion. She is strangely reticent about the subject.'

'Well, well, it is no doubt her shyness. She will be more relaxed when she sees Allison among the family.'

'So much rests upon it.' There was a pause. 'Dickie's commission?'

He laughed, but it sounded sour from her always cheerful Papa.
'Wilbert has promised to buy it from his next win at Faro.'
'Hah!' said Mama bitterly.
Honoria was free. She went towards the breakfast room rather noisily.
'Are there muffins?' she asked gaily.

'How on earth do you come to be engaged to *him*?'

Honoria was jolted back to the present by Serena's outcry. She gazed in dread over her sister's dark curls and saw a sober figure in a black coat and dull breeches, with a wide-brimmed, antediluvian hat walking towards the house. She gave an involuntary giggle.

'Oh, that is only Mr Scribster, his friend.'

'*He* you remember!' laughed Serena. 'Is he as dull as his hat?'

Honoria remembered Mr Scribster's long, miserable face, framed with two lank curtains of hair, at several parties. She thought it odd that a gentleman so patently uninterested in the events should bother to attend. And indeed her mother had whispered the same to her. Honoria must be present where her parents willed her - but surely a gentleman should be free not to? But Mr. Scribster attended in company with Lord Salcomb or Mr Allison with a face suitable for a wake.

'Yes,' said Honoria. 'He never looks happy to be anywhere. And generally converses with no one. Though occasionally I saw him speak to Mr Allison in his grave way and Mr. Allison *laughed*.'

'Maybe it's like when Sir Henry Horton comes to dinner.' Sir Henry was nicknamed among the children "The Harbinger of Gloom". 'Papa laughs so much at his doomsday declarations that he is the only man in the county that actually looks forward to him coming.'

Honoria spotted another man exiting the chaise, this one in biscuit coloured breeches above shiny white-topped Hessian boots. His travelling coat almost swept the ground, and Serena said, 'Well, he's more the thing at any rate. Pity we cannot see his face. You should be prepared. However, he *walks* like a handsome man.' She giggled, 'Or at all events, a rich one.'

The door behind them had opened. 'Serena, you will guard your tongue,' said their mama. Lady Fenton, also known as Lady Cynthia (as she was the daughter of a peer) was the pattern card from which her beautiful daughters were formed. A dark-haired, plump, but stylish matron who looked as good as one could, she said of herself, when one had borne seven bouncing babies. Now she smiled, though, and Honoria felt another bar in her cage. How could she dash her mother's hopes? 'Straighten your dresses, girls, and come downstairs.'

Benedict winked and walked off with his parent.

There were no looking glasses in their bedroom, so as not to foster vanity. But as they straightened the ribbons of the new dresses Mama had thought appropriate to the occasion, they acted as each other's glass and pulled at hair ribbons and curls as need be. The Misses Fenton looked as close to twins as sisters separated by two years could, dark curls and dark slanted eyes and lips that curled at the corners to give them the appearance of a smile even in repose. Their brother Benedict said they resembled a couple of cats, but then he would say that. Serena had told him to watch his tongue or they might scratch.

The children, Norman, Edward, Cedric and Angelica, were not to be admitted to the drawing room - but they bowled out of the nursery to watch the sisters descend the stairs in state. As Serena tripped on a cricket ball, she looked back and stuck her tongue out at the grinning eight-year-old Cedric. Edward, ten, cuffed his younger brother and threw him into the nursery by the scruff of his neck. The eldest, Norman, twelve, a beefy chap, lifted little three-year-old Angelica who showed a disposition to follow her sisters. On the matter of unruly behaviour today, Mama had them all warned.

As the stairs turned on the landing, the sisters realised there was no one in the large square hall to see their dignified descent, so Serena tripped down excitedly, whilst her sister made the slow march of a hearse follower. As Serena gestured her down, Honoria knew that her sister's excitement came from a lack of society in their neighbourhood. She herself had enjoyed a London season, whilst Serena had never been further than Harrogate. She was down at last and they walked to the door of the salon, where she shot her hand out to delay Serena. She took a breath and squared her shoulders. Oh well, this time she should at least see what he looked like.

Two gentlemen stood by the fire with their backs to the door, conversing with Papa and Dickie. As the door opened, they turned and Honoria was focused on the square-shouldered gentleman, whose height rivalled Benedict's and quite dwarfed her sturdy papa. His face was nearly in view, Sir Ranalph was saying, 'These are my precious jewels!' The face was visible for only a moment before Serena gave a yelp of surprise and moved forward a pace. Honoria turned to her.

'But it's you!' Serena cried.

Everyone looked confused and a little shocked, not least Serena who grasped her hands in front of her and regarded the carpet. There seemed to be no doubt that she had addressed Mr Allison.

Honoria could see him now, the dimpled chin and strong jaw she remembered, and topped by a classical nose, deep set hazel eyes and the hairstyle of a Roman Emperor. Admirable, she supposed, but with a smile dying on his lips, he had turned from relaxed guest to stuffed animal, with only his eyes moving between one sister and another. His gaze fell, and he said the most peculiar thing.

'Blue slippers.'

To read on click : getbook.at/ Honoria

Printed in Great Britain
by Amazon